Molly Evans ... ... has taken her experiences as a travel nurse and turned them into wondrous settings for her books. Some of those assignments were in small rural hospitals, the Indian Health Service in Alaska and in the American southwest, as well as a large research hospital and many other places across the United States.

After rambling for many years, the high desert of New Mexico is now where she calls home. When she's not writing or attending her son's hockey games she's obsessed with learning how to knit socks, visiting with friends, or settling down in front of the fireplace with a glass of wine and her two hounds who are never very far away.

Visit Molly at mollyevansromance.wordpress.com to keep up on her latest releases, book events, and what's going on in Molly's life at any given moment.

Abigail Gordon loves to write about the fascinating combination of medicine and romance from her home in a Cheshire village. She is active in local affairs, and is even called upon to write the script for the annual village pantomime! Her eldest son is a hospital manager, and helps with all her medical research. As part of a close-knit family, she treasures having two of her sons living close by, and the third one not too far away. This also gives her the added pleasure of being able to watch her delightful grandchildren growing up.

Emily Forbes is an award-winning author of Mills & Boon Medical Romance. She has written over twenty books and has twice been a finalist in the Australian Romantic Book of the Year Award, which she won in 2013 for her novel *Sydney Harbour Hospital: Bella's Wishlist*. You can get in touch with Emily at emilyforbes@internode.on.net, or visit her website at emily-forbesauthor.com

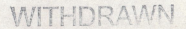

Their Forever Family

MOLLY EVANS

ABIGAIL GORDON

EMILY FORBES

MILLS & BOON

First Published in Great Britain 2018
by Mills & Boon, an imprint of HarperCollins*Publishers*
1 London Bridge Street, London, SE1 9GF

THEIR FOREVER FAMILY © 2018 Harlequin Books S. A.

Her Family For Keeps © 2015 Brenda Schetnan
A Father For Poppy © 2015 Abigail Gordon
His Little Christmas Miracle © 2015 Emily Forbes

ISBN: 978-0-263-27466-0

1118

MIX
Paper from
responsible sources
FSC® C007454

This book is produced from independently certified FSC™ paper to ensure responsible forest management.

For more information visit: www.harpercollins.co.uk/green

Printed and bound in Spain
by CPI, Barcelona

HER FAMILY
FOR KEEPS

MOLLY EVANS

CHAPTER ONE

REBEL TAYLOR ROLLED her shoulders against the heat. Sweat tickled and trickled down her back as she crossed the steaming parking lot. It was a very hot day for the first of June, even for New Mexico.

Movement in the backseat of a small sedan drew her attention. As an ER nurse, she was highly trained in skills of observation. Even the smallest detail made the difference between life and death. Frowning, she moved closer to the back window.

Rebel dropped her backpack as she hit full ER nurse mode. "Hello?" She stepped closer and the bottom dropped out of her stomach.

A toddler was strapped in the backseat.

Alone.

"Oh, God." Panic flooded her, and her limbs went limp for half a second. She looked around at the parking lot full of cars but devoid of people. "Help! Someone help!"

Tugging on the door handle brought her no results. The windows in the front were down a crack, but not enough to squeeze her arm through.

The child's cries grew into screams as he pulled on his hair. What Rebel had first thought was a seizure was the frustration of the toddler imprisoned in the heat.

"Hold on, baby. Hold on!" She jerked her cellphone out of her pocket and called 911.

Dr. Duncan McFee strolled across the parking lot toward the hospital, but had to pass through the lengthy, car-filled parking area. When the doctors' car park was full, he parked with the rest of the staff. Heat bubbled up from the black surface and seemed to take on a life of its own, reaching out to drag passersby down into the dark depths. Days like this, he always wondered why he'd passed on that exotic job offer in the Caribbean. An ocean breeze would have been very welcome at the moment. If the desert had an ocean, it would be perfect.

Up ahead, he noticed a woman with long, luxurious, curly red hair who apparently had locked her keys in her car and was bent on beating the life out of it as a result. He decided to see if he could help the lovely damsel in distress. Not every day presented an opportunity to meet such a stunning woman.

"Lock your keys in?" he asked.

She turned, true panic in her incredibly green eyes, and took in a gasping breath. Duncan frowned. Something was wrong with this lady, not just keys locked in her car.

"There's a *baby* in there!"

"How long has he been in there?" Duncan dropped his briefcase, instantly understanding her panic.

"I don't know, but he's in trouble."

Duncan knew he needed to get that child out of there. Time was the enemy right now.

"Call 911."

"I did, but he'll die before they get here. We've got to *do* something." She hit the heel of one hand against the window in frustration.

Duncan looked around for a rock or anything he could

use to break into the car. People started to gather, attracted by their activity. The woman grabbed the closest person. "Go get Security. We have to break into this car. It's an emergency. Go!"

The man raced away into the building.

Frustration mounted in Duncan, and he felt the same emotion emanating from this unknown woman. She was obviously a caring and concerned person, as well as stunningly beautiful. She stuck her fingers through the space in the front window and pulled. The window didn't budge. "Dammit."

Duncan joined her and managed to slide his fingers in alongside hers. "On three, pull. One, two, three…pull." Together they put their muscles to work, but the window simply didn't move. They couldn't get enough leverage on it.

"Dammit! Where's Security?" He glared toward the building, but there was no rescue party racing up the hill. "We're going to have to do this ourselves." One glance in the backseat was all he needed to realize she was right. The baby would die in the next minute unless he was rescued.

And then what they both feared happened. The child had a seizure, its little limbs jerking uncontrollably in response to the high temperature in the car forcing its body temperature too high. The brain could only take so much before reacting badly.

"There has to be something we can use to smash the window." The woman glanced around. "There!" She ran a few feet to grab a landscape rock nearly hidden by shrubbery.

"Give it to me." He took the rock, and she turned her back, but stayed close. With everything, every ounce of strength he had, he smashed the rock into the driver's window, determined to get this baby free. Never again was he going to let someone die in a car. Not if he could help it.

Glass shattered. She shoved the window in with the heels of her hands and released the door lock. "Got it."

Duncan yanked open the back door. In the last few seconds the baby had lost consciousness after the seizure. With quick thinking, she released the car-seat clasp and Duncan pulled the child free.

"We have to cool him quickly." She pulled off his shoes and socks and stripped him down to his diaper.

"Let's go." Duncan raced into the ER with the woman at his side. "Pediatric code! Call a pediatric code," he yelled as they sprinted through the doors, the baby clutched against his chest.

This man was obviously known here and thank heaven for that, Rebel thought as she raced into a treatment room with him, her hand supporting the baby's head.

Once she had her hands on him, she refused to let go, as if her touch could infuse life into him. Staff arrived quickly and took over the scene. Once on the stretcher, the baby was flaccid, his breathing erratic.

"Get an IV in him." Duncan gave orders and the staff were already responding. Performing in code situations was something these people did routinely and were obviously accustomed to working together.

Out of her element and uncertain what to do, Rebel wet a towel at the sink and draped it over the boy's head.

Duncan looked at her with dark brown eyes filled with dangerous anger, and she nearly stepped away. Had she overstepped her boundaries? He didn't know she was a nurse or that she had any medical knowledge whatsoever.

"Good idea. Cool his brain off." He gave a grim nod and continued to give orders, orchestrating the scene. After the boy was hooked to the respirator, Duncan took a stetho-scope and listened to the little chest as it rose and fell in synchronization with the respirator. "This will rest him a bit."

Rebel tried not to give in to the awful sense of dread crawling into her limbs and stomach. These heroic efforts may have been too little, too late. The baby had had a *grand mal* seizure, the worst kind. His immature brain had gotten too hot too fast and might not recover from the insult. Even if he survived, he could have lifelong brain damage.

Rebel pressed her lips together as emotion overwhelmed her. Images of her family flashed into her mind. "We didn't get to him in time." He was going to die. Just the way her father and three brothers had.

"We don't know that yet," Duncan said, and clasped Rebel's shoulder in a reassuring gesture that failed to bring any comfort. She knew that no matter how good medical care was, people still died. Her father had been the first, then her brothers. Nothing had been able to stop the disease that had taken them all.

"Time will tell," she said, defeated by the rescue efforts she knew were probably futile. If there were miracles in the world, they hadn't been given to her family. Each of her brothers had died a slow, agonizing death, leaving behind holes that could never be filled.

Duncan looked at her as if trying to read something into her words. "Yes. Time *will* tell." He moved to the side and drew Rebel with him. "Is this your child?"

"What? No." Rebel's eyes widened, surprise on her face. "I just happened to come along at the right time." She looked away. "I guess it was the right time."

"I see. Just doing business in the hospital?" He normally didn't stick his nose into the business of others, but this was an unusual and very traumatic situation. One he wanted to figure out now.

"Actually, I'm here to finish up some pre-employment paperwork. I'm a travel nurse. Start tomorrow."

They moved into the hallway as the staff finished stabilizing the boy to transfer him to the pediatric ICU. There was always hope. There had to be for him to carry on with this work as a healer, a physician, as a human being. If there was no hope, what was the point in even trying? Even when his fiancée, Valerie, had been near death, he'd had hope she'd survive. Unfortunately, he'd been wrong that time.

"Where will you be working?" Curiosity made him ask.

"Here. In the ER." The sideways smile she gave said it all.

Duncan nearly chuckled at the irony of the situation, but held back. This was no laughing matter, and he could see in her expression that she thought the same thing. "Quite a trial by fire you hadn't expected."

"It's the life of an ER nurse."

"Yes, for ER doctors, too. I'm Duncan McFee, one of the physicians here in the ER." He paused a moment and watched her soulful green eyes follow the child as he was wheeled toward the elevators. "How are your hands?" He gestured for her to hold them out.

"My hands? What do you mean?" She frowned and looked down at them.

"Your palms, I mean." He placed his strong hands over hers and turned them over. His touch was firm and warm and a little tingle she hadn't expected rushed through her. "You pushed the glass in with your hands, and I'd like to make sure you don't have any cuts. Glass can go deep before you even know it."

"I did? I don't remember doing that."

"You did." He stroked his fingers over the heels of her hands and her palms, using his sensitive fingertips, looking for any irregularities. "Guess we'll be working together if you stay." He released her. "Looks good. What's your name?"

"I'm Rebel Taylor and what do you mean, *if* I stay?" Rebel raised her brows and leveled her intense eyes on him. "I'm not going anywhere."

"Good. Then I'll see you tomorrow. Don't worry about the paperwork. You can finish up in the morning. Go home and de-stress after this. You need it."

After a deep sigh, Rebel's shoulders drooped. She knew the benefits of letting go or destressing or whatever you wanted to call it, after such an event. Time to take a breather on duty was often a luxury, rather than the necessity it should be.

"Maybe you're right." Conceding felt like weakness, but her mind overrode the emotions. She wasn't officially an employee yet, so she had no real place here.

"I'll walk you out. I have to recover my briefcase anyway."

"I hope it's still there. My backpack is there, too." She shook her head, having forgotten about it in the rescue crisis. What a pain that would be to replace all of the items in her wallet if it had been stolen.

"I'm sure it is. This hospital complex doesn't have a lot of crime and there were plenty of people around."

As they approached the exit, Duncan turned to her. "So where'd you get such an unusual name? You don't look like a rebel to me."

She smiled, some of the tension lifting, even though she recognized his distraction technique. She'd used it many times on her patients, and she appreciated his efforts for her now. "It was something my father gave me when I was a kid. Apparently, as a toddler, I was *quite* the rebel and the nickname stuck." She gave him a slant-eyed glance.

"My given name is Rebecca, but if you ever call me that, I'll slap you silly."

Duncan laughed and some of the tension seemed to let go of him as well.

"Agree." He offered an arm for her to move ahead of him. "I think Rebel suits you better anyway. Rebecca is too tame for all that wild hair." Curiously, that hair made him itch to touch it, feel its texture and softness. Check that. Not gonna happen.

They left via the double doors that whooshed open on quiet hydraulics. They approached the parking lot, now alive with police and security.

"Wow." Rebel looked at the area now packed with fire trucks, rescue vehicles, an ambulance and a police aid directing traffic away from the area. "Guess we'll have to file a report, won't we? And someone's got to find out who that baby belongs to." The person probably worked in the building and had forgotten to leave their child with the sitter.

From behind them, Rebel heard a gasp. A young woman dashed past them toward the car and the police officer putting up yellow tape.

"What happened to my car?"

The officer faced her. "Is this your vehicle, ma'am?" He set down the crime-scene tape and stepped closer to her, the sun glinting off his reflective sunglasses. He removed them and wiped his forehead.

"Yes, what happened?" She gestured to the mess it had become.

"Can I see some ID?"

"Oh, for heaven's sake." She dug into her purse as Duncan and Rebel moved closer. "Someone breaks into my car, and *I'm* the one who has to show ID?" She shook her head in obvious disgust. "I was only at work for half an hour and someone broke into my damned car."

"We broke into your car," Duncan said, his voice soft, and Rebel shivered with anticipation as to what his next words would be.

That confession got the officer's attention, and he looked between Duncan and Rebel, keen eyes putting together the scenario.

"You broke into my car?" The woman looked him up and down, then at Rebel, completely baffled. "Why?"

"Because your son was in there." Even though his voice was as soft as silk, the words were hard to hear.

Rebel took a deep breath and gritted her teeth, certain she'd have knots in her shoulders later. Duncan held her gaze and gave her a nod and she moved a little closer to him. The close proximity brought her some comfort and feeling some of his strength made her realize she was going to get through this difficult situation. With the power this man exuded, she thought she might just be able to get through anything.

CHAPTER TWO

"WHAT DO YOU MEAN, *my son?* Eric's at daycare." She swallowed, her blue eyes wide with fear and uncertainty. She looked between Rebel and Dr. McFee trying to figure out if they were telling the truth or if this was some sort of sick joke.

"No, ma'am. Your son was discovered in the backseat of this vehicle." The officer took her ID from her limp fingers.

"N-no, he wasn't. He's at daycare." She looked at Rebel and Duncan, and then at the car as she put the pieces together and completed the horrifying puzzle.

The back door hung open.

The car seat was empty.

The diaper bag lay upside down on the floor.

She focused on Rebel. "Isn't he?"

"Did you forget to stop on your way here?" Duncan asked as gently as possible.

"Did I forget…? Of *course* I didn't forget." Anger flared in her face, then was quickly replaced by fear. She began to hyperventilate and her grip on Rebel's arms loosened.

"Then you left him in the car on purpose?" the officer asked.

"No! I would never…" Her eyelids fluttered.

"She's going out." Rebel held on to the woman's arms as the purse and wallet thudded to the pavement.

"Go get us a gurney," Duncan instructed the security guard, who ran into the building, and took some of the woman's body weight from Rebel.

"As soon as she wakes up she's under arrest," the officer said, and shoved his shades back on.

"As soon as she wakes up she needs to see her child, so back off." Dark anger flashed in Duncan's eyes, and Rebel held her breath.

"She put her kid in mortal danger. He may die."

"I understand. She's not going anywhere, so you can arrest her later."

For the second time in less than an hour Rebel and Duncan entered the ER with an unexpected patient.

"Can you start an IV?" Duncan asked. "The others are working on a new trauma."

"Yes," Rebel said, ready to be helpful and hide the fear surfacing in her veins. Facing her fears was what had led her to ER nursing, but some days the fear nearly did her in.

Duncan pointed to the counter behind her. "Supplies are there. Get some saline going."

In seconds Rebel had everything prepared and inserted an IV into the back of the woman's hand.

Duncan rummaged in a cabinet beside her. "Aha." He moved closer to the patient. "Make sure that's taped down well."

"Why?"

He held up the small mesh-covered capsule. "Old-fashioned smelling salts."

"Haven't seen those used in years." Thinking outside the box was what kept ER nursing interesting. "Let 'er rip."

The instant Duncan popped the capsule with his fingers,

the noxious scent invaded the room. He waved it beneath the woman's nose, and she jerked away.

"Wake up for me," Duncan said, and patted her cheeks.

"Her name is Amanda Walker." The police officer arrived from outside with her belongings.

"Amanda? Amanda. Wake up now." Duncan spoke to her.

Rebel leaned close to Amanda's ear. "Eric needs you."

Amanda's eyelids fluttered, and she jerked away from Duncan's hands. "Yuck, what is that?" She struggled to wake from unconsciousness and coughed.

"Amanda, I'm Dr. McFee, and you're in the ER. Do you remember what happened?" Amanda kept her eyes closed and frowned.

"Eric? What about Eric?" She opened eyes that appeared to have no memory of the recent events in the parking lot. Not unusual. The brain provided wonderful coping mechanisms to assist in dealing with emotionally painful situations. None of them were going to help her now.

"You were on the way to work and what happened?"

"What do you mean? I parked and came into work like I always do." She focused more on Duncan and glared. "Why are you asking about Eric? Did the daycare call?"

"No, ma'am…" Duncan interrupted the officer with a glare. He clenched his jaw, not wanting to verbally castigate the officer when he had a patient on his hands. "No. Daycare didn't call."

"I was… No. Is Eric okay? What's happened?" She tried to sit up. "What's going on?"

Rebel stepped forward and glanced with hesitation at Duncan. He didn't know her, had never worked with her before, so he had no reason to trust her or her abilities as a nurse. Then again, he had no reason not to trust her. He nodded.

Rebel placed her hand over Amanda's with a gentle touch. Compassionate energy pooled around Rebel in such waves that Duncan felt them. This woman was made of tough stuff. So far turning out to be a damned good ER nurse. Gorgeous and smart. Hard combination to find.

"I'm Rebel, one of the nurses. I…discovered Eric…in the back of your car."

"No, you didn't." Amanda shook her head in denial and jerked her hand away from Rebel. "He's at daycare." Amanda placed a trembling hand over her mouth and tears spilled from her eyes as trickles of the truth emerged from her subconscious. "You're scaring me now." Amanda looked around the room, at the glaring overhead lights, at the medical equipment, at the IV in her arm. Then she took a deep breath.

The wail that followed emerged straight from her soul.

The hair on Duncan's neck twitched in reaction to the agonizing cry no amount of comfort could touch. He looked at his newest coworker.

Tears overflowed Rebel's eyes as she stood with hands clenched in front of her. Even the cop turned away.

"N-o-o-o. No. No. No." She hopped off the gurney, her eyes wild. "You people are crazy! His dad *always* drops him off." Her breathing came hard and fast.

"Amanda. Think back to this morning. Was there a change in your routine? Did you deviate…?" Rebel asked questions designed to trigger her memory.

"No!" She pointed a finger at Rebel. "Wait till I call my husband. He's a lawyer, and he'll… My husband… is…sick…today." Amanda collapsed to her knees. Sobs croaked out of her in an unrelenting torrent of realization.

Rebel knelt beside her. "What happened? Can you tell me?"

"His office has daycare." She huffed in a few breaths. "He always takes Eric. *Always*."

"And he's home sick today?"

Amanda nodded, then slumped over onto the floor. "I killed my son! Oh, God, I killed my son."

"Eric is alive, Amanda. He's not dead."

Amanda sat up and grabbed Rebel by the shoulders. "You found him in time?" She hauled Rebel into an exuberant hug. "Oh, my God." Now, sobs of relief overflowed. "I don't know how to thank you."

Rebel placed her arms around Amanda and looked at Duncan. Those beautiful green eyes of hers pleaded for his help and something inside him emerged. Whether it was the trained physician in him, the male protector of women and children, or he was just reacting to the pain in Rebel's face, he didn't know. He just knew he had to respond.

"Amanda, sit up. I'll tell you about Eric, then we'll take you to see him." He assisted her to her feet, protecting Rebel from being overwhelmed. He offered a hand down to Rebel and brought her by his side. His instinct was to place his arm around her waist, to shield her from the pain they both knew was yet to come, knowing the story before it was even told. Instead, he took Rebel's hand and led her to a chair. She was pale and her hand was clammy. Though she didn't look it on the outside, he knew she was having great difficulty with this situation. Officially she wasn't even an employee, and she'd gone above and beyond what was expected of her. She could just as easily have walked away, but she hadn't. What heart she must have.

Duncan placed his hands on the shoulders of the sobbing woman. This was going to bite. "Amanda, pull yourself together. You need to be strong for Eric. Now take a breath and stop crying."

In a few minutes she'd managed to subdue her emotions. Tears still dribbled from her eyes, but she could look at him. That was a start.

As the noon hour approached, Rebel felt about a hundred years older than her actual thirty. Days like this were why people left healthcare. Some days being a nurse just wasn't worth it.

She'd been sitting outside the PICU where Eric had been taken. She didn't know why, but she didn't want to leave just yet. Dr. McHunky had taken the mother inside to see Eric.

Rebel had plopped herself into a chair outside the unit and hadn't been able to get up. Sitting outside an intensive care unit brought back so many overwhelming memories it shut her down. For years she'd been an unwilling participant in her family's inherited illness, Huntington's disease. Watching her brothers struggle to survive had forced her to grow up too quickly, to be too old too soon, to leave childhood behind too early. Events like today sucked her back in time to when she had been a frightened little girl watching her family be taken from her one by one.

The door to the unit swung open, and she shoved aside her past to dive into the present again. That's what adrenal glands were for, right? Surges of adrenaline kept her going from one crisis to another in the ER, and that ability didn't fail her now.

"So, how is he, Doctor?"

"It's Duncan, please." Though he patted her on the shoulder in what was supposed to be a comforting gesture, he looked as if he needed some comforting himself.

"Okay, Duncan. First tell me how he is then tell me how you are. You look like someone beat you with a hammer." Lines of what could be grief or fatigue showed on his face. Though it was mid-morning, he looked like he'd been up all night.

A small smile twisted his lips and a little relief appeared in her eyes. Mission accomplished.

"I *feel* like someone beat me with a hammer." He looked at his watch. "And it's not even lunch yet." He took a deep breath and let it out in a very long sigh. "I'll be okay. I think. Eric's critical, on a vent, the works. I've never seen so many tubes hooked up to a kid that size, and I thought I'd seen it all."

"I'm so sorry." She gave his arm a squeeze, intending to offer him some of the comfort she'd offer to any of her patients and families. His arm beneath her hand was warm and firm. Though this child wasn't related to either of them, he was special and bonded the two of them together.

Duncan turned his dark-eyed focus fully on her, and she gulped at the intensity of him. When he focused on something, it was something else. His dark, dark eyes seemed to have no pupils. His aura nearly reached out to her, like some invisible cloak trying to cocoon her into its warmth.

"And how are you holding up?"

"I'm okay, I guess." She shrugged. "Are you ever okay after an event like this?" She'd been through many traumas in her career as an ER nurse and some patient situations stuck with her, no matter how long ago they'd happened.

"You might want to go home. The paperwork for employment can wait until tomorrow."

"I'm good, really—" Denial had gotten her through many tough situations in life, why not one more?

He gave her such a doctor look, knowing she wasn't all right, knowing she'd been through the wringer today, and knowing she wasn't telling the truth, that she actually felt a flash of shame.

"Rebel. We don't always have time to shake off the

vibes from work while in the midst of it. Take the time to relax and shake this off." Duncan spoke like a man who had been on the front line of healthcare for a long time. That kind of experience didn't come without a toll on the body and the psyche.

"Thanks. You're right." She nodded. "I usually like to meet with the charge nurse the day before I start and introduce myself to see who I'm going to be working with. Stuff like that."

Duncan gave a snort as the elevator doors whooshed open. "I think you've had quite an introduction already. The entire staff knows who you are by now, so just go home. I'll tell Herm."

"If you're sure it's going to be okay…"

"It'll be fine." The elevators took them to the first floor, and they exited. "Today is an admin day for me, so I'm going to do the bare essentials and head to the gym. Always helps me blow off the stress of the day."

"My apartment complex has a pool. Maybe I'll take a swim."

"Good idea. Don't forget the sunscreen. At this elevation the rays are more intense. See you tomorrow." He'd hate to see all that luscious skin damaged by the sun. It was beautiful and she obviously worked to keep it that way.

Rebel turned and held out her hand. Duncan took it. "I'd like to say it was a pleasure to meet you, but I'm not sure that's the right thing to say." She met his eyes and held his gaze. This was a very interesting man. Unfortunately, she hadn't come here to be sidetracked by gorgeous doctors. Men and emotional relationships didn't go with her long-term goals, so there was no use in establishing a short-term one either. Men were fine as friends and the occasional lover. Too many times she'd counted on a man and had been disappointed. She needed to be in control and if she were in a relationship, she lost that. Plain and simple.

"How about 'See you tomorrow'?"

"Good enough." They shook hands, and Rebel untangled her sunglasses from on top of her head and walked out into the bright June sunlight, determined to make it to her car before another disaster happened.

Hitching her backpack across one shoulder, she tried not to look at the scene of where they had found Eric. That, like so many other bad memories, already had a permanent place in her brain.

Thoughts of Duncan, however, lingered. How would it be to work side by side with such a dynamic man? She'd worked in many types of hospitals and clinics, and there had been plenty of handsome doctors to be had, but this one was different. Somehow, deep in her gut, she knew something was different about Duncan, and she itched to know what it was. Could it be that the intensity of the situation they'd just been through was making her see things that weren't there?

She didn't think so, as she'd been through many tough situations with many doctors in the past. Today, however, made her think more about what it would be like to have a man like that around her more often.

Those dark, dangerous eyes of his remained in her mind.

CHAPTER THREE

THE NEXT DAY dawned as bright and shiny as any she'd ever seen.

Until she arrived just before her morning shift to find the ER in complete chaos. This ER was shaping up to be just like most of the ones she'd worked in. Either it was complete bedlam, or the staff were falling asleep from sheer boredom.

She took a deep breath, shoved her backpack beneath the desk and hurried to the first busy room she found. "I'm your new traveler. Someone give me a job."

A Hispanic man strode over to her with his glasses perched precariously on top of his graying hair and shoved a clipboard into her hands. "Here. Run the code. I'll be back in ten minutes."

Gulp. Running a code within thirty seconds of arriving. That was a record, but this was something she was fully capable of managing. She squeezed behind staff members who were performing all kinds of tasks around a patient who had been in a traumatic accident.

She looked at the clipboard. Pedestrian. Hit by a high-speed vehicle, thrown forty feet in the air. Possible neck and spine injuries. Probable head injury. Punctured one lung. Blood in the abdomen.

If he survived, he'd spend the next year in rehab all

because someone hadn't looked both ways. She read the cardiac monitor. His heart rate was fast, rhythm good.

"What do you need next, Doctor?" She hadn't met any of the physicians yet, so she didn't know who she was working with.

"Glad you're here, Rebel. Call Radiology. Need a chest X-ray, abdominal films." She knew the voice and a little bit of her relaxed, and a little of her got excited at the compliment. Although she couldn't see his face behind the mask and goggles, she knew Duncan was in charge of this case. The sound of his voice was reassuring and made a funny squiggle in the pit of her stomach at the same time. The man had definitely made an impact on her senses yesterday.

"Got it." She turned to the phone on the wall. Fortunately, there was an extensive phone list posted nearby. After the first call, she checked the monitor again. The heart rhythm had changed. Not looking good.

"Doctor. He's had a rhythm change."

Duncan twisted around and looked at it for himself. "Dammit. I was hoping we could get him to the OR before he crashed. Get a chest tube set up."

She set the clipboard down. "Where are they?"

"There. One of the other nurses pointed to a cabinet right behind Duncan. Rebel squished her way through the bodies in the room to fetch the sterile tray, dropped it onto a portable tray table, opened it, and donned sterile gloves.

"I'm back." The man who had given her the clipboard returned to take over.

"We're putting a chest tube in on the left." Rebel called out the information so he could catch up to where they were in the situation and record it. "Rhythm is V-tach. Rate one-eighty." She prepared to assist Duncan with the procedure. Duncan removed his gloves, and she held out a new, sterile pair for him. A collapsed lung would be deadly along with all of his other injuries.

After insertion, blood poured through the tubing into the collection container and the heart monitor settled down. Rebel drew a deep breath. Yet another save before eight in the morning by a doctor she was coming to have confidence in very rapidly. "Good going, Doc."

The only response was a connecting of glances and a nod. The tension of the code dwindled as the patient stabilized and was being prepared for transfer to the operating room for surgery.

"Rebel, right? What a name. I'm Hermano Vega, but call me Herm. I'm the charge nurse in this madhouse for today. You're with me for orientation. The others can get him upstairs."

Rebel shook his hand, liking his gentle, fatherly demeanor immediately. "Nice to meet you."

"Quite the first day, *no*?" He echoed Duncan's statement from earlier. "Come on. Let's get you settled." He turned and motioned for her to follow. Though she looked back as Duncan removed his protective gear, she went along with Herm. Somehow that man had gotten under her skin, and they'd only met yesterday.

"Great. What sort of torture do you have planned for me this morning?" There was *always* torture involved at the beginning of a new assignment.

Herm gave her a stern look over his glasses, and her gut twisted a little. Maybe she was being too flip too soon. Eek.

"The evil policy and procedure manual."

Rebel relaxed. Yep. This was going to be just like every other ER she'd worked in. Torture with orientation material then release her to the wild.

"You've got the expedited orientation training to go

through for travelers. Fire safety, infection control, HIPPA, etcetera. All online now. I'll set you up with a computer terminal then we can talk about your schedule." Schedule. The most important thing to keep staff happy. Aside from payday. And good coffee.

"Got it." She looked around the station. "Is there by chance a cup of coffee somewhere I could snag first?"

"Oh, sure." He gave a nod down the hall. "Grab what you need, then back here for the mind-meld the rest of the day. If you get it all done today, you can go home early."

"Awesome."

Rebel wandered down the hall to the staff-only area and the crazed energy of the main unit eased a bit until she opened the door to the small lounge. Then her heart fluttered when she saw Duncan in his blue scrubs, coffee in hand, leaning against the counter.

His eyes were closed, and he seemed lost in his thoughts. She paused a moment, uncertain whether or not to disturb him, but the smell of coffee called to her.

"Come in. I know someone's there. I'm just perfecting my sleeping while standing up technique."

With a little smile, Rebel entered the lounge. "I thought that's what you were doing. Maybe you can give me some pointers for the next time I work a stretch of night shifts."

Duncan opened his eyes a little, glad to hear her voice free of tension. Obviously she'd been able to let the stress of yesterday go. That was a good thing. Today she looked as gorgeous as she had yesterday. But her hair was up in a clip with little strands handing down to tease her face. He had to resist the urge to push some of that mass back behind her ear. Those weren't the kinds of thoughts he should be having about a new coworker, but he seemed powerless to resist. He cleared his throat. "Not scared off after yesterday and walking into that trauma today?"

"Nope. You?"

"Nah." His smile was self-deprecating. "I grew up with four sisters, four brothers and twenty-five cousins. I saw more trauma and drama than you'd guess by the time I was twelve."

"I see. That's a huge family." Indeed. Hers had dwindled down to just her mother and herself, with a few cousins in the Mid-West somewhere.

"I'm guessing you didn't come in here to chat, but need some liquid fortitude to get through the rest of the day Herm has planned for you." He raised his coffee cup toward her.

"Psychic, too." She nodded. "I'm impressed by your extensive set of unusual skills."

Playful and flirtatious, she appealed to his lighter side. Duncan shoved away from the counter and poured her a cup of coffee, then handed it to her. "Additives are over there." He indicated the powdered creamer and sweetener selection on the counter.

"Sorry, I'm a creamer snob." She pulled out her own stash of flavored creamer and added it to the mug.

"Good to know." He grinned.

Rebel noticed that Duncan watched her intently as she prepared her coffee. She wasn't accustomed to such attention and she was a little uncomfortable with it. She'd spent years avoiding the intimacy of relationships, apart from a very occasional and very brief fling. Right now she wasn't certain whether she was appreciative of, or offended by, Duncan's focus.

The silence that hung between them went on for a few seconds too long as she ran out of things to say. Her charm only lasted so long.

"Well, I'd better go before Herm thinks I've run off." She raised her mug. "Thanks." Dropping her gaze away from him, she headed out to the safety of the unit and the dreariness of orientation.

Rebel sat in a corner of the ER away from the hustle and bustle around her, answering the incessant questions of the computer program. *Have you located the fire alarms and fire extinguishers in your area?*

She clicked "Yes," although she was pretty certain she'd just raced by them on the way to the trauma this morning. That counted, didn't it?

Staff occasionally would give her a wave, but no one stopped to chat. She supposed that was best for the moment. The next three months would give her plenty of time to make friends. These relationships were only temporary, lasting only as long as her assignment, then she moved on, to another hospital, another set of temporary friends, to relive the same life over and over again.

This lifestyle was one she'd chosen after losing most of her family to Huntington's disease. There had been no hope for her father or three brothers, and they hadn't even known it. Here, at least, she could save someone once in a while. Like yesterday.

Herm peeked in on her after a few hours. "Had enough yet?"

"Have a barf bag?" Humor in the workplace was a necessity for survival.

"Enough said. Come with me." Rebel followed him to the nurses' station and wondered what it was that he had for her to do.

"Am I going to like this job?"

Herm peered at her over his glasses again. A gesture she was coming to associate with him. Kind of like a beloved teacher overlooking his charges.

"Hard to say, but one set of papers is a follow-up from yesterday and then a scavenger hunt." He handed the papers to her. "The ER is required to follow up on patients to see how successful our efforts have been."

"I'm not quite getting that."

"Did the patient survive the first twenty-four hours, any infections, any further injuries as a result of being resuscitated? Those sorts of questions that risk management people love to drool over."

"Okay, now I'm with you." She took the paper. It was filled front and back with questions. The flow chart from hell.

"See if you can find these departments without cheating, then you can take lunch. Cafeteria's pretty good, coffee shop is close by, then come back up here."

"Got it."

Rebel didn't know how, but she knew the instant Duncan approached them. Whether it was his energy, his cologne or some unknown force she was attuned to, she turned slightly, already knowing he would be there. Maybe it was having gone through the situation together yesterday, but she felt a strange connection to him. She was probably imagining things. Men like Duncan didn't go for women like her. That was for sure. He was too much, too exciting, too dynamic, too over the top for a woman like her.

The same scenario had played out over and over on various travel assignments. Dashing doctor and super-nurse work side by side, saving lives, and one day they discover a new spark that has nothing to do with work and everything to do with the heat crackling between them. She'd seen it dozens of times, but it had never happened to her.

She rolled her shoulders against the twinge of guilt that nestled uncomfortably there. If she was honest with herself, it wasn't that she hadn't had opportunities, she'd run from them when someone had wanted to get close to her. Right now, it didn't matter. Duncan was here to do a job, just like her. It didn't matter how handsome he was or how much her heart fluttered when she thought of him.

In some dark place deep down inside her, if she was really, *really* honest, she'd admit that something about Duncan made her want to stop running, to take a chance on a relationship, see if there was a man who could love her despite the problems of her past, someone who would just love her and not worry about the time bomb ticking inside her. Loving someone again who would then reject her because of something inside her would be her worst nightmare.

Looking down into that place scared her. Made her afraid no one would be able to love her the way she needed to be loved. A man like Duncan made her want to take a chance.

CHAPTER FOUR

"Oh—hi, Doc. Maybe you can help, too." Herm included Duncan in the conversation, and Rebel turned toward him. Yes, he was definitely as handsome in scrubs as he was in street clothing. Possibly more, because scrubs had a way of stripping a person down to their basics—no frills or high-priced clothing to hide behind. From her first encounter with Duncan, she'd concluded he certainly had that. He didn't skimp on his clothing. Not that she minded. She did admire a sharp-dressed man.

"Sure. What is it?" He stepped a little closer, and Rebel's senses squealed. Oh, the man was too close for comfort. Though she could talk herself out of engaging in any sort of liaison with him, her senses reacted on their own volition.

Duncan looked at Rebel. She was tall, nearly as tall as he, and he could meet her clear green eyes almost head-on. Curious that she didn't realize how attractive she was. Maybe she'd been burned, just like him. He gave a mental shake. No one had been burned like him. The arguments, the fights. And then the wreck. That was something he'd never get over. Refocusing, he looked away from Rebel.

"It's a follow-up on the boy you two rescued yesterday. Within twenty-four hours we need to lay eyes on them." Herm muttered a few things under his breath. Probably about more documentation. Seemed it was the same situation everywhere in healthcare. Do more with less.

"Sure. I thought about him most of the night."

"Me, too." Rebel admitted what had kept her from having a good night's sleep, other than first-day jitters and thoughts of Duncan. She took the paperwork, and Herm pointed to the brightly colored map in her hands.

"That's the scavenger hunt. Find these places in the hospital so when you need to know where they are at three a.m., you can find them." He glared at Duncan. "No helping her."

"Who, me?" Duncan placed a hand on his chest and raised his eyebrows and, despite herself, Rebel responded to his light-hearted attitude. It was so essential for their work. How could she not?

"Yes, you. Get out of here for a while and take a break." Herm turned away as another staff member called for his attention.

With papers in hand, Rebel drifted toward the exit and Duncan moved with her. "You'll have to lead the way, I don't even know how to get to the PICU yet." Rebel kept her gaze on the papers, not really seeing the words. She was suddenly atwitter at spending time with Duncan. He was her coworker, but he was also a disturbingly handsome man. And one who smelled like a dream.

"This way." He ushered her with one arm ahead of him, as if he were escorting her. "We'll take the staff elevators to the fifth floor. PICU is up there." Duncan swiped his badge to call the elevator.

In just a few seconds they entered the empty car, and Rebel pushed the button. The idea of staff elevators appealed to Rebel. They helped keep the staff separated from the visitors at important times. Taking a bloodied and battered patient upstairs in view of the public did not make for good surveys. And it also protected patients' privacy.

Nervous, she kept her eyes focused on her papers. They arrived at the PICU and approached Eric's room. Duncan had gone quiet beside her, his energy dark and serious. His anticipation of what they would find was palpable, and she reacted in much the same way.

Nothing was ever quiet in an ICU. Bleeps, alarms, and the noise of respirators, although quiet in and of themselves, together made quite a racket.

A nurse in cartoon scrubs and a bouncy blond pony-tail approached. "Can I help you?" She was perky in a way Rebel could never hope to be. Her skin was flawless, and she had applied just the right amount of makeup to enhance her features. She was buxom and curvy, where Rebel barely had breasts. Or at least that's what she felt like sometimes. This was the kind of woman Duncan prob-ably went for, not someone as uninteresting as her. She didn't wear much makeup, her hair kept its own schedule of events, and she didn't have a curves in the places men liked. Even though she had flaming red hair, she thought it was a detractor. Men like Duncan didn't go for women like her, but then again she didn't date, so it didn't matter, and she needed to focus on things other than her dashing coworker.

The nurse's bright blue eyes looked between them as she spoke, but lingered on Duncan. Rebel could hardly blame her, he was something the eyes could linger on and not become fatigued.

"We have some paperwork to fill out for the ER as follow-up to see how Eric's doing," Rebel said, focusing once again on the task at hand, the only reason she was here with Duncan.

"Oh, you must have been the first responders." A light

of sympathy entered her blue eyes. "I heard about your efforts in report this morning." She pouted out her lower lip and placed a gentle hand on Rebel's arm.

"Yes, we were." She looked at Duncan, who seemed impervious to Becky's beauty and sympathetic manner. Maybe he already had a squeeze on the side and wasn't interested in anyone else. She mentally yanked herself back. Maybe it was none of her business.

"How awful it must have been to find him."

"Yes, it certainly was a shock." Rebel showed Becky the form. "Can you give us an update?"

"Sure."

Duncan observed the interaction between the two nurses who couldn't possibly be more different in looks. Though Becky was certainly attractive, his gaze kept returning to Rebel. What an unusual woman she was. Of course, he'd run across unusual women before, but there was something about Rebel that kept taking his mind down a path he'd sworn never to go down again. Romance and dating was something he'd thought had died when his fiancée had been killed. His interest in sex had been on hiatus, but now was beginning to return as he watched Rebel beside him.

"Excuse me. I want to go see him first." He stepped forward, leaving the two nurses to do the paperwork.

Rebel watched as he placed a hand on Amanda's back, startling her from sleep in the chair. He exuded compassion and Rebel swallowed hard, crushing down the memory of being on the receiving end of such a gesture some years ago.

In a few minutes, Duncan returned, the lines in his face serious. "Can you tell me where your intensivist is? I'd like to speak to him or her."

"Her. Dr. Barb Simmons. She's in the charting room

behind the nurses' station. Drop-dead gorgeous blonde. Can't miss her."

With only a nod and no lingering glances of interest, Duncan left them.

"Let's see your paperwork. I can help you fill it out," Becky said.

As Rebel stretched out her arm to hand the paperwork to Becky, her arm seemed to go numb, and she lost her grip on the pages. They fluttered to the floor. "Oh, rats!" Hastily, she grabbed them and shuffled them back together. "Sorry about that. Lost my grip for some reason." She knew the likely reason and it frightened her more than anything in the world. She was starting to show symptoms of the disease.

"That's okay," Becky said, and opened her bedside computer chart, distracting Rebel from her self-focus. Becky's fingers flew over the keyboard and pulled up the data on Eric's case.

"Any sense of how he's doing overall?" Rebel asked, nurse to nurse. Experienced nurses developed senses that couldn't be learned in a classroom or in books.

"Well, he's deeply sedated right now." She gave another sympathetic look. "I hate to even give you a guess because patients surprise me all the time. These little ones are so amazing. They spring back when you least expect it." She sighed. "Then again, they take a downturn just as fast." She gave that pout again. Once, Rebel got, twice was just unattractive.

"Thanks." She looked behind Becky. "Can I go in and see him?"

"Absolutely. Just let me know if you need anything."

Rebel could see Amanda half sitting on a chair, half lying on the bed beside Eric. Across the room a man sat with a computer on his lap, leaning back in his chair, fast asleep. "Amanda?"

The mother turned to Rebel, her face splotchy and swollen. "Yes?"

"It's Rebel, the nurse from the ER." She knelt beside the bed and placed her hand on Amanda's back, the same way Duncan had. "I came to see how you and Eric are doing." The words sounded trite. After all, how could any of them be doing after such a life-altering event?

"He's going to die. I know it." Her voice was just a whisper that spoke to Rebel's soul, which had seen so much pain in her own family. Somehow, there had to be hope, even if it was just a little.

Trying to be encouraging without giving false hope was a tricky dance. "I just reviewed his chart with Nurse Becky and things look pretty stable right now." That was the truth. At least for the moment.

"Then why hasn't he opened his eyes? Why doesn't he respond to me?" Frustration shot out of her like electricity.

"He's being heavily sedated. When kids are on the respirator they get wiggly and won't let the machine do the work." That was true, too.

"Why didn't anyone explain this to me?" She raked a hand through her hair in frustration then clenched her fists in her lap. She looked as if she wanted to hit something.

Rebel knew this information had likely been explained more than once, but due to stress of the event she hadn't remembered it.

"Just keep talking to him. He can hear you." Hearing was the last sense to leave before death. People who returned from seemingly unrecoverable events often did, and were able to relate stories of hearing everything going on around them but being unable to respond at the time.

"I didn't know whether he could hear me or not."

"He does. Just give him your love. Just let him hear your voice." That was the one hope she'd held on to when her brothers had died, that they had heard her voice and had known she loved them. "He may not respond to you right now, but he will hear you. It will be your voice he recognizes and responds to. If anything is going to pull him out of this, it will be you."

"Really?" Shocked, Amanda looked at her child, then back at Rebel, trying to determine the truth.

"I've worked with many patients who have awakened from comas, and that's the thing they all had in common. They heard their families and knew there was someone with them."

"Do you think he can…make it?" She pushed her hair out of her face.

"I don't know, but for me to go on as a nurse I need to have some hope." Rebel squeezed Amanda's hands as she echoed Duncan's sentiment and choked down her own emotion that wanted to swallow her whole. This moment was not about her own grief and loss but about the recovery of Amanda's child. "It's never easy, but don't give up."

"I don't want to…but I'm not getting much support…" she glanced at her husband "…from anyone."

"Men like to fix things and feel powerless when they can't." She thought about Duncan. He was definitely a fixer.

"You are observant." Amanda offered a smile at that bit of wisdom.

She leaned over and spoke into Eric's ear, then gave him a kiss on the forehead, careful not to bump any of his tubes. "Just remember, there is always hope."

Eagerness and a little hope now showed on Amanda's face.

"I will." She stroked Eric's forehead. "I'll talk to him all the time now. Thank you." Tears welled again in Amanda's eyes. "Thank you. You've given me more hope than I've had since this all happened."

Unable to bear the onslaught of emotions dredged to the surface by this situation, Rebel pushed them aside. She backed away before she lost control and turned to dash out the door.

And ran right into Duncan's arms.

CHAPTER FIVE

DUNCAN REACHED OUT just as Rebel crashed into him. The only way he would not bowl her over was to grab hold of her hips and bring her close against him. The papers in her hands flew into the air and seemed to drift in slow motion to the floor.

He pulled her against his hips with one arm and braced them against the doorframe with the other. Eyes wide in shock, she clutched his upper arms with both hands and caught her breath with a squeal.

With her trim frame and lower body weight, she would certainly have bounced off of him and landed on the floor had he not caught her. Now that he had caught her, he found himself in a very interesting position. Holding her was inappropriate, yet letting go of her seemed equally so. She was tiny beneath the figure-erasing scrubs. It was a crime against man to cover up such a beautiful body. He looked down at her and realized that if he'd wanted to kiss her, she was in the perfect position to do so.

He watched as she licked her lips and pressed them together. What an enticing mouth she had. Unfortunately, he had to release her before any opportunity to taste those lips occurred. As a man experienced in the ways of romantic coworker relationships, that was a treat best left unsavored. "Sorry about that. Are you okay?" Reluctantly, he released her. With some amusement he watched a vivid blush cruise up to her neck and into her cheeks. She was not as unaffected as she pretended to be. Interesting. Off limits, but very interesting.

"Yes, sorry about that."

They retrieved her paperwork, and she shuffled it back in place. They left the room with a respectable two-foot distance between them. Duncan had had enough of losing the women in his life. His mother, a sister and his fiancée. The last one had about killed him, and he'd sworn off of emotional relationships for a while to rest his heart and soul. Rebel was the most interesting woman he'd run across in a long time and, still, he hesitated. That last relationship had burned him to the core, and he hadn't really recovered from it. She'd been a colleague, too. He paused, thinking. Perhaps it was time he at least tested the waters again.

"It's Duncan, please. And it was just a little accident of timing. No fault."

She cleared her throat, focusing on the tile pattern on the floor. "So are you going to help me cheat on this scavenger hunt, or what?" She quickly diverted the conversation.

"No." He snorted. As if. But he did like a challenge.

Her gaze flashed to him. "No? So how am I going to get through all of this without dying of hunger or thirst? We are in a desert, you know."

He gave a quick laugh. He liked humor in his coworkers. Made shifts a lot more interesting. And it was safer than where his thoughts had been going. "Isn't there a map on there?"

Now *she* snorted. "If you can call it that. The copier must have run out of toner at an inopportune time. I need a GPS to get through this hospital."

"If you can navigate to the cafeteria I'll buy you some lunch." His stomach had been reminding him of his skimpy breakfast for some time now.

"You're on." She started toward the elevators, and he followed along behind, admiring the view. Puzzled, he frowned as he observed her gait and the way she moved her body.

"What do you do?" Now, more curious than ever, he began to ignore that finely tuned alarm system in his head. Pursuing her might be worth the pain.

She hit the elevator button. "Do about what?"

"For exercise. Working out." He gave her a once-over glance and liked what he saw. "The way you walk and the way you carry yourself is different. I can usually pick out how a person stays fit by the way they move and their body shape. It's a little game I play with myself. Swimmers look one way, runners look another way, cyclists another way, but you I can't figure out." The feel of her body beneath those scrubs had been firm, yet still very feminine. "You aren't a body-builder either." He frowned and tried not to ogle her in public. Administration wasn't kidding about sexual harassment.

At that, a genuine grin covered her face. "Yoga." She stood on one foot and clasped her hands together over her head with the paperwork flattened between her palms. "Like this."

"Yoga?" He glanced over her again, dumbfounded. "Really? Just yoga? I thought you just sat in impossible situations and chanted to the universe for enlightenment."

Rebel laughed. "That would be meditation. You should try yoga sometime. Strengthens the mind and spirit as well as the body." She resumed her standing position without even a wobble. Show-off.

Duncan tried to mimic her pose and was able to get his

hands over his head, but standing on one foot at the same time was *not* happening, and he almost crashed into the wall. Very uncool.

"I'm a more brute strength, linear kind of guy, like running, hiking, that sort of stuff. If I have to think about it too much, I won't do it." He laughed. "Just put me on a bike in a straight line, and I'm good."

"So how do you get back, then, if you just go in a straight line?"

He laughed, liking her quick wit. "Eventually, I stop, turn around and go in another straight line until I'm back where I started."

"You need to expand your horizons, Doctor."

"I like skiing."

"Skiing in the desert—really?" The bemused look on her face betrayed her skepticism at his statement.

"Yes. Ice hockey, too. You'd be surprised what kind of landscape the desert has to offer. We're considered high desert since we're higher in elevation than other desert areas of the southwest."

"Oh, so not like Phoenix or Death Valley?"

"Right. Way too hot for me. Went there for a conference once and about cooked my brain."

The elevator arrived, and they were off on the scavenger hunt. Rebel successfully negotiated her way to the blood bank, lab, central supply, and finally to the cafeteria.

Duncan sniffed appreciably. "I can smell the green chili from here." He closed his eyes, savoring a fond memory. "I'm in the mood for green chili cheese fries, how about you?"

"What's that?" Innocent curiosity showed in that gorgeous face of hers. Stunned, Duncan looked at her. She was *serious*.

"You've never heard of green chili cheese fries?"

"Nope. Or green chili anything." Duncan's jaw dropped, and he swore his heart skipped several important beats. He may have seen stars, but he wasn't certain. "I think I may have a coronary right now." He placed a hand over his chest. "Get the AED."

"Why? What did I say?" Eyes wide with concern, she pressed her lips together. "Did I say something totally stupid?"

"I know you're new in town, but green chili is the number one agricultural crop of the entire state and has been the foundation for my family's holdings for the last two hundred years." He took a breath and frowned. "My grandfather should never, *ever*, hear you don't know what green chili is or it could start another highland war."

"Oh, is that all?" She turned away.

"What?" Stunned, he froze in place.

"Kidding." She gave a sly grin over her shoulder. "Got it. Important stuff around here."

"And, besides that, it tastes really, *really* good."

"Okay, can we get some, then?"

"Absolutely. Your orientation would not be complete without a sampling of green chili cheese fries." Another sign of her adventurous spirit if she was willing to try an unknown food on his recommendation. That was very attractive to him. But he remembered his fiancée had also had an adventurous spirit and look where that had left them. Her dead. Him with a broken heart.

Minutes later, they had a pile of steaming French fries in front of them, topped with green chili sauce and shredded cheddar cheese. The consistency of gravy, the sauce was absolutely amazing, as far as Duncan was concerned, and he was an expert.

"If you don't like this, I'm afraid your contract will have to be terminated."

"Oh, give me a break, it will not." She gave the first natural-sounding laugh he'd heard out of her since they'd met. That was a good sign. This was fun, showing her something she'd never seen or even heard of before. Gave him new appreciation of it, too, to experience it again through her eyes, and his heart lightened.

Duncan watched as Rebel took a fry, dripping in chili sauce and cheese, and put it in her mouth. She closed her eyes as she chewed. What was it about eating a meal with some people that was so erotic? He didn't care as he took in how Rebel's face changed and her eyes popped open, surprise filling those incredible green eyes of hers. His mouth began to water and it wasn't for food but a taste of her. Even against his better judgment, the longer he spent with her, the more intrigued he became. Could he engage in a casual relationship with her, knowing she'd leave in a few months? Could they have a simple, sexual relationship and let the rest go? It was worth thinking about.

"That is spectacular. You're gonna have to get your own, pal, 'cos I'm not sharing." She slid the plate closer to her.

"I'll tell Herm you cheated." He slid the plate in front of him.

"I did not." The plate returned to Rebel.

"Who's he gonna believe, you or me?" Duncan reached for the plate but Rebel narrowed her eyes and held on to it.

"You are evil. And I believe that's blackmail."

"Then you have to share." He slid the plate into the middle again. "And it's actually extortion." He shrugged at her look. "Got a cousin who's a lawyer."

"Fine. But you know what they say about payback."

"I do. And it is." He grinned and dug his fork into the bliss on the plate, deciding to shove away thoughts of a casual sexual relationship for the moment.

"So you have a hobby farm?"

Duncan tried not to choke at her description. "If you can call ten thousand acres a hobby farm." That was in Hatch, New Mexico alone. Cousins in surrounding areas worked ranches half that size, but every acre produced quality chili in dozens of varieties.

"Shut. Up." Disbelief covered her face.

"I will not. I'm highly offended at that." Not.

"I mean, really?" She paused and looked at the chili on her fork. "Is *this* from your…ranch?"

"Probably. We ship all over the world."

"I'd love to see this place."

"I'd love to show it to you." Showing off the family estate was a piece of cake, and he'd taken a few lady friends there. Unfortunately, once they'd seen the size of his family holdings, they'd changed, expected more out of him and offered less. Sharing the money was part of the reason he enjoyed it. He was just a regular guy whose family had created wealth by working hard. His fiancée hadn't cared, and it hadn't changed their relationship, but she'd been an exceptional woman. She'd been his friend as well as his lover. And he missed that, wanted it again. But was he as appealing on his own without the draw of the wealth? With some women he hadn't known, but it had been a factor over and over again, enough to make him hesitate, less likely to take risks on a woman. Especially with a woman who might not even be around in a few months.

He wanted a woman who had heart and soul and a passion for living that equaled his own. So if he was honest with himself, he wanted the whole package, the soulmate deal, not just a sexy roommate he had nothing else in common with.

"It's obviously not here in town." Rebel's statement brought him back to the conversation.

"No. South of here. Just follow the river and stop before you hit Mexico." A place his heart lived.

"Cool. Maybe someday I can see it. I love to take day trips when I'm on my assignments to see places I never would be able to otherwise."

Just as Duncan put a forkful of the heavenly stuff in his mouth, his phone received an emergency text. He looked at it quickly, then back at Rebel. "Grab the fries. We gotta go."

Rebel took her newly discovered dish with her as they raced back to the ER and back to saving lives.

Two hours passed before Rebel surfaced from the trauma room. What had come in had been a tractor trailer versus motorcycle. Neither had won.

Rebel combed back the hair of the young man lying on the gurney while awaiting the arrival of his parents. He was only twenty-five and brain dead. She hoped his parents would consent to organ donation as there was no indication on his driver's license.

"How are you?" Herm entered the room.

"Okay." She sighed and looked at him. "I was thinking about how many people this one person can help, and he won't even know it."

"It's true." Herm pursed his lips in contemplation for a moment. "If it's a match, it's a match." He rubbed his eyes and turned away from the patient, who was being kept alive on a respirator. "Unfortunately, I've seen too many young folks like this."

"You'd think that it would get easier over the years, but it doesn't. We just learn to get through it, shake it off, and do it all over again." Fatigue swamped her. Herm was a very observant man, and he didn't miss that.

"You're sure you're okay? I can have someone else monitor him for a while and give you a break."

"Nope. I'm good."

"His folks are on the way. Should be here within the hour. You can finish your orientation materials in here and keep an eye on him at the same time, can't you?"

"Sure." Nurses were forever being tasked with multiple duties at one time. Part of the job and part of the way nurses were built.

"Is there something you need to tell me about? If there is, I'm a good listener." He turned his full attention to her.

"No." She placed a hand on his arm. "I appreciate the offer, though." A sigh escaped her. "He reminds me a bit of my brother, Ben. He died a few years ago. Now and then the memories spring up for me."

"I'm sorry, Rebel. If I had known…"

"You couldn't have, and I'll be all right." With a nod, Herm left her to her thoughts.

After the situation was tended to and the parents had given consent, the patient was taken to the operating room. It was a somber time, and she needed some fortitude to get through the rest of the shift.

She entered the staff lounge and poured herself a cup of coffee, wishing for something strong to put into it, like Irish whiskey or coffee liqueur Kahlua. After the last couple of hours she could use a stiff drink.

Just as she was about to have her first sip, the lounge door opened and Duncan entered. He stopped short when he saw her. "Don't drink that. It'll kill you."

"What? It's coffee, not hemlock."

"It's awful." He rummaged in a cupboard over the sink. In just a few minutes he'd put on a new pot of coffee and the brew smelled heavenly. Her mouth even watered. "I keep a stash of the good stuff for just the right occasion."

"And this is it?"

"Seems good enough for me." He gave a sideways smile that made her heartbeat a little irregular.

"Wow. That smells like Jamaica, or what I imagine it to be." She'd never been there, so she could only imagine.

"It does, and that's why I like it."

"I've never been there, but it's on my bucket list for sure." It was a very long list.

"Seriously? Your *bucket* list? What are you, thirty?" He peered at her, trying to figure out if she was serious.

"Yes, I'd like to go there before I die. That's what a bucket list is about, right?" She'd go there and go other places her family hadn't been able to go to. Someday. Before she died. Hopefully.

"You're out of your mind." He stared at her as if she was.

"Why?" She frowned. "Didn't you say you liked Jamaica?"

"Jamaica isn't a place you go before you *die*. It's a place you go in the prime of your life, with a lover on your arm, taking long walks on the beach. Hell, even sleeping on the beach." He shook his head and sipped some more, considering her. "You need to move Jamaica up on that list." He tipped his empty coffee cup at her. "It's for young people. Long days at play and longer nights in your lover's arms. *That's* what Jamaica is for."

Though the description sounded fantastic, she'd put away fantasies of having a normal, loving relationship with a man a long time ago. No man would willingly go into a relationship knowing his partner could die any time, and waiting until she was well into a relationship before telling a man wasn't fair either. It would be starting a relationship on a lie, and she wouldn't do that. "That's all well and good, but I don't have anyone to go with." She shrugged as if it didn't matter to her when it really did. "I don't date, so I'd end up going by myself anyway. It can wait." Something about his description of Jamaica scratched at a door she'd locked long ago. With her family DNA she wasn't a marriage candidate. She'd accepted it. Explaining it wasn't going to change it.

Duncan nearly spilled the coffee he was pouring. "What do you mean, you *don't date*? A woman with your looks, your smarts should be beating men off with a stick. Why wouldn't you have someone whisk you off to Jamaica for a week of passion?" The thought was ludicrous. Even he, who had serious commitment issues, had been to Jamaica with a woman before now.

Rebel glanced away and got fidgety. Uh-oh. He'd offended her.

"It's not something you'd understand, but I just don't date very much." Her smile was tight and that open door to communication they'd been enjoying had just slammed shut. He poured her coffee and brought it to her at the table where she sat.

"You should. You'd live longer."

She looked at him then, doubt covering her face.

"It's a documented fact that people who have a regular sex life live longer than those who don't."

"Now, that's just not true." She flat out didn't believe him.

"Sure it is. Read it in a men's health magazine. Three orgasms a week, and you'll live longer."

Flabbergasted, obviously uncomfortable with the topic, she delayed by adding some milk and sweetener to her coffee. "Yes, well. I'll take that into consideration should the occasion arise."

He sat at the table with her and hid a grin as he pursued the topic against his better judgment. What was it about Rebel that was making him take more risks, want to take even bigger risks, than he had in, like, forever? "As a traveler, you control your own destiny, right? Your own schedule?"

"In theory. I can always refuse an assignment or take a break between. But being a traveler is like being on permanent vacation and having a full-time job at the same time." She shrugged. "I don't take vacations either."

"That's a serious infraction against adding fun to your life." He took a sip of the steaming brew, but his gaze remained intently focused on her. "This is definitely what I remember from Jamaica." He closed his eyes, and instantly an image of walking with Rebel on the beach at night surfaced in his mind. The wind teased her luxurious hair against his skin as he reached out to bring her closer to him. That was too easy, so he opened his eyes.

"Sounds like it was a good experience for you." She wished she could say the same. There was nothing else going on in her life so she just worked. Although some people might call that sad, she saw it as a necessity to get through her painful life. If there was too much extra time she thought too much of her family losses.

"It was." He focused his full attention on her in that probing way she was coming to associate with him. "But what you said concerns me, Rebel." He got all serious then.

"Oh, don't be. It's the way I live my life. Quiet, unassuming, devoted to work." Avoiding emotional intimacy and relationships along the way. They only resulted in loss and she'd had enough of that in her life.

"I get that. You can be all that and still date, maybe add a layer of fun to your life. It doesn't have to be all about work, does it?"

"At this point, it does." She put down her cup. "I'm not comfortable having this discussion with you, Duncan, so can we table it and just have a nice cup of coffee together?"

"Sure." He nodded. "Sure." Wow. That was a very strong boundary she'd erected around herself in seconds flat. She'd obviously been doing it for some time. Most people were willing to talk a little about themselves, some people talked entirely too much about themselves, but Rebel was a different issue and that intrigued him. He loved a good mystery, and Rebel was cocooned in it.

"You mentioned your family has lived here for some time." She was changing the topic away from herself. That was okay for now, but he wanted to know more about her and one day he would find out. For the moment, he let it go.

"Yes. Although I favor the Hispanic side of my family in looks, the other side is Scottish. If you talked to my grandfather, you'd think he'd just gotten off the ship."

"What do you mean?"

"His grandparents were from Scotland and immigrated here, so he learned English with a heavy Scottish accent." Even the memory of the man made him smile. He was an old codger, but lovable. Sometimes. On occasion. If he felt like it.

"Oh, wow." A small smile curved her lips upward.

"Yes, you should hear him when he gets going on something."

"Like what?" She leaned forward, her green eyes sparkling now.

"Like formal introductions when you meet someone for the first time." He'd had that pounded into his brain over and over as a kid, so it wasn't something he'd ever forget.

"Come again?" Her brows twitched upward.

Duncan set his coffee cup down, cleared his throat as if preparing for a stately oration and struck a dignified pose.

"Hoo d'ye expec' people t' remembe' hoo ye are if ye don' intr'duce y'self?" Duncan gave a plausible Scottish accent, rolling his tongue in all the right places.

Rebel laughed out loud and covered her mouth with her hand. "In this day and age? He's still stuck on introductions and proper manners? Are you kidding me?"

Wide-eyed, Duncan gave her a serious look. "Absolutely not. When I was a kid he was tough on all of us when it came to manners. We thought he was from another planet. I now have a highly tuned reflex to open a door if a woman even *thinks* of going through one."

"I'd like to meet this grandfather of yours sometime. He sounds like a kick in the pants." She sipped her coffee and Duncan picked up his cup, too.

"He is. And that's something I'd like to see. You and all that red hair could give him a run for his money." He leaned forward and peered intently at her. "I'm willing to bet there's a bit of a temper hidden down in there somewhere in the right circumstances."

"What are you talking about?" She played it up, wide-eyed, and blinked innocently at him. "I'm just a simple lass of Irish descent."

Duncan barked out a laugh. "Like I'm going to believe *that* anytime soon." He shook his head, enjoying this repartee. "But I'm willing to bet you didn't come in here for a chat about my family history."

"Nope, but that's okay. It's been an interesting chat."

Duncan tilted his head as an even more interesting thought entered his mind. Why not? "I'm going to see him this weekend if you'd like to come along. He won't go see his doctor, so I have to give him the once-over a couple of times every year, make sure everything's still ticking the right way."

"Oh, sure. I'm off this weekend. Sounds like fun." She pointed a finger at him. "But it's not a date, just a field trip."

"Great. I'll pick you up on Saturday morning for a non-date field trip." He looked at his watch then sighed. "Guess I'll let you get back to your reading."

Rebel nodded. "Thanks for the coffee." She smiled, but it was less exuberant than her laughter had been only moments ago and he could see she was fading away. Whatever had happened to her still had enough pull to drag her away.

"Anytime." Duncan watched her go out the door, careful to avoid any coffee spillage. More puzzled and intrigued than he'd been about a woman in some time, he wondered what was going on with Rebel Taylor that she'd left romance, relationships and thoughts of romantic islands behind. She was too dynamic to wither away her youth. How in the world could he help her when she wouldn't cop to what was really going on? One way or another, he'd find out.

That thought stuck with him for most of the day. Rebel was in the prime of her life, had her career path laid out, obviously single without children or she wouldn't be working as a travel nurse.

As he moved through his day in the ER, seeing patients with spring flu or a kid with serious road rash on his right arm and leg after crashing on a bicycle that was too big for him, to writing up notes and reviewing radiology reports, he'd see Rebel in a corner of the nurses' station seemingly engrossed or hypnotized by the computer screen. Probably bored out of her mind.

He'd been pursued by women of many cultures and from unfathomable wealth, but none had captured his interest the way Rebel had. Women in his social circle were generally predictable, demanding, and spoiled rotten, and he wanted nothing to do with that anymore. After the death of his fiancée, he'd changed. The experience had changed him. But he was interested in a trim woman with flaming red hair and sad eyes that made him want to know why.

CHAPTER SIX

TWO DAYS LATER, Duncan's muscles felt every bit of the workout he'd just performed. Running. Swimming. Biking. As if he were preparing for a triathlon. But it was just his way of working off the stress of the job. It wore him out, but filled him up at the same time.

Thank you, endorphins.

No, thank you, yoga.

Duncan prowled his living room after getting something to eat and hitting the shower. Television news was the same old hash with a human interest piece thrown in, so he preferred to read it online. Usually a few miles on his stationary bike or elliptical machine kept his mind focused and helped him to decompress from the day, but not tonight. Tonight was different. Restlessness seized him.

Nothing distracted him from the unusual green eyes that kept flashing in his mind, and the deep sorrow hidden within them. Somehow, the world must have hit on Rebel Taylor's life. She'd assured him there was no ex-husband, about to jump out of her past into her future. So what was it that drove her, kept her going from assignment to assignment without a break? People behaved in predictable ways, and he could figure them out pretty quickly, but Rebel was not being predictable at all.

Though he'd had a few relationships over the years, the last one had about done him in. A woman he'd loved enough to be engaged to had died in his arms. He'd been unable to help her and that had destroyed him for months. Now the memory burned in the back of his throat and prevented him from having another deep relationship.

Just then the phone rang, and he answered it. His cousin Rey was on the other end.

"Hey, man."

"What are you up to?"

"Heading down to Hatch on Saturday to see him." He paused, knowing he was going to get some stick from his cousin, but they were like brothers, so he could deal. "And taking a lady friend with me. She's Irish. Should be interesting."

"A lady friend, eh?" The tone in Rey's voice hinted he thought she was more than a lady friend. "Irish, eh? You're asking for trouble." Rey laughed.

"There could be sparks for sure."

"You're tempting fate. Remember the last chick you took down to meet him? Disaster from the get-go." Duncan couldn't argue that. Rebound relationship after Valerie had died.

"This one's different, and she's not a romantic interest."

"Why not? She ugly?"

"No." She was gorgeous.

"Overweight?"

"No." Fit and athletic.

"Smell bad?"

"Hardly." She smelled like a lavender garden.

"Bad breath?"

"Not that I can tell." He hadn't gotten close enough to really know. Yet.

"Then you have some explaining to do, cuz, 'cause she sounds fine to me. Why aren't you interested in her?"

"*She* actually isn't interested in *me*. She doesn't date."

Rey laughed out loud at that one. Duncan could hear the wheeze as he struggled for breath. "That's a good one. Maybe she likes ladies instead."

"No. She's straight for sure, but she doesn't date. Now someone who is as gorgeous as she is should have men standing in line for her, but she doesn't, and isn't interested." He paused a moment. Rey was a cop and had finely tuned instincts. He definitely knew how to read people. "Does that make sense to you?"

"Not to me, but to her it does. Something probably happened to her she's not over yet." Rey snorted. "You're the doctor, not me. Aren't you supposed to know this stuff already?"

"Yes, but it just doesn't make sense." Seriously.

"Not to me either, but you know women, they can change on a dime. Maybe she just doesn't like *you*." He laughed that one up big time.

"What?" Seriously? He was nice, had a good job and—

"Come on, man, lighten up. I'm just kidding. What lady in her right mind wouldn't like you?" He knew all about Duncan's romantic escapades since they'd both discovered girls were cool.

"Sounds like you need to have a heart-to-heart with this lady. If she's like you say, you can talk to her, right? And if you can't talk to the woman you're in love with, there's something wrong."

"Whoa. I'm not in love with her." But he would admit to being intrigued by her. And very attracted *to* her.

"Maybe she just has a broken heart you need to fix. Some ladies have tender hearts, even the tough ones. You're a doctor, so heal her." There was mumbling on the phone and the sound of children giggling in the background. "I gotta go, bro'. The wife's out with her lady friends tonight, and I have dad duty. Homework, baths, the works."

"Sounds like fun." Duncan knew Rey loved being a dad, and he hoped to be one someday, too. Having grown up surrounded by cousins, he wanted a big family of his own. He had wanted to marry Valerie and be a dad, too. That's what had been the last straw in their relationship. They'd argued. She hadn't wanted children. Period. She'd taken off in her car and crashed. He'd followed behind her and pulled her from the wreckage, but she'd died in his arms.

"So what's your lady friend's name?" More giggling in the background, and Duncan knew his time with Rey was just about up.

"Rebel Taylor." Even as he said it, her name lingered in his mind, and he wanted to see her again. Soon.

"Okay, okay, wait. Her name is Rebel? Seriously? Maybe she was just born bad with a name like that." In his culture superstitions were everywhere, so it wasn't a surprise his cousin said that.

"She's a perfectly nice woman, Rey. She has a proper name but it doesn't suit her at all." The thought of using her given name didn't feel right.

"Then why don't you just ask her? You've never been shy about getting what you want, even if it's just information."

"I don't know." He ran a hand through his hair. "There's something with her. A vulnerability or something that's deep. When I talked about Jamaica, she said it's on her *bucket list* to do before she dies."

"So?"

Was his cousin brain dead? "Seriously? Would you want to wait till you're old to go to a place like that?"

"Good point. That's messed up."

"And she had never heard of green chili."

Silence on the other end for a moment. "You're *serious*?"

"Unbelievable, isn't it?"

"You should marry that woman."

Duncan blinked. "That's a hell of a leap. From 'This is green chili' to 'Will you marry me?'"

"Well, you know this lady isn't out for your money if she's never even heard of green chili, and she certainly doesn't know about the family business." There was a snort of indignation in the background. "Just need to find yourself a woman like my Julia. She's the best."

"Of course she is, but you've known her since we were kids."

"True."

"I'll keep that in mind, should the occasion arise. For now, I'm just bringing a coworker to the ranch for the weekend. No big deal."

After signing off with Rey, he did his best to settle down for the night. A pair of haunted green eyes kept appearing in his mind's eye. There was something, some pain, some regret, some…something she couldn't hide. He wanted to help, wanted to take her in his arms and hold her close.

Was it only curiosity holding him captive? Was it the shared experience of rescuing Eric bonding them when otherwise they'd have just been acquaintances? Or was he imagining something that wasn't there, simply because he was lonely?

Flopping facedown onto his bed, he gave up for the night. He didn't know what the answer was, maybe Saturday would tell, but right now he needed some shut-eye.

* * *

After a few more days of chaos in the ER and seeing Duncan only briefly, Rebel was ready for a weekend of peace and quiet, with a small side trip to meet Duncan's elderly grandfather. Duncan had called and said he'd pick her up at eight a.m., so she was ready to go.

She flitted around her apartment, waiting for Duncan. Was she out of her mind? Had he really invited her to meet his grandfather? What had she been thinking to agree to that? She didn't meet the families of people she worked with. She didn't even socialize with people she worked with. She didn't know how many invitations she'd turned down or avoided over the last six years of her travel nursing career that had been offered by coworkers.

The echo of their words rang in her mind.

Come on, it'll be fun.

It's just one cocktail.

You work too much.

Why don't you want to come?

They were all well meaning, and she certainly could have made more friends, but people who extended offers like that expected something in return. They wanted something from her. Wanted to get to know her, and that was out of the question.

The doorbell rang, and Rebel's pulse kicked into high gear. If she didn't move, maybe he'd go away. Maybe he'd think she'd forgotten. Couldn't she just say she'd changed her mind or gotten called into work?

"Stop being silly, Rebel. You're a grown woman. You can do this." She opened the door and realized she wasn't being silly at all. Her senses were instantly overloaded by Duncan, the epitome of a sexy Hispanic New Mexican man. A black T-shirt hugged muscles that hadn't been apparent beneath his scrubs. It molded to his torso and defined his shoulders and trim waist. Jeans that were well loved, a little worn around the edges and fit him to perfection. A tan chamois shirt with sleeves rolled up to his elbows, revealing muscled forearms and strong hands. And scuffed cowboy boots that seemed a perfect fit to his heritage and personality.

She swallowed and took in one of those deep yoga breaths she practiced every day. She'd told Duncan yoga was good for the mind, body and spirit. She needed some of that now. Gulp.

"Wow. Don't think I'd have recognized you out of the scrubs." Seriously, and he smelled like a dream. "Come in."

She huffed out a little breath.

This was *s-o-o-o-o* wrong.

She was in *s-o-o-o-o* much trouble.

"Thanks. Same to you," he said, and indicated her state of dress in white clam-diggers that exposed her calves, a Kelly-green top, and her family tartan thrown over one shoulder.

"You do realize you're going to start a war with that." He nodded to the tartan and gave a full-out grin.

"Oh, really? Then I won't bring it." She reached to remove the plaid and gasped when Duncan clasped her wrist tightly in his hand.

"Absolutely not. Don't change a thing." He leaned closer to her and looked down as she could only stare into his eyes. "I wouldn't miss that for anything. It's about time the old man had a challenge."

Somehow she ended up closer to Duncan with his one hand still clutching her wrist and his other pressed against her hip, reminiscent of the position they had been in the other day. Only this time there were no constraints of work, no witnesses, nothing to stop him.

Then his gaze dropped to her mouth. Without thinking,

she parted her lips and tilted her face toward him, silently begging him to kiss her.

This was a woman who had no idea how beautiful she was and how that intrigued him. If there was no flash between them, then he'd know they were destined for friendship. But if there was a spark, that could lead them down another, more dangerous, yet much more interesting, path. Needing no further encouragement, Duncan closed the distance between them and pressed a simple, chaste kiss to her lips.

Spark.

Definite spark.

Duncan's mouth was soft and firm against hers and her lips actually tingled. The surprise of the kiss flashed all the way to her toes. Something she'd heard about but had never experienced. Then he moved and pulled her more firmly against him. One hand dove into her hair and held her head as his mouth opened over hers.

Inside she gasped as his tongue touched hers. Oh, God, she was in trouble. Without being aware of it, she moved her arms and clutched his shoulders, easing closer to him, if possible. The glide of his silky tongue nearly made her want to abandon her morals and her clothing, but she restrained herself. She tasted cinnamon on him and the lingering essence of coffee. Two of her favorite things, but right now she didn't care as she gave herself over to the kiss that overwhelmed her senses.

Duncan nearly forgot he was going to just kiss her to test the situation. As she moved closer, bringing her body against his, he realized how well she fitted him from nose to toes. The taste of her was shockingly sweet. As he cupped the back of her head and dove deep into her, he sensed a depth of passion she probably wasn't aware of. Tremors shot through him, and he wanted to abandon the planned trip to take her down the hall to her bedroom instead.

Not a good idea. Yet. He eased back and watched in delight as her eyelids fluttered and surprise covered her face. She was as turned on as he by the surprising power of the kiss. Her lips were red and plump, face flushed and breathing slightly erratic. He imagined he looked about the same. He'd love to see her all rumpled from making love all afternoon but had to grit his teeth and pull away.

She was relieved when he moved back, but at the same thoroughly confused by the kiss. Then again, Duncan wasn't going to be someone she'd date. They were just coworkers and friends.

Who maybe kissed on occasion. That happened, didn't it?

"That was very nice, Rebel." His eyes glittered.

"Uh, very." She cleared her throat and blew out a breath, trying to get herself under control.

He placed a light kiss on her lips and reluctantly withdrew. He clasped her shoulder, then let his hand stroke down her arm and take her hand. "Let's get going, shall we?" He straightened the tartan over her shoulders. "This looks perfect on you."

Despite her experience as a nurse, she was such a babe in some ways. He liked that. Not sure why, but he did. The innocence she exuded was really quite alluring. Her own siren song she didn't know she sang.

"Thanks." With her senses still humming, she grabbed her handbag and locked the door. Duncan took her hand and escorted her to his vehicle. The pickup truck seemed totally *Duncan*. It was black and unassuming on the outside, but inside it had all the bells and whistles one could ask for. It looked like a small airplane. She wasn't surprised when he put on aviator sunglasses.

"We'll be there in a few minutes."

"Where does he live? In a retirement home?" There were probably lots of them in Albuquerque. It was a retirement hot spot.

Duncan snorted, then choked on a laugh. "Him? In a facility? Not on your life. He'd throw himself in front of a bus first."

"More self-sufficient than I imagined, then?" Some elderly lived independently well into their nineties.

Duncan gave her a slant-eyed glance then turned his attention back to the road. "You have no idea."

In short order, they arrived not at a private home, as she'd expected, but at a private airfield.

"He lives at an airport?" Now she was more confused than ever.

"No, he lives in Hatch, like I said. It's about three hours by car, but only about forty-five minutes by plane."

Her stomach churned. "This isn't a good idea. Why don't you just take me home, and we can forget it? Or we could drive." Panic began to set in. How the hell was she going to get out of this? Get into an airplane with him after he'd just given her the kiss of a lifetime? How was she going to sit *that* close to him and not reach out?

"You don't get air-sick, do you?" He parked the truck and got out. She bailed out of her side and slammed the door.

"N-no, I don't think so, but I've never been in a plane that small before." It looked like a toy. Seriously, where was the wind-up device?

"Well, here's your chance." He began to remove the padded covers from the propeller. "You're not afraid to go up with me, are you?" He moved closer to her. "You are. You're uncertain about going up in a plane with a man you just met."

What a relief. He understood, and they could end this now.

"No problem." He resumed his preparations and anxiety resurfaced.

"You're a pilot?" That surprised her. Most people she knew were just what they appeared to be. A doctor or nurse or plumber. Duncan was starting to have more depth than she'd imagined, but that didn't mean she wanted to get into a flying tin can with him.

"I've been flying since I was fourteen. Got my junior license when I was sixteen, flew my grandfather back and forth from Hatch to Albuquerque I don't know how many times, then got my full pilot's license so I could fly day or night. Been flying for almost twenty years now."

"Uh…that's nice." He was still preparing the plane, like he thought she was getting into it.

"Don't worry, Rebel. I'll get you there safely, and I'll get you back safely." He grinned and looked at her over his reflective sunglasses. "Trust me. I'm a doctor."

Now, that made her laugh, and she relaxed. "I think that's the cheesiest line I've ever heard."

"Yeah, but it made you laugh and that's a beautiful thing."

He approached her and took her hand gently in his. "It's going to be okay. You said you wanted a field trip." He led her to the small plane, opened the door and assisted her into the passenger seat, tucked the plaid around her and buckled her in. After securing her door, he rounded the plane and settled himself in the pilot's chair.

Duncan helped her to adjust the headphones so they could speak to each other over the headset and started the plane. The hum of the engine whined in her ears and the vibration pulsed through her. Excitement and eagerness fought with equal parts of anxiety and nausea inside her as Duncan got all serious and went through his preflight checks.

"Any mishaps over the years?" Although it was wise to ask, it also felt impolite.

"Only one. Daisy got sick every time." Though he answered the question honestly, he didn't elaborate and continued his preparations.

"Oh, I see." A sick, jealous feeling surged inside her, and she pushed it down. Though he'd kissed her, she didn't have any right to be jealous. Knowing he'd flown another woman multiple times put a damper on the day. Another yoga breath to clear those thoughts. And she ignored the tremor in her hands. It was nothing.

"She hated flying, but once she got her paws on the ground she was a whole new dog. Raced through the fields like a puppy."

"Paws?" That opened up a whole new dimension to the situation.

"Yes, she was my dog. Chocolate lab. Never had another dog like her." A wistful sigh escaped him. "She was a gift from my mother when I was twelve. Said I needed to learn how to take care of a four-legged female before I could ever consider taking care of a two-legged one."

Relief flowed through Rebel and a warm pulse in her chest followed. A dog.

Someone spoke into the headset, and Duncan responded. Rebel remained quiet as they bumped out onto the runway and prepared to take off.

Her heart raced and her mouth went dry. Clenching her hands on the seat didn't relieve her anxiety, but she couldn't help it, just as she couldn't help the grin that exploded on her face when the tires left the pavement and they were airborne.

CHAPTER SEVEN

A TOTALLY GIRLISH squeal erupted from her throat. "Oh, my, this is incredible!" There were so many things to look at all at once out of every window of the plane, she felt as if her head were on a swivel. There was the river, the mountains, cars on the highway, and all kinds of buildings that were growing smaller and smaller.

Duncan's chuckle sounded warm in her ears. "Keep that up and you're gonna barf. Pick one side of the plane to look out of."

That got her attention. So uncool to barf in front of witnesses. "Good to know."

"Look to your right, there's the Rio Grande. Locals say it *without* the emphasis on the e at the end. And I've heard people add the word river at the end. It literally translates to river big, so no need to add river on the end."

"Dead giveaway for tourists, right?" Note to self.

"You got it."

For the next hour Duncan kept her entertained by pointing out the sights below and didn't make her one bit nauseated. She was fascinated by all the knobs and dials he tended to. No wonder his truck looked like a small plane on the inside. He was used to it.

"We're coming in over the property now."

Rebel looked at a beautiful patchwork of red dirt and

green vegetation, whirls of dirt kicked up by a tractor adding another dimension to the scene below. The engine changed tone, and Rebel clutched the seat.

"Don't worry, just have to slow the plane so we can land."

"Down there?" She raised her brows and didn't see a thing large enough to land on. "Uh, where?"

He chuckled. "Yes, down there. Don't worry. I've never missed the airstrip yet."

"That's reassuring."

Duncan expertly guided the plane down until they were just a few feet above the dirt. Rebel cringed and closed her eyes tightly, held her breath.

Then a few bumps, the pressure of the brakes pressed her forward into the seat belt and then flung her back into it as they came to a dusty, bouncy stop unscathed.

"You okay?" Duncan asked, and looked at her.

"I'm okay."

Duncan reached toward her, his hands cupping her face as he pushed off the headset. "Welcome to Hatch."

Both doors were flung open from the outside and two young men, bearing a strong resemblance to Duncan, peered in at them.

"Come on, he's waiting for you."

Rebel smiled as she stepped out onto solid ground again.

"Rebel, these are my nephews, Jake and Judd," Duncan said as he introduced them. They rode in a golf cart on a dirt track that paralleled a field of chili. In minutes, they approached a huge, two-story home that reminded her of pictures she'd seen of historic old Mexico. Beautiful, traditional and exotic.

"There he is."

Rebel noticed a hunched-over old man standing on the porch. He raised a hand, and she waved back, though she knew he couldn't see her. The old man appeared to lean on something, and she thought it might be a cane or a walker. With the sun bright overhead, she shaded her eyes with one hand and as they neared the house she realized she'd fallen victim to a trick of light and shadow.

The man was six feet tall and as robust as she could imagine any ninety-year-old could be. Duncan had said he was impressive, and Rebel believed him. The cart stopped at the edge of the patio, and Duncan stepped out, then offered a hand to assist her. "Don't be afraid."

"I'm not afraid," Rebel said, and straightened her spine. "I've taken on many patients his age. I can handle him."

A snort erupted from one of the nephews in the front seat, but Rebel didn't know which one.

Duncan walked beside Rebel with anticipation humming through him. He didn't really know why. They weren't a couple, they weren't even dating. The last time he'd introduced a woman to his grandfather it had ended in disaster. The man had seen right through her and had made no bones about what he thought of her.

They'd broken up the next day.

"So this is the lady friend you were tellin' me about?" he asked, and stepped forward.

"Yes. Allow me to introduce my friend and a nurse, Rebel Taylor. Rebel, this is my grandfather, Rafael McFee, current owner of this impressive empire."

Rafael held his hand out to Rebel, and she didn't know whether to shake it or curtsy, so she went with a firm grip. She'd seriously have to amend her mistaken assumption he was going to be elderly, frail and *cute*. This man was anything but, and she could see how Duncan had inherited his strong, commanding presence and control.

"It's a pleasure to meet you, sir. Duncan has mentioned you several times." She hoped that was okay.

Without releasing her hand, he gave Duncan a narrow-eyed look. "I'll bet he did." His accent was soft with a mixture of Spanish and Scottish inflections. Rafael tucked her hand into his elbow and led the way to an outdoor patio, a *portál*, if she remembered correctly. "Did he tell you I chased off his last girlfriend?"

Rebel gave a panicked look at Duncan's enigmatic expression, then returned it to Rafael. "No. No, he didn't. But as I'm not his girlfriend, I don't have to worry about you chasing me off, do I?"

"Well, there's still the matter of you walking into my home brazenly displaying the colors of a rival clan, now, isn't there?"

Rebel laughed and patted him on the arm. "Now, that's a whole other issue."

They settled at a large wooden table with chairs made of wood and cowhide, and an older Hispanic woman emerged from inside, carrying a tray of iced tea. She didn't have the manner of a hired member of staff, but carried herself as if she had been around this family for a long, long time.

"I'm Lupe, and I run this madhouse," she said, then turned to Rebel. "Now, be on your best manner."

Rebel raised her brows and Duncan said, "She's talking to him, not us."

"Oh." She paused. "Oh! So you've made a habit of misbehavior, have you?" Rebel asked, innocently setting her chin on her hand and looking right at Rafael.

Duncan tilted back in his chair and roared out a laugh. "I knew this was going to be fun."

The scowl on Rafael's face should have made her cringe, but she only smiled, comforted by Duncan's relaxed demeanor. He was right. It was fun.

"So, tell me, why *aren't* you dating my grandson? Don't tell me he's not good enough for you either." Rafael turned to face Duncan. "Don't tell me she's like that last one. Only seeing dollar signs." He paused, thinking. "Or was that the one before that? The last one didn't make it to the altar either." He slapped his hand on the table and Rebel jumped. "Dammit, Duncan. You're supposed to find a woman you can make babies with. I want to make sure my favorite grandson has his life in order before I die." The scowl on his face was enough to make anyone cringe, but Duncan hardly looked disturbed.

Duncan snorted and reached out to take Rebel's hand for a second. "That's about enough of the grilling." He leaned forward, getting into Rafael's face. "And I've *never* been your favorite grandson."

"Duncan certainly is a fine doctor and a fine man, but the fact is I don't date. It has nothing to do with him." There. She said it out loud, and she hadn't been struck by lightning. She looked overhead. It could still happen. Looked like thunderheads were coming their way. Outrageously huge ones, racing across the horizon.

"Why not?" The frown grew even more fierce. "Don't you like men?"

"I like men just fine." She glanced down and fiddled with her glass. "Things just haven't worked out that way for me. So I've decided to let go of that part of my life."

"Why? There must be something wrong with the men you're picking, then."

"Yes. Well." Rebel's insides tightened a bit, not wanting to get into her tragic family history the second they arrived, but it seemed they were on the edge of it.

"Seriously, Rafael. Enough." Duncan defended Rebel. She didn't need that sort of treatment. "Rebel's decisions are her own and it's not for us to pry. She hasn't even had a cup of coffee, and you're jumping down her throat."

"It's not natural, that's for sure," Rafael said, and eased back into his chair.

"If I've offended you, sir, I apologize, but, as Duncan says, this is my own business." She stood and wrapped the plaid around her shoulders as if it would protect her. "You'll have to excuse me for a while," she said, and walked away from the table, back out the gate they'd entered and away from the house. Where she was going, she didn't know, but she needed a breather. Now.

Her strides lengthened until she was almost running away from the house. If she'd worn better shoes, she would have raced, but her flats weren't designed for that. And there were too many rocks and stickers on the road.

Minutes later she heard the crunch of tires on the dirt, but no engine. She kept going, not looking behind her. It was probably one of the field workers she'd seen, and she wrapped her tartan around her shoulders tightly. Certainly wouldn't be Duncan chasing after her. He wasn't the kind to chase.

"Rebel, wait."

It really was him. "No."

"Seriously, please wait." He drove the golf cart closer and pulled alongside her as she huffed along the dirt road. A small rock had gotten into one shoe and now she limped along, pain in every step. But it was nothing to the pain in her heart. She didn't want to have to explain herself to anyone. Her lifestyle was a choice. A personal one. Telling it didn't change it.

The sky darkened further as the thunderclouds raced closer and drops of rain began to fall all around her while Duncan was safe in the little golf cart.

"I'll stop if you'll stop." What a ploy.

"I'm not stopping." It was a matter of stubborn pride now. The Irish always could out-stubborn the Scottish.

Or at least that's what her mother had told her. Rebel was about to find out.

"Then I guess I'm not either."

When the skies opened up minutes later and lightning sizzled too close, she jumped into the golf cart. "Let's go. I can be mad at you later."

Duncan guided the lumbering golf cart toward a large barn, which looked really far away. Rain pelted down on them and Duncan began to drive slower.

"What are you doing? Go faster, not slower."

"The battery is dying. Damned kids never plug anything in. We're going to have to run for it."

"Oh, no." She got out of the questionable shelter of the cart and ran alongside Duncan. They were getting closer to the barn when mud engulfed one of her shoes, and she was forced to stop.

"Come on!" Duncan raced back to her.

"I'm stuck!" She was *not* leaving her shoe.

Like any superhero ready to save the damsel in distress, he bent at the waist, put her over his shoulder and ran for it.

Rebel screamed the whole way.

Duncan stumbled into the barn and collapsed into a pile of hay as he lowered Rebel down. Or tried to. It was more of a controlled fall than a gracefully executed maneuver. Seemed like he was always stumbling into something when he was around Rebel.

"Are you okay?" Riding on his shoulder couldn't have been comfortable.

"I'm fine. Just soaked." She pushed her dripping hair up and out of her face. "That storm came up quickly."

"Welcome to monsoon season."

"Seriously?"

"Seriously, but that's not what I mean. I meant okay about what happened back there. He's a cantankerous old buzzard, but that was going overboard, even for him." Duncan slid his hand down her arm until he reached her hand. "I'm sorry. I should have stepped in sooner, but I didn't realize he was going for the jugular until too late."

"It's okay, really. I should be used to people asking me questions like that."

"Well, no, you shouldn't. Your personal decisions are nobody's business, not even mine. Though I don't understand, it's really none of my business." He wanted to, but it was such a waste of life to not fully enjoy it. And for someone as vibrant and lively as Rebel, it was equally sinful in his eyes. Especially when that life could be ripped out from under you at a moment's notice. Like in a car wreck.

"Thank you." Giving herself a verbal shake, she sat on a bale of hay and patted the space beside her. "Sit down. Why don't you tell me about this monsoon season? I've never heard of it."

Duncan shook himself like a dog. He dropped onto the spot beside her. "It's the rain this time of the year that makes or breaks a chili season." Though he was soaked to the bone, it didn't bother him. He was warming up watching Rebel try to make headway with her hair, which was a wild tangle. He itched to dig his hands into the mass and test it for himself.

"I had no idea." She huffed one last strand out of her face.

Pieces of straw poked out from her shirt, and he reached to remove that. She looked up at him, and she'd never looked more beautiful, more alluring than she did sitting there soaking wet on a hay bale in his grandfather's barn.

"Rebel." He reached out and cupped her face so she looked up at him. "I want to kiss you again."

She didn't say anything, but held his gaze. He wanted her with everything he had in him, but she was much more fragile and vulnerable than he'd known. Hiding behind all that fire and sass was a profoundly bruised soul. He leaned closer, drinking in the sweet fragrance of the hay, the fresh aroma of the rain falling around them, the unique perfume of Rebel's body, and he leaned closer still. Her eyes dilated, and her gaze dropped to his mouth.

He'd only intended to give her a small kiss. But his appetite to taste her had been whetted that morning. When his lips touched hers, she took a deep breath, as if scenting him, breathing his essence, and he was lost. Wrapping his arms around her shoulders, he brought her fully against him. She tasted sweet, like the rain on his lips. Pliant, she relaxed beneath his touch and parted her lips to his questing tongue.

Lord, the man could kiss. Unable to deny herself this moment, she wrapped her arms around his middle and hung on as he kissed her like he couldn't get enough of her. His hand dove into her hair and cupped her head while his mouth explored hers.

She'd been kissed plenty of times, had had a few short-term relationships that had been purely physical, but she'd never been kissed like this. Warmth began with his lips pressed against hers and spread to her chest and abdomen, inspiring surges of pleasure that made her want to stay in his arms forever.

Duncan could stay here, just like this, wrapped up with Rebel for the rest of the day, the rest of the night. Doves cooing overhead only lent to the atmosphere. Making love all afternoon would be something he'd never forget, but he knew she wasn't ready for that yet.

Rebel wrapped her arms around his neck and drew him closer, aching to have him against her skin. When his hand cupped her breast and his thumb traced her nipple, she knew she was in over her head. Telling him no or pulling away wasn't one of the options she was thinking of right now.

The lights of a vehicle shone in the doorway, and they broke apart.

"Someone's come to get us, I think." Duncan pressed a kiss to her nose and helped her to sit. "Dammit."

The SUV raced down the road and nearly drove into the barn. Rebel watched as Duncan changed, his radar on full alert. This wasn't the usual rescue of people stranded in the rain.

One of the boys burst from the vehicle and dashed into the barn. "Come quick. He's in trouble."

CHAPTER EIGHT

DUNCAN GRABBED HER hand and they hurried through the rain and into the SUV.

"What's wrong?" Duncan leaned forward from the backseat.

"He's having another spell." Jake skipped the road and drove right through the middle of what had once been a promising field of chili, but was now a straight shot to the house.

"Another spell? What do you mean, *another*?"

"Last week he couldn't breathe, but it passed, and he wouldn't let anyone call you."

"Dammit."

"He's so stubborn, he thinks he's invincible."

In minutes the SUV stopped in front of the house. "Go to the plane and get my medical kit from the outside cargo hold."

"Got it." Jake sped away before Duncan even closed the door.

Rebel waited, anxious, for him. He was more serious than she'd ever seen him. Concern for his grandfather was evident on his face and the grim set of his mouth.

"It'll be okay. We'll take care of him." Somehow she wanted to reassure him.

Duncan nodded and led the way inside. Lupe met them

at the door. She clutched her hands in her apron. "Where is he?"

"In the den. He can't breathe, *mijo*, just like last time."

Without a word, Duncan strode to the den, with Rebel steps behind him. If his grandfather died it would be because of pure stubborn pride. Or Duncan would strangle him. One or the other. Rafael could inspire the most patient of men to murder.

He sat on the couch, eyes closed, his color a waxy, greenish-yellow. That indicated a cardiac issue. "How long has this been going on?"

"'Bout...half...hour." His breathing came in short gasps, and Duncan could hear crackles in his lungs, even without a stethoscope.

Rebel sat on the other side of Rafael, and she placed his hand in her lap, her fingers on his pulse. "He's clammy, tachycardic, and I can hear fluid in his lungs."

Her demeanor snapped him out of grandson mode and into doctor mode. "Where's Jake? I need that kit."

Lupe dashed to the door. "Here he comes now." She pulled the door open as the young man ran through.

"Here it is." What he set down looked to Rebel like a giant black fishing-tackle box with a red cross painted on it.

Duncan flipped the double clamps on it and opened it to reveal a stash of medications and equipment equal to any ER crash cart she'd ever seen.

"I'm going to call my mother and let her know," Jake said.

"Dear God...not...your mother," Rafael gasped.

"Just go for now," Duncan said, and Jake hurried from the room but lingered in the doorway, his eyes wide.

Duncan extracted a stethoscope from the box, and Rebel fished out a pulse oximeter, a small monitor that fit on a finger to check the oxygen level and whether a patient's condition required supplemental oxygen.

"Sat's seventy-two—way too low." That meant his lungs were full of fluid and oxygen wasn't getting into his bloodstream the way it was supposed to.

"Get an IV in him. There's a butterfly setup on the left side." Quickly, Rebel got an IV access in the back of his right hand.

"Got it."

As she dug into the kit for the proper equipment to administer the medication, she noted that the room had started to fill with people. Lots and *lots* of people. Migrant workers, whose lives and livelihoods depended on this man, showed up and stood at the threshold of the room. Others stood inside the door. All were grim-faced and staring.

Rebel began to feel uncomfortable with so many strangers staring at her. Fumbling with the packing of the IV insertion supplies, she dropped it twice before being able to open it properly. What was wrong with her? She was a skilled nurse, and she could perform an IV setup in her sleep. So why now were her hands trembling like she was a new nurse fresh out of school?

That little voice in a dark place in her heart told her she knew why. It told her she was beginning to get sick. Just like her family had. Just like she'd known she would.

"Do you think someone could make coffee?" she asked Duncan.

His gaze flashed to her, and he frowned. "Seriously? You need coffee now?"

She wanted to whack him one for his lack of insight, but she refrained. Given the circumstances with his distress over this grandfather's sudden illness, she had to cut him a break. He wasn't thinking as clearly as he normally would if he were in the ER with control of the situation. "*N-o-o-o*. It will give them something to do and ease the tension in the room, which is about to strangle me. We also need oxygen. Is there any sort of oxygen machine we could hook him up to?" It would give her a little space to control her own racing thoughts and steady her hands again before she put in the IV.

Duncan closed his eyes for a second as he realized her suggestion was brilliant. "Sorry. You're right." He'd been too focused to see a solution to the congestion in the house. Turning slightly, he spoke to Lupe in Spanish, and then to the people gathered in the room.

Lupe clapped her hands like a drill sergeant and shooed everyone out. One man stepped forward. "I get the oxygen." He raced from the room, plowing through the rest of the crowd now that he had a mission to accomplish.

The atmosphere eased as people filed out, each offering a quick sign of the cross for Rafael's recovery. Rebel could take a deep breath for the first time since she'd sat down.

"I'll take your blood pressure, too." She applied the cuff to his left arm and performed the short procedure. "One-eighty over eighty-five."

"Give him a diuretic."

"How much?" Rebel was already reaching for the vial. The tremor in her hands was less visible, but she still felt it on the inside, down in her gut.

"Twenty now, twenty more in thirty minutes if he doesn't respond."

Rebel dropped the vial in her lap, cursed quietly as she wiped the perspiration from her palms and picked it up in a tight grip.

"Don't worry, Rebel. It's an unexpected situation, but don't worry. Take a breath, and we'll get through this together." Duncan gave a glance at his grandfather, who had not opened his eyes. "We'll *all* get through it."

Finally, she drew up the prescribed dosage in a syringe and administered it through the IV, grateful Duncan was putting the shaking of her hands down to nerves. He couldn't know what she knew. Someday, she knew she was going to get sick, but it was like a time bomb, waiting to go off. Distraction and focus on the task at hand was the way out of her mental chaos.

"This will ease your breathing by pulling the fluid from your lungs, but it's going to make you pee like a racehorse." She gave him the information she'd give to any patient.

"If you…say…so."

"I do." She patted his knee, knowing he needed comfort, even if it was the last thing he'd ask for.

She glanced at Duncan. His gaze was glued to Rafael's chest. She wanted to comfort him, too. This was what she did, what she was good at, and she shoved aside her own tremors to give them her best.

Leaning over, she placed a hand on Duncan's arm until he looked at her. "He's going to be okay."

After placing a hand over hers, he gave a terse nod. Not that he didn't believe her, but as a physician he knew too much. People who knew too much worried even more. They knew what could happen, knew the worst-case scenario, and always went there mentally. Plan for the worst, hope for the best, was her motto. Personally and professionally. She'd had her will made out for ten years now and had purchased life insurance with a long-term care rider for when she became ill. She just hadn't expected it to be now.

A shiver made her twitch and their dash into the rain was starting to reveal its unforeseen consequences. Though the room should have been warm, she felt chilled. The effect of adrenaline only lasted so long and the kick she'd gotten was fading.

Duncan's phone rang. "It's Juanita. One of my sisters," he added for Rebel's benefit.

Rafael clucked his tongue, just as one of the men returned with a very dusty oxygen tank. If it worked, who cared what it looked like? Duncan stood and answered the phone, leaving them to the task of getting the oxygen hooked up.

After pulling a tubing package from Duncan's kit, Rebel placed it on Rafael's nose and turned on the tank. "Now take some deep breaths. Slow and steady."

Amazingly, Rafael did what she said and slowed his breathing, though she knew it was very difficult. "Listen to the sound of my voice. I'll tell you what to do." She kept up the light chatter for Rafael, but watched as Duncan wandered away, listening to Juanita pontificate in his ear.

Lupe entered the room with a tray of coffee and sat it on the table in front of them. "He trusts you, you know?"

Rebel reached out for the warm cup Lupe handed her and added a few drips of creamer, not too picky about the flavor at the moment. "I'm not sure what you mean."

"Duncan. He trusts you, or he wouldn't have left you alone with him." She nodded at Rafael.

"I...can hear...you," Rafael said, and opened his eyes to slits, glaring his displeasure.

"Oh, you." Lupe inhaled a tremulous breath and gave him a light rap on the wrist, then took his hand and held it. "Be quiet, you old goat." The words she said were at odds with the concern and love in her eyes. Rebel was starting to get a clue there was more going on between them than a professional relationship.

Who was she to pass judgment? Her family had been full of oddities. Rafael turned his hand over to clasp Lupe's in his. What a sweet gesture, to see their aging hands intertwined. Something she had accepted would never happen to her. Especially not now, since she'd noticed a tremor. There was nothing to stop her illness now.

Rebel cleared her throat and placed the oxygen monitor back on Rafael's finger. "I'm sure Duncan just believes I'm a competent nurse."

Lupe raised her brows and gave her a look that made Rebel reconsider. "I don't think so, *mija*. I know him. He trusts no one to care for Rafael."

"I see." Another shiver made Rebel twitch. This time Lupe saw it.

"Oh, *mija*, look at you. Sitting here like a drowned rat!"

Duncan wandered in, still listening to Juanita rant on the phone, but his gaze remained sharp and focused on the scene.

"It's okay." She clutched the cup. "The coffee will warm me up."

"Nonsense. You'll have a shower, and I'll make you both some of my special hot chocolate." She motioned for Duncan to come closer.

"Juanita, get a hold of yourself and take a sedative or something. I gotta go." He closed the phone, but Rebel could still hear the voice on the other end as he cut her off.

"Everything okay?" Though he spoke to Rebel, he watched Rafael.

"His color is better and his breathing is, too."

"And she's soaked to the bone, *mijo*!" Lupe said with great concern.

For the first time since they'd entered the house, Duncan grinned. "Well, so am I."

"Bah!" Lupe waved away his statement. "Rebel needs a shower and dry clothes before she gets a cold." The housekeeper stood, once again in charge of herself and the situation. She took Rebel's hand and led her away. "You take care of things for a while."

Rebel went with Lupe, but cast a look at Duncan, who could only stare as the most interesting woman he'd met in years was being held hostage by his grandfather's girlfriend. They soon disappeared upstairs, and a door slammed.

"Duncan! Get over here. She's right. I have to pee like a racehorse!"

A light-hearted sensation filled him. All was well in the world if his grandfather could yell again. He shivered, casting a longing glance upstairs. He was going to need a shower, too. Too bad it would have to be by himself.

After helping Rafael to the bathroom then returning him to the couch and the oxygen, Duncan took a shower of his own. He dressed in clothing he'd left on a previous trip, but he wondered what Rebel would be wearing as she hadn't brought anything with her. It was too much to hope that it would be skimpy.

As he descended the stairs and scraped his hair back from his face, he expected to see Rebel sitting with Rafael, but she was nowhere in the vicinity. And neither was Rafael.

"I put him to bed, and she's out on the *portál*," Lupe called from the kitchen. "I'm making my hot chocolate for you. I'll bring it out in a few minutes."

He found Rebel ensconced on one of the settees, with her feet tucked beneath her and covered by a Pendleton blanket.

What a picture she made. After the shower, her hair seemed curlier and luxurious. He wanted to sink his hands into it and pull her closer to him, pull her fragrance into his mind so he would never forget it. The firelight cast a golden glow over her and he paused, absorbing the image of her quiet beauty. He knew he didn't make a noise or hardly breathed, but she turned. A few beats of his heart went missing.

And then she smiled.

And he knew he could *never* be her friend. He wanted way more than that. Especially after that kiss that afternoon had set his blood on fire.

Without directing his feet, they moved him over to where Rebel sat, and he settled beside her. Placing a hand on the back of the settee, his hand tunneled beneath her hair so he could make contact with the skin on her neck. She was such a beauty. Vastly different from the women he'd known from society who'd only seen the prestige in his name and the dollars in his pocket, convinced their beauty alone would win him over.

Rebel had none of those issues. She had others, but he was willing to work on them. She needed a friend, and he wanted to be that for her, as well as something else he wasn't quite willing to name. Lover? Best friend? Partner? He didn't know and didn't want to think about it right now and pushed aside thoughts of his fiancée. Although it had been a long time ago, guilt from his inability to save her resurfaced. Right now, all he wanted to do was put his arms around Rebel and never let go.

"This is lovely. Who knew there would be a need to have a fire on a summer night?"

"Summer nights are the perfect time for a fire." There was a fire in him that he wanted to explore. Leaning closer, he stopped just short of placing his lips against hers. "There's been a fire between us since we met, whether you want to admit it or not."

A small gasp came from her mouth, but she didn't pull away and she didn't deny it. How could she when the proof was in front of her face? The proof was in that kiss and the way her body reacted to his.

Slowly, she moved her hand up and she placed a palm on his cheek. "I'm not the one you want, Duncan." Sadness crept into her eyes again and it maddened him when things were going so well between them. He didn't want to stop, and he didn't want anything to get in his way.

"You *are* the one I want." He hardly had to move and his lips would be against hers. Every breath she took tingled against his skin.

A sudden interruption on the *portál* ended the conversation.

"Here it is. I told you my special hot chocolate would be just the trick to warm you up from the inside out." Lupe hustled across the patio stones and placed a serving tray in front of them. She handed each of them a huge, steaming mug.

"Lupe, this smells incredible."

"It is!" She clapped her hands together once. "This recipe has been handed down for generations in my family. You will love it."

"Thank you, Lupe. How's he doing?"

"He's asleep and looks peaceful for the first time in months." She leaned over and kissed Duncan on the forehead. "Thanks to you, *mijo*." She moved to Rebel and gave her a kiss as well. She smiled and for the first time tonight he saw the fatigue and the fear in her eyes. "Thank you, *mijo*. It's time for bed for me. You two enjoy the evening."

"Goodnight," Rebel said.

Duncan watched her as she stared into the fireplace, cupping her hands around the mug of hot chocolate he already knew was a gift from the gods. "Somewhere along the way, Lupe's family must have made a Mayan sacrifice to get that recipe." He'd been drinking it since he was a child and it never ceased to impress him.

"What?" She frowned. *"What?"*

"Kidding." He clinked his mug gently against hers. "It's magical. The Mayans were the first to use chocolate and chili in their cooking."

"This whole place is magical, Duncan." Hesitation in her eyes, the stiffness in her posture indicated a level of discomfort he wanted to put at ease.

And he really wanted to kiss her.

Clearly there were events in her past that continued to haunt her in the present. If they were going to be friends, or anything else, he needed to know some of them. Patience had never been his way, but right now he knew it was the only way. The way he tended to plow right through things worked in some ways, but not now. Not with Rebel.

She blew on the steaming hot chocolate, and he noticed a tremor in her hands he'd not noticed before. Maybe he made her nervous or just talking about her past made her tense up.

"Want to talk about what happened earlier?"

Shy, she looked down at her mug and avoided the question for a few moments. Then she nodded, as if having come to a firm decision. The mug rattled against the table as she set it down and then turned to face him. "You deserve the truth. To know the truth about me and my family."

"What, are you descended from a line of circus performers, or bank robbers or something?"

She gave a sad smile. "No. Much worse."

"You have the plague?" Seriously? What could it be?

Tears sprang into her eyes, and he had to confront the fact there might be something seriously wrong he'd not been aware of. He dropped the attempt at humor. Obviously, now was not the right time for it. "Tell me what it is. Some things are best told straight out. Why don't you try?"

After a few breaths, she looked at him and held his gaze. "My family has Huntington's disease."

Duncan closed his eyes, immediately feeling sadness for her and understanding her grief—her behavior now made perfect sense. Genetically, it was a death sentence. There was no getting around that. At least for some people.

"I'm so sorry, Rebel. Truly." He leaned closer to her, intending her to see how serious he was. "But you can't give up your life because of an illness that may or may not strike. Have you been tested?"

"No. I don't need to, I know I have it." She looked down, shamed. "I've begun to have symptoms."

"What? How long has this been going on?" That thought sickened him. She was in the prime of her life, and they'd just met.

"It started in the last couple of days. Things like this have never happened to me before, so I'm certain it's the Huntington's." She brushed away a tear that was making its way down her cheek.

"Tell me what your symptoms are. I'm not a genetic expert, but I know a bit about the disease."

"Over the years, I've become one. I've got tremors in my hands, shortness of breath, headaches, and I've been losing control of my extremities."

"How so?" He hadn't seen anything unusual.

"The last few days I've been dropping things more than usual. Paperwork mostly, but I dropped the vial in my lap three times when I was preparing it for Rafael."

"Have you checked your blood sugar? Simple things like dehydration and moving to a higher elevation can make you behave in ways your body isn't accustomed to." The panic in him started to settle down. "You haven't been here long enough to have acclimated. I'm sure it's something like that."

"It's not. It's can't be *just* that. I'm accustomed to traveling." She picked up her mug again and avoided his gaze. "I appreciate you trying to help, but—"

"But nothing, Rebel!" Anger snapped inside him, and he had to rein it in. He normally didn't have much of a temper, but when injustice occurred in front of him, his temper roared. "You can't just sit here and say you're giving up. Unless you've been tested, you can't know you're going to develop the full-blown illness."

"Haven't you ever just *known* something in your life? I mean, just known it down in your gut without anyone ever having to tell you?" She looked into her mug as if she were going back into her memories, seeing them now as if they were a movie in front of her eyes.

"Of course, everyone has. But I've also been wrong about some of those things too. That's a sign you're thinking with your emotions and not logic." He'd been there and done that, in spades.

"Logic? Research shows a full fifty percent of people develop the disease. The pattern in my family is well over the fifty percent mark. So far, seventy-five percent. There were four children and three have died of it."

"Rebel, you're not interpreting the research properly. A full fifty percent of people then *don't* develop any symptoms and go on to live beautiful lives." He raked a hand through his hair, frustrated at her thinking process and her unfounded belief. "Have you thought that you've got those sort of statistics on your side? Those are quite positive in my book."

"No." She sighed and clutched her hands in her lap. "It's just always easier to believe the bad stuff, you know? How can I even consider thinking I might not have it when the proof is in my symptoms?"

"You are a stubborn one, aren't you?" He sighed, not wanting to run over her beliefs, but he wouldn't be satisfied until she obtained the proper testing. Her symptoms could be anything from simple fatigue to stress from work.

"Why haven't you gotten the testing done to know for sure?" That's what he would have done, immediately.

"I'm..." Her breathing came in short huffs and tears sprang forth in earnest. Duncan patted her shoulder but remained silent. "I'm *afraid*! God, I'm so afraid to have what I know confirmed." She covered her face with her hands. "I can't take knowing that every tick of the clock is leading me closer to my death."

Duncan pulled her against his side, offering her some comfort as the fire in the *kiva* fireplace snapped and crackled, offering its warmth to her as well. He pressed a kiss to her temple.

"Science may equally *disprove* what you think you know, too."

"I don't know if I want to know. It's like I can feel it coming on, what more proof do I need?"

"What you may be feeling is the stress of unrelenting anxiety from years of worry." Squeezing her shoulder, he leaned back into the settee, pulled her closer, tucked her head beneath his chin. "Tell me about it. Tell me the story that's locking you up inside."

A few minutes passed before she took a deep breath. "My dad died when I was eleven, and he was forty-five. We had no idea what had happened to him, but a few years later when my oldest brother got sick and showed the same symptoms we had a clue it was the same thing." She cuddled against him and allowed her body to relax. One hand drifted over his abdomen, almost shyly, as if she hesitated to hold on to him. He placed his hand over hers and held it against him.

"Then what happened?"

"My grandparents finally told us that dad was adopted and they had no idea what his family history was. But when Ben became symptomatic, we started digging. Mom got all of the boys tested as they were the ones showing symptoms. I didn't have any symptoms yet, so she decided to wait for me." She paused as a tear ran down her cheek. Duncan caught it with the back of his fingers and wiped it away. "Seemed like every couple of years all we did was plan funerals. All of them were dead by the time they were twenty-five." She huffed out an irritated breath. "I have three nephews and so far they are doing okay." She took a deep breath and looked up at him. "They might be okay, then, right?"

"I'm so very sorry, Rebel. That's a lot of pain to go through." He could only give the odds science had already established. The guilt she felt for surviving such tragedy now explained everything. Why she ran from one assignment to the next and why she was so reluctant to make friends.

"I know." She nodded. "It's awful. But it was part of the reason I became a nurse. I couldn't help my family, but I wanted to do something to help someone else's."

"No matter the reason you entered healthcare, you're an excellent nurse." He paused for a second. "But you are entitled to have a life of your own, no matter what your family history is."

"How can I even think of having a relationship or a family with such history?" Anger blazed in her eyes at the suggestion, but it was part of the process of letting go.

"By living your life you honor your family, and you don't let a disease, something you have no control over, live your life for you. That's how." Anger surfaced again, and he struggled to choke it down. Wasting a life was unconscionable. His fiancée had wasted her life, died after a stupid argument, and he wasn't going to let Rebel just as surely destroy herself.

"That's a very different way of looking at it." She turned away and reached for her mug on the table in front of her, clearly not comfortable with that way of thinking.

"I'm challenging your thinking, Rebel, not your commitment, or loyalty, to your family." He pushed her hair back from her shoulder.

"You haven't mentioned your mother at all. Where is she in all of this?" Mothers were a driving force in the lives of children. His had gone from his life entirely too soon.

"I don't know. We haven't spoken in a while." She shrugged and looked away. "It's hard for me to be around her. I think, whenever I'm with her, I remind her too much of everything she's lost."

"She may be sad over her loss, but I think she would be overjoyed at being with you."

"She's married again. She's moved on." She made a face. "I don't think she really needs me."

"Look at me, please?" Her pain was almost tangible, and he wanted to ease it, but he didn't think he could right at the moment.

It took a few seconds, but she turned her face toward him. The anger still blazed inside him, but it was tempered by compassion. "The question really is, do you *want* a relationship and a family? If you don't, then it's simple, you carry on the way you are. But if you do, then you have to make a change."

"I did want a family. I grew up loved, and I wanted that for my own children. But when my brothers died, I knew I couldn't face such pain ever again or bring it to anyone

else." She sighed. "I've already tried to have myself steril-
ized, but no doctor would do it because of my age."

"You don't want children?" That would be a crime.

"I would. I did. I do." She shook her head and her hair
caught the firelight. "I gave up thinking about it. It's not
like there have been many men lining up, wanting to father my children. All I could do was have the birth control
implant placed in case of accidental pregnancy. It lasts for
three years. It's a pain, but it works."

"We all have pain. It's just different for everyone."
Thoughts of the night his fiancée had died surfaced again,
but he pushed them away. It was the past and should remain there, though it hadn't stayed there, ever. She hadn't
wanted children and it would have ended their relationship
had she not died that night.

"You have an incredible family with a history like
something out of a story book." She gestured around the
patio, encompassing everything.

"True. But it wasn't perfect." He had to concede that.
"You don't know about how many of them were killed or
died on the trip to the United States, how many of them
died from starvation and disease until the ranch got established, how many died in raids or in gunfights with early
settlers, Indians and bandits from Old Mexico."

She smiled. "I can just see Rafael hanging out with
Pancho Villa if he'd been around then."

Duncan snorted out a laugh, admiring her spirit once
again. "Actually, we have a photo of my *great*-grandfather
with Pancho Villa."

"No way!" Astonishment showed in her eyes.

"Way." He pressed a kiss to her temple. "My ancestors
not only fought disease but Mexican revolutionaries, as
well as Mother Nature. It's not the same thing, but every
family has their trials, their grief. My mother and a sister

have both died from breast cancer." He sighed, not letting the pain of their loss intrude on this conversation. "It's what you do with the pain, how you learn from it, that counts." He paused for a second. "And growth hurts. It's uncomfortable, but it challenges you in places you'd never thought about, but in the end it's worth it." Like he'd been challenged so many times in his life.

"Wow. I'm so sorry about your losses. I'll have to think about that." She dropped her gaze to her mug again and remained lost in thought for a long time. "It's been quite a day, hasn't it?"

"Yes, it has. Tomorrow will be crazy, because the family is going to come to check on him."

"They don't just call?"

"You've obviously not been involved with a large Hispanic family before." Call? They descended *en masse* from all corners of the state when there was a family crisis.

"Um, no. No, I haven't."

"Just wait. You'll see."

Sipping again from her mug, she realized she'd just about consumed the whole thing, but clutched the mug like it was some sort of protective chalice.

He caught her gaze. She was frightened, yet curious. Very intriguing mix this Rebel was. And she had his complete attention.

When she lowered her mug, he placed his left arm around her shoulder and drew her close against his side. With his right hand, he lifted her chin and closed the distance between them. Slowly, he pressed his lips against hers when he really wanted to ravage her mouth. Gently, he squeezed her shoulders when he wanted to clasp her tightly. Easily, he parted her lips with his tongue when he wanted to consume her with his mouth.

She was as sweet as any woman he'd ever tasted, but she

was such a frightened, delicate thing he knew he'd have to be gentle, though his body insisted otherwise.

When she pulled back, confusion, curiosity and arousal warred in her face. "I don't know what to think about this, Duncan. I'm not a virgin, but if I were more worldly, more experienced, I'd know how to deal with this." This was the first time she'd truly opened up to him, and he didn't want to let go of it.

"With what?"

"With what's going on between us."

"What, exactly, is going on between us?" He knew. He just needed to hear her say it.

She lowered her eyelids. "You know."

"What I know is this has been brewing since the day we met." Truly. From the second he'd seen her in the parking lot, she'd held him captive.

"What, exactly, is that?" she asked, turning his words around on him.

"This attraction. This need to touch you, kiss you. This desire to hold you in my arms and never let you go."

Rebel blinked, uncertain whether he'd just said the words she'd wanted to hear. But she'd never let any man get close enough emotionally to her to say them. She'd always run before she could be disappointed. Could she let Duncan past the barriers she'd erected and held so firm?

"I had a boyfriend in college who I loved dearly. When I finally told him about my family, he broke up with me. Said he couldn't deal with someone who might die at any moment."

"He was an idiot to let you go. And it was probably just an excuse." He reached for her mug and set it aside on the table with his. "Well, it's been a long day. Why don't I see you upstairs, and we'll call it a night, then?"

After removing the Pendleton blanket and setting it

aside, he took a look at her, let his gaze wander down over her body, and sighed. Reluctantly, she allowed him to lead her up the curving staircase to the gallery. She stopped at the third door. "This is where Lupe put me, I think."

"It's a nice room." He led the way inside and tugged on her hand, then shut the door.

From the inside.

"Duncan? What are you doing?" She paused, her gaze questioning. She was blossoming right in front of him, opening and tremulous. She was like a new angel just getting her wings.

"Rebel." He stepped closer, his mind and his body aching to touch her, but this was a moment of great importance. If he scared her, if he hurt her, there would never be any turning back. "Let me stay with you tonight." He urged her closer. "Let me hold you tonight and let what happens between us happen." He tilted her face up. "It's been happening since we met, and I don't want to let go of it, of you."

He could see the pulse in her neck thrumming away and his heart raced at a similar pace. He wanted her without a doubt, his body was aching and hard already. But could she accept the intimacy of baring her soul and her skin in one night?

"Duncan." She closed her eyes and rubbed her face against his hand, allowing herself to accept him in small measures. Their bodies were millimeters away from each other. Her fragrance and the electricity surging between them were almost overwhelming. He had to pace himself or he'd frighten her more than she already was. "I don't know what to say."

"Say you want to make love with me tonight."

CHAPTER NINE

WHEN HE CUPPED his hands around her face and tilted it up to his, she didn't resist. She couldn't. How could she resist the one right thing that had happened to her? This moment, this time, this man were all perfect. Pushing away thoughts that she didn't deserve this, deserve Duncan or to be loved fiercely, she brought her hands to his shoulders and hung on.

There was a change in him, a tuning in, a focus that was intense and overpowering. A chain reaction occurred in her, and she was on fire.

With impatient hands, he whisked the black sweatshirt off, over her head, baring her upper half.

"Wow. I hadn't expected that."

"What?" Her breasts weren't big, but they did the job.

"I expected a sensible white bra, not gorgeous pink nipples with nothing covering them." His thumb strayed to tease one.

"I *was* wearing a sensible white bra, but it was wet and I didn't want to put it back on." There was no way to hide the flush that covered her entire body.

Watching her face, he cupped both of her breasts in his hands and stroked her nipples. Tingles of desire raged through her, and her eyelids dropped. She didn't know if she was going to live through this night, but if she didn't, at least she'd die happy.

"I would like to extrapolate on that idea."

"Uh… What?" She was nearly delirious with desire, and he was talking theories?

"Since you aren't wearing a bra, I'm guessing you aren't wearing panties either." His right hand explored beneath the waistband and discovered nothing but skin. "I thought so."

"What?" Brain function minimal. Comprehension vague.

"You are a woman full of secrets." He leaned closer, his breath hot in her ear. "At first look, one would never guess there's such a sexy, passionate woman hidden inside you."

She was about to tell him there wasn't when she realized it might true. At least when she was in his arms. He kissed her deeply, and she wrapped her arms around his shoulders, wanting to draw him inside herself.

Duncan eased her onto the bed and pulled off her sweatpants. Now, naked, anxiety began to surge, and her breath burned in her lungs.

Bouncing up onto her knees, she was about to call the whole thing off when Duncan dragged his shirt off and popped the button of his jeans. His eyes glowed with want for her. She wanted to touch him, feel his skin, put aside any uncertainty of tomorrow and just live in the moment. When her palms touched his chest, all thought of leaving fled.

This was where she needed to be and in this man's arms.

"Rebel," he said, gently holding her face, "let's enjoy right now and let the rest of the world just go away for a while."

There was no need for an answer as his mouth covered hers and plundered. Hot and wet, his kiss took away her breath and her control. Eagerly, she shoved his jeans down over his hips, exposing more of that tawny skin she wanted against her.

Easing her back, Duncan covered her body with his, pressing her down into the cottony softness of the bedding. He slid one knee between hers and parted them gently. The movement gave her the opportunity to feel how hot and hard he was. Kisses ranged everywhere, and he suckled her nipples into intense peaks, hard and tingling with desire. She was on fire. Duncan was both the cause and the cure.

When his hand roamed over her hip and downward to the core of her, she instinctively parted her thighs, giving him greater access. Shyness had no place here. He released her nipple from his mouth and blazed a hot trail of kisses across her ribs and down past her abdomen.

She was the beauty of his dreams. Soft, luscious and passionate. Each stroke of her body, each restless moan that escaped her throat urged him on closer to that moment when he joined with her, when he was able to let go, to let her take him away. Moving downward, he nuzzled his way to the apex of her thighs. This was what he wanted.

When his hot mouth opened over her core, she stiffened, the sensations taking her to a completely new level of arousal. Her hands dropped to the bedding and clutched it in tight fists. Suddenly, her body wasn't her own, and she allowed him to do with her anything he wanted.

When Duncan knew she was his, he dove upward and kissed her long and luxuriously, exploring with his tongue. He wanted to know every part of her.

Opening her legs wider, he allowed the tip of his erection to ease into her. She was a delicate thing, and he didn't want to hurt her in any way. But he was trembling inside, eager to be inside her, eager to feel her heat all around him.

The demands of his body were growing impatient as he eased inside her slick sheath. Waiting for her body to accommodate to his was sexual torture. Sweat popped out all over him, straining with the effort to control himself.

"Duncan." She breathed his name, and that was all he needed. He kissed her and was lost. He didn't know if he was falling in love with her, but he was definitely smitten when her arms went around him and she clutched his back, her legs raised to wrap around him.

Easing in and out of her was a pleasure he'd never expected. Liquid fire encased his body and was about to take over his mind. Unable to control the sensations Duncan roused in her, Rebel gave up and let the feelings take her under. The sparks that had begun at his first kiss now raged through her and spiraled to an explosion within.

Spasms of pleasure rocked her. As long as he touched her, moved within her, teased the reaction from her body, she responded. Each touch, each thrill bonded her more thoroughly to him and she pulled at his hips, dragging him into her body again and again.

Unable to stop them, cries of pleasure escaped her throat. She buried her face in his neck, trying to quiet the noise.

"Let me hear you, Rebel. Let it go."

She cried out and allowed the experience of Duncan to rock her.

Unable to control his body any longer, Duncan clasped her hips and drove hard into her, taking his pleasure in hers, letting the glorious spasms of her sheath take him over the edge into his own bliss.

He poured his passion into her as sweat broke out over his body and he savored every sensation, every moment with her. He sent light kisses over her face, her eyes, her nose and finally again on her mouth.

Turning onto his side, he dragged her against him, not

wanting to let go of her but not wanting to crush her small frame beneath the weight of him.

"Are you okay?" He pressed a kiss to the top of her head. This was Nirvana.

Snuggling against him, she nodded. "Better than I ever expected to be."

"Me, too."

A yawn caught her.

"It's been a long day." He pulled the comforter over them and closed his eyes, allowing the fatigue of his body and the day to overtake him.

Rebel lay for a few moments savoring the sensations of her body and her mind. None of her previous sexual encounters had prepared her for the full onslaught of what she'd experienced tonight. Duncan filled her, mind, body and soul.

She splayed her fingers over his chest, savoring the feel of her skin against his, how her body had fit with his intimately and how they now curved around each other, limbs entwined to perfection. This was a night she'd never forget.

Rain began to fall again on the metal roof, providing a soothing backdrop against Duncan's regular breathing. Yes, this was a night, and a man, she'd never forget.

Early dawn roused Duncan as a car door slammed shut outside. He smiled. Probably his sister, Juanita, who'd gotten up at three a.m. to be the first to arrive. She really was a drama queen.

Turning toward Rebel, he delved beneath the covers to find her glorious body and pulled her against him. Even in sleep, she aroused him.

The first time they'd made love had been urgent with need. This time, soft sighs and softer kisses fell between them and their bodies joined with ease as limbs entwined and tangled together.

Rebel startled at the slam of another car door. And the sounded was repeated with disturbing regularity.

"What's going on out there? Sounds like an army has arrived."

"There is." He sighed. "You're in for a shock if everyone shows up."

"How many people are in your family?" She could count hers on one hand.

"I have no idea. People keep having babies."

A brisk knock at their door came seconds before it opened and Lupe entered. Rebel squealed and jerked the sheet over herself, but Lupe seemed nonplussed to see her and Duncan in bed together, and naked.

"Here you go. Your clothes are nice and fresh. Get dressed and come down. Everyone's here." She turned and left as quickly as she had come.

"She seriously didn't stay up all night, doing our laundry, did she?"

"No."

"That's good."

"She probably started them last night and got up at five to finish them."

"What?"

"That's normal around here. She gets up before the chickens." He patted her on the arm. "Let's take a shower." Striding across the room naked, Duncan appeared to have no issues with his body, the way women did. In seconds the spray of the shower drew her attention, and Duncan beckoning from the doorway enticed her from the bed.

They dressed and composed themselves. Rebel prepared to meet his family and then they'd check on Rafael, see how he'd fared overnight.

Duncan opened the door and Rebel almost ran back to the room when she saw how many people were down there. She'd never seen so many people in one home before. Or even a stadium!

"This is your family?" She blinked, certain she wasn't seeing this right. "Just *your* family?"

Duncan paused for a look. "Most of them, I think." He gave her a quick hug. "Don't worry. They'll love you."

When they entered the foyer, Rebel noted it had been set up with long tables and was laden with every sort of food she could imagine and some things she'd never seen before.

"Where did all the food come from? Surely Lupe didn't do all this."

"No. Rule is if you want to eat, you bring something to share."

"But we didn't bring anything!"

"You provided a very valuable service last night, so you're off the hook."

Rebel gaped at him. Was he serious? Had he really just said that?

Duncan let out a full-blown belly laugh at her response. "I meant about helping with my grandfather."

"Oh, my. I thought you meant—"

"I know what you thought." His chuckle was warm in her ear. "Get your mind out of the gutter, and let's go see how he is. Then we can eat and enjoy." With a squeeze to her shoulder, he released her.

"I'm so embarrassed." That awful flush she hated race from her chest up over her neck and cheeks.

"Don't worry about it. I'm not offended."

"Okay. So let's go see him before I say anything else stupid."

"Tio Duncan!" a young male voice called out, seconds

before a little body launched himself at Duncan. He caught the young man up in his arms with a laugh.

"Pablo! *¿Como está?*"

Duncan spoke in a mixture of Spanish and English to the little boy, then turned to Rebel. "Pablo, this is my friend, Rebel. She's a nurse and helped me to take care of Great-grandpa last night."

"Gracias, amiga." He leaned over and pulled Rebel into a one-armed hug from his perch in Duncan's arms. "Is Great-grandpa okay?"

"We're going to check on him right now. He'll be just fine, you'll see."

"Come here, monkey." Another male voice approached them from behind, and Pablo released his stranglehold on Rebel's neck. The little boy reached for the man Rebel assumed was his father, who placed him on the floor. "Go find your cousins." Pablo raced off toward a small table set up for the young ones, heedless of the art and artifacts on nearby tables.

A man about the same age as Duncan approached. Instinctively, Rebel drew back a little. The man was intense with eyes that seemed to look deep down inside her.

"Rey, stop scaring her." He gave a handshake, a fist bump and a hug to the man, then turned to Rebel. "He's a cop and likes to intimidate everyone."

"Well, it worked." A hesitant smile covered Rebel's face. "I'm Rebel Taylor."

Rey shook her hand and the cop eyes disappeared as he gave her the once-over in obvious appreciation. "Nice to meet you, Rebel." Then he pulled her into a quick, unexpected hug. "Thank you for helping him last night. He's a tough old bird, but I don't know what we'd do without him."

"Hey man, back off. She's taken, and you're married." Duncan tapped his cousin on the shoulder.

"Okay, fine." He reached for a plate, more focused on the food than Rebel.

"We're going to check on him. Don't eat everything before we get back." Duncan gave his cousin a warning.

"No guarantees." He took a plate from the large stack and got into the line behind his relatives.

"Come on. I'm sure he's been waiting on us since dawn."

"He's an early riser, then?"

Duncan snorted. "Late to bed, gets up early, I don't know how he does it at his age."

After a quick knock on the bedroom door, Duncan pressed down on the handle and pushed the door wide.

"About damned time you two came to see me. I could be dead a week before you'd know." His booming voice thundered through the room.

Duncan grinned. "I see you've survived your night and are back to your usual charming self."

Rebel hid a smile and bit her lips together. It was good to see the man's coloring had improved, the oxygen was nowhere in sight, and he was dressed and ready for the day.

"Charming?" He offered a crooked smile and a foxy gleam in his eyes. "I don't think I've ever been called charming in my life."

"You can be sure of that!" Lupe said from the bathroom. "He's never even *pretended* to be charming as long as I've known him. Maybe my English word is not right, but cantankerous sounds good."

At that, Duncan laughed out loud and met Rebel's gaze. There was something in that moment, a shared intimacy that tugged at Rebel's heart. Then it occurred to her. She was building memories with Duncan. Her heart thumped and her breath hitched. Looking into his eyes, with the laugh lines fanning outward, she knew she was falling for him much harder than she'd ever expected.

Then, in seconds, the moment was gone as he turned to Rafael.

"Let's have a look at you." Duncan opened the medical kit beside the bed and extracted the stethoscope, listened to his heart and lungs and gave a sharp nod. "All that fluid you had in your lungs is gone."

"It damned well better be. I spent half the night in the toilet." He glared at Rebel, but she only raised her brows. "Yes?"

"No thanks to you." He held his hard stare at her.

"I didn't do anything." The stare was returned with equal intensity. She could handle herself again this morning, and he wasn't going to shake her up like he had yesterday.

"You gave me that medicine." He glared harder, but she was nonplussed.

Rebel snorted and nodded at Duncan. "He told me to!"

Rafael snorted right back. "And you do everything he tells you to?"

"Not hardly. But it was the right thing to do at the time." She raised her chin, holding his gaze, and her confidence strengthened.

Rafael held a hand out to her, and she crossed the room to take it. "Thank you, my dear. I appreciate your help." He leaned over and pressed a kiss to her cheek. "You've made an old man feel good again." He gave a sigh. "And I do apologize for my behavior yesterday. It was uncalled for, and I hope you accept my deepest regrets. Maybe, if you come back, we can have a better time."

Her gaze sought Duncan, and he stood there, his mouth hanging slightly open. A piercing wail from the bathroom drew their immediate attention. Lupe stood, holding her apron over her face, sobbing into her hands.

"Lupe, what's wrong?" Rebel released Rafael's hand to comfort the woman.

"Why didn't you tell me he's going to die?" She covered her face again and sobbed her heart out.

"No, he's not. Why would you say that?" In desperation, Rebel looked at Duncan for help.

CHAPTER TEN

"He's not dying." Blandly, Duncan confirmed her statement.

"But…he's being…*nice*, he *apologized*, he never does that!"

Rebel gave an eye-roll and then looked at Rafael. "You really should be nicer."

"Why? She'd cry more then." He glared at Lupe, but softened it with a little smile and held out his hand to her. "Come here, woman. I'm fine."

"Oh, please, everyone. It's just fine. He's fine, and I'm starving." Duncan took Rebel's hand and led her to the door. "Come out so no one thinks you're dying, okay?"

Rafael just grinned. The old goat.

"He's such a pain sometimes." Duncan shook his head but his touch on her was gentle as he took her to the table. They made their way along the line, filling their plates, and Duncan introduced her to entirely too many people. Their names would never stick in her brain, she was certain of it.

After lingering over the meal and sharing coffee with the family out on the *portál*, Lupe approached Duncan and Rebel.

"The clinic is set up."

"Clinic, what clinic?" Rebel had no idea what they were talking about.

"When I come for a visit, I run a health clinic for a few hours. These folks are the poorest of the poor, most of them come from Old Mexico and have never had regular health or dental care. They have issues stemming from lifelong malnutrition and chronic illnesses. We hope we can help them out and the children that are born here will be better cared for right from the start."

"I didn't know any of this." She frowned. New Mexico was not a developing country, but what he was describing certainly sounded like it. "Most people I come into contact with in the ER have health insurance."

"These folks don't." He shrugged and looked away, but she could tell he cared deeply about these people who worked on his family ranch. "Some of these folks have worked here their entire lives. Poverty, lack of education, and cultural biases have kept them this way. Slowly, we're helping change their outlook. The kids are blossoming." He tried to hide it, but a burst of pride pulled his shoulders back. "We even have a daycare and an elementary school on the ranch."

"That's amazing." She leaned I closer to him. "I'm so proud of what you are doing here." Truly she was. She'd never met a man like Duncan.

"I wish we could do more, but there aren't enough resources and it's a seasonal business."

"Well, what can we do today?" Doing things for others had always helped keep her focus off her family tragedy and doing good works never went out of style.

"Let's go see what the troops have set up." Duncan took her hand in his firm grip and led her out to the staging area.

"During chili season we use this open-air shed to roast the chili and get it ready for locals. There's nothing fresher than produce just picked and roasted within a few hours. Today I have a clinic in it."

"So, what kinds of health issues do you see with your workers?" Though she'd worked in the ER for years, farming accidents weren't something she'd had a lot of experience with.

"A lot of things are farming related, like cuts and other injuries sustained from using heavy machinery. Other things are minor, like tetanus shots, or colds and flu." He shrugged. "The usual stuff."

"You do good work, here, Duncan." Indeed. He was not just some pretty face playing around at being a doctor. He had a heart dedicated to service to others that was very appealing to her.

"I'd like to do more of it, but at the moment there's just not enough of me to go around." That brought some pain to him. This was a group of people who could use his skills, not the people who held fund-raisers and had never set foot in a *barrio*.

They stepped around the large machine shed to a line of people that looked a mile long and her eyes widened. "Wow. That's a lot of people."

"I know." He grinned. "Not doing anything else the rest of the day, are you?" He patted her shoulder, then let his hand linger there for a second. She was so different from women he'd known. That little alarm inside him started to go off, reminding him again that she could leave him at any moment and he'd best not set himself up for getting hurt again. Then he shook it off, reminding himself there was work to do now.

"Uh, no. No, I'm not." She straightened her shoulders, ready for whatever would come up. She was an experienced ER nurse. She could handle whatever they had. Except… "I don't speak Spanish. What do you want me to do?"

"The boys will help with translation for you. You can

start with vital signs and triage, get a little info, then send them over to me. You're over there." He pointed to a long table where hand sanitizer, index cards for writing down information, and a blood-pressure cuff lay.

Duncan's area even had a screen so people would have some semblance of privacy.

Jake and Judd stood by, ready to help with translation. With a last look at Duncan as he walked away, she put on her best nurse smile and accepted the first patient into her triage station.

They spent about four hours on mundane issues before a patient of concern surfaced. As Duncan had foretold, the majority of the issues were farm related or other minor complaints. Then a boy with a serious face was plunked down into the chair by his father.

"Hi, there." Her welcoming smile faded. Usually she liked working with pediatric patients because they always had some interesting take on their situation or made up a grand and glorious tale about their injuries.

But not this.

Something was seriously wrong about his situation. She didn't know what, but, watching the boy interact with his father, she knew something was off.

This little boy of about six years old was too thin for his age and bone structure. His hair had been cropped very short, as was the custom, but she could see scratch marks on his scalp, and a little bald spot where the hair was worn away. The child didn't look at her but kept his eyes downcast, a sure sign of insecurity. He was not as frisky as the other children. Then the boy looked up at her and his eyes widened, fixating on her red hair that the wind had begun to tease from its clip.

"What's the problem?" she asked his father, who had

distant black eyes. He made eye contact but dropped his gaze quickly.

"He…no…" Frustrated with his attempt at English, he launched into a monologue in Spanish about the boy's problems, pointed to the bald spot on his head and then at the boy's back.

"His father says that he's always hurting himself, falling down or tripping, and then the spot on his head, he keeps rubbing it, and if he doesn't stop is going to be bald before he's seven years old."

A smile curved up her lips at that last statement. "It's okay. He won't be bald, but we do have to figure out the reason he's rubbing the spot." She held out a piece of candy to him. First his gaze flashed to his father, then he accepted it and focused on unwrapping the little sweet. "Kids his age, especially boys, are accident prone. They run full blast and don't see the hazards, so he'll stop falling if he stops running so fast." She waited while Judd interpreted that part.

"What's your name?"

"Alejandro." He bobbed his head politely.

"Is his mother here? I could talk to her about some things she can do to help keep him calm, from a woman's perspective." She'd had lots of training in pediatrics, and now seemed a good time to share some of it.

Judd hunkered over and whispered to her. "Mother's not in the picture. Died last year. He's raising the boy alone."

A sick feeling turned in Rebel's gut. No child should have to suffer the loss of a parent at that age. She knew exactly what it was like. An ache formed inside her, and she just wanted to reach out, gather the little boy against her and never let go of him. He was an innocent victim and his injuries may have been an attempt to gain his father's attention.

"Let me check him and listen to his lungs, look at his injuries and then we'll have the doctor look at him, too." She set about her tasks, but when she placed the stethoscope on his back he winced and cried out.

Rebel pulled up his shirt to look at his back. "Oh!" She nearly cried out in pain for the boy. "What happened?" She shot a questioning look at the father. "This time."

"He fell from the high loft in the hay barn," Judd translated. "He and the other kids were playing a game, and he lost his grip on the rope and fell."

"You're kidding, right?" She reached for the boy's hands. Healing rope burns gave evidence to Pedro's explanation. With a shake of her head, she took Alejandro's chin in her hand and gently tilted his face up until he looked at her. He blinked, as if coming back to himself, and rolled the candy around in his mouth until he'd tucked it into one cheek. "You have to be more careful, little man. You hurt yourself too much."

After Judd had interpreted for the boy, he shrugged. "I…okay," he said, demonstrating some understanding of English.

"You can hurt yourself doing things like that."

He only grinned and resumed playing with the candy in his mouth.

"If his mother is…gone, then what does he do during the day? Who takes care of him?"

The father offered an explanation, which was then translated. "He goes to school during the day, then comes home and one of the neighbor kids looks out for him while Pedro is still working. He won't stay in the daycare."

Rebel couldn't help but imagine what she would do if she were closer at hand. Children were at risk for injuries and death if left unsupervised as they didn't have the capacity to determine risk compared to what the perceived fun would be. She pressed her lips together and tried to resist the primal mothering urge that had begun to surface. If only...

"Pedro says he doesn't know what to do with him. The boy won't stay in the house after school, just runs and runs and runs as soon as he's off the bus. That's why he's so skinny." Judd listened again to Pedro. "He wants to know if there is a medicine or something Duncan can give him to make him behave better."

"I'm sorry, Pedro. This isn't a matter of medication, but may be the only way for him to express his grief at the loss of his mother." Pedro nodded, opened his mouth as if he were going to say something, then pressed his lips firmly together and turned away. Rebel could see the frustration and anger in him. "Children often need to cry in order to get those feelings they don't understand out of them."

Pedro pointed at his son, anger blazing in his eyes. "No cry. He no cry." He launched into another explanation to Judd.

"When Pedro's wife died, it was because she was an alcoholic. He doesn't want Alejandro to cry for a woman who chose the bottle over them."

So misunderstood. Grief had grabbed this family by the throat and hadn't let go. They needed to be in counseling, but how to suggest it to a man still entrenched in the angry phase of grief was beyond her comprehension.

"Duncan, I need your help." Though she spoke to him, she busied herself with taking Alejandro's blood pressure.

"What's up?" Duncan stepped closer and nodded to Pedro, spoke a few words of greeting.

"Kid's got a case of Superman syndrome."

"A what?"

"Superman. Thinks he's invincible, and is into serious risk taking."

"What is he, six?" Duncan glanced at the kid and frowned.

"Still thinks he's Superman. Just needs a cape." After relaying the list of injuries his father had reported and the escalation of them, she turned his hands over to show the rope burns to Duncan.

"So what's really going on?" That was the question. There was always something behind a person's behavior, a motivation, even if they were six years old and didn't know it. She explained the loss of his mother and the emotionally distant father to Duncan as quickly as possible.

He sat with a sigh and examined Alejandro, speaking in Spanish. Pedro seemed to relax a little as he listened to Duncan. Then Pedro stiffened. "No." He grabbed Alejandro by the hand and began to walk away. Rebel let out a gasp of distress and looked at Duncan.

"You can't let him just walk away like that. We have to do something more." There was always something to be done. Alejandro turned to look over his shoulder at her and her heart nearly broke at his big brown eyes beseeching her to do something.

"*Uno momento*, Pedro," Duncan said, and the man stopped, but his leg twitched in his eagerness to get away from the situation. Some men couldn't handle emotion and either ran from it or covered it with anger. Pedro was obviously a runner, so his son came by it naturally. Duncan motioned for the man to return the boy to the chair and spoke to him in Spanish.

Fortunately, the man responded, nodding now and then. Rebel gingerly lifted the boy's shirt to have a better look at the wounds he'd sustained in the fall while Judd translated. "It's okay, little man. I'm going to take care of you, don't worry about anything." She applied a non-sting wound spray to cleanse the open areas on his back and then a soothing ointment to prevent infection. The wounds on his hands were nearly healed, but she was sure they had hurt like crazy.

Responding to her gentle touch, the boy looked at her, hesitation in his eyes, as if he'd not known much mothering in his short life. He reached out to touch a stray lock of her hair. With careful focus, he took the strand and wrapped it around his finger. A curious expression covered his face, as if he hadn't ever seen such a thing, and he probably hadn't. Then he released it and it sprang back against her shoulder, and he grinned.

"Nice to meet you, Alejandro. I'm Rebel." She shook his hand and noted he had a pretty strong grip. But she could tell he was definitely underweight.

He bobbed his head, but didn't take his eyes off of her hair. "*Buenas dias, señorita.*"

Duncan patted Pedro on his shoulder. The man still stood stiffly with his arms crossed, his back to the child, but at least he hadn't left.

"What did you say to him?"

"I told him he and the boy both needed some support. We'll pay for it, but we'd really like him to go." Duncan cast a glance at Pedro. "He's not happy about it, but says he will try. At least it's a start."

He took a breath and let it out in a huff. He squatted by Alejandro and spoke to him, getting more information than Rebel could. She didn't know what he was saying, but in a few seconds Alejandro gave a grin and then looked up at Rebel, his eyes sparkling for the first time since he'd arrived.

"What did you say to him?" She played along, pleased to see a light of humor in those defeated eyes.

"I told him you were an Irish fairy come here just to

help him." Though his face was stoic, there was a playful light in his eyes she responded to.

"Me? A fairy?" Seriously? At her height? "Aren't they tiny little creatures and have tiny little wings?"

"I told him the only way you could tell a real Irish fairy was that they had beautiful, curly red hair and an impish gleam in their remarkable green eyes, but you had to look closely to find it."

"Duncan," she said. Her heart fluttering wildly at his words. The only glint in her eyes had recently been put there by him. And a fresh beating of her heart.

"Hey, you made him smile again, and that's a beautiful thing." He held her gaze for a second longer then broke away to answer Alejandro's next question. "The other ladies around have tried to offer some mothering, but he hasn't bonded with any of them. Until you."

Alejandro distracted Duncan with another question, and he turned to answer the boy.

"He really likes you, you know?" Judd said, and gave her a playful poke in the arm.

"Well, he's a sweet kid."

"I mean Duncan. He really likes you."

Rebel gave an assessing look at Judd. Was it true? Did Duncan really like her in the way Judd meant or was Duncan just having a good time while she was present and would move on to the next woman when he realized she could never give him what he needed? Was that reality or just her own fears surfacing?

"Oh. Yes. Well." Flustered, she didn't know what to say.

Duncan stood and the moment was over.

The tension that had eased resurfaced again when Pedro collected Alejandro. There was nothing to be done at the moment. Time would heal, eventually, but Rebel wanted to do something else to help him. To take him in her arms and rock him to sleep, the way he should have been all of his life. The boy went reluctantly with his father, casting longing glances at Rebel. As if the Irish fairy could help him.

A pain filled her heart as she watched him walk away.

What had started out as a lovely day had faded into a low hum of concern for Alejandro. Somehow she needed to figure out a way to get back here and help. Something in her called to this little boy, and she wanted to be around for him. Farming accidents were fairly common and if something happened to Pedro, what would happen to Alejandro?

She imagined she and Duncan would be heading back to Albuquerque soon and this lovely weekend would be committed to the memory books of her mind. She couldn't imagine another weekend being more wonderful. Or more impossible to hang on to. There was just no way she could be what Duncan wanted or needed. After seeing him, his family, the way they were, this had to be just a one-time event. She just didn't have it in her to be what he needed, and there was no way she would taint this family with her genes.

"Come here, children," Lupe instructed, and ushered them from the heat of the outdoors to the cool interior of the home. Ceiling fans ran in every room and the windows were left open a few inches in order to facilitate circulation. The adobe structure needed no artificial cooling.

Rebel and Duncan settled at a large wooden table where several of Duncan's older female relatives sat. Duncan introduced her to the matriarchs of the family, who all seemed to study her.

"They mean no harm, they're just curious about you." He took her hand. "As I've not brought many lady friends here, they are taking the opportunity to determine whether I'm worthy of you." These ladies who had helped to raise him loved him, but didn't always trust his judgment in women. That made him laugh. They were so right. At least up until now.

"Don't you mean that the other way around?"

"No. Once you helped out with Rafael, they decided you were made of gold and can do no wrong." He grinned. "I'm the one in the hot seat."

"I see. I like them already." Was she really seeing this? Was his family already taking her under their wings as one of their own? He looked at her as if he saw her, saw who she really was. That frightened her. She sipped her coffee and realized Lupe must have put a dash of red chili in the coffee as well. It had a nip to it. Or maybe it was the close proximity to Duncan and all he represented that made her sweat. The temperature was definitely going up.

"Tell me, dear, where are you from?" one of the aunties asked her. Before she could respond, Duncan's phone rang, and he got up to answer it then glanced at Rebel and moved farther away. That was curious. Made her wonder if it was work.

Lupe made the introductions as to who was the oldest and the youngest and the ladies began to argue about who looked the best and who had the best hair and the fewest wrinkles among them. Rebel couldn't help but be engaged and put at ease by these women.

The laugh in Rebel's throat caught when Duncan reentered the room. Something was wrong. It was in his eyes, in his walk, in the energy around him. He looked only at her, and her heart sank. Somehow she knew this news was only for her.

And it was bad.

She stood, nearly knocking over her chair. "What is it? I know it's bad, just tell me."

The smile that he'd been suppressing burst out from his heart. Unable to contain his joy any longer, he had to share it with the only other person who would understand and appreciate it. He embraced her, and he felt the trembling of her body against his, as if she could already read him and know there was something going on. "I'm sorry, Rebel. I didn't mean to scare you. Eric was taken off life support this morning." He felt her go stiff in his arms, and he hurried to tell her the rest. "He's breathing on his own, and stable." A rough laugh escaped him. He didn't know if it was relief or what, but it felt good to let it out.

"Are you *serious*?" She pulled back from him, her gaze frantically searching his. Unknowingly, she reached out to him, clutching his arms with both of her hands.

"Totally serious. That was Dr. Simmons who called just now. She wanted to tell me the news herself." Another laugh of relief rushed out of him. "I can't believe it. I had little hope for his recovery."

"Oh, my God, Duncan. I can't believe it." She grabbed him around the shoulders and held him close. The feel of her body against his was such a relief, such a wonder. He didn't care if there were fifty witnesses, he wasn't going to let go of her.

"What's going on? Did someone win the lottery?" Lupe asked, reminding him of where they were. He was on such a high he'd almost forgotten. Duncan moved to face them but tucked Rebel against his side, wanting to hold on to her and give her some support. He knew she was as gobsmacked as he was at the moment.

"It feels like it. The little boy Rebel and I rescued from the car last week is off life support." He rested one hand on the table to support himself. "It's such a relief."

"Tell us what happened," Auntie Matilda said. "I didn't hear the story."

Rebel looked to Duncan and made a chagrined face. "You tell it. I'm not a very good storyteller."

"Bah, both of you sit down and tell us what happened. We want to hear how you rescued this little boy. You did it together, no?" Auntie Esmeralda patted the seat beside her and urged Rebel into it. Duncan dropped into the chair beside her and rested his arm on the back of her chair.

"Okay. I'll get it started, but then you have to join in and add your piece of it," Duncan said. "You were as important as I was in this."

"No, I wasn't." She shook her head in that self-deprecating way she had.

"Actually, you were more important because you found him. If you hadn't found him, he would have died."

Saying nothing, Rebel pressed her lips together to keep them from trembling, and he saw the flash of tears before she looked away.

Duncan recounted the tale, with Rebel adding details here and there.

"What will happen to him? And what will happen to the mother?" Those questions were posed by Auntie Esmeralda again.

"We don't know yet, but at his age the brain is very resilient." He certainly hoped so.

"As for the mother, she's probably suffered enough for her mistake." Rebel shrugged.

"We generally don't get so attached to our patients, but this situation…" Duncan tapered off and looked at Rebel. He swallowed a few times, controlling his emotion.

"That's how you met? By saving the life of a child?" Esmeralda leaned forward in her chair.

"Yes." Duncan confirmed her statement.

"You will have a special bond forever because of this."

Duncan held Rebel's gaze. "We already do." His voice dropped and he cleared his throat again, somewhat embarrassed to admit such a thing in front of the ladies, but it was true.

"How about I show you around the ranch now that there are no thunderstorms or medical emergencies?" Duncan was after any excuse to be alone with Rebel.

"Wonderful. I've love to see more of the place since we'll leave tonight, right?"

"Let's see what the rest of the day brings. I'm in no hurry to go back to the real world, are you?"

Shy, she dropped her gaze, but squeezed his hand. "No. I'm not."

That warmed Duncan's heart as nothing else had today. This was a wonderful weekend, and he was so glad he'd convinced her to come with him. With an arm around her shoulder he led the way to the golf cart, which had been charged overnight, and sat out front.

He cupped the back of her head and pulled her closer for a kiss. Her lips were soft and pliant beneath his, letting his tongue search for hers and reveling in the sensations of her passionate response.

After several minutes of lingering kisses, stroking her face and listening to her soft sighs, he seriously wished the house wasn't still full of people. Pulling away, he let his hand drift down her arm to clutch her hand. "Let me show you some sights."

"I think I've already seen quite a few," she said, and gave a quick laugh.

"Are you enjoying yourself?" He placed his boot on the gas pedal, and they lurched forward onto the path to the farthest reaches of the farm. Away from people and truly alone.

"I am." The sound of her voice was a little shy. "I'm just amazed at how friendly and open your family has been when they don't know me at all."

"They know a good soul when they see one. You will always be welcome here, Rebel. Always." He just hoped she would see it that way.

They rounded a bend in the road that seemed to go off to nowhere. "What's out here?"

"A whole lot of nothing." He knew every inch of this ranch and there was nothing to draw anyone out here for a while.

"Seriously."

"We have some herb fields I thought you'd like to see. Herbs, as you know, are the basis for all medicine, and we still hold on to the belief that herbs grown and used locally are the best. We have quite a few herbalists and aromatherapists who use our plants in their concoctions."

"That's fascinating. I love lavender."

"Then you are in for a treat. We happen to have an incredible crop of it this year. Let me take you to the drying shed. It's amazing in there."

The low building ahead was where they were apparently going. When he pulled to a stop beside it, she knew she was in trouble again. After kissing him again, she wanted more of it. Though she knew this relationship wasn't likely to last, she wanted to immerse herself in every moment of it while she could. To live in the moment because she wasn't sure she'd have a future.

"Take me inside, will you?"

The *double entendre* wasn't lost on Duncan. "Gladly." He paused as she rounded the cart. Something in him changed and intensified as she approached, as he responded to the electricity between them. Each step she took toward him, each movement that took her closer to him filled her with desire and longing, the power of which she'd never felt before. The alarm bells in her mind grew dimmer.

He took her hand and pulled her closer until her chest touched his, until she tilted her face upward and her lips were millimeters away from his. His breath came as quickly as hers, his focus on her intensifying.

"Is there something going on I need to know about?"

"Yes," she whispered, her breath mingling with his. "I want to be alone with you." She cleared her throat. "And naked."

As soon as the words left her mouth his lips were on hers, his tongue searching, seeking, parting her lips and devouring her.

Her desire ripped free as Duncan clasped her hips and lifted her to wrap her legs around his hips. "God, you're so tall, you fit me perfectly." He cupped her bottom in his hands and held her close as he entered the drying shed. The dim lighting was no issue as he made his way through rows and rows of lavender hanging from the ceiling. The fragrance only added to the primal feelings stirring within her.

He found a suitable place to set her down, whipped his shirt off, then arranged it quickly on the floor of the shed. "Come here."

She let him lead her down as he lay back on the shirt and dragged her willingly over him. Kisses and hands ranged all over her and soon he had her shirt and bra off and was working on her slacks. Never having been an exhibitionist, nerves started to fray as he unclothed her, but when he pulled back to remove his jeans she forgot her shyness and reveled in the outrageously glorious image of him completely naked and completely aroused. For her.

"You're beautiful, Duncan." Unable to hold herself back, she nearly launched herself at him. He pulled her hips up to meet his and abruptly joined with her, sinking his erection deeply into her.

She stilled and savored the sensation of him inside her and allowed a moan low in her throat to escape.

"Tell me," he said, breathless. "Tell me what you feel, what you want, what you need."

Hissing her breath in through her teeth, she clutched his forearms while he held her hips, digging his fingers into her flesh. "Oh, God, Duncan. I don't know." Her hair clip flew free as she tossed her head back, giving in to the arousal of her body, of Duncan filling her, of him moving strongly against her as he pulled her hips toward him, then let her rock back.

Each movement, each pulse of pleasure pushed her closer to the edge. Each time her hips moved forward she stroked her sensitive flesh against Duncan's. The pleasure built until the pace moved faster, harder, more intent toward a shared goal.

When it hit, the wave of pleasure overcame her, and she cried out with it, unable to contain the joy of her body and heart joined with Duncan's. Wanting to bring him the same release, she rocked her hips faster and his sensitive flesh responded the way hers had. Explosively. Duncan cried out and dug his fingers into her hips, clutching her tightly to him as the climax washed over him.

CHAPTER ELEVEN

SHE'D HEARD ABOUT sex as a release of emotion, but she'd never experienced it before. Now it made complete sense as she lay there, contented and at peace in Duncan's arms. Even though they were lying on the floor of an outbuilding, there was no more perfect place to be.

She pushed her hair out of her face. "I still can't believe it. About Eric, I mean."

"Neither can I." He pressed a kiss to her temple and then kept his face close to hers. "I was surprised. Somewhere down inside I thought he couldn't survive, that there was no way. I was never so happy to be wrong about something." He paused a second, touching his forehead to hers and sharing his emotion with her. For the first time in a long time he was able to feel and share it with someone. Someone who knew exactly what he was feeling. Somehow, he knew the more he stepped forward, the more Rebel would step forward, too.

"So what happens now?" She settled against his shoulder, the length of her body against his, as they lay on the floor, looking overhead, soothing him. After today, he'd never get the fragrance of lavender out of his mind.

"I'm sure there will be an investigation. For the family's sake, I hope it's not bad. They've been through enough."

"Something like this can destroy a family." Her voice

suddenly changed as if she was recalling a memory, then she shook herself and came out of it.

"We'll likely be called as witnesses, but I'm hoping that Amanda isn't prosecuted. I thought she really just forgot about him."

"Do you think it's that simple?" She tilted her head back as she asked the question. His gaze dropped to her mouth and the intensity of him changed.

"Nothing is ever as simple as it seems." Moving in, he closed the distance between them, pressed his lips against hers and kissed her.

This slow exploration of her mouth, the heat of him against her, the emotional day all sought to rob her of her control, of her rationale, and her will to resist everything she knew she shouldn't have. Shouldn't want. But she did. With all her heart, she wanted it.

Duncan's mouth against hers, his lips soft and hot over hers, his tongue exploring hers, created tangles of confusion in her mind and tingles of desire in her body. Overwhelmed, she pulled away.

"Duncan, I'm so confused by you. You make me feel things I shouldn't be feeling or thinking. Or wanting." Unable to hold his gaze, she looked away. He wished he could impart some of his strength into her.

"Don't be. I'm a pretty simple man." He cupped both hands around her face and forced her to look up at him. "What's going on here is pretty simple, too. It doesn't have to be complicated."

"You mean making love?" Some people thought of it that way.

"I mean everything." How could he tell her he was crazy about her, about her wild red hair and the beauty in her face, the humor in her green eyes and the compassion in her heart? How could he tell her all of that when they'd only known each other for a few weeks?

He didn't fall for women that way. *Ever*. Opening himself up like that wasn't in his rule book. But now it was happening and it had taken him by complete surprise. People were predictable and usually disappointed him. She was everything he wanted in a partner, he only had to convince her of it. And not listen to the voices in his past telling him he was an idiot for falling for an Irish redhead so quickly. Right now, all he wanted was her skin against his, her heart beating in time with his, her breath hot in his ear.

"You're just in time to help put the food on the table." Lupe handed each of them a bowl to take from the kitchen to the table in the dining room. The majority of people had taken off and returned to their homes, satisfied the patriarch of the family was doing well.

Rafael looked as if he was back to his usual ornery self.

After a short dinner, and a lovely walk in the garden, Duncan realized their fairy-tale weekend was coming to a close.

They sat on a wooden bench with the scent of roses, lavender and other things he didn't know swirling around them. It completed his picture of the perfect evening.

"I know we have to go back tonight, but do you think we could see Alejandro again before we go?"

"Yes." The thought of the situation with that family put a damper on his buoyant mood, but it was part of life. It was surviving the bad times that made the good times even better.

"What will happen to Alejandro if his father doesn't go through with the therapy?" She sighed. Concern and resignation flashed in her eyes.

"I'm going to think positively, that Pedro will go, and

both of them will benefit." He squeezed her hand. "You know time is the only true healer of grief, and it hasn't been very long."

"I'm sorry his mom died. No kid should have to go through all of that at Alejandro's age. He's so sweet." He knew she was thinking of her own family losses, and he wished he could ease the pain in her heart. Given time, and the opportunity, maybe he would be able to.

Duncan rose from the bench and with Rebel's hand in his they left the garden. When they reached the machine shed and rounded the corner to the row of tenant housing, tension in both of them rose.

They arrived at the *casita* where Alejandro and Pedro lived. Before he could knock, the door swung open, and Alejandro bounded out, a happy smile on his face. *"La mujer está aqui! La hada Irelanda esta aqui!"* He threw the words over his shoulder to his father and raced over to Rebel.

She knelt and gave him a hug. Yes, the giant Irish fairy had arrived.

"Rebel and I wanted to say goodbye before we go. I think Rebel has a soft spot in her heart for him." He nodded to the boy.

Duncan watched Rebel trying to communicate with Alejandro. They needed a little interpreting. The sight of her with the boy invited visions of her with her own child in her arms.

"Oh, Duncan. He's really trying to tell me something, but I just can't get it. If I stick around here for much longer, I'll need to take a course in Spanish."

That was the first indication she'd given about not moving on to another assignment and his heart lightened. "That would be great. We always need bilingual nurses." He stooped beside them and spoke to Alejandro. The boy became very animated in his face, his words and his gestures. Duncan laughed.

"What's he saying? I asked him about his back, and he gave me a two-minute answer."

"He says his back still hurts a little, but he's much better since you, the Irish fairy, applied the magical cream to his back and his hands." He gave her a sideways glance. "He's enthralled with you." And so was he, but he couldn't put words to what he was feeling.

"Only because you told him I'm magical." She gave an eye-roll as if doubting his assessment of her magical abilities.

"To him, you are." Duncan wanted to believe in magic right then, too. He'd learned to mistrust his instincts where women were concerned and the situation with Rebel had *mistake* written all over it. But there was something deep in his gut that made him want to kick his judgment to the curb.

The plane was ready. They just had to get into it and return to reality. He sensed reluctance in Rebel as he buckled her into the seat. She was quiet, her eyes downcast, and she clutched her tartan around her shoulders.

When they were airborne and he had tipped his wings to those watching from below, he spoke to Rebel in the headset. Mostly it was just pointing out landmarks, how the sunset glinted off the Rio Grande and mindless chatter. He wanted to put her at ease, but it wasn't working. Though she nodded and responded politely, she had gone deep inside herself again.

The remainder of the trip was quiet except for the whine of the engine. Maybe the little voice in his head was right after all. Rebel was a bad bet. Not just because she was a coworker but because her family model was so different from his, her emotional status was fragile, and she just shut down.

That wasn't how he operated. Although he didn't like to fight, on occasion the situation demanded it. He taxied the plane to its space and cut the engine. Rebel had removed her headset and was reaching for the door.

"Wait. We need to talk."

"There's nothing to talk about. It was a moment in time, Duncan. You'll go back to your life and I'll go back to mine. We'll work together, and that's it." Her eyes remained downcast.

"I don't want that." He shoved a hand through his hair in frustration. "Since we got into the plane you've been withdrawing, and I don't want that either. We need to talk about us."

"There's no us." She shook her head as if trying to convince herself. "You've got a vastly different life than I do. Meeting your family, your *huge* family, has made me realize how different we really are. I appreciate the weekend away and meeting your family and all, but nothing has changed for me."

"What?" Incredulous, he reached for her shoulders to turn her to face him. "*Nothing* has changed for you? Are you kidding me?" She tried to pull away from him, but there wasn't much room in the plane. "*Everything* has changed, Rebel. I'm not going back to my life and pretend nothing happened between us. I don't know how you can."

Her tearful gaze met his for the first time in hours. "It won't be easy," she whispered, then yanked away from him and pushed out of the plane.

No. Way. There was no way he was leaving things like this. He shot out of the plane and the wind slammed the door shut behind him. Monsoon season wasn't over and the wind swirled leaves and dust around them.

She stood beside his locked truck, unable to get into it and unable to avoid him. This was where it all came down to the wire. She had to face her demons and maybe he was the one to *make* her do it.

"We're not leaving things this way." He stood a few feet from her. "What do you mean, 'It won't be easy'? If that's the case, then why don't you at least *try* to have a relationship with me? All I'm asking for is a chance, Rebel." Demons of his own resurfaced at the word. He'd begged Valerie to take him back, and she'd laughed. He'd vowed never to beg another woman to be with him, and he was on the verge of doing it now.

Pressing her face against the glass of the door, her shoulders trembled. Her pain was escalating, but so was his. "I can't do this, Duncan. I can't do it. I don't have what it takes. I can't be what you need, and I can't give you what you want. It's better to end things right here and now, and just say we had a weekend we'll never forget."

"Why? Why pretend? And what makes you think you know *what* I need or *what* I want?" Miscommunication led to disaster, and he was done with that, too.

She turned to him, anger and disbelief in her eyes. "*Really*? I'm not that stupid. One look at you with your family and it was all there. You want what you have, what everyone there has. A home, children, a family. I can't give you *any* of that." Her voice cracked and her lip trembled. "I can't give you children, and you know you want them."

"I do want them. But I want an amazing relationship with an amazing woman first." That was true, and the amazing woman in front of him was drawing into herself, moving further and further away from him. He didn't know if he could bring her back.

She pressed her back to the truck door as he moved closer to her. This was not going to be the end of it. No.

Way. "Are you listening to yourself? You've talked yourself into giving up your life, any chance of a happy relationship because of your family history. So. What. Everyone has bad stuff in their lives. It's what you make of it that makes your life worth living." He grabbed her by the shoulders as lightning flashed overhead. "I want that with you. I want to build a life with you, Rebel."

"It's *not* just a bunch of bull, and you know it!" Now she was getting angry and that was good. Time to spew it all out rather than letting it fester inside. "I've lost nearly my whole family. You have no idea what that's like. None! You and your perfect family, have no clue."

"Perfect? *Really?* You think you've cornered the market on despair? I could tell you some stories that would rival your family for losses. I've already told you about my mother and my sister, but what I haven't told you is that I also lost my fiancée. Her name was Valerie and I loved her, she was both my lover and my friend. But we argued. I wanted kids, she didn't, she had her reasons, and I let her drive away knowing she was distressed. She crashed the car and died. I blame myself and I couldn't save her. But I can save you, and make you happy, Rebel. I don't want to lose another woman I love. Please listen to me…"

The closer he got to Rebel, the harder it was for her to get away, to run away from her past when confronting it right here and now was going to heal it. He knew it. He just had to make her believe it. "Don't belittle someone else's experiences because you don't think they're as tough as yours. Open your eyes, Rebel. There's plenty of pain and suffering for everyone. We see it roll through the ER every damned day. There's also enough joy and love and faith and hope for all of us. *Including you*, Rebel. Come out of the darkness for just a second into the light that's right in front of you." Like he was. Standing right in front of her, and she couldn't see him. See the potential right in front of her face.

At that moment lightning flashed again, followed quickly by a roll of deep thunder. The gods themselves seemed to want to have some input into their discourse.

"I. Can't." Tears now fell, and she covered her face with her hands. "Oh, Duncan, I'm sorry, so sorry that you lost your fiancée and for all the pain your family has suffered. But I don't have your courage. It's too painful. Everyone leaves or dies, and I can't take it. I couldn't take it if I lost you, too."

"So you won't even try? You are worthy of being loved, worthy of having the greatest thing ever happen right here, right now." He wanted to comfort her, but it wasn't what she needed right now. He also wanted to shake her to make her see how crazy her thinking was.

He stepped back as the first raindrops fell. There was nothing else he could say right now to change her mind. He'd put it all out there. There rest was up to her. Vanquishing her demons was within her power. He just didn't know if she would pick up the sword. He unlocked the door to the truck and let her in, then returned to the plane to lock it down and put the covers on.

Soaking wet, he got into the truck and started it, not looking directly at Rebel. She sat with her eyes closed, as if that would prevent her from seeing the world around her.

"I'm sorry you got wet. I should have helped you."

"It's fine." He negotiated the wet streets until he arrived at her apartment complex.

"Thank you for the amazing weekend. I won't forget it." She straightened, then unbuckled herself and opened the door. "I'll see you at the hospital." The smile she tried to paste on was pathetic. His words had apparently had no impact on her.

He watched as she dashed through the rain to her front door, waited until she entered her apartment, then drove away into the deepening night knowing that once again he'd bet money on the wrong horse.

CHAPTER TWELVE

WORK SUCKED. THE SUMMER was shaping up to be one of the hottest on record. Tempers flared. People lost their patience on the freeways and crashed like dummies, drank to levels of idiocy and got into fights with their relatives, or committed acts of stupidity that landed them in the ER.

For the next few weeks all staff worked overtime, gave up their summer fun to take care of the never-ending stream of patients rolling into the hospital, and became the most tightly knit group Rebel had ever seen.

"I knew this was a busy place, but this is as crazy as some of the big city hospitals I've worked in." Rebel sat at the desk with Herm and a few other nurses, taking the opportunity to have a quick lunch.

"We're a level-one trauma unit for the entire state. No one else has the ability to care for trauma the way we do here." Herm nodded, obviously proud of the work this hospital performed.

"How long have you been here?" She was curious. In her life, relationships and jobs were all short term. People who stayed in one place fascinated her.

"I was born in this hospital, and I feel like I never left!" Shared laughter warmed a little of the ice in her chest.

The fragrant and distinct smell of green chili got her attention, and she froze as Duncan joined the conversation. A plate of green chili cheese fries sat in front of him as he stood at the counter.

"Hey, Duncan. When's the chili going to be ready?" one of their coworkers asked.

"Very soon. Report from the ranch is that things are looking good." His gaze honed in on Rebel, and he tipped his head to her. "Things are looking very good."

"What's the heat level? I can't find the extra-hot stuff in town." Another person posed the question.

Keeping his eyes on Rebel, he answered the question. "Yes, we have the hot stuff. So hot you'll need a cold shower."

"That's the stuff I'm talking about. I want it to make me sweat."

"Oh, you'll definitely be sweating." Everyone at the table got animated, eager in their anticipation of the new crop of chili. Everyone except for Herm, who raised his brows at Rebel.

"What?" She cleared her throat. "Um… I like green chili, too." The flush up her neck betrayed her lie. It wasn't only green chili she liked, and Herm knew it.

"I see."

And then the moment was gone when the doors burst open with an ambulance crew, fire crew, and police all looking like they'd been at some smoke-filled rave.

Strapped on the gurney lay a firefighter, having succumbed to burns and inhalation of smoke during a structure fire. She'd never seen so many impressive men and women at one time.

"Trauma one," Herm instructed, and pointed to the room. "Gina and Candy, you're on it. Duncan, you're it for now. Rebel, crowd control, then suit up and come in."

Everyone sprang to action at the direction of the charge

nurse. He knew who he had working with them, their skills and where they would best be utilized.

The overpowering stench of smoke invaded the entire emergency room. The highly sensitive sprinkler system clicked on and purged the main area with water from the ceiling.

"Out! Everyone who smells like smoke, take it outside!" Rebel waved her hands to get the attention of the firefighters, whose only focus was on their fallen comrade. "I'm sorry, everyone. Please go outside and ditch the stinky stuff, then come back."

She dialed the operator. "Please call off the 911 alarm, half the department is here. We need Maintenance for water cleanup." She herded the first responders to the waiting area reserved for VIPs. There was nothing like the support of your peers, who in this case were like family, to help through the tough times.

"I want to know what's going on in there." The tallest woman she'd ever seen emerged from beneath protective gear. She was strong, fit, but highly agitated. Her hair was a wild, iron gray and her steel-blue eyes pinned Rebel in her spot. Tension filled the posture of her shoulders and the tightness around her lips. This was a woman who was used to being in control and had suddenly gotten lost in unfamiliar surroundings.

"I'm Rebel, one of the nurses—"

"Kat Vega, Station Nine Commander. What's going on with Jimmy?" There was no handshake, no polite query.

"Right at the moment he's being assessed by Dr. McFee and the trauma team." She held her hands out to stop the tirade of questions she knew was going to be coming. "I can't answer any more questions, because I just don't know. I'll go in there and check his condition. When I have something to report I'll be back."

"You'd better be, or we'll be coming in there to find you." The woman with pain in her eyes turned away from Rebel. She held her hands out to two of her crew members, who clasped them and pulled her into a tight hug. Though she was obviously tough, she depended on these men to hold her up in times of need.

These people weren't afraid to feel. They embraced every second of it because they never knew if it would be their last. Rebel hurried from the scene and hoped she would have good news to share. Her meager concerns and needs dropped away in the face of real tragedy. She hoped this firefighter was made of strong stuff, because he had a long road to recovery.

"I'm back."

"What's going on out there?" Herm asked. "I heard alarms."

"Those firefighters set off the smoke alarms."

"What?"

"Yeah. Those guys were so hot they set off the sprinkler system. Literally." Rebel contained herself, knowing the situation was serious, but any chance at levity helped people perform better by cutting some of the tension right out of the air. "What do you need?" To prevent the chance of bringing any infection to this patient, she pulled on a protective gown and mask as she entered the room that stank to high heaven of smoke.

"He's got one IV in, but we can't get another one in. Both arms are burned and Doc's going to put in a central line." Herm supplied the information. Though his voice was casual, tension filled the lines on his face and the concern in his eyes. The man was not immune to the stress of the job.

"Have you checked his feet?" she asked, and began the process of removing his protective boots. "Sometimes the feet are good, especially since he's had these big honkers on."

Both boots thudded to the floor, and Rebel reached for an eighteen-gauge IV catheter. In seconds she felt the tip enter the vein. "Got it!" Carefully, she secured it and connected the bag of fluids.

"Get one in the other foot, and we'll hold off on the central line for the moment." Duncan spoke to her from behind his protective gear, his voice calm and professional. "Good job, Rebel."

"Thanks. I worked burns in a few places and the feet are usually a good bet." She grinned, excited to share this moment with him, forgetting she was supposed to be maintaining a wide boundary from him and any emotions she didn't want. He nodded and turned back to the patient. "Need to intubate him right now. I don't like the look of his saturation level."

"He's got soot in his nose and mouth. Sure sign of inhalation injury." Rebel clucked her tongue and shook her head. Inhalation injuries destroyed lung tissues if the fire was hot enough, but inhaling smoke suffocated the patient at the blood level.

"What about a blood transfusion?" Duncan said aloud, almost talking to himself, trying to puzzle out the problem and the solution.

"That would add fresh oxygen-carrying ability right away, wouldn't it?" she asked Duncan.

"Yes." He nodded and smiled at her and gave a nod of approval that made her flush.

"Brilliant idea, Doc! You two are quite the team." After receiving Duncan's nod, Herm called the blood bank. "Need two units of packed cells right now. I'm sending someone for it." He hung up and turned to Rebel. "See why that scavenger hunt is so important?"

She removed her protective gear and dashed toward the blood bank, but skidded to a halt, changed direction and raced back to the waiting room.

"Do you have news?" Kat crossed the room in two strides.

"Yes." Rebel caught her breath. "We've got good IV's in him, I'm going to blood bank now, and we're going to transfuse him."

"I'll go." A blond firefighter stepped forward.

"Me, too." Another one approached.

"I can donate." And another.

Several people rushed her at once, willing and eager to donate their life-giving blood to help their friend. Their eagerness and intensity impressed Rebel. Never in her life had she had friends the way this Jimmy did. And she wanted them. More than almost anything else, she wanted to belong, wanted people to call her own, friends to depend on.

"It might not all go to him, but come with me, and we'll see if they can take your donations now." Rebel led the way to the basement, negotiating the way as if she'd run this route a hundred times.

In minutes she had the two units of blood in her hands, the proper paperwork, and had set up two donors with the blood bank.

Rebel returned to the ER, huffing and puffing, out of breath. "I have…it…here." She held up the two pints of red stuff.

"Are you okay, *chica*?" Gina asked.

"Out…of breath…for some…reason." She was in good shape. Why running up a few flights of steps should wind her, she didn't know.

"It's the elevation. We're over five thousand feet here,

and you aren't used to it yet." Gina verified the blood type was correct with Rebel.

"How long does it take?" she asked, and took some deep breaths, beginning to feel better. At least the stars spinning around her vision had vanished. Maybe Gina was right. Her gut churned. Maybe Duncan was right too. He'd told her the exact same thing and she hadn't believed him, hadn't been willing to believe it. Maybe she was overreacting to symptoms that really weren't related to the Huntington's. Maybe.

"About a month. You might have headaches, hand tremors, too." Herm supplied the answer. "Keep up the fluids, exercise slower and eat more green chili."

"That doesn't help. Don't listen to him." Gina gave her a look of disbelief.

"Okay, but it won't hurt anything, will it?" Rebel asked.

"Green chili never hurt anyone," Duncan said, amusement in his voice.

"Good to know, thanks." She paused and took a step back from him. "Think I'm going to see Jimmy's friends again. Give them an update."

"Oh, his parents are on the way from Belen. The fire chief lady called them." Herm made a notation on his notepad as he spoke.

"Where's Belen?" She had no idea. There were so many little towns around the area.

"Don't you remember? I pointed it out to you in the plane—" Duncan began, then stopped talking when the other staff became very interested in the conversation.

Gulp. Secret out. "Oh. Yes. I remember now." Face flushed, she returned to the waiting room to escape the knowing looks of her coworkers. They had questions she was *not* going to be answering. She would be professional.

She would do her job, and she would *not* be caught alone again with Duncan.

Ten minutes later she was alone with Duncan.

She went to the staff lounge for coffee and a short break. Burn patients were always intense. Seconds after she turned the coffeemaker on the door swung open and Duncan entered.

"Oh. Hi." He paused for a second when he saw her, then recovered and approached. "Coffee?"

She didn't make eye contact or even look in his direction, but kept her gaze on the drips of java that came way too slowly out of the pot. "Yes. Coffee." She was *so* skillful at trite conversation. She amazed herself. So *not*! How embarrassing. Did the elevation make her heart beat fast now, too? Or was that Duncan's presence?

"You were great." His voice was low and sexy and rattled her nerves.

"Oh. Thanks." Work related…phew! Then she looked at him.

Mistake.

The longing in his eyes almost brought her to her knees. The feeling was mutual. "Don't look at me that way," she whispered.

"Why not?" With his gentle hand, he reached out and pushed her hair behind one ear. The gesture was so sweet she wanted to cry.

"You know how I feel." Despite her words, her resolve lacked the strength to resist him.

"I do." He stepped closer, his voice dropped. "I know how you feel in my arms. How you feel when you put your arms around me and squeeze me." He moved closer still. Though he didn't touch her, he pressed his face into her hair and spoke into her ear. "I know how you feel when you let yourself go and how you feel when you let me inside you."

"Oh, God, Duncan." She whispered his name in protest. What was he doing to her? "Please don't."

"Don't what? Remind you of how good you felt when we were together? Of how you laughed and how you loved me?" He took her hand and moved it around his neck, his chest and abdomen. "Did you forget what I feel like when you touch me?"

"No, I haven't forgotten." She looked up at him, longing now in her own eyes, but curled her hand into a fist. "But it can never be."

"Only because you think it can't." He pressed a kiss to her palm. "I won't forget how you felt, and I hope you don't forget what you felt like because it was real, Rebel, not just some fantasy for you to bring out when no one is looking."

Tears pricked her eyes. Images of them together at the ranch, in the plane, in the barn in the rain, and snuggled together beneath the covers, skin to skin, bombarded her mind and her heart. This man cared deeply for her. How could she walk away from him, from what they could have? How could she love him and then die too soon?

The door to the lounge swung open, and Herm stuck his head in. "He's crashing."

They all raced to the trauma room where fifteen firefighters stood around the stretcher of their fallen one.

"Everyone back up." Duncan, in command again, pushed his way through the pack of people. "What happened?"

"His parents arrived and there was a scene," Gina said. "His mother got hysterical and fainted."

"Dammit. Let's get him settled down again. Give him some more sedation and pain control." He issued the orders as Rebel ushered everyone from the room.

"Everyone except Kat has to go." She led the woman to the head of the bed. "Sit here." Rebel indicated a stool by the stretcher. "Talk to him. Tell him everything that's going on, everyone is safe, use their names."

"But—" She looked down at Rebel, but sat as directed.

"Just do it, Commander. He needs to hear a familiar voice to tell him everything out there is okay so he doesn't worry and can focus on himself."

Kat began to talk low, directly into his ear. "Jimmy? It's Kat. I'm going to tell you what's going on, like the crazy Rebel nurse said, but you have to relax and let me do the talking and the worrying right now." She took a breath and gave a questioning look at Rebel. "Trust me to take on your burden."

Rebel nodded and backed away from Kat. Even though they were in a room full of people, there was a little privacy she could give them.

"Rebel, you're just brilliant," Herm said as he watched the scene unfolding in front of him. "His oxygen level is better and his heart rate is slowing down."

"It's probably the sedation." She denied any responsibility for his improvement.

"Every bit helps, remember? And stop putting yourself down. You're a highly skilled, if unconventional nurse, and I'm very pleased to be working with you." Herm patted her on the back.

"Me, too," Gina said, and the other staff nodded. A flush of warmth rose in Rebel's chest at their words and their obvious sincerity. This was what she needed and craved. This was the kind of place she'd been looking for but had had little hope of finding. Could she take the plunge and actually stay put? Stay in Albuquerque and build a life for herself here, instead of running the way Alejandro ran and ran and ran? She didn't know, but it was getting harder to be on the road all the time. Slowing down and resting her head on the same pillow suddenly became very appealing but very frightening, too. Change. She knew it was change that scared people the most.

"We're going out for drinks afterward. Maybe you want to come along this time." Gina nodded as she spoke. "We all can use it."

"Maybe," she said, unwilling to commit to anything yet. Was this an opportunity to make a few friends staring her right in the face, and she'd been blind to it previously?

Finally, the shift ended, about an hour late. Her feet ached, her back hurt, and she had a headache. Gina was right. The elevation took some getting used to.

"Ready? We're going to meet at Roscoe's. It's a dive, but we like it." Gina nodded toward the door. "Come on, Rebel. You deserve a break as much as the rest of us."

Rebel bit her lip in indecision, but as she watched the staff walking out the door, a bubble of excitement made her stomach squirm. Just like the firefighters, the nurses and other staff were like family. She'd noticed it the first day when she'd met Herm and his fatherly way.

"Okay." She nodded, eagerness bursting inside her, giving renewed energy. "I'd like to come if I won't be intruding."

"Intruding? Where'd you get that idea?" Gina gave a snort. "You're one of us, kid."

CHAPTER THIRTEEN

Nervous, but excited to be inducted into the group of friends, Rebel followed Gina to the parking lot and then to the little restaurant. It was a low, adobe-style building with twinkling lights in the windows and festive chili-shaped lights hanging from the ceiling.

Everyone straggled in and gathered around a central wooden table that wobbled on its uneven legs. Pitchers of drink were ordered and the servers placed baskets of handmade tortilla chips and bowls of salsa on the table. She was coming to realize this was a staple in all New Mexican restaurants. Chips and salsa. The staff devoured them as if they hadn't seen a meal in a week. People kept plopping into the chairs and then her pulse raced when Duncan took the one beside her that magically opened up. Jokes and stories were told as more people contributed to the conversation. Then something happened to Rebel that hadn't happened in a long time.

She relaxed. And she laughed. And she enjoyed herself. And she began to let go of the tight coil holding herself together. Life was messy, but when you had friends to help clean up, it was okay.

She leaned back in her chair, a smile on her face as she sipped a margarita and watched these people interact. In the past she would have been alienated by such a tightly knit group.

Could she really have relationships like the ones she'd seen in the firefighters? Covertly, she watched Duncan, casual and comfortable, despite the grueling day they'd had.

"Rebel? How about it?" Herm patted her arm.

"What? Did I miss something?" Apparently.

"Yes. Gina asked what your most interesting assignment has been." He snagged another chip and signaled the server for more. There was never enough.

"Oh, sorry." She paused and tucked her hair behind her left ear, remembering how Duncan had done that just a few hours ago and a flush warmed her insides. Or was that the margarita? "Every assignment has its perks, but I have to say Hawaii was the prettiest place I've been."

"I've heard it's really amazing."

"It is. I worked on Maui and when you drive around, the whole place smells like pineapples." She smiled with a fond memory of the islands.

"Well, stick around here long enough and there will be plenty of stuff here to get hooked on. There's skiing in the winter, all kinds of outdoor stuff to do year-round, loads of great food, too."

"Sounds great. I'm here for two more months, then I guess I will have to decide where to go from here." But in her heart she knew there was going to be no other assignment like this one. She didn't want to go, but she didn't know if she had the courage to stay.

"We always have a need for nurses with your skills, so you can stay another three months before deciding." Herm patted her arm. "I already know you want to stay."

Only Rebel saw the small nod he made in Duncan's direction. She leaned closer to Herm. "Please don't say anything about what you think you know." She glanced at

Duncan, who was listening intently to another staff member. "I hate to ask you to keep my secret, but I am." Her lip trembled. "I don't even think it's real."

"No worries, Rebel. I'll keep your confidence." He lowered his voice. "Just know that he's a *good* man. He doesn't hook up with women the way you might think." He patted her on her shoulder in a comforting gesture. "Listen to your instincts and do whatever you think is right."

"I appreciate that." The burn of tears flashed in her eyes at his kindness. "You don't know how much." She had no father or older brothers she could go to for comfort or to help explain men to her. She'd not had the best of experiences in love. Muddling through things had been too difficult and so she'd given up on love, just focusing on her career. At least until now. Until coming to Albuquerque had completely upset her goals, and her beliefs about love, life and family. Until Duncan.

Now she didn't know what to think. The one person she wanted to go to for comfort, for love, for friendship and understanding was the person most likely to hurt her. Trust and vulnerability were so hard for her. The universe seemed to enjoy taking people from her.

"I don't know what's been going on between the two of you, but I know neither of you have looked happy these last couple of weeks." He shrugged. "I have three daughters of my own, and I recognize the signs of heartache."

"It's complicated."

Herm laughed. "Every great love story has complications. Have you ever heard of one that was *easy*?" He shook his head. "No, my young friend, there are always issues, no matter who you are or how long you're in a relationship." He downed the rest of his drink. "Trust me on that one. If you find someone you can laugh with and love with, there's no better relationship than that. The rest, you work out." He patted her hand again. "I'm going to challenge you to think about what it would take to get through the complication. I don't need to know what it is, but you need to think of solutions, not stay stuck on the problem."

No matter what happened things would be okay. How had she forgotten that? As her family had disappeared one by one, it had become harder and harder to remember. Then, instead of trying to remember, she'd tried to forget. The guilt of surviving hung around her shoulders every day. What should have driven her closer to her mother, had only driven her further away.

"Hey, you okay?" Gina tossed a wadded-up napkin at her and struck her in the chest.

"What?" She blinked and realized where she was. "Oh, sorry. Guess I'm tired or something." Or something.

"You looked like you were out there somewhere."

"Yeah. Somebody said something that made me think of something. You know how it goes when your brain takes off on you and leaves your body behind."

"No kidding. Just don't do it when you're driving, okay?" Gina interjected with an understanding nod.

Rebel shifted her position in the chair, then yawned and stretched. "This was great, but I'm going to call it a night." She stood. The day had been long and intense. Fortunately she was off for a few days.

"I think we're all ready to call it a night." Herm stood and waited for her to extricate herself. "You take care, Rebel."

"You, too."

Herm surprised her by putting a friendly arm around her shoulders and pulling her against his side. "I don't know what's going on between you two, Rebel, but you won't find a better man than Duncan."

Breathlessness overcame Rebel, and she placed a hand

over her chest, nodded at Herm and left via the back door. She didn't know what was wrong with her, but she definitely needed some fresh air. Too many things were getting to her all at once, and a sense of panic churned in her gut.

Herm's words, her memories, the day's fatigue, the crowded restaurant all seemed to close in on her. Something was wrong, something was changing. Everything she had known and accepted for so many years was changing. Could she have been wrong about her entire life? Her livelihood and the lives of countless people depended on her making the right decisions in an instant. What if she'd been making the wrong decision in her life over and over and over—

"Rebel?" Duncan's voice made her jump.

"Duncan! What are you doing?"

"You're in an alley alone, at night, in a town you don't know. I'm not going to just let you walk alone." He emerged from the shadows. Lines of fatigue looked as if someone had drawn on him with a marker. These last few weeks had been very difficult.

"I appreciate it. I hadn't thought of it, because I do so many things by myself." Maybe she'd done too many things by herself.

"No problem."

Tension filled the air between them. She didn't know what to say as she led the way to her car a few blocks down the street.

"How are you?"

"I've missed you."

They spoke at the same time, and she turned to face him instead of opening her car door, as she should have. Some part of her wanted to reach out to him, but she'd trained herself for so many years not to touch, not to want, not to need. Just survive. That's all she needed. At least that's all she'd needed until Duncan had blazed his way into her life and set fire to her beliefs.

Without another word, he cupped his hands around her face. He hesitated a second with his mouth just an inch from hers, looked deeply into her eyes and kissed her.

Surprise and the shock of his action shot overwhelming desire all the way from her lips to her feminine core. Oh, the man could kiss. His hot lips opened over hers, and she stroked his tongue with hers, unable to hold back her response.

He pressed her back against the car and his hips pressed into hers. She felt the strength of his body and his erection through the scrubs and wanted him with everything she had in her. Breathless, she pulled away, thankful she was supported by the car. Desire nearly swamped her resolve to stay away from him evaporated.

"Will you stay with me tonight?" His breath came in quick little pants, his desire for her seeping out everywhere.

"What?"

"Will you stay with me tonight?" He was serious. "Come home with me. Stay with me. I need you, Rebel. I don't want to let you go."

"I don't know what to say." She gave a nervous laugh. "My body says one thing, but my mind says another."

He stepped back from her, and shook himself a little, creating the distance she needed. "When you figure it out, let me know. I'm heading to Hatch in the morning. Sounds like you're off for a few days. If you want to come with me, you can."

"Rafael's okay, isn't he?"

"He's fine. I'm the one who needs you." He took another step back. "I'll be gone for a week."

I need you. I just don't want to need you.

"Okay. Well. Goodnight, then." Fumbling with the door

and her keys, she finally got into the car and started it. She watched Duncan walk away through blurred vision. It was better this way. If he wasn't going to save himself, she would do it for him.

The night had to be the longest on record. She sweated despite the cool air in the apartment. Her heart raced despite doing thirty minutes of yoga breathing. Desire filled her body despite her best efforts to channel it elsewhere.

Once she'd had a dose of Duncan McFee, he was in her blood, and she didn't know how to get him out. Finally, after a restless and unfulfilling night, she slept for about four hours, awakening to a bright day full of promise.

And five days off with nothing to do but feel sorry for herself. Her schedule had been arranged by Herm and with a couple of staffing changes she'd agreed to she now had five entire days off. Alone.

Normally she would be excited about exploring the area, hiking the foothills outside town, taking in museums or movies, but now all of that sounded incredibly boring and dull without Duncan to share it with. She'd never shared anything with a man and now that she'd had a taste of Duncan, she wanted to share everything with him. But how could she when her life was a ticking time bomb?

Had she blown the best part of her life by being alone? Was Duncan right? She didn't want to think so, but some part of her knew it was the truth. She'd turned into an old woman well before her time. Tears pricked her eyes. She was such an idiot, unable to see outside her own pain.

When her phone rang she jumped for it, hoping it was Duncan, but it was work. Maybe she wasn't going to have five days off after all.

"Rebel, this is Herm."

"Hi. Do you need me to come in?" She hoped not, but it might keep her mind off of Duncan.

"No. I want to tell you not to come in."

She laughed. "Why is that?"

"It's Duncan."

It only took a nanosecond for her to imagine the worst-case scenario, and she gripped the phone tightly. "What happened? Has he been in a car accident? God, he didn't crash his plane, did he?" She bombarded him with questions.

"No. He's okay, physically." She heard the concern in his voice, but there was no panic as if something bad had happened.

"Then what's going on?"

"He's gone."

"Yeah, he went to Hatch for a few days." Whew, what a relief.

"He came in, was very serious and the *way* he did things, said things made me think he's not coming back."

"*What?* He loves the ER! Why would he resign?"

"I don't know, but he came in this morning, said good-bye to everyone and left." Herm paused. "Maybe this thing between you two is more serious than you know."

"I'm dumbfounded that he would do that, but why are you calling me?" Seriously. What was she going to do?

"You're the only one who can talk him into staying. We need him here and, frankly, Rebel, we need you here, too. For good." He sighed. "Truly good ER docs are hard to come by, and Duncan is just about the best."

"I don't know what I can do. He'll never listen to me if his mind is made up. That Scottish blood of his is as stubborn as any Irish I've ever met."

"If there's anyone he will listen to, it will be you."

"Herm, what am I supposed to do?" She knew he was going to the family ranch in Hatch today, but that's all she knew. After her refusal of him last night, he might not want to see her. Ever.

"He's always taken a week off during the height of the chili harvest, so I'm sure that's where he will be."

"He told me last night that's where he was going."

"I know it's none of my business, but can't you give the man a chance?"

"It's not just about him or me. It's—"

"Yes, it's complicated. But when isn't life complicated? Don't you want to have someone to hold your hand through those tough times? A shoulder to lean on, and cry on, when you need it?"

Rebel paused, a pulse of regret warming her chest. "I never thought of it that way."

"Well, it's time you did. I've seen your résumé, Rebel, and it's appalling."

"What? It is not. I have an excellent résumé." It clearly outlined all her travel experiences and her references were flawless.

"Clinically it's perfect, but there are no gaps where you took time off for vacation or to climb a mountain or anything like that. That's just wrong."

"I see." She thought about it a second, and he was right. She'd gone from assignment to assignment over the last six years without any pause. "How did you get to be so smart?"

"I'm old with a lot of miles under the hood. Now write this down. I'm going to give you directions to get to Hatch, and you can find the ranch from there."

Rebel wrote down the directions and signed off with Herm. How in the world was she going to talk Duncan into returning to work?

CHAPTER FOURTEEN

AFTER GETTING AN early start, Rebel drove to Hatch, hoping she could find the ranch. Having been there only one time, only by air, she faced uncertainty. Herm's directions were great, but they only led her so far. There was a whole lot of nothing out here for her to get lost in. She knew people died in the desert all the time, and she didn't want to be one of them. In preparation for the trip, she'd tossed a case of water and some snacks into the car, so hopefully she would survive the day.

Then she smiled, her heart a little lighter. All she had to do was ask a local where the best green chili in all of New Mexico was grown, and she was sure they would send her right to Rafael.

The drive was beautiful, following the river south, the massive cottonwoods green and white against the dark shadows beneath and the red clay below.

The scenery, the air rushing in the window brought the scent, a fragrance of things new, fresh and exciting. A memory bubbled up within her that began in her gut and flooded upward, surprising her with the intensity, the passion. She gasped as pain made her heart pause, then race in reaction.

Tears she'd buried, emotions she'd forced down for

years unhinged in her. Braking hard, she pulled to the side of the road, raising a cloud of dust.

Images, hard and fast, raced through her mind. An outing with her brothers, her father, their mother. The joy of the occasion. She didn't even remember where they'd gone that day, but the sense of safety, security, of family overwhelmed her, and she sobbed into her hands.

The pain, the grief, the loss flowed through her and the rock-solid shell around her heart shattered.

That was the last time she remembered them together. And happy.

Ben had pushed her on a swing.

Collin had carried her on his back.

Patrick had played tag and chased her around the park.

The pain she'd held back would no longer be ignored. After the storm of tears passed she rested her forehead on the steering-wheel and caught her breath. All this pain, these memories were thanks to Duncan.

The sound of tires crunching on gravel alerted her that she wasn't alone. Panic emerged on the heels of Duncan's warning in the alley last night. She was on a back road in a place she didn't know. She straightened and wiped her face with her hands, now alert.

A black sedan pulled up behind her. Red and blue lights flashed from the grill of the slow-slung car and a police officer emerged from the vehicle.

"Great. It's always something." She rolled down her window.

"Are you okay, ma'am? You've been pulled over for some time." The man took a wide-legged stance a few feet from the car and rested his right hand on the weapon at his hip. It was probably just habit, as she'd seen many cops take the same pose in the ER.

"Yes. I'm fine." Her voice cracked, and she cleared her throat. "I'm...I was just...resting...for a bit."

"Resting?" His dark eyes narrowed. "Are you impaired?"

Only by emotion. "Am I what? No." She blinked and looked down, wondering what to tell him that didn't include her whole life story.

He gave a long-suffering sigh, as if he'd been through this many times before. "Registration, ID, and proof of insurance."

Silently, she handed the items to him.

His brows went up and the expression on his face changed.

"You're Duncan's girl?" He relaxed his stance and handed her paperwork back. "Yeah, for sure, you're Duncan's girl."

"How do you know that?" This time her brows raised in surprise.

"Rey told me." He grinned. "It's a small town and cops talk, you know?"

"I see. Yes. Well. Hi. I'm fine. Really." Maybe knowing Duncan would get her out of a ticket she didn't need.

"Now, that's not true." He gave her that cop look again.

"Why do you say that?" Was she *that* obvious? She didn't deny it, but she wanted to know how he knew.

"Easy. Pink nose. Pink cheeks. Swollen eyes." He clucked his tongue. "Unless you're having an allergy attack, something's wrong."

"Oh."

"Did you and Duncan have a fight or something?" He gave her a brotherly look.

"No."

"Men can be a pain, you know. But you ladies have to forgive us. It's our nature." He gave a shrug that said it all.

"Your nature?" That was a new one. Now they could blame everything on their DNA.

"We want to be right all the time. So, whatever he did, cut him a break. He can't help it." He patted the window frame twice and stepped back. "Have a good day."

"Okay. Thank you, Officer…"

"Gutierrez. But my friends call me Tito."

She smiled, unexplained relief in her belly. "Thanks, Tito." She held out her hand, and he shook it.

"*Mucho gusto.*" Nice to meet you. He nodded, then returned to his car and drove away, leaving little swirls of red dust in his wake.

Maybe there was something to small-town living she hadn't seen before. She'd spent years running from one big city to another. If an assignment became too easy, too familiar, too tempting, she headed off to the next one.

Looking ahead to the small town of Hatch, she was beginning to wonder if her travel-nurse plan was a good one any longer. She pulled back onto the road with a renewed buoyancy of spirit, with a flicker of hope in her soul that she didn't have to run any more.

But Tito was wrong.

She didn't have to forgive Duncan, and she wasn't going to.

He'd been right all along. She just hadn't been able to face it.

After a few wrong turns and a few course corrections, otherwise known as U-turns, she found her way to the ranch.

But something was wrong.

Something was different.

An unusual and chilling quiet cloaked the land around the *casa*. When she'd been there before there had been activity and noise everywhere, but not now.

Something was very different.

Everything looked the same—the house, the grounds, even the tire tracks through the chili field was familiar—but her senses were on alert. Maybe it was her ER nurse experience or the personal protection classes she'd taken. Learning to be aware of her surroundings had saved her a time or two, and her senses were on high alert now.

She knocked on the front door, but there was no answer. No Lupe coming with open arms to greet her. No Rafael to loom over her. No goofy nephews causing chaos. Mysteriously absent was the persistent fragrance of cooking.

And no Duncan. If he were here, wouldn't his truck be parked in front?

Then a sound she never wanted to hear caught her attention.

She ran toward the sound of a screaming child. "Where are you?" The sound echoed off the buildings, and she ran in circles until she figured out where it was coming from.

Underground.

"Oh, God." It must be one of those old wells Duncan had told her about. Racing forward, she dropped to her knees beside what looked like a bunch of old wood stacked up. Lying on her belly, she pushed aside the planks to see into the dark. "Hello?"

The crying stopped for a moment. "*Señorita? La Irelanda hada?*"

"Yes, Alejandro, it's me."

He began screaming and crying at the top of his lungs and Rebel nearly broke down too. Determined to save this little boy, she pulled out her cellphone and dialed Duncan.

"Hel—"

"Duncan, it's Rebel. We need your help!" Quickly she explained what had gone on.

"Where are you?" The confidence in his voice calmed her a bit.

"I don't know. Somewhere behind the machine shed." She rose up onto her knees, looking toward the main house, and relief struck her as she saw him come out into the yard. She waved with one hand. "I see you." She stood, waving her hand.

"I can't see you. Where are you?"

She placed the phone on the ground, jumped up and down and waved with both hands. "We're over here!"

Duncan responded to her voice and saw her disappear. Fear like he'd never had twisted in his gut and sliced like a knife through his heart. She'd fallen into the hole, too. Prayers that he'd long ago forgotten moved his lips, and he whispered to the saints for strength.

"So, where is she?" Jake asked, scanning the horizon with his hands shading his eyes.

"Go get the backhoe and bring it behind the machine shed. There's an old homestead site there, and I think they've fallen into the old root cellar. We're going to need the horse sling, the winch and cable."

"What—?"

"Just do it!" Duncan raced to where he'd last seen Rebel, running as fast as he could, and his heart felt like it was going to burst. Panic set in when he couldn't see her, couldn't find her. "Rebel! Where are you?" He cupped his hands and kept calling for her. He didn't know if she didn't hear him or couldn't call out. Hastily, with hands shaking, he dialed her number. Maybe it was still above ground and he was close enough to hear the ring. If it wasn't on vibrate.

Dammit. After two tries, he finally got it right and heard the faint music. Listening intently, he moved around, going closer, hanging up and ringing again until he saw the pile of wood that was supposed to have covered the hole from one of the original homes built on the ranch. There was no way she could have known it was there. "Rebel?" He skidded to a halt and fell to his belly, then scrambled to the edge of the opening.

Below was a scene he never wanted to see again. Rebel lay crumpled up, with Alejandro shaking her shoulder and crying.

"Alejandro?" The boy looked up, frightened but not hurt.

"I'm coming to get you. Don't be afraid."

"*La mujer? La hada?*"

"She'll be okay, too, but you have to help me."

The little boy nodded. "I help."

Though Duncan didn't know how at the moment, he knew he had to get them out of there before the whole room collapsed on top of them. The vibrations of the backhoe reached him and he stood, directing Jake. Workers arrived, hurrying after the heavy machine, and Duncan derived some comfort from having such a knowledgeable group coming to help. Pedro raced ahead of the group, his face distorted with worry and fear. He gasped for breath, trying to question Duncan in between breathing.

"Pedro, calm down." Duncan motioned for the other men to come closer. "We're going to need the ropes and pulleys set up. Strap it to one of the horse harnesses and use the backhoe to be the support." Everything was done quickly and Duncan looked over the edge again.

Rebel was rousing. The little Superman patted her shoulder and spoke to her softly. Duncan noticed spots of blood on the back of her shirt and hoped she wasn't badly injured. With that kind of fall, it was hard to predict.

"Rebel. Honey, are you okay?"

She turned at the sound of his voice then winced. More

slowly, she pushed her hair out of her face and looked up at him. "Duncan? How did I get here?"

"You fell into the hole when you called me to help get Alejandro out." He paused to take a breath and calm himself, but his heartbeat thundered in his ears. "Can you tell what kind of injuries you have?"

That information was necessary to ascertain before putting her into the harness. If she had serious injuries, they'd have to get the rescue squad and dig her out.

"I hurt everywhere. My back is scraped, but I don't think I've broken anything." Experimentally, she moved her limbs, testing for injuries, then shook her head. "No, everything seems okay." She took a gasping breath that sliced through his heart. "I'm scared, Duncan."

"Don't worry, darling. I'm here, and I'll get you out." One of the men called to him. "Hold on. I think we're ready up here. I've got a horse harness I'm going to lower down to you. Put Alejandro into it first, then we'll get you up right after." Though it nearly killed him to do it this way, the child had to come first.

"Okay." She nodded, as if trying to convince herself of the plan. "Okay." Crawling to her knees, she slowly rose upright, swayed, then caught herself. "Just a little dizzy."

"You'll be fine. Once we get you topside, you'll be fine." And he would be too. Everything was in readiness, and the harness was lowered down to her. Though her hands shook, she was able to get it loosely around the boy. He was so small Duncan was afraid he'd fall out of it. "Hold on tight and up you go."

Duncan gave the signal and the men began to pull the boy up. As the rope sliced through the ground at the edge of the opening, dirt and other debris were dislodged and fell down onto Rebel's head.

She cringed and turned away from the dust and dirt,

coughing as she tried to breathe. In seconds, though, Alejandro was topside and Duncan untangled him from the harness. Pedro fell to his knees and hugged the boy between kisses and curses.

Duncan lowered the harness down to Rebel. "Put this on somehow and we'll get you out." His heartbeat faded away, his breathing faded away, the sounds of the machine and the other people faded away until all that was left was Rebel. "Come back to me, darling."

Flinching from pain, Rebel was able to get the thing mostly around her torso and gripped it with both hands. She looked up at him and her eyes met his. The trust, the need in them humbled him. It all came down to this moment with Rebel putting her life in his hands. He couldn't, wouldn't let her down. Never again.

"I'm ready. Get me outta here." She gave a thumbs-up signal and Duncan signaled the men. They hauled on the ropes, pulling and easing Rebel up through the opening. Dirt and more small rocks rained down on her as the rope dug into the dry ground.

The second he could touch her hair he knew she was going to be okay. And so was he. "I've got you. I've got you." Helping her over the ledge and onto the ground, he reached for her, and he wasn't ever going to let go again.

"Oh, Duncan." She reached out, still tangled in the harness, and he brought her against him. He was trembling inside. He couldn't help it. The fear he'd had in the last thirty minutes was like nothing he'd ever experienced in his life. And he never wanted to go through that again.

"Oh, my God, Rebel. Are you okay?" He pushed her away from him to look at her. She was a mess. Scrapes and scratches covered her face and arms, and dirt and dust covered everything.

"I think I'm okay. My head is starting to hurt, though.

Where's Alejandro? Is he okay?" She clutched Duncan's arms, her eyes wide.

"He's okay. He raced off to his father, so I think he's okay."

"Good." She nodded and pressed a hand to her forehead. "Can we go to the house now? I need to sit down."

"Yes." He unbuckled the harness and ropes as the men gathered around, smiling and laughing, offering good wishes and many thanks for her finding Alejandro. Someone gathered up the ropes. Someone else got the harness and Jake drove the backhoe to the machine shed while everyone else followed them to the house. Lupe met them at the door with a screech and a litany of orders that everyone scrambled to get going. "What happened, *mija*? Oh, you are such a mess."

The tremors he felt from Rebel intensified, her eyes fluttered, and he knew she was going into shock. Moving quickly, he scooped her up in his arms and hurried into the house.

"Lupe! Have one of the boys get my kit from the plane. I need warm blankets and a bottle of whiskey."

"Whiskey or tequila?"

"Both." In a Scottish-Hispanic household both libations were always available.

Lupe gave orders to the women of the household and before he could even get Rebel settled down onto the couch someone had arrived with pillows, an electric blanket, a heating pad and a bottle of electrolyte water.

Judd arrived with his medical kit, and Duncan's hands trembled as he tried to start an IV in Rebel's hand. He missed the vein and the IV blew.

Lupe placed a hand on his shoulder. "Take a breath, *mijo*. It will be okay. You have the power in your hands to heal her. It's not like before. Give her your love, and it will all be fine."

Duncan nodded and, without looking up, he addressed his nephew. "Judd, go get a bit of the herbal mix we use on the horses. She's gonna need some."

"Seriously? The stuff for the *horses*? It stinks. Really bad." He stood, though uncertainty remained on his face.

"Just go." Judd raced off and Duncan took that breath Lupe had suggested, releasing the tension in his shoulders and his hands. He did have the power to heal her and it was right in front of him.

Focusing again, Duncan successfully inserted the cannula into a vein in the back of Rebel's wrist. Relief swept through him as he connected the IV fluids, letting them infuse quickly.

A small hand appeared on his arm. Alejandro stood tearfully beside him, and he hadn't even noticed. Duncan put his arm around the boy and drew him closer.

"*La hada*, she bad hurt?" Alejandro spoke in soft Spanglish. Duncan could see the little man adored her.

"*La hada* is hurt bad, but she's going to be okay." Duncan hugged Alejandro, who tried to hide a wince. "Let me see your arm."

Alejandro shook his head and looked down, holding his left arm across his middle.

"Alejandro, *es bien*. I want to see if you have any injuries." He took a breath, trying to calm the fear and adrenaline racing through him. "You're not in trouble, *entiendo*?"

Tears welled up in the boys eyes as he looked at Duncan. "My fault."

"No, it's not your fault *la hada* is hurt. She came to rescue you with her magic. Sometimes when the magic runs out the fairy has to rest a while, *entiendo*?"

"*Sí, entiendo*." Still downcast, Alejandro held out his

arm to Duncan. A purple bruise had begun in the middle of the forearm. Probably broken, at least deeply bruised, but they'd need an X-ray to determine it, which meant a trip to town.

"Lupe? Can you take him to the kitchen and get him some of your special hot chocolate and some ice for his arm?"

"Come, Alejandro." Lupe held out her hand to him, but he refused to take it.

"No. Stay *con* Rebel. *Por favor*?" Trembling, he made the request to remain in the living room with Rebel, the only woman who had put her life on the line for him. Even at his young age, he knew how special she was. Even if she wasn't a magical fairy.

"Okay. Lupe, can you bring those things in here for him?" Duncan nodded to the end of the couch at Rebel's feet. Alejandro climbed up carefully and placed one hand on her foot, patting it gently.

A groan from Rebel and a twitch of her arm indicated she was coming round, which was a good sign after the trauma she'd sustained.

"Can you sit?" Duncan knelt beside her and put an arm behind her shoulders. As careful as he was, she winced anyway.

"Oh. Ow!" She sat up abruptly and put a hand to her forehead. The second her legs hit the floor Alejandro scooted closer to her, not touching, but needing her nearness to comfort him. Pedro plopped into a chair across the room, and dropped his face into his hands.

"Easy, love. Take a few breaths." Though Duncan understood there was an unofficial rule in medicine that you never treated those you were emotionally close to, he didn't give a damn.

With Rebel lying limp and in pain in his arms, he would

trust no one else to care for her, even if they had been in Albuquerque in their own ER.

Whatever needed to be done was going to be done by *him*.

CHAPTER FIFTEEN

REBEL RAISED HER HEAD and looked into his eyes. "My back is on fire. Got anything for that, Doc?" Her smile was as stiff as her movements, but she curled her left arm around Alejandro.

"Judd is bringing me a special herb concoction we use on the horses. It will help as soon as I get it on you."

Her brows shot up. "The horses? You're using a horse liniment on me?"

"Sure. If they like it, I don't see why you shouldn't." A small smile lit him up. If she was starting to crack jokes, she was going to be okay.

"Yes. Lupe makes a salve out of the herbs we grow."

Judd arrived, skidding to a halt beside them. "I got it." He shoved the container, the size of a mint tin, into Duncan's hands. "Here."

Lupe arrived at that moment with a tray for Alejandro, laden with her special hot chocolate, a few cookies and a picture book. "Come over here, Alejandro, so Duncan can tend to Rebel."

This time, when she held her hand out to him, he took it and allowed her to lead him to the chair across the room beside Rafael, whom Duncan hadn't even seen come into the room. The great man said nothing, but Duncan could see the tension around his eyes and in the set of his mouth, firm and displeased. Duncan nodded to him and received a return gesture.

"Let me see your back. You'll be amazed at how well it works. The horses make a fuss at the medicinal smell as it's camphor, but I don't think you'll mind."

Rebel turned her back to him, and he raised her shirt over her shoulders. Red welts covered her back, swollen in places and already deep bruises showed themselves. He dipped his fingers in the salve. Starting at her trim shoulders and moving downward, he applied the ointment. She winced several times, but it couldn't be helped. After settling her shirt again, she sat on the edge of the couch so her back didn't touch anything.

Jake shuffled into the room, carrying two neoprene packs of some sort. "When the horses get hurt we put these ice packs on them. I figured you and Alejandro could use them, too." He cleared his throat and blushed gloriously as he approached Rebel.

Duncan raised his brows. Apparently, Rebel had made quite an impression on the men in the family, no matter what their age. He obviously had some competition for her attention. That made Duncan smile. She'd already been accepted by the family, and she didn't even know it.

"Thanks, Jake." Duncan took the cold gel pack from him and placed it gently on Rebel's back. She closed her eyes and gave an audible sigh.

"That's fantastic. Thanks, Jake." She reached out for his hand without opening her eyes.

The young man shook her hand roughly and turned a florid shade of red, matching Lupe's scarlet trumpet vine on the *portál*. "Glad to help." He dropped her hand, and then she opened her eyes. "I…uh…got something to do." He backed away from her, prepared to bolt from the room.

"What's the status out there?" Rafael questioned, and hit him with a stern stare.

"It was the old homestead foundation, sir."

"I thought we blocked that well off some time ago."

"It wasn't the well, sir, but some sort of storage room. Maybe the root cellar." Jake said. "The backhoe's still out. I can just plow the whole thing over if you like and cover it for good."

"Go ahead. Then we need to start going to the other old home sites and making sure there aren't more death traps we've forgotten about."

"I'll get it done right now." Jake left to do the job.

Rebel leaned against Duncan's shoulder, and he was glad to be her support. Her gentle breathing against his skin was something he wanted to savor for years to come. This woman who had no qualms about putting herself in harm's way for others deserved to be cherished and adored.

He'd been so determined to have his own way he hadn't been able to see there was another way to be had! He'd been so determined to make Rebel see things *his* way, to do things *his* way, he'd nearly driven off the woman who excited him, inspired him, and stirred his passion for living.

Lupe paused in front of him until he looked up.

"She deserves your best, *no*?"

"She does, and she's going to get it." He stroked Rebel's hair and pressed his cheek to the top of her head.

Rafael stood. "Come on, kid, let's go see if you can help me figure out this new cellular phone." Alejandro looked with longing at Rebel. "She's in good hands but needs to rest right now. Come on, Pedro. You too."

"Okay." Alejandro took Rafael's hand and allowed the man to lead him away, Pedro following behind.

"Rebel, you are an amazing woman. I wish you knew

that." As Duncan held her, her breathing changed from the easy, restful pace to rapid and anxious.

"Duncan."

She leaned her head back and looked up at him and all he wanted to do was kiss her. So he did, dirt and all.

Leaning in to her, he opened his mouth over her parted lips. Somehow, he wanted to put all his fear and all his love into that one kiss. He cupped the back of her head gently and kissed her. She allowed him to take what he wanted, the glide of her tongue over his assuring him she was no longer upset but needed him as much as he needed her.

Breaking the kiss, he held her close, the tremors surging through him coming as a surprise.

"You can't leave."

"I'm not going anywhere." This was where he wanted to be for now. With a hand that still shook he brushed some of the dirt from her face.

"Herm told me." She sat upright, urgency in her expression. "You love that place. You can't leave."

"What exactly did Herm tell you?" He frowned, puzzled by this. Did she have a concussion?

"He said you resigned this morning. You can't do that."

Duncan smiled and gave a head shake. "He exaggerated a little." Warmth stirred in his chest at her reaction.

"You didn't resign?" Confusion warred with relief in her eyes.

"No. I came in to say goodbye to everyone as I decided to take the rest of the month off to help with the chili harvest. Not resign the whole thing."

"Oh, that man! He made me believe you'd resigned and weren't ever coming back, and I was the only one who could talk you into keeping your job!"

Speechless for a moment, Duncan pulled her against his side. "And you thought you could do that?"

"I thought I might be able to help, yes." She placed one arm around his waist. "You aren't leaving?"

"No, I'm not going to leave the ER, but I do need to spend some more time here. The situation today with Alejandro and the lack of serious healthcare here has made me wake up to where I am needed just as much."

"I see." She looked away. "That's good."

"But we need to talk about us, Rebel." He stroked the hair back from her face, extricated a chunk of dirt. "I know you're in pain right now, but I can't wait any longer." Here goes. This was going to be the hardest conversation he'd ever had with anyone, but for both of them it had to happen, it had to be done. And if he couldn't make her see, couldn't convince her of his sincerity, then he would have to move on. Again.

Her chin trembled, but she nodded. "Go ahead."

"I know you're still grieving about your family, and it sucks." He wanted to touch her, comfort her, but making it easier wasn't going to help either of them.

"Grieving?" She took a deep breath and let out an agonized cry, as if coming to a conclusion on her own for the first time. "I'm not grieving, Duncan. I'm feeling *guilty!*"

"For what? You didn't do anything."

"I. Survived." Emotions choked out of her. "I was *supposed* to help my mother, I was *supposed* to make things better for her, and I didn't. I couldn't! All I did was live and remind her every day of what she'd lost." Painful though it was, she stood and began to pace.

"None of that was your fault, Rebel. None of it." He punched a fist against his thigh, unable to contain the temper that ate at him on her behalf. "You were a child. And if your mother expected you to do anything else, then she was out of her mind with grief, too."

"It was my job to be *good*, to be *quiet*, to help take care of them when my mother needed a break." Tears streamed down Rebel's face, making muddy tracks, and the memory took her deep.

Duncan paused, wanting to reach out to her, to hold her, to comfort her, to make it better in some way, but he knew he couldn't. He couldn't take away her pain, but he could be there when she let go. He stood and watched as she moved through the pain that had shaped her entire life.

"I did what I could, and it was never enough. It was never going to be enough. *I* was never going to be enough. Even as a kid I could see that." She took in a breath, her eyes still glazed as she whispered her pain out loud. "I emptied trash cans and vomit basins, and stood up on an old wooden box so I could reach the controls on the washer when I was eight. I went to school in the day, but when I got home I became the mother, the nurse, the caretaker, and my mother went to work."

"So you stayed home with all of them?" Incredulous, he could hardly conceive of the responsibility heaped on the tiny shoulders of a child.

She nodded and reached up to tug on a strand of her hair, wrapping it round and round one of her fingers. "Yes, but they weren't all sick at the same time. The first one, my dad, went on for three years."

Duncan closed his eyes, unable to fathom the pain and the loss of a vital part of her youth. No wonder she was such a strong nurse. She'd been at it since childhood. "What happened after that?"

"Well, I don't remember much from some of those years. Just going to school and staying up with my dad until my mom got home." She shrugged. "Fortunately, he died at the beginning of my summer break when I was eleven, so I had the whole summer to recover."

"You don't really recover from the death of your father, though, do you?"

"No, I mean from the exhaustion of caring for him. I had a few months to recover before school started again."

"I see." He settled on the arm of one of the couches. "What did you do then?"

"The boys were okay for a couple of years, then when I was about thirteen or fourteen, I don't remember, the boys started showing symptoms, and we got a clue it wasn't just Dad." She let out a heavy sigh. "Ben had a stroke when he was twenty-three. He was the oldest." She shook her head and tears flowed again. "My mother was so proud of him when he got this job working construction. He loved to build things, and she was so happy he was doing what he wanted." A sad smile curved the corners of her mouth upward. "He was in a heavy equipment accident at the construction site where he worked. No one ever figured out if he had the stroke first and then the accident happened or the other way around."

Duncan didn't think it mattered, chicken or egg, the result was the same. "So that's how you found out he had Huntington's?"

"Yeah. When the neuro symptoms lingered longer than the rest of his injuries, and he couldn't go back to work. After that it was bam, bam, bam." She hit the back of one hand against the palm of the other for emphasis. "They all became symptomatic within three years and died within five." Though her breathing had settled, she inhaled an erratic breath as her body calmed and she told her story.

"The emotional pain must have been excruciating." He couldn't conceive of it. Even though he'd faced his own pain and saw the pain of others on a daily basis, he just couldn't wrap his head around what she'd gone through as a child.

"It doesn't matter now, but there it is. You know what my deal is and why."

Without responding, he stood and placed his hands on her cheeks and lifted her face upward until she looked him in the eye. Hers were the saddest eyes he'd ever seen, and now he knew why. "Did your mother ever thank you, or tell you she was proud of you?"

The green darkened and the tears she'd managed to contain welled again and overflowed. "No." Her chin quivered, and she began to cry in earnest.

Then he did comfort her, held her against him and gave her the support of his body as he held her and let her cry against him, let her cry for the childhood she'd never had and the family she'd lost. "I'm proud of you, Rebel. I'm so proud of the woman you've become, of the humor you've maintained, of the compassion you share, and the insight you've developed. Of your passion when we make love." He stroked her hair and didn't know if she heard him, heard his words or the things he meant when he said them.

"I'm such a mess, how can you be proud of me?" Pressing her face against his neck, she hid her face from him.

"Because I love you, Rebel. With all my heart, and all my soul, I love you." At those words, she stiffened, stilled, and he didn't know if she even breathed. With gentle hands, he pushed some of her hair back and bared her face. "There you are."

"You must be delusional or something." Red, blotchy-faced, with tears still flowing, she was the most beautiful person he'd ever known.

"Why? Because I love you?"

"Yes," she whispered, and the seemingly endless fountain of tears continued. "You've seen the real me, all of me, and you can still say you think you love me?"

Using his thumbs, he wiped the tears from her face and

placed a kiss on the tip of her dirty, red nose. "I don't think I love you, I *know* I do. You're one of the strongest women I've ever known, Rebel Taylor, and I want to know more of you every day."

There were no words to describe her feelings. Relief, guilt, loss, confusion, but most of all love for Duncan. The kind of love she'd heard about and read about but had put down to good fiction, wild fantasy, or drunken debauchery. Never in her life would she have thought she could find that kind of love for herself. "I don't deserve you, Duncan. Or this family or—"

"Shh. Yes, you do. From the second you set foot on this property, you've been welcome. From the second you looked at me in the parking lot when we met, I've been unable to get you out of my mind, and you've found a place in my heart. I want you in my life."

"I don't know how you see all of those things in me, but I'm so…glad…you do." She clutched him against her and this time there were tears of joy, of happiness along with the pain left in her, but if Duncan was beside her, she knew she could take at least one step forward to having a normal life, to having a great love in her life and putting behind her the pain of her past, the childhood torn away from her by death and disease. "I don't know how to say the words." She looked at him, begging him to understand.

"The words 'I love you'?"

Nodding, she pressed her lips together.

"Then I'll say them for you, every day, until you can say them to me." He pressed his forehead against hers, holding her, trying to help her see she was worthy of his love. "I love you, Rebel Taylor. Will you stay with me, will you love me, and be my wife?" He felt her stiffen again. "It's not too soon, it's not too fast, it's barely fast enough for me."

Then she smiled, and he knew they were going to be okay. Even if she couldn't yet say the words, she loved him.

"Dr. McFee, what will people think? We've only know each other…for how long?"

"It doesn't matter how long we've known each other." He curved some of that wild hair behind one ear. "People will think I'm damned lucky you agreed to be my wife. Say you will?"

"I will be your wife and stay with you and…love you."

"Will you be part of this crazy family and help me to open a free clinic here in Hatch? I know it's a lot to ask all at one time, but when you see your dreams right in front of you, how can you not grab hold with both hands?"

"I… I never thought I would marry or have children, so I cut that dream out of my life a long time ago."

"I want to take you on all those trips you never took, and I want to check everything off that long bucket list of yours, and experience with you all the things you've never done."

"Well, that's quite a lot," she said with a laugh, and she knew she would be okay. Really okay on the inside. With time, with love, maybe a little therapy and his support, but she would be okay. Now, she could breathe again and for the first time she inhaled a sense of relief she'd never had.

"Duncan McFee, I will marry you and be part of this crazy family of yours and travel anywhere you want to go. As long as you're with me, it will be home."

Duncan held her close, mindful of her injuries, and the tremor of fear inside him began to subside. All was going to be well with them, and he'd spend his lifetime ensuring she knew it. "I love you."

"But what about children? I can't give you any babies." He knew her history, but would he accept it? That could be the deal-breaker for them both.

"You don't know that. Not for sure." He took her hands in his. "I think it's time for you to know."

"To know wh—? No." She shook her head and tears filled her eyes. "I can't, Duncan. I just can't. I already know."

Though she tried to pull away from him, he held on to her hands. "Darling, you don't know, and neither do I." He drew her a little closer. "What I do know is that I love you. The results won't stop me from loving you. It will give you some peace, and that's what I want for you more than anything."

"Peace? How can you say that when having the test will determine how long my life is?" Her eyes were wide with fright he'd put there, and her chest rose and fell quickly.

"No, it won't. That test is what it is, and that's all. It doesn't determine how long your life is or how well you live it. I'll be with you every step of the way, and I will love you through whatever happens."

"I've never known anyone like you, Duncan McFee. I can't believe you love me enough to want to know the truth about me."

"I already know the truth about you. You are a wonderful, caring, vibrant woman who loves deeply. *That's* the truth of you. What I want is to bring you peace, to ease your mind, and take away the pain that's been in your heart for too long."

"That's a pretty tall order." One she'd never been able to fill on her own, but now, with his help, his guidance and his love, she could.

"I know, and I may not be able to do it all, but I want to try. And I want to spend whatever time we have on this earth together."

"So what happens if I'm positive? I won't be able to

give you children, and you so deserve to be a father." Her voice had gone soft, fear filling it again.

"And you deserve to be a mother. I've seen you with Alejandro, and I know you would love to have your own. I know. But there's more than one way to be a parent. And that's more important than having a pregnancy, isn't it?"

Rebel wrapped her arms around him, feeling like there was hope for her future. "Yes, yes, it is." She took in a deep breath and huffed out the remaining doubts and uncertainty. "If you'll be with me and help me, I can be strong enough to find out the truth."

"You're already stronger than you know." He stroked her cheek. "And I'll be with you every step of the way."

EPILOGUE

TROPICAL BREEZES HEAVY with the smell of the ocean and flowers surrounded Rebel. She emerged from the small commercial plane and was enveloped by the welcoming arms of Jamaica. This was something she'd never imagined, stepping out into such paradise. Now that she'd received the test results, life could go on. Beautifully, peacefully.

She did not carry the gene, as she'd thought she did. She'd been able to tell her mother the wonderful information on her wedding day. What a joy that had been, to be reunited with her mother, introduce her to a huge new family, and share the perfect news of being negative, all in one brilliant day.

"You were so right to tell me I was nuts."

"I never said that." He looked at her over his aviator sunglasses as he had when she'd flown with him for the first time.

"When we first met and I told you Jamaica was on my bucket list. You didn't say it quite that way, but you inferred it." She smiled up at him. "And you were right. This is unbelievable. We haven't even left the airport and I'm speechless."

Duncan stopped and placed a well-deserved kiss on her lips, then took her by the hand and led the way through the airport. "Our luggage will be delivered to the bungalow, there will be fresh fruit on the table when we get there, with a bottle of rum and a lovely breeze bringing the smell of the ocean through the windows."

"It sounds heavenly." As she let him lead her through the colorful airport, the sun glinted off the ring on her left hand. It was a plain silver band, but she hadn't wanted anything else, much to Duncan's disappointment. What was the use of having money if he didn't spend some of it on her? She'd said he could spend the money on making memories with her, rather than on a sparkly token. He'd taken her at her word and booked the honeymoon trip immediately.

"It is." He kissed her hand then pulled her closer for another kiss. "Just like you."

"My birth-control implant runs out in another few months. Maybe we should think about baby-making." That was another thing she'd never considered before meeting Duncan. But now life had opened up into a new world since meeting him.

"It takes more than *thinking* to make babies." He smiled. "While we're here in Jamaica, I think we could work on perfecting our technique, so when the time comes we'll have it down pat."

She laughed, feeling freer than she'd thought she'd ever be, more loved than she'd ever thought possible, and happier than she'd ever thought she *could* be.

"Thank you, Duncan McFee." How else could she put it? She was grateful for his presence in her life and for the joy he gave her every moment of the day.

"For what?" He stopped and other people in the airport just moved around them, as if accustomed to lovers stopping spontaneously.

"For loving me." Tears distorted her vision, and she happily blinked them away.

"Always." He put an arm around her shoulders and drew her close against his body, then led her out into paradise.

* * * * *

A FATHER
FOR POPPY

ABIGAIL GORDON

For my dear friend Jill Jones.

CHAPTER ONE

THEY HAD MADE love for the last time with the evening sun laying strands of gold across them. It had been as good as it had always been—sweet, wild and passionate. But there had been sadness inside Tessa because deep down she'd known it was the end of the affair, although neither of them were prepared to put into words that it was over.

It had been the agreement when they'd met—no commitments, take what life offered and enjoy it. Wedding rings were a joke, brushed to one side with babies and mortgages. Having spent her young years amongst her parents' quarrelling, unfaithfulness and eventual divorce, she was wary of the kind of hurts that a gold band on the finger could bring.

So she'd kept her distance from the men she'd met until Drake Melford had appeared in her life and everything had changed. He hadn't asked anything of her except to make love and when they had it had been magical. There had been no suggestion of any kind of commitment and in the beginning she'd been totally happy.

The attraction between them had been intense. So much so that when they'd been together at either of their apartments they'd made love on the rug, the kitchen table, and even once on a park bench in moonlight when the place had been empty, giving no thought to the future. Only the present had mattered.

So what had gone wrong? Something had changed the magic into doubt and misgivings, telling her in lots of ways that it was over, and whenever she'd wanted to ask Drake what was happening to them there had been the 'no strings' pact that had made the words stick in her throat.

Her only comfort had been in knowing that she wasn't competing against another woman, that it was his career that was going to take him away from her, and ever since then Tessa had kept the memory of that time buried deep in one of the past chapters of her life.

But a fleeting glimpse of the back of a man's neck and the dark thatch of hair above it as he'd got into a taxi outside a London railway station had been a reminder that anything as memorable as the time she'd spent with Drake Melford would never stay buried.

She brushed a hand across her eyes as if to shut out a blinding light. It wasn't the first time she'd given in to wishful thinking, and she knew how hard she had to fight to keep sane once the raw and painful memories were allowed to intrude into the life she had worked so hard to build in Drake's absence.

She groaned softly and an old lady next to her in the taxi queue asked, 'Are you all right, dear?'

Managing a smile, Tessa told her that it was just a stitch in her side instead of a thorn in her heart.

It was a Friday. She was in London for an important meeting and at the moment of seeing the man at the front of the queue getting into the taxi her thoughts were on what lay ahead and any surprise announcements that might be made.

She'd travelled up from Gloucestershire, where she was employed for the yearly AGM that was held in the city, and intended on staying the night at a hotel and catching an early train back in the morning.

Horizons Eye Hospital was on the edge of the elegant town of Glenminster, with the green hills of the county looking down on it, and was renowned for its excellence in specialised treatment. Tessa was employed there in a senior management position and was deeply committed to every aspect of it.

She'd heard it said that the health service had more managers than doctors. Though she, of course, respected the fantastic work done by the medical teams, at least a doctor didn't have to get up in the middle of the night when a patient who had arrived with valuables in their possession and asked that they be put in the hospital safe was unexpectedly being discharged and wanted their belongings returned to them. As the only key holder, this meant a deal of trouble for Tess.

It had also been said that she must wish that her position there was more connected with healing than organising. But Tess had always believed that a clean, healthy and efficient facility with good, wholesome food did as much for a patient's recovery as the medical miracles performed there.

As her taxi pulled up outside the building where the meeting was to take place, she was remembering a veiled comment that the chairman of the hospital board had made to her.

The top consultant of the hospital was retiring, so would be saying his goodbyes at the AGM, and the chairman had remarked that, much as the hospital was already famous, the man who was to replace him was going to take it even higher on the scale of excellent ophthalmology. When she'd asked for a name he'd just smiled and said, 'All will be revealed at the AGM.'

And now here she was, still too bogged down with the past to be curious about the present, until she walked into the conference room and realised that this time she hadn't been wrong in thinking she'd seen him. Drake Melford was there, chatting to some of her colleagues in his usual relaxed manner. It was history repeating itself.

Tessa turned quickly and made her way to a powder room, where a face devoid of colour stared back at her from the mirror. She closed her eyes, trying to shut out what she'd seen out there, telling herself that she should have known it was Drake that she'd glimpsed at the taxi rank.

She'd caressed his neck countless times, pressing kisses on to the strong column of it, raking her fingers through the dark pelt of his hair... But the meeting was due to start any moment and the chairman would not be expecting her to be skulking in the powder room.

The hospital board was already seated around a big oval table when she went back into the room, with Drake, the chairman and the retiring consultant seated centrally. When he saw her, Drake felt his heartbeat quicken and wished that their meeting—after what felt like a lifetime of regret—had been a more private one. But a part of him knew it was better this way, as a casual meeting of old friends, rather than... Rather than what? he asked himself.

As she eased herself into a seat at the far end of the table, Tessa listened to what was being said as if it were coming from another planet.

The chairman was making a presentation to the retiring consultant, who was following it with a short farewell speech, and then Drake would be introduced to those who would be working with him at the famous hospital.

He received a warm welcome from the chairman, who described him as a local man, top of his field in ophthalmology, and who, having fulfilled his obligation to a Swiss clinic, had agreed to accept the position of chief consultant at the Horizons Hospital.

There was loud applause. Tessa joined in weakly. Then Drake was on his feet, speaking briefly about the pleasure of being back in the U.K. and how he was looking forward to being amongst them. For

Tessa it was like a dream from which she was sure she would awaken at any moment.

After that, routine matters were discussed and soon the assembled members retired to a nearby hotel where an evening meal had been arranged for all those present.

So far the two of them hadn't spoken, but when she was chatting to one of the members of the hospital board, Drake went past with some of the bigwigs and called across, 'Hi, Tessa. You're still around, I see.'

She made no reply, just smiled a tight smile at the thought of being referred to as part of the fixtures and fittings. It was hardly the reunion her fevered brain had imagined during all those nights of tossing and turning.

As the evening wore on it seemed that quite a few of those at the meeting were booked in at the hotel for the night, Drake amongst them. Every time she thought of him being under the same roof she had to pinch herself to believe it.

Leaving most of them settled in the bar after they'd eaten, she went to her room and tried to come to terms with the day's events. The first time she'd met him had been mesmerising and today had been no different, though for a different reason, she thought, lying wide-eyed against the pillows.

The most mind-blowing thought was that after three years of being denied his presence, she would now be seeing him on a daily basis. How was she going to cope with that? Their agreement had made it easy for him to leave her when the opportunity for a promotion had landed at his feet, and there had been no word of any kind from him since he'd left. Not one. And now they would be colleagues again. Tessa groaned into her pillow.

Drake had gone to his hotel room shortly after her and there was no smile on his face now. When he'd received the offer to work in Switzerland everything else had faded into the background. It had been a chance to improve his expertise and he'd been so keen to get over there he had given no thought to what he and Tessa had shared, so obsessed had he been with his own affairs.

It had only been as the months had become years without her that he'd realised what he'd lost in his arrogance. Too much time had passed for him to get in touch with her again, and he had felt…what? Regret? Shame?

For all he knew, she might be married with a couple of little ones, he'd told himself whenever the desire to be with her had surfaced. He'd hoped it wouldn't stop him from making amends if the opportunity ever presented itself, and almost as if the fates had read his mind had come news of the vacancy at Horizons Hospital. Discovering that Tessa was now a senior manager at the hospital was only an additional bonus, he told himself.

He'd been anticipating her arrival at the meeting and observed the dismay in her expression when she'd seen him. There would be no warm welcome or happy reunion.

Then, fool that he was, he had made it a certainty by the patronising manner in which he'd greeted her when the meeting was over, as if she had been stagnating while he'd been on top of the world. Some of the Swiss Alps had actually seemed like the top of the world, but he'd had no chance to explore them because he'd always been too busy fulfilling his contract. He could no longer deny that he had been hoping for a different homecoming, and was plagued by flashes of memory of how things had once been between them.

In her room just down the corridor Tessa was also remembering when she and Drake had first met. It had been at a hospital staff meeting when he'd come to talk about some advances he had made in his work.

She'd arrived not intending staying long as her job was in Administration, but had been curious to see the man who was making a name for himself in eye surgery.

He'd been chatting laughingly to a group of nurses who'd been hanging on his every word as they'd waited for the meeting to begin, and Tess had been struck by dark good looks.

Having seen her arrive, he'd stepped to one side to get a better look and from the way his glance had kindled she'd known that he'd liked what he'd been seeing. Slim, elegant, with hair the colour of ripe corn, and wearing a black suit with a white silk top, Tessa Gilroy had been used to the appraisal of the opposite sex, but had rarely allowed it to proceed further than that. Her job had taken up most of her time and she'd accepted that.

But the stranger, tall and straight-backed with eyes of warm hazel and a thick, dark pelt of hair, had seemed different from any man she'd ever met, and when he'd been introduced to her as Drake Melford she'd known why.

His name had been mentioned frequently in medical circles because he'd been new, different, with a vivid, unorthodox approach that had got results, and she was to find that his attitude towards her would be the same.

Their only contact on that occasion had been a brief handshake on being introduced, and when the meeting had ended she'd left, leaving him encircled once again by admiring medical folk.

Her doorbell had rung at six the next morning and she'd found Drake Melford on the step. 'I couldn't sleep for thinking about you,' he said. 'Can I come in?'

Barefooted in a white cotton nightdress, she nodded and stepped back to let him pass, as if welcoming a man she barely knew into her apartment at that hour was something she did all the time.

She made a breakfast of sorts and they ate without speaking, eyes locked over every mouthful of food, and halfway through he pushed his chair back, lifted her up into his arms and carried her into the bedroom.

The first time they made love was rapturous. She was so in tune with his desires and the magic of his presence that it felt as if she had been waiting all her life for him to appear in it.

For the rest of the time it was slower and more sensual, and when at last Drake lay on top of the silk coverlet with his arms behind his head, he said with a slow smile on his face, 'Wow! I haven't felt like this in years, Tessa. You are incredible.'

It was then that they made the pact, still drowsy with fulfilment but not so sated that they couldn't think straight.

They would take it as it came, they agreed. No ties, no commitments, no promises. There would be no babies or mortgages.... An open-ended affair.

And when Drake got dressed after that last time and slung his things into a couple of suitcases Tessa watched him in mute misery, eyes shadowed, mouth unsmiling. She didn't speak because there was nothing to say. It had been what they'd agreed from the start...no ties.

But one of them had discovered that they didn't want it to be like that any more and it hadn't been him. She'd fallen in love with him, totally and for all time, and to find him back in Glenminster and part of her working life was going to take some adjustment.

Whether Drake's life had changed since then or not, she didn't know. But hers certainly had, because now there was Poppy. Poppy was the small bright morning star that Tessa had adopted after getting to know her while she'd been in the children's ward in Horizons. On the strength of that, Tessa had done two of the things that they'd vowed to steer clear of all that time ago: allowed a child into her life on a permanent arrangement and taken out a mortgage.

She had moved out of the apartment where she'd lived and loved so passionately, bought a cottage built of golden stone not far from the hospital and life had been good again because there'd been love in it. A different kind of love, maybe, but love nevertheless.

Drake was standing by the window of the hotel room, gazing out to where theatres and restaurants were sending out a blaze of light onto the main street.

In the background was the everlasting drone of the traffic that would be far more noticeable when daylight came, and was a far cry from the silence of the mountains and the soft white snows of Switzerland.

But his yearnings weren't for those. He'd left Glenminster without a second thought three years ago with an easy mind, because Tess had seemed willing enough to keep to the pact they'd made on the night they'd met.

So why was it, he asked himself, that the moment his contract in Switzerland had come to an end he'd caught the first London flight available to be there for the meeting? And why had he hired a car to take him directly to the place where they'd lived and loved until his ambition had come between them?

It wasn't like he'd been expecting Tessa to be all dewy-eyed and panting to take up where they'd left off three years before. If he had, she would have soon put that misconception right when she'd seen him at the meeting and observed him so joylessly that the attention he'd been receiving from everyone else had seemed claustrophobic.

If she was going straight home in the morning, would she let him give her a lift? he wondered. For all he knew, she might be turning the occasion of the AGM into a shopping trip or a theatre break and he could hardly go knocking on her bedroom door to question her plans after three years of silence and all that had passed between them...

He had planned on making an early start because he had to find somewhere to live when he got to Gloucestershire. He wanted to be settled into some kind of accommodation before appearing at the hospital in his new role on Monday morning. So it would seem that unless they met at breakfast their first proper encounter would be at work, under the eagle eyes of their colleagues. It was hardly ideal, but they were professionals and they would make the best of it.

It turned out that Tessa was already in the dining room amongst a smattering of other early risers when he went downstairs at six o'clock the next morning, and before he could give it another thought he stopped by her table and said, 'I've got a hire car and will be leaving shortly. Can I give you a lift to Gloucestershire?'

'No, thanks just the same,' she told him levelly, in the process of buttering a piece of toast. 'I have a seat booked on an early train. The taxi that I've arranged to take me to the station will be here soon.'

'Are you still at the same address?' he asked casually, letting the rebuff wash off him.

'No, I've moved recently,' was the curt reply, and then to his surprise she followed up with 'If you haven't got any accommodation arranged, there is the house in the grounds of the hospital that the retiring consultant has been living in.

'The property was bequeathed to Horizons in the will of some grateful patient and is now vacant. I'm sure it could be made available to you if you wished.'

Drake was frowning. 'I don't want any fuss, Tessa, I'm here to work.' He realised his tone had come across perhaps a little harshly, so he added, 'But I suppose living so near work could be very useful.'

In truth, he was amazed. After her tepid reaction to his return he hadn't expected her to do him any favours. He was the one who'd been a selfish blighter all that time ago and anyone observing them now would find it hard to believe they'd been lovers.

'I will most certainly look into that,' he assured her, dragging his mind back from the past.

Meanwhile, Tessa's only thought was whether

there would be anyone sharing the place with him if it was available.

It was an old house that its previous owner had cherished, with high vaulted ceilings, curving staircases and spacious rooms all furnished with antique objects, with its biggest benefit being that it was only a matter of minutes away from the hospital for the consultant in charge when needed.

'Now that you mention it, I seem to remember something about being offered it when I accepted the position,' he said, 'but I had so much on my mind at the time I'd completely forgotten about it. So thanks for that, Tessa.' Could he sound more like an idiot? Drake thought to himself.

She shrugged as if it were of no matter. 'You would have heard about it sooner or later.'

'Yes, well, thanks anyway,' he told her, and as a member of the dining room staff came to show him to a table, added, 'Until Monday morning, then.'

She nodded and turned back to her tea and toast, hoping that she hadn't given any sign of the fast-beating heart that the turmoil inside her was responsible for. Having already settled her account, when her taxi arrived she left the hotel as swiftly as possible, and without a backward glance.

So far so good, Drake thought sombrely as he watched her go. At least they were on speaking terms *and* Tessa had taken the trouble to tell him that his accommodation arrangements might soon be solved. But who was it that *she* had moved house for?

She wouldn't have left her beloved apartment

for no reason, and he could hardly expect that her life had been on hold while he'd been away. She'd watched him leave that day without a murmur. Or could it have been that he hadn't given her a chance to get a word in with his obsession about the job in Switzerland, and the opportunities for developing new techniques it had presented?

But he'd made his choice and paid the price. It had been over then and nothing had changed. It wasn't like he'd returned to Horizons for her. He'd wanted the job—and to see her for old times' sake, not to rekindle what had once been between them.

But that wasn't to say that he'd forgotten the passion they'd shared, or how it had felt to lie in each other's arms. So much so that he hadn't slept with anyone since, hadn't found anyone he'd wanted to share that with. Now that he had some distance, he could see that what they'd had was without equal— but he didn't regret taking the Swiss job, which had developed his skills and offered him a once-in-a-lifetime opportunity. Now, for better or worse, he was back and he couldn't deny that a part of him was curious to see if there was anything left of it.

He could tell from Tessa's manner that his return hadn't sent her into raptures—far from it—but perhaps beneath her frosty reception she was as curious as he to see whether any of the old passion remained. The old Tessa certainly would have been.

On the train journey home Tessa rang her friend Lizzie, who was Poppy's childminder and the only person she would entrust her adopted daughter to stay with overnight, and was told that she'd been fine. A little bit weepy at bedtime but a couple of stories had made her eyelids start to droop and then she'd slept right through the night.

'I should be with you by lunchtime and will come straight to your place,' Tessa told her, but Lizzie suggested bringing Poppy to the station to meet her, knowing how she would be longing to see her again. Tessa was anxious to hold her little girl in her arms again, and thanked Lizzie, who was mother to two cute little ones of her own. But when her friend asked if the meeting had justified the long journey and overnight stay in London, Tessa could only reply that it had been full of strange surprises.

She didn't regret refusing Drake's offer of a lift home, even though it would have been faster. The thought of being in close contact with him for three to four hours had been inconceivable.

Until yesterday he had been out of her life completely and now he'd come back into it with the same ease as when he'd appeared at her door at six o'clock in the morning an eternity ago, and now she was wishing him far away… Or was she?

With Drake back in her life he would no longer be a shadowy figure from her past. She would be able to see him and hear him, but would also have to keep him at a distance.

Her life had been transformed with Poppy in it. The little one had been in care, waiting to be adopted after losing her parents in a car crash, and when she'd been brought into Horizons soon after with a bleed behind her eye from the accident, Tessa had been drawn to the solemn little orphaned girl and had spent much of her free time beside Poppy's bed.

'*You* are just what the child needs,' her social worker had said.

'What! A single mother!' she'd exclaimed. 'Hardly! My life has never been planned to include children.'

But the seed had been sown and the more she'd thought about it the more she had known that she wanted to take care of Poppy. So the proceedings to adopt had begun, with every step along the way feeling to Tessa more and more that it was the right thing to do. If she needed any confirmation of it, the happy little child that Poppy had become was proof.

If Drake had any recollection of the pact they'd once made, he was in for a surprise, she thought, and as the train left the station on the last leg of her journey home she was wishing that he had stayed in the place that he'd been so eager to go to, because now she had her life sorted.

They were waiting for her on the station platform, Lizzie holding Poppy's hand tightly as the train stopped, and when she saw her, the little one cried, 'Mummy Two!' It was the name that Tessa had taught Poppy to call her so that 'Mummy One' wasn't forgotten, and as she held her little girl close her world righted itself.

'So where are the boys?' she asked Lizzie, whose twins were the same age as Poppy.

'They are at home with their daddy. He's taking a few days' leave from work so I didn't need to bring them,' Lizzie explained, as she pointed to where her car was parked. As they walked towards it she asked, 'So what went wrong while you were in London, Tessa? You didn't sound very happy when you phoned.'

'You aren't going to believe it when I tell you,' she told her. 'Guess who is taking charge at Horizons from Monday?'

'I haven't a clue. Who is it?' she asked.

'Drake is to be the new chief consultant. Drake Melford!'

'What?' Lizzie cried. 'He's back here in Glenminster? How do you feel about that?'

'Honestly, I'm shattered at the thought. My life is sorted, Lizzie. I'm happy as I am with Poppy and my job. They fill my days.'

'Have you actually spoken to him?'

'Yes. He's on his way here in a hire car and offered me a lift, which I refused…needless to say.'

'And he's taking over on Monday?'

'Yes, giving me no time to compose myself after our London meeting,' Tessa replied, looking down at Poppy, who was holding her hand tightly, 'but nothing is going to interfere with my life and Poppy's. Drake will be in my working life—that I can't help—but for the rest of it he will be just as much out of it as he has been during the years we've been apart.'

* * *

Her first thought on awakening on Monday morning was that she would be in the same place as Drake today. Indeed, it was a while before she could focus on anything else. For not only would she be in the same place as Drake *today*, she would be for the foreseeable future. While their professional goals would be aligned, she could imagine him making his entrance into the life of Horizons Hospital with his usual charm and confidence, while she would be struggling just to keep afloat.

But at least she wouldn't be on the wards or in Theatre, where he would surely be. That would be intolerable, so if the chance came to stay in her office all day she would take it. *Coward*, she couldn't help but think.

What about all the other days when she would be out there, arranging and improving the standard of care that the hospital provided for its patients? She couldn't hide in her office every day.

She'd risen through the ranks because of her expertise, efficiency and professional manner. She had years of experience, having worked in a similar capacity on cruise ships, and wanting to revert to dry land for a change had gone into hospital administration. She couldn't help but wonder how her life would have been different if she'd never met him, if she'd stayed on cruise ships perhaps.

But there was no point going over what couldn't be changed. And, anyway, she could never regret the road that had brought her darling Poppy into her life.

Her friend Lizzie lived on the other side of the hospital, at the edge of a town that was endowed with the beautiful architecture of bygone days and wide shopping promenades. It was an arrangement that suited both mothers. As well as putting Tessa's mind at rest, knowing her little adopted daughter was cared for by someone she could trust during working hours, it provided Lizzie with an income of her own and gave the two friends an excuse to see each other very often.

Tessa had to drive past the hospital to get to Lizzie's and as she took Poppy to be dropped off she saw what must have been the hire car that Drake had indicated when he'd been offering her a lift at the London hotel.

It was parked amongst other staff cars and she wondered where he had stayed over the weekend, and how she could possibly be so disinterested after the way she'd adored him. Had her feelings eventually turned to pique because she'd been discarded so thoughtlessly for a promotion and a trip to Switzerland?

When she arrived at her office, which was part of the hospital's administration complex, her secretary, middle-aged Jennifer Edwards, was already there and eager to inform her that the new senior consultant had called to say hello on his way to the wards and what did she think of that?

'I don't think his predecessor even knew we existed,' Jennifer said in a tone of wonder, and Tessa's hopes of a busy day in the office without sightings of Drake began to disappear. But Jennifer went on to say that he'd stopped by to explain that he was calling a meeting of *all* staff who were free to attend at five o'clock that afternoon and hoped that the two of them would be there.

'But will you want to stay behind?' she asked Tessa, knowing that normally she would be setting off to collect Poppy at that time.

It was a tricky question. Her dedication to her job demanded that she be there to support the new head consultant, and deep down she knew that if it wasn't Drake she would be phoning Lizzie to explain that she would be a bit late. She'd already been away from her little one for part of the weekend on hospital business and felt that she had given enough of her free time, but Tessa knew that was just an excuse. It would be worse if Drake thought she was being difficult because he had come back into her life unexpectedly—perhaps she should go to the meeting just to show him that he was fine. *Stop it, Tessa*, she told herself severely.

She was free of the spell he had cast over her. And she wasn't going to the meeting. If they didn't speak today she would explain tomorrow that she'd had another commitment that had been equally important.

It had been a hectic day, Drake thought, as he made his way to the main hall of the hospital at five o'clock, but it was to be expected with patients and staff all new to him…with the exception of one.

Would Tessa be there when he spoke briefly to his new team? He hoped so. There was no way he would want to cause her pain or embarrassment, but they were adults—and professionals, for goodness' sake—and could surely behave that way.

If his restlessness and discontent while he'd been in Switzerland had been because he'd made a big mistake by not cementing their relationship, there was nothing to indicate so far that *she*'d been missing *him*. If she was now living with someone else, he had only himself to blame.

He was crossing the hospital car park to get to where the meeting was being held and caught a glimpse of her in the distance, about to drive off into the summer evening. He quickened his step but she was pointed in the opposite direction and as the car disappeared from view he had his answer.

She had better things to do, it would seem, than stay behind to hear his few words of introduction to the staff. It was going to take more than just showing up, or his charm, to get to know her again. Did he even want that?

Minutes later he faced a varied assembly of the workforce and with complete sincerity assured them that every aspect of the day-to-day challenges that Horizons Hospital was confronted with would have his full attention. Relieved that the meeting at the end of their working day had been brief yet reassuring, most of them went on their way, leaving just a few who wanted to meet the new chief consultant.

CHAPTER TWO

AFTER THE LAST of the staff members had left Drake's thoughts turned to food.

He was starving, and the thought of relaxing over a meal in a good restaurant in the town centre had no sooner surfaced than he was on his way there.

He had to pass a park on the way and happened to cast a glance at a certain bench that had memories of a time that was as clear in his mind now as it had been then. Did Tessa remember? he wondered. Did she think of it each time she passed this spot?

As he drove along a country lane not far from the hospital he unexpectedly found his curiosity satisfied about where she had moved to. It was in the porch of a cottage by the wayside that he saw Tessa, and he almost ran the hire car into the hedgerow in his surprise.

She was chatting to a guy of a similar age to himself and as he drove past Tessa reached out and hugged him to her. Drake's first thought was that this had to be the man who had replaced him in her heart. His second thought, which took a while to summon up, was, So what? But at least he knew now where she was to be found out of working hours.

As for himself, he'd wandered into the house in the hospital grounds that she'd mentioned, after remembering the keys on his desk and the chairman's note offering him the use of it, and thought it wasn't his type of place. It was too drab and he thrived on light and colour. But he had already decided that its proximity to Horizons would be perfect in an emergency, so was going to take advantage of the offer. He'd look for something else when he had time.

The food was fine when he found a restaurant that was his type of place; it battened down his hunger with its goodness, but Drake hardly noticed it. He'd got the job of a lifetime back in his home town and a place to sleep that plenty would die for, yet he wasn't happy.

It had been a mistake to come back to where he and Tessa had been so besotted with each other, so right for each other in every way. He'd had three years to realise in slow misery that he'd thrown away a precious thing without a second thought to satisfy his ambitions, and would have been even more selfish if he'd expected that time might have stood still where she was concerned.

She was just as beautiful now as she'd been then, but there was no warmth in her towards him, and as the night was young—it was barely seven o'clock— he decided to call on her on the drive back. If possible, he would wipe the slate clean by apologising for his past behaviour and assure her of his intention to stay clear, with the exception of their inevitable coming face to face sometimes in a professional capacity at Horizons.

When Tessa opened the door to him the shock of what he was seeing rendered him speechless. Standing behind her on the bottom step of the stairs and observing him unblinkingly was a small girl in a pretty flowered nightdress with hair dark as his own and big brown eyes.

'Who is *she*?' he questioned, standing transfixed in the doorway.

'She's my daughter,' Tessa told him. 'Her name is Poppy.'

'How old is she?' he asked hoarsely.

'Three.'

There was a pause. 'Is she mine too?' he asked in barely a whisper as the colour drained from his face.

She shook her head and watched the dark hazel of his eyes become veiled. 'Who *is* her father, then?' he choked, as the small vision on the bottom step rubbed her eyes sleepily.

'Poppy is my adopted daughter,' she told him. 'Her parents were killed in a car crash and we got to know each other when she was brought into Horizons with a bleed behind her eyes from the accident.

'She was with us for quite some time and we became close. I used to sit beside her whenever I got a spare moment and take her a little surprise every day. In the end I applied to adopt her and was successful. So there you have it. No cause for alarm.'

Turning, she scooped Poppy up into her arms and held her close. As their glances met she told him, 'Poppy has brought joy into my life.'

'Yes, I'm sure that she must have,' he said flatly, turning to go. But then thought that before he did he might as well ask another question that could have a body blow in the answer. 'So is the guy I saw leaving earlier her new daddy?'

'No, of course not,' she replied, her voice rising at the question. 'There are just the two of us and we're loving it. The man you saw was the husband of my friend Lizzie who minds Poppy while I'm at work. When I picked her up this evening we left her doll behind, and he brought it, knowing that she would be upset without it.'

'Ah, I see,' he said, and added, with a last look at the child in her arms, 'I'll be off then, to let you get on with the bedtime routine and maybe see you somewhere on the job tomorrow.'

'Yes, maybe,' she replied.

She was relieved to see him go. Her heartbeat was thundering in her ears, her legs were weak with the shock of his surprise call, and she didn't know how she was going to cope with having Drake so near yet so far away in everything else. He probably thought she was crazy to be taking on the role of mother to someone else's child.

As he walked down the drive to his car she

couldn't let him go without asking, 'Did you find somewhere to stay?'

He turned. 'Er, yes. The keys for the mausoleum, along with a welcoming note to use it if I so wished, were waiting for me, and as it's so near where I'm going to be working, and I didn't feel like looking for anywhere else, I took advantage of the offer.'

'You don't sound too keen on the accommodation,' she commented.

'It's a roof over my head, I suppose, but it's rather dark and dreary. I'm more into light and colour, if you remember.'

She remembered, all right, remembered every single thing about him from the moment he'd knocked on her door early one morning until the day he'd packed his bags and left. But the memories had been battened down for the last three years and she wanted them to stay that way.

He had his hand on the car door and as he slid into the driving seat and waved goodbye, she carried a sleepy Poppy up to the pretty bedroom next to hers. Looking down at her, the feelings that being near him had brought back disappeared as her world righted itself again.

Tessa didn't sleep much that night. She usually went to bed not long after Poppy to recharge her batteries for the next day, but not this time. Her moments of reassurance when Drake had gone and she'd carried Poppy up to bed hadn't lasted.

She kept remembering how his face had changed

colour from a healthy tan to a white mask of disbelief when he'd thought that Poppy was his, and when she'd told him that she wasn't, she could tell that he'd thought she was crazy to adopt a child. Clearly nothing had changed with regard to what he saw as *his* priorities, and they obviously didn't include parenthood.

Why did he have to come back into her life and disrupt her newfound contentment? she thought dismally as dawn began to filter across the sky.

In her role as health and safety manager Tessa went round the wards each week, chatting to patients at their bedsides about what they thought of the food, cleanliness and general arrangements of the famous hospital, taking note of any comments that were made. The morning after Drake's surprise visit it was down as her first duty of the day.

As she made her way to the children's ward, where it would be parents she was chatting to rather than the small patients, one of the nurses who had been there when Poppy had been admitted caught her up on the corridor and asked when she was going to bring her in to see them.

The plight of her small adopted daughter had pulled at all their heartstrings when she'd been admitted frightened and hurt after the car crash that had taken the lives of her parents. But Tessa had experienced a strong maternal feeling towards the little orphan that had made the promises she and Drake had made to each other seem selfish and immature.

At that time she'd had few expectations of ever seeing him again, but she'd been wrong and thought guiltily that she should be happy for the hospital's sake that he had taken over, instead of complaining about the effect he was having on her life.

'I'll bring Poppy the first chance that comes along,' she told her. 'It is just that the days seem to fly.'

On the point of proceeding to wherever she was bound, the nurse said, 'What about Drake Melford? Wow! If I wasn't so fond of my Harry I'd be tempted. That man is every woman's dream!'

He was certainly that, Tessa thought, and when she looked up the man himself was moving quickly along the corridor in their direction and the nurse made a swift departure.

She felt her shoulders tensing, but then reminded herself it was Drake the surgeon coming towards her, not the dream lover of the past, and with a brief 'Hello, there,' he was gone.

Drake had driven the short distance back to the hospital car park the night before in a state of amazement. The scene he'd just been confronted with at Tessa's cottage had revealed that the person she'd moved house for was a parentless child, a small girl without a father. *He* could hardly get his head around what was certainly the last thing he'd expected to find on his return to Glenminster.

A husband and a child of her own wouldn't have been too much of a surprise, but the dark-haired

little tot at the bottom of the stairs had been nothing less than a shock to his system, and after seeing
Tessa in the corridor just now, he had to admit that
he was still reeling.

She had done the rounds of patient appraisals and
been closeted with the laundry manageress for the
rest of the morning. Then, after a bite of lunch, she'd
spent the rest of the day in her office, dealing with
the demands of the busy eye hospital, and it wasn't
until Tessa was leaving at the end of the day to go to
collect Poppy that she saw Drake again on his way
to Theatre. He nodded briefly in her direction, but
instead of accepting thankfully that it was a sign he
was keeping the low profile that she wanted from
him, Tessa was filled with sudden melancholy.

It came from the memory of strong passions and
their fulfilment in a relationship that for her had
been transformed into a love that was strong and
abiding, and not according to the promises they'd
made to each other when they'd first met. If she'd
told Drake back then how she'd felt he would have
seen it as not keeping to her part of the pact they'd
made and so she'd stayed silent.

And now when he had finished for the day, whenever that might be, he would be alone in the huge
house that he had reluctantly opted for, while she
would be alone in her living room, Poppy asleep
upstairs. It was a matter of minutes between their
respective homes, but an unimaginable distance in
every way that mattered.

Why couldn't he have stayed away, she thought anxiously as she set off to Lizzie's, instead of coming back to awaken memories from the past that she'd finally been able to put aside because her life had been made liveable again since she'd adopted her precious child.

She'd seen his expression when she'd explained who Poppy was, as he'd observed her at the bottom of the stairs, and he'd actually gone pale.

Yet there was no one better than Drake for bringing a smile to the face of a frightened young patient in the children's clinic, having them laugh instead of cry while he was making a shrewd assessment of their problems.

They'd been in a similar professional situation when they'd first met. He'd been on the staff of a less famous place than Horizons but had been moving up the ladder fast, already a name that was well known in the profession, and she'd been employed as a mid-level manager where she was now, which had brought her into his line of vision when he'd been the speaker at Horizons that night.

His had been a personality that had drawn her to him like a magnet. From the moment of their meeting she had been enraptured, and, being just as much a free spirit as he was, had thought that the pact they had made would survive any hazards or setbacks.

But lurking in the background had been his ambition, his determination to be at the top of his profession, and he'd gone and left her to pick up the pieces, taking her silence on the matter as her acceptance of the open-ended arrangement they'd agreed on.

Tessa had been thankful they hadn't lived together, had each kept their own space, that there had at least been one aspect of his going that she hadn't been left to face.

As days had turned to weeks and weeks to months she had felt only half-alive until Poppy had become part of her life and her own unhappiness had seemed as nothing compared to what had happened to the little orphaned girl.

When she arrived at Lizzie and Daniel's to collect her after each working day, she felt joy untold to hold her close and know that she was hers.

'So how has another day with Drake around the place gone?' Lizzie questioned when she arrived.

Her friend had been there for her during the long months after his departure, and knowing how much Tessa had been hurting, she had admired her when she'd adopted the small girl that she was holding close.

'Not bad' was the reply. 'I've seen him briefly a couple of times but not to talk, so I guess he's getting the message.'

'And are we sure that it is the right one?' Lizzie questioned, raising an eyebrow.

'Yes,' she was told firmly.

'Good for you, then. He hasn't brought anyone with him...maybe a wife or fiancée?'

'It would appear not,' Tessa told her, and went on

to say, 'I haven't told you, have I, that when Drake called last night and saw Poppy, he asked if she was his. Something that would never have been on his agenda, and he seemed quite overcome with relief to be off the hook when I explained that she wasn't.'

'So nothing changes, then?'

'No, it would seem not. And now that he's taken over at Horizons I'm just grateful that I'm not on the wards or in Theatre. With my job our paths won't cross that much.' She smiled and took a breath. 'He's living in the big house in the hospital grounds at present and not liking it all that much, which I can believe. He is too much of a socialising sort of person to enjoy living on his own in that sort of place, but once he gets into his stride we shall be seeing the real Drake Melford.'

Later that evening, sitting alone in the cottage garden with Poppy fast asleep upstairs, Tessa was watching the sun set over the hills that surrounded the town in a circle of fresh greenery and letting her mind go back to that other time when its golden rays had embraced her and Drake on their last night together.

She'd vowed then that never again would she leave herself open and vulnerable to that sort of pain and loss, and had kept to it, relying on a polite but firm refusal when other men had sought her company.

There had been no expectation in her to hear from Drake again so she hadn't been disappointed.

But a part of her was still hurt that he hadn't even dropped her a quick line to let her know how the new job was going, if nothing else.

Then out of darkness had come light. Poppy had come into her life and she'd begun to live and love again, and nothing was going to interfere with that, she vowed as the sun began to sink beneath the horizon.

On Saturdays she took Poppy to see her maternal grandfather in the town centre. Tessa had met him at her bedside when the little girl had been brought into Horizons after the accident, and had been aware of his frustration at the thought of his granddaughter being taken into care because he was too old to look after her.

When Randolph Simmonds had heard some time later that the smiley blonde hospital manager loved Poppy and wanted to adopt her, he had been overjoyed and looked forward to their weekly visits.

He had an apartment in a Regency terrace overlooking one of the parks not far away from the town's famous shopping promenades, and always on Saturdays insisted on taking them out for lunch and afterwards driving them up into the hills, where pretty villages were dotted amongst the green slopes.

Randolph was due for eye treatment soon in Horizons and his first question when they arrived on the Saturday was whether the new fellow had arrived yet, as he wanted Drake Melford to be in charge of any surgery that might be necessary.

'Yes,' Tessa told him. 'He has been with us a week, but, Randolph, you need to be on his waiting lists, or do you have an appointment to see him privately? Drake is extremely busy.'

'Oh, so it's Drake, is it?' he said, twinkling across at her. 'You're on first-name terms?'

'I knew him way back before he was so much in demand, though he was already making a name for himself,' she explained flatly. 'I hadn't seen him for quite some time until the other day.' Then she steered the conversation on to a different topic. 'Do you want me to sort out an appointment for you privately? Or you can see him through your optician or GP, if they think it is necessary.'

'You could make me a private appointment if you would,' he said immediately. 'I'm getting too old to be shuffling around waiting rooms and clinics.' With his glance on Poppy, who had gone out into the garden to play, he asked, 'How is the little one? Does she still cry for them in her sleep?'

'Not so much,' she told him. 'I've taught Poppy to call me "Mummy Two" so that your daughter isn't forgotten, and she seems happy with that.'

'And maybe one day there might be a "Daddy Two", do you think?' he questioned.

'There might, but don't bank on it,' she told him. 'The three of us are happy as we are, aren't we?'

He sighed. 'Yes, you were heaven-sent, Tessa.'

When they went for lunch to Randolph's favourite restaurant Tessa was dismayed to see Drake seated at one of the tables. But, she thought, having already promised to speak to him on Randolph's behalf, and not looking forward to any kind of one-to-one discussions with him, it seemed an ideal opportunity to put forward the old man's request.

'Isn't that the man himself?' Randolph exclaimed. 'I saw his picture in one of the local papers.'

'Yes, that's him. I'll introduce you while he's waiting to be served and you could mention an appointment now if you like,' she said, as they approached his table.

'Yes, why not?' he agreed.

Drake had seen them. He rose to his feet as they drew near and Tessa saw that his glance was on Poppy, who was holding onto her grandfather's hand and looking around her.

'This is a surprise, Tessa. I wasn't expecting to see you here,' he said, with a questioning smile in Randolph's direction.

She ignored the remark and changed the subject by saying, 'Can I introduce Randolph Simmonds, Poppy's grandfather?'

As they shook hands the old man said, 'We have just been discussing my need for a private appointment with you, sir, which Tessa was going to organise, and here you are.'

It was a table for four and Drake pointed to the three empty seats and said, 'Why don't you join me for lunch and tell me what it is that you want of me.' Beckoning a nearby member of staff, he asked them to bring a child's chair for Poppy.

Tessa felt her heartbeat quicken. This wasn't what she'd expected, but there was nothing she could do about it now, and while Poppy's grandfather was engaged in explaining his eye problems to Drake she talked to Poppy and pretended that she wasn't shaking inside.

Until Drake's voice said from across the table, 'I've just been explaining to Mr Simmonds that I'm going to do as my predecessor did before me and use the same facilities that he had put in place for his private practice in the big house in the grounds. So, yes, I will ask my secretary to get in touch with him first thing on Monday morning, if that will be satisfactory.'

This is ludicrous, he was thinking. Across the table from him was the woman he'd once romanced and made love to in a torrent of desire and had had it returned in full, and they were behaving like strangers. But he'd forfeited the right to anything else and was now paying the price. It was hellish, making polite conversation when he'd adored every inch of her way back in what seemed like another life.

Fresh menus were being brought to the table for the extra diners and as Tessa gazed at the selection of foods available the print blurred before her eyes.

She would have the fish with the creamed potatoes and fresh vegetables, she told them when they came for her order, with a child's portion for her daughter.

Once they had eaten they would go their separate ways, and this would all be over. But soon it seemed that, like everyone else who met Drake, the old man had fallen under his spell and wanted to chat.

Yet Randolph had no problems about them moving on when she made the suggestion at the end of the meal, but to Tessa's dismay Poppy had. She had wriggled down off her chair and gone round to the other side of the table, and climbing up onto Drake's knee was sitting there, sucking her thumb. After a moment of complete astonishment on his part, his arms closed around her.

This is madness, Tessa thought wildly. Not only was Randolph impressed by Drake's easy charm, but her beautiful Poppy must be seeing in him something she hadn't seen in any other man since she'd lost her father. It had to be him of all people, him, for whom babies and mortgages were no-go areas.

Drake was reading her mind as clearly as if she was speaking her thoughts, and putting Poppy gently back onto her feet he led her back to where Tessa was sitting and said softly, 'Yours, I think.'

'You think correctly,' she told him levelly, 'and now, if you will excuse us, Poppy's grandfather always takes us up into the hills when we've had lunch, don't you, Randolph?'

'Er, yes,' he replied uncomfortably, and turned to their host. 'It has been good to meet you, Mr Melford. Maybe next Saturday *we* could take *you* for a meal, if you aren't too busy.'

Tessa noted that he didn't say either yes or no, just smiled, and she thought, Please, let it be a no when next I see him.

When they were clear of the restaurant Randolph asked curiously 'So what is it with you and the man back there, Tessa? What have you got against him? I thought he was most pleasant. We butted into his mealtime with our requests and interruptions and he never batted an eyelid.' He looked down at Poppy's dark curls. 'Whatever *you* might think of him, our young miss took to him like a duck to water.'

'Yes,' she admitted. 'I saw that. It is just that Drake and I had a misunderstanding a few years ago.'

'And you still bear a grudge?'

Not a grudge, she thought. It was scars that she carried, mental and physical ones, but she wasn't going to tell Randolph that, so she just let a shrug of the shoulders be the answer to that question, and he let the matter drop.

Randolph was very fond of both Poppy and Tessa, whose loving role of a second mother to his granddaughter took away some of the dreadful feeling of loss that he had to live with, and no way did he like to see her unhappy in any way.

But as he drove the last stretch homewards he was reminding himself that all he knew of her was what he saw now, in her early thirties and beautiful. There had to have been men in her life previously, if not at the present time, and it seemed that Drake Melford might have been one of them, though clearly not any more.

* * *

When the little family had left the restaurant after the uncomfortable moments when Poppy had been drawn to him, Drake sat deep in thought. It had been a mistake to come back to where his roots were, and where he'd had the mad fling with Tessa. Yet what was it he'd been expecting when he did? That nothing would have changed and Tessa would be waiting, patient and adoring, after the abrupt way their affair had ended?

One thing he certainly hadn't expected was that she would have a child in her life. Not his, of course, not a child born of a 'no responsibilities' type of guy, but a sweet little thing that it would be easy to love, given the chance.

He'd liked her grandfather, had been relieved to see that there was someone else connected with Tessa and the child. Whatever the old man's problems with his vision, he would give him his best attention when he came to see him, and with the thought of an empty weekend ahead he paid for their meals and went to see what was on at the theatres and cinemas in the town centre.

There was nothing that appealed and on a sudden impulse he drove to the place not far away where he had lived when he'd met Tessa.

It was an apartment in a block of six and if it had been up for sale he would have bought it for the sake of the memories it held, and to get away occasionally from the big cheerless property in the hospital grounds.

Seeing that it wasn't on the market, he turned the car round, drove back the way he'd come, and settled down for the night in the mausoleum once more.

Back at the cottage Tessa was wishing that they hadn't come across Drake in the restaurant and that she hadn't suggested that Randolph should speak to him about an appointment, because if none of that had happened Poppy wouldn't have gone to sit on his knee and given *her* food for thought.

She had been content in her new life until that moment, but now the future seemed blurred instead of clear, and Randolph hadn't enjoyed their time together so much after that because she hadn't been able to face telling him the truth about how she'd come to know Drake Melford.

CHAPTER THREE

Saturdays spent with Randolph were pleasant and relaxing, but Sundays were precious, when Tessa had Poppy to herself all day. She did chores in the morning while her small adoptive daughter played with her toys, and in the afternoon they went to the nearby park, where they picnicked either inside or out, according to the weather.

Again Tessa hadn't slept. She'd twisted and turned restlessly as the memory of their meeting with Drake in the restaurant had kept coming back to remind her that it had been a crazy and intrusive idea to confront him with Randolph's request for an appointment.

But as usual he had brought his charm into play and come out of it on all sides as the relaxed and understanding host who had been swift to hand her child back into her keeping. An apology from her was going to be due when next they met which would be at the hospital in the morning. That was her last thought before the patter of tiny feet and a small warm body snuggling in beside her indicated that breakfast-time was approaching.

As the day followed its usual pattern Tessa began to relax. Worries of the night always seemed less in stature in the light of day, she decided as she drove to the park on the edge of the town.

She'd parked the car and as they walked the short distance to the children's play area she was hoping that she might have a day without any sightings of Drake.

Her wishes were granted. The day passed happily, as it always did, except for the fact that she couldn't help wondering what he was doing in his absence. One thing she felt certain about was that he wouldn't be spending the time in his over-large accommodation if he could help it.

But Tessa was wrong. He was doing just that because he wanted the arrangements for seeing private patients to be sorted for Monday morning, with a secretary installed. Especially after the request he'd had from Mr Simmonds the previous day.

He was still bemused by his meeting with the three of them, especially with little Poppy's entrusting climb up onto his knee, and if he hadn't been so aware of Tessa's dismay he wouldn't have handed her back to her mother so quickly.

By the time he had finished rearranging part of the house he was hungry but resisted the urge to dine in the town again. He knew it would afford a glimpse of Tessa's cottage on his way there, as well as a sighting of a certain park bench, so he took a ready meal out of the house's well-stocked refrigerator and made do with that.

During a long night spent amongst creaking boards and the smell of mothballs he'd decided that, after looking up Poppy's case notes from the time Horizons had treated the eye injury she'd sustained in the car crash, he was going to suggest to Tessa that he should check her over to make sure that all was well with her vision and the surgery that she'd had.

It wasn't anything to do with how he'd felt when the little girl had climbed up on to his knee. It was his job for heaven's sake, to bring the far horizons closer to those who might be denied the sight of them.

On his very first morning there he'd been faced with a child that he might never be able to do that for. A five-year-old boy with an eye missing, born with just an empty socket, had been there for a regular check-up, and if it hadn't been so sad it would have been amusing the way he could remove the artificial eye he'd been fitted with and put it back with so little fuss at such a tender age.

If there had been no sightings of Drake during Sunday it seemed that he was making up for it on Monday morning, Tessa thought when she arrived at the hospital. No sooner had she positioned herself behind her desk than he was there, observing her with a dark inscrutable gaze that made her heart beat faster.

But there was no way she was going to let him see how much he still affected her. It was different from her wild passion of before—now she saw him more as a threat than a joy, jeopardising the new life she'd made for herself with Poppy. As she observed him questioningly, what he had to say took her very much by surprise.

'I've had a look at your little girl's case notes,' he said without preamble, as if he had guessed the direction of her thoughts. 'Would you like me to check the present state of her vision and the area where she had the surgery to make sure that all is still well there?'

'Er, yes,' she said slowly. It was an offer she couldn't refuse for Poppy's sake. Drake was the best, but she didn't want to be in his debt in any way, didn't want any relighting of the flame that she had been burned with before she'd learned the hard way that what they'd shared had meant nothing to him.

She often thought that if they'd spent less time making love and more getting to know each other in the usual way of new acquaintances, if she'd got to know his mind before his body, she could have been saved a lot of hurt and humiliation.

But maybe that was how Drake liked his relationships to be, and if that was the case there was no way she was ever going to let him know the degree of her hurt when he'd taken thoughtless and uncaring advantage of the pact they'd made after those first magical moments.

Tessa doesn't trust me with her beautiful child, he thought. Can it be that the little one coming round to my side of the table to sit on my knee in the restaurant on Saturday is rankling?

'You don't sound so sure,' he commented, turning away as if ready to leave. 'It seems about time she had a check-up, just to make sure all is still well with her vision.'

'I'm sorry if I sounded dubious about your offer,' she told him awkwardly. 'It was just that you took me by surprise. Yes, I would be grateful to have your opinion about Poppy's vision and anything that might be going on behind her eyes. So far she's had a clean bill of health regarding that, but I do worry sometimes.'

'Then do I take it that you will trust me on that?' he wanted to know.

'Yes, of course I will,' she told him hurriedly, and wished that their conversations were less overwhelming.

'Good. I'll get my secretary to ring you to arrange a time when you and I are both free for me to see your child.'

'She does have a name!' she said dryly. 'I suppose you think I'm crazy adopting Poppy after all that we vowed?'

'I'm not in a position to be making judgements,'

he replied, 'but as far as that's concerned it's clear to see that you're happy in the life you have chosen, that you have no regrets.' *Which is more than I can say for myself*, he thought. And then, from nowhere, he found himself saying, 'It would be nice if I could take you for a drink somewhere, for old times' sake.'

'I don't go out in the evenings,' she said, her colour rising at the thought.

'You haven't got a childminder, then? What about your friend Lizzie?'

'Lizzie sees enough of me and mine, and after being away from Poppy in the daytime I want to be where she is in the evenings.' With her cheeks still flushed at the thought of being alone with him, she continued, 'My life these days is very different from when I knew you. It has sense and purpose and...'

'All right!' he said. 'You don't have to justify yourself, Tessa. It was only that I thought it would be nice to bring ourselves up to date with each other. How about I buy you lunch one day in the hospital restaurant if you don't want to spend time away from your child? Not very exciting, I know, but it might be more convenient for you.'

'Yes, of course,' she said, smiling across at him, and thought there wouldn't be much time for chatting if they did that, which would suit her fine. The last thing she wanted to accompany the meal was memories of the good times they'd had blotting out the misery of how it had all ended.

At that moment her secretary came bustling

into the outer office, ready for the week ahead, and Drake departed, striding purposefully back to the ward.

When he'd gone Tessa felt like weeping. Since Drake had arrived at Horizons he hadn't had a moment to spare from his consultancy, yet he'd taken the trouble to check Poppy's records and offer an appointment.

It was only in his attitude to his private life that she'd ever found him to be less than generous, but she had known the risks that came from that sort of affair. If only she hadn't been so mesmerised by him, and remembering his startled questioning about whether Poppy was his when he'd seen her that night at the bottom of the stairs, she wondered what his reaction would have been if she'd had to tell him that she was.

Would he have been horrified at the responsibilities that would have come with her and dealt with them from afar?

Jennifer in the outer office was fidgeting to get started on the day ahead, so putting her mind games to one side Tessa called her in and the mammoth task of keeping the hospital clean, hygienic and well supplied with food and clothing began.

Meanwhile, somewhere else in the picturesque old stone building that had once been a wool mill Drake and his staff were preparing to perform what would have been impossible in bygone days, and as he scrubbed up for whatever surgery lay ahead after his stilted conversation with Tessa he would have been grateful for a minor miracle of his own.

If she had shown distress at the thought of him leaving her behind all that time ago he might have taken notice, but the euphoria he'd felt at being head-hunted by the Swiss clinic had made him oblivious to things around him, and apart from her being a little quiet and withdrawn during his last few days everything had seemed normal. If she *had* said something, would he have taken notice with his head so high in the clouds?

The time he'd spent in Switzerland had been the coldest and loneliest he'd ever known. The experience and knowledge he'd gained over the three years had been excellent, but he hadn't been able to stop thinking about Tessa and the magic they'd made together, which he'd cast aside as if it had been nothing.

When the position at the Horizons Hospital had been his if he wanted it, he'd accepted the offer without a second thought.

He hadn't flattered himself that time would have stood still for her, had accepted that she might have someone else in her life, but had never expected it to be a child that she'd adopted. He had to admire her for that, while at the same time shuddering at the thought of what it would entail.

As Tessa was on the point of leaving at the end of the day he rang her office and said, 'Sorry to be last minute with this, Tessa, but I haven't had a moment all day. It's just a thought, but how about your daughter coming to be checked over on Saturday? I've given Mr Simmonds an appointment in the morning and have accepted his invitation to have lunch with you folks afterwards. So if she's at all apprehensive, maybe her having watched my treatment of him will help to stop her from being upset. What do you think?'

'Er, yes, I suppose so,' she said hesitantly, with the feeling that since his surprise appearance he already featured too much in her life. She went on to say, 'Although Poppy does know you already, doesn't she?' And isn't afraid of you…and I'm not looking forward to another uncomfortable meal, she thought in silent protest.

He almost groaned into the earpiece and said, 'I'll leave it with you, but it would be better from both our points of view if she came on Saturday as my time on weekdays is soon filled', and rang off.

When she arrived at Lizzie's her friend said, 'You're looking very solemn.'

Tessa dredged up a smile. 'Ashamed would be a better description. Drake is being kind and thoughtful and I'm as prickly as a hedgehog when I'm in his company. He's offered to check Poppy's vision and the back of her eye where she had the bleed just to make sure that all is well there, and—'

'Surely you didn't refuse?' Lizzie exclaimed.

'No, of course not, but I wasn't gushing, and he wants me to take her to Horizons on Saturday morning while her grandfather is having a consultation with him to reassure her if she isn't happy about him doing some tests.'

'I don't see anything wrong with that,' Lizzie said gently.

'No, neither do I.' she agreed, 'except that I feel as if he's too much in my face.'

'And you definitely don't want that?'

'It's a matter of my not being able to cope with it, but obviously I'm not going to refuse anything that's beneficial to Poppy, so when she's asleep tonight I'm going to phone him and accept his offer.'

Randolph rang in the middle of Poppy's bathtime and while she splashed about happily he informed Tessa that a secretary had been on to him, offering an appointment with Dr Melford on the coming Saturday morning, and he'd accepted it with pleasure.

'So that's good, isn't it?' he said. 'And she informed me that he's pleased to accept our invitation to dine with us when the consultation is over. I hope that's all right with you, Tessa, as I know you're not a member of his fan club.'

'Drake has offered to check Poppy's eyesight along with any scarring from the bleed she might have and will generally give me an opinion on the state of her vision,' she replied. 'He wants me to bring her to the clinic on Saturday so that she can watch him examining your eyes, and hopefully she won't be too fretful when it's her turn. Needless to say, I'm most grateful for the offer but that is all. After what Drake has done for you and Poppy I can hardly refuse to join you for lunch. But, Randolph, please don't expect me to be the life and soul of the party on Saturday.'

'So the rift runs deep, then,' he said disappointedly, and having no intention of explaining just how deep it was she left it at that.

She didn't tell him that she hadn't given Drake a definite answer regarding Saturday because in spite of his thoughtfulness in offering to check Poppy's eyes she still felt as if she couldn't communicate with him.

But for her little one's sake she would accept his offer, and take her to his consulting rooms at the same time as Randolph.

When he'd gone off the line and Poppy was asleep Tessa sat deep in thought as the summer dusk that would soon be tinged with autumn colours fell over the town and its surroundings. She'd been so happy in her newly found contentment, she thought as she looked around her. Why couldn't Drake have stayed away?

But if he had it would have been Horizons that would have been the loser, as well as herself, and she couldn't wish that on the patients in need of a specialist eye hospital who lived in Glenminster and the surrounding areas.

She was just going to have to keep a low profile where he was concerned—as if she wasn't doing that already. And if it got to be too difficult? Well, she would just have to move somewhere else where he wouldn't be always under her feet as a reminder

of a time in her life that she'd once wanted to last
for ever.

When she finally rang Drake there was no reply,
so she concluded that he must be eating out somewhere, and for the briefest of moments she let memories of the past, the passionate never-to-be-forgotten
past that had left her hurt and aching for him, intrude into the present. But then the sight of Poppy
sleeping the sleep of the innocent brought calm to
her stressed mind.

When she phoned again and said that Saturday
morning would be fine for her to bring Poppy for
a check-up he said, 'That's good. If she watches
me with her grandfather first, she should be happy
enough when it is her turn.'

'Er, yes,' she said hesitantly, and waited for a
comment about the four of them doing a repeat of
the previous week's lukewarm meal together, but
there wasn't one coming, so maybe she was exag-
gerating its importance.

When she told Lizzie about Drake's suggestion,
that they catch up for old times' sake, her friend said,
'So what do you think it means, that he's sorry about
the past? Or that he's just trying to mend fences with
a colleague?'

'He did refer to the past while we were discussing it,' Tessa told her. 'A mild comment along the
lines of why didn't I say something if I wasn't happy
about him leaving, But we'd agreed that it was to
be a no-strings affair and he'd been so on top of
the world about Switzerland I think he would still

have gone, even if we'd been in a proper relation-ship.' She sighed and finished with, 'So, as far as I'm concerned, Lizzie, nothing changes, and that's how I want it to stay.'

When Saturday came Tessa dressed with care in a blue linen dress and jacket and shoes with heels in-stead of her working flatties.

She had dressed Poppy in a pretty pink dress with shoes to match and as the minutes ticked by she could feel tension rising inside her at the thought of what lay ahead. But it was also bringing back mem-ories of how badly hurt Poppy had been, orphaned and injured, and those first moments of seeing her when word had been going around the hospital about her plight.

There was also the thought that the morning's events were everything she'd been trying to avoid with Drake as much as possible. An eye examina-tion for Poppy, yes, but dining with him afterwards was a different matter, an ordeal to be faced, and the sooner it was over the better.

There had been no signs of any long-term after-effects of the bleed and bone fracture, but to have him—of all people—check that all was well behind those beautiful dark eyes had been something she couldn't possibly have refused and as she and Poppy watched while he dealt with Randolph's vision, they were all making light of it for her daughter's sake.

But not enough, it seemed. When Tessa would have settled on the chair that he had just vacated with Poppy on her knee she rebelled, and sliding down, said, 'You first, Mummy Two.'

When she seated herself reluctantly into a make-believe position in front of Drake and his instruments she saw amusement in his glance. This wasn't part of the arrangement!

'Don't touch me,' she said quietly.

'Of course not. I have no intention of doing any such thing,' he said smoothly. Pointing to nearby instruments, he said, 'These are what I will be using, my hands don't come into it, but that isn't going to persuade your daughter to do what we want if she's set against it, unless I can rustle up some of the charm that I keep on hand for this sort of fraught occasion.

'But first we have to convince her that you are also having an eye test.' He raised his voice. 'So put your chin on the ledge in front of you, Tessa, and look straight into the green light for me.'

It worked, and after watching Drake actually giving her an eye test Poppy came over, climbed up onto her knee and allowed him to do the same thing for her. When it was over and Tessa had lifted her down and sent her to sit by Randolph, he said, 'I've looked at the backs of her eyes, Tessa, all is well there, and her vision is excellent too.'

He was serious now, amazingly so, very much the ophthalmologist instead of the ex-lover as he said, 'I'll write you a report and let you have it first thing on Monday if you'll come to my office before my day gets under way.'

'Yes, of course,' she told him. 'Thank you for giving us your time this morning, Drake, and I'd like to settle your account at the same time on Monday if you will have it ready then.'

'There's no rush,' he said absently, with a frown across his brow as if his mind was elsewhere, and she hoped he wasn't going to use the occasion to bring them back onto a better footing.

'So, are we ready to eat now?' Randolph was asking. 'I've booked a table at one of the restaurants on the promenade.'

'Yes,' Tessa said, watching mesmerised as Poppy went to stand beside Drake and put her hand in his.

Aware of her reaction, he looked across, shrugged his shoulders and followed Randolph to the car park of the hospital, leaving her to bring up the rear with a strong feeling that the meal ahead was going to be exactly the nightmare she'd feared.

As they neared the cars he said, 'Obviously, I haven't got a car seat for Poppy, so if she stays with you and Mr Simmonds, I'll follow on behind.' The glint in his eyes told her that he could read her mind, but what was she supposed to do when her adorable child made a beeline for him?

'So Poppy's eyes are good, then?' Randolph said, turning to Drake as they were shown to a table in one of the town's best restaurants. 'That's a relief, isn't it, Tessa?'

'It certainly is,' she agreed, and was ashamed of her reluctance to sit down to eat with the man who had given them such welcome news. For the rest of the time she let her gratitude show by smiling across at him whenever their glances met, but wasn't rewarded by any warmth coming from Drake's side of the table. Just a brief nod in her direction was all that was on offer.

The answer to his strange behaviour was waiting for her when she presented herself at his consulting room on Monday morning. 'I have something to tell you that you won't like,' he said levelly, when she'd seated herself across from him, and he watched dread drain the colour from her face.

'You've found something wrong with Poppy's eyes after all?' she questioned anxiously.

'No, she's fine,' he told her reassuringly.

'So it's Randolph who has a problem?' she questioned as relief washed over her in a warm tide, knowing that he would rather it was him than anything happen to his granddaughter.

'No, all he needs are a couple of cataracts removed,' he said sombrely. 'It's you that I'm referring to. It was fortunate that I gave you a proper eye test, instead of pretending for Poppy's sake, as it has shown an eye defect that may need surgery.'

'Me!' she gasped. 'That can't be right, surely!'

'I'm afraid it is,' he said levelly.

'No,' she said, fear rising inside her. This was what single mothers must dread, she thought, not being there for their child when the unexpected threw their lives into chaos. All right, Lizzie would look after Poppy for her if she was hospitalised, but it wouldn't make it any less agonising to be away from her.

As he observed her dismay Drake thought that her eyes, as blue as a summer sky with golden lashes, were one of the things he remembered so clearly from their time together. During the test his attention had been drawn to the fact that on one of them the pupil had been forcing her eyelid apart, which was an indication that there could be over-activity of the thyroid gland—also known as hyperthyroidism.

As he explained the situation, pointing out that it was a problem that could restrict eye movement and cause double vision, Tessa's pallor deepened and her dismay increased as he went on to say, 'Sometimes it can be solved by medication to relieve the pressure, but it isn't always successful and then surgery is required to bring the vision back to normal. But first I need to arrange some tests.'

'And will I have to be hospitalised if I need surgery?' she asked tightly.

'For a short time, yes,' was the reply, 'but you can always go somewhere else if you don't want to be treated here.'

'Of course I want to be treated here!' she protested, and as her voice trailed away weakly she added, 'By you.'

'Fine, so under the circumstances I am going to treat you myself while the relevant clinics do their bit, and with regard to that will take some blood from you now to go to the endocrine folks for testing. The results should be back by tomorrow morning and when I get them I will know better what I am dealing with. Have you not noticed any discomfort in and around your right eye?'

'Er, yes, I suppose I had,' she told him. 'It felt tight in the socket, but not enough to cause alarm as I haven't had anything like double vision, but I don't have much time to fuss over myself. My world revolves around Poppy.'

Drake longed to take her in his arms and tell her that he would make it all right for her, that he'd been a prize fool to have left her like he had, and since he'd found her again was aware of the depths of her hurt.

But he knew that a few hugs and kisses wouldn't wipe out the past, the decisions they had both made, and the awkward situation they now found themselves in. Even though Tessa had said she wanted him to perform the surgery if the need arose, he knew that she didn't want him in any other part of her life. How did he feel about that, especially now she had a daughter? He shook his head at the thought. How had a simple affair between co-workers become this complicated?

'Be prepared to make yourself available first thing in the morning Tessa, and we'll take it from there,'

he'd told her, and she'd nodded with the feeling that they were being thrown together whether she liked it or not. But there was also relief, a warm tide of it inside her, because Drake of all people would be there to see her through the nightmare that had just unfolded in her life.

'I have to get back to the office,' she said weakly.

He nodded. 'Yes, of course, by all means. I'll give you a buzz in the morning when I have the results of the blood test and Tessa, don't worry, I will be with you all the way'.

It seemed as if she had no reply to that, and nodding she went back to her daily routine with a heavy heart. What was happening to the contentment that she'd cherished so much, she wondered miserably as she sat hunched behind her desk.

First Drake had come back to stir up the past that she'd thought lay buried deep, and now she might need surgery. But there was one happy thought that came to mind. He'd said that Poppy's vision was fine and Randolph's would be too once the cataracts had been removed.

So with those comforting thoughts and the knowledge that whatever was wrong with her eyes was going to be treated by the top ophthalmologist for miles around, she had to be grateful that he had come back into her life, if only for that.

About to start his Monday morning clinic, Drake was imagining the kind of thoughts that must be going through her mind. How cruel a twist of fate that he should have to tell Tessa that she had a problem that might be serious, on top of everything else still unresolved between them. Yet there was relief in him too, because it was sheer luck that he had been examining her eyes and had therefore spotted the problem early. There was every chance that it could be treated without the need for surgery.

Still hunched behind her desk, Tessa was reminding herself just how much expertise there was under Horizons' roof, how dedicated these medical professionals were in treating those who relied on them. Whatever her personal feelings towards Drake, nothing could compete with that. So as calm settled on her she called Jennifer into her office and began to face the day's duties, doing her part to look after the health and safety of the hospital and its patients.

When she called at Lizzie's that evening to pick Poppy up it was her first opportunity to tell her the results of their Saturday morning appointment at the clinic with Drake.

'So everything is fine, then,' she said delightedly, when she heard what Drake had said about Poppy's eye test, but her expression sobered on hearing of Tessa's problem She held her close and told her, 'Between us we'll cope. Daniel and I will look after Poppy if you're hospitalised, and this time Drake will be doing what he does best and not disappearing into the sunset. But, Tessa, how do you feel about seeing him so often, about having him feature so much in your life? Do you still have feelings for him?'

She shook her head. 'Not really, but now that I've got some of the hurt out of my system I remember how fantastic it was, being loved by him. Drake appeared in my life from nowhere and went out of it just as quickly.

'Knowing him, his stay at the hospital might be brief now that he's in my company once again. He won't want to be confronted by an old girlfriend everywhere he turns, and I don't want to be reminded of how I became surplus to requirements when Switzerland beckoned.'

Back at the hospital Drake had just finished for the day and was making his way towards his accommodation with little enthusiasm. What to do during the evening, he wondered. A boring ready meal and then an early night was what it would most likely be. He'd had a few of those of late and had lost the taste for them.

His mind kept going over those fraught moments with Tessa. It was typical in the present climate between them that he should have to take the sparkle out of her life with the news about what might turn out to be a worrying problem, with the only good side to it being that *he* was going to be in charge of it.

That was how he saw it, but in spite of her appearing to be happy about the arrangement he'd known that to her it would be just a means to an end, that the sooner it was sorted the sooner her fears that she might be separated from Poppy would be gone. If he could promise her *that*, she might just let him into the life that he now had no part in. But was that what he wanted, especially on such terms?

If ever she let him back into her life he would want it to be because it was him she needed, not his expertise.

In such cases as Tessa's, medication was usually tried first to slow down the over-activity of the thyroid gland. Surgery was only resorted to when it didn't solve the problem, and if he could save Tessa the stress of an operation he most certainly would. Not only because he cared about her as a patient but because he cared about her for old times sake...

CHAPTER FOUR

AFTER PARTAKING OF the inevitable ready meal, Drake felt restless. It was a clear, calm evening. The sun was about to set over the town and the hills that encircled it, making him feel stifled inside the big house. It had been another hectic day and he needed a break. So, prescribing himself some fresh air, he set off to enjoy what was left of the day.

What would Tessa be doing at this time? he wondered, and leaving the hospital behind he walked towards the town. Would she be sitting alone in the cottage while the little one slept up above, with the news about her condition lying heavily on her and no one to discuss it with?

He would be there in a flash if he thought she would welcome it, but at this point he ought to consider himself lucky that she'd agreed to let him treat her. She had been quite willing to hand over Poppy and her grandfather into his care, but he hadn't known what to expect when it came to herself.

The cottage would be coming into view soon and if he had any sense he would pass it without stop-

ping. But sensible he was not, because he found
himself pressing the doorbell within seconds of it
appearing in his line of vision.

It wasn't opened to him and, restraining himself
from going round the back in case Tessa had seen
him and didn't want to be disturbed, he went on his
way, shaking his head at how disappointed he felt.
It stood to reason that she was inside as small children were usually asleep by the early evening, and
there would be no opportunity for lie-ins for that
small family, with her having to take the little one
to her friend's house every weekday before going
to the hospital. Why she had lumbered herself with
that kind of responsibility he really didn't know.

When they'd met up again a part of him had
hoped they might fall back into the easy agreement
they'd had before he'd got his values all mixed up.
But it was turning out to be a lesson in endurance
because there were no signs that she still had feelings for him. Instead, a small brown-eyed, dark-
haired child was bringing Tessa more happiness
than he ever had.

He was passing the park once again, but this time
his glance fell on a group of parents watching over
their small offspring in the children's play area.
Amongst them was Tessa, looking pale but composed as she pushed her child backwards and forwards on one of the swings.

She hadn't seen him, but Poppy had and she was
indicating that she wanted to get off the swing.
When she'd lifted her down Tessa glanced up and

saw the reason why. It looked like she didn't know whether to be happy or sad, but there were no signs of any inward tumult as she greeted him.

'I called at your place as I was passing and got no answer,' he told her, 'and now I know why.' Poppy held out her arms to be picked up. 'Isn't it somewhat past the young miss's bedtime?'

'Yes and no,' Tessa told him, as he bent to lift the small figure up into his arms with a wary glance at her mother. 'Lizzie said that she'd had a long sleep this afternoon and wouldn't be ready for bed at the usual time so we came out here for a breath of air and some play time for her. Why was it that you called at the cottage?'

'Just to check that you were all right after the upsetting news I had for you earlier today. But now that I've seen you and am reassured, I'll be on my way.'

He put Poppy gently back on her feet and when she was standing firmly said, 'I've been in touch with her grandfather today, and I'm going to remove one of his cataracts some time next week.'

'You didn't tell him about *my* problem, I hope,' she said. 'If Randolph gets to hear about it he'll start concerning himself about my not being there for Poppy as he's too old and frail to take on the responsibility.'

'Of course I didn't tell him,' he told her dryly. 'I would have thought that you would have been around hospitals—and me—long enough to be assured of patient confidentiality. At the moment he doesn't need to know anything as tests need to be done on your eye first.'

His glance was fixed on what lay behind her and she knew why. The bench where they'd once made love in the moonlight when the park had been empty was in view.

'Don't even think of it,' she said in a low voice.

'Why not?' he questioned, 'You're asking me to forget something as special as that?'

'Special for who?' she asked, and when she took Poppy's hand in hers and began to walk away he didn't stop her, just watched her go and continued his walk into the town grim-faced.

With no reciprocation from Tessa regarding the pleasures of the past, Drake brought his thoughts to the treatment of her condition. If it was an overactive thyroid gland that was affecting her eye; it might react satisfactorily to medication, but didn't always. If it didn't work and surgery was needed because the pressure in the orbit area was so severe that it was restricting the blood supply to the optic nerve, possibly leading to blindness, it would become a more serious matter. He had no doubt that Tessa would have read up on it by now and must be tuned in to what lay ahead, so he could imagine just how much she would want some definitive results on the situation, for her child's sake more than anything else.

Back at the cottage, with Poppy now asleep beneath the covers in her pretty bedroom, Tessa was allowing herself some moments of reflection. If she and

Drake had been together in the way that they'd once been, and Poppy had been their own child, it would be so much easier to face up to this thyroid thing, she thought bleakly.

But in the present situation she was using him because of who he was—the top man for eye problems in the area—knowing that there was none better. Part of her was imagining it as payback time, when the truth of it was that Drake owed her nothing. He had merely kept to the pact they'd made and had moved on when the Swiss job had come up. Could she really blame him for that?

And now he was back, having gained the expert reputation that he'd sought so eagerly. It was fine, just as long as he hadn't any ideas about taking up with her where he'd left off. It was too late for that. Her life was so different now, she had different priorities and a casual no-strings hook-up couldn't be further from her mind.

The next morning there was a message waiting for her in the office asking if she could spare him a moment. When Tessa explained to her secretary that she would be missing for a while and would Jennifer proceed with the routine of the day in her absence, the older woman was surprised but asked no questions.

She found him seated behind his desk like a coiled spring, ready to face the day's demands. But he was clearly prepared to put her first amongst his commitments as he said with a keen appraisal of the offending eye, 'How are you feeling this morning?'

'Not on top of the world,' she said flatly.

'I can understand that. How is Poppy?'

'Happy. She loves going to Lizzie's to play with her twin boys, who are a similar age,' she told him, and wished he would leave out the small talk.

As if he'd read her mind Drake said, 'I have the results of the first blood test.'

'Yes?' she questioned anxiously.

As she faced him across the desk, what he had to say was both was good *and* bad. Aware of the distance between them, and how different it was from the intimacy they had once shared, he needed to tread carefully because he knew just how much she didn't want to be in his debt in any shape or form, yet she was having to rely on him because he was the most senior eye surgeon at Horizons. Their past only complicated what should have been a purely professional relationship, and he couldn't let it affect the care he would be giving her.

'Your thyroid gland has become overactive,' he said, 'and that is causing the swelling of the eye socket, which could be dangerous if left untreated. In cases such as yours another doctor would normally be in charge of prescribing the medication to slow it down. But in this instance everything has to be centred on not interfering with the optic nerve. As I've already promised, I am going to deal with every aspect of the problem myself, and if there is no improvement over the next few weeks and the eye problem is worse rather than better, we must consider surgery.'

Aware of her distraction the previous day he said, 'I was sorry that I had to deliver such news, Tessa,' his voice softening. 'I'm tuned in to your opinion of me and all I can say is that protecting your sight will be my prime concern.

'At the sign of any further change in the eye socket please don't hesitate to get in touch. I'm available day and night and I have already sent down to the pharmacy for the medication that you will require. Someone from there will deliver it to your office.'

She was on her feet. 'Thanks for that, Drake,' she told him steadily. 'Needless to say, I will trouble you as little as possible as my vision isn't affected so far.'

With that she went, trembling after the attempt at calmness that she'd just presented him with, and praying that nothing would stop her from looking after Poppy.

When she'd gone Drake got to his feet. His busy day was waiting and nothing that was to come could possibly make him feel so concerned as the moments he'd just spent with Tessa. So much for a happy reunion. He must have been out of his mind for even thinking of it, but at least the fates had given him the chance to be there for her in her hour of need. For the present, what more could he ask?

He had longed to put his arms around her during the conversation they'd just had and hold her close to let her see that she wasn't alone in the moments of stress and fear that had appeared from nowhere, but he could imagine the kind of response he would have got. Tessa might have thought he was using her distress to hit on her. Aside from being professional misconduct, that couldn't have been further from his mind in that moment. She was a friend and colleague receiving bad news, that was all.

When she arrived at her friend's house that evening Lizzie was watching anxiously for her arrival and her first words were, 'Have you got the test results?'

'Yes,' Tessa told her, dredging up a wan smile. 'It is my thyroid gland that has become overactive and is causing the problem. Drake is going to try me on medication first. If it doesn't work it will mean surgery,' and went on to say with her voice thickening in an unexpected moment of yearning, 'I would have given anything for him to have held me close for a moment.'

Lizzie's eyes widened.

'No, I'm not weakening in my determination never to let him take me for granted again. I'm just so grateful that Drake is on my case.'

'Why don't you and Poppy stay here for the night?' her friend suggested. 'I don't like to think of you on your own after today's news. You know the spare room is always ready for visitors and when Poppy and the twins are asleep you and I could pop out for a change of scene. You need some light relief and Daniel will keep an eye on them.'

'Maybe you're right,' Tessa agreed. 'I need to unwind, and get what is happening into perspective. It will be a few weeks before Drake can clarify any improvement in my eye condition and until then I need to live as ordinary a life as possible. But I'm still in my work clothes, which are hardly suitable for going out.'

'We are the same size,' Lizzie said. 'You can have the run of my wardrobe if you wish.' And while the children were having their bedtime drink the two women went to see what would be suitable for Tessa to wear on her first night in the town for as long as she could remember.

It seemed strange to be out in the nightlife once again, she thought. It brought back memories of the time when she and Drake had lived it up there at every possible opportunity and then gone back to the apartment where they'd made love.

It was incredible how different her life was now, but she had no regrets. It had more purpose, more giving than taking and she was happy with that, not that it stopped her from remembering what it had been like to be romanced by Drake.

Where was he tonight? Tessa wondered as she and Lizzie approached one of the town's famous nightspots. The Bellingham Bar was a popular meeting place for those who liked to relax in pleasant surroundings with good food and a cabaret for anyone who liked that sort of thing.

It had been a favourite haunt of the two lovers and as they paused outside the place Lizzie said, 'Shall we throw away our cares for a while at Glenminster's top spot? Or will it upset you?'

'No,' Tessa told her. 'Having Drake back in my life is just coincidental, so why not? What about Daniel, would he want you in a place like this without him?'

'He wouldn't mind. Daniel knows I'm safe as long as I'm with you and anyway our marriage is solid.'

Lizzie's throwaway comment hurt for no accountable reason. Tessa guessed she was just feeling fragile and sensitive because of the difficult news. She refused to admit that she was affected by Drake's sudden return to Glenminster, and she couldn't regret the life choices she had made. Poppy was the best thing ever to happen to her and nothing, not even thoughts of Drake, would change her mind on that.

Without further conversation she led the way into the bar and looked around her, almost as if she was expecting to find him there. After all, he was appearing in every other aspect of her life. But there was no sign of him, and she pushed firmly from her mind her earlier desire to have him hold her in his arms and comfort her.

She wasn't to know that he had been round to the cottage to check that she was all right and on finding her missing was at that moment on his way to Lizzie's house to ask if they knew where she was.

He'd had to drive through the town centre to get there and was dumbstruck to see the two of them, smartly dressed, going into the Bellingham Bar as he was passing.

Before he'd had time to think about what he was doing—or indeed, to ask himself why—he'd parked the car and entered the bar. The thought uppermost in his mind was that Tessa wasn't exactly moping after the day's dark moments, and he was some fool to think that it would have been him that she would have sought out if she had been.

She was studying the menu with head bent when he stopped at their table. As his shadow fell across her she looked up, startled. 'Drake,' she breathed, 'where have *you* appeared from?'

'I've come from trying to find you to make sure you were all right,' he said dryly, 'but it would seem that I needn't have concerned myself. I'll leave you to what is left of the evening.' Then a thought suddenly struck him and he blurted out, 'Where's Poppy?'

'She's safe at my house with Daniel and the boys,' Lizzie hastened to tell him as Tessa sat speechless.

'Right, I see,' he commented, and went striding out of the place with every woman's glance on him except hers.

'Would you believe that?' Lizzie breathed. 'How could he have known that we were in here?'

'I don't know,' she said, 'Maybe he was passing and saw us outside on the pavement. I feel dreadful. He will have been working hard all day at the clinic but still took the trouble to drive out to check how I was feeling, and now finds me about to start

living it up in this place. How embarrassing!' Tessa
put her head in her hands and groaned. Could this
night get any worse?

'Let's go home.' Lizzie said gazing around her as
the tables were filling up with would-be diners. 'It
was a mistake to come here, though seeing Drake
was the last thing either of us would have expected.'

'You're early!' her amiable husband said, when
they reappeared. 'What happened to the night on
the town?'

'Drake Melford happened to it,' Tessa told him
flatly. 'He'd been to the cottage to see how I was
after him giving me the results of my test today, and
of course I wasn't there.'

'Lizzie and I think Drake was on his way to see
if I was here and when he saw us going into the Bellingham Bar he wasn't pleased to find me there instead of being at home having a quiet evening,' she
said ruefully. 'Not that it's any of his business what
I do or where I go. All my evenings are quiet and
I'm happy with that, knowing that Poppy is sleeping
in dreamland only a few feet away.' Lizzie nodded
and squeezed Tessa's arm in support. 'But tonight
was different, Daniel. I needed something to take
my mind off everything and didn't want to be alone,
brooding over it.'

When she went up to check on Poppy a few
moments later and stood looking down at her sleeping child, Drake's questioning of the little one's
whereabouts came to mind and she thought won-

deringly that he'd sounded almost father-like in his over-zealous concern for her well-being.

If the next thing he did was take on a mortgage she would have to eat her words, but in the meantime she felt she owed him an apology. His thoughtful gesture had clearly caused him further fatigue at the end of his busy day. It was the least she could do after his numerous attempts to reach out to her, and his kindness towards her little family.

The next morning she rang his office several times and was told by his secretary that Drake would be in Theatre for most of the day and asked whether she wanted to leave a message.

The answer to that was definitely no. What she had to say wasn't for anyone else's ears. But say it she must, and the first opportunity came when Tessa saw him coming towards her in the main corridor of the hospital at the end of the day.

'I've been trying to get in touch with you,' she said, stopping in front of him, 'but I understand that you've been busy. So can I take a moment of your time now to apologise for last night. I'm so sorry that I wasn't there when you called at the cottage and for my rudeness in the bar. If I had known to expect you I would have been there.'

Tessa rushed on, hardly able to look him in the eye as she delivered her rehearsed speech. 'As it was, I was feeling really low when I arrived at Lizzie's house and she suggested that Poppy and I stay the night. When the children were asleep she came up with the idea that we should go into town for a change of scene and some night life—which is never normally on my agenda—and I suppose it was as we were going into the bar that you saw us.'

He was smiling. 'The main thing is that you were safe and *I* owe *you* an apology for being so abrupt when I saw you. Shall we call a truce and make up with a kiss?'

When she took a quick step back he laughed. Taking her hand, he opened a door nearby that led into a quiet rose garden that was rarely occupied, and once they were out of sight Drake tilted her chin with gentle fingers to bring her lips close to his and kissed her.

It was like coming in out of the wilderness, magical and blood warming for the first few seconds, until Tessa pushed him away and with pleading eyes said, 'Please, don't do this to me, Drake. I want a relationship that has substance, one that will last.'

'And ours didn't, of course?'

'No, it didn't,' she told him, holding back tears at the memory of those last sun-kissed moments before he'd gone out of her life.

Turning, she went back through the door and was gone. As he followed her at a slower pace he thought bleakly, So much for taking things slowly.

'Did you see Drake to apologise?' was Lizzie's first question when Tessa arrived that night.

'Yes,' she told her, having scooped Poppy up into her arms the moment she'd arrived. 'But it was a rather hotch-potch affair as he said it was all his fault. He took me into a rose garden at the side of the hospital and I was like putty in his hands.' She shook her head at the memory. 'But the thought of this little one and all she means to me brought me to my senses.'

'What does Drake think about you adopting Poppy?' Lizzie asked.

'I don't know. I can't think he approves but he hasn't said anything. I imagine that he thinks I'm crazy. Part of the pact we made was to stay clear of exactly these sorts of responsibilities and it would appear that his ideas haven't changed like mine have. No doubt he will think that adoption is even more of a trap than an ordinary family. But if he does he's missing so much.' And with that, Tessa gave her gorgeous little girl a hug and silently counted her blessings for the way things had turned out.

Back at the big house that was so not to his liking, except for its nearness to Horizons, Drake was sitting on the terrace at the end of another busy day, reliving the moments with Tessa in the rose garden.

He could have gone on kissing her, kept on kissing her over and over, if she hadn't pleaded with him not to, and it had brought him swiftly down to earth. They were living in different worlds, he thought, and for once it occurred to him that she must be far more content than him.

Tessa had gone into the town for the evening to try to clear her head, and had had to face his bullish interruption just as her night of freedom had been beginning, and yet, incredibly, *she* had sought *him* out to apologise for not being at the cottage when he'd called to check on her. She was different. Tessa seemed sorted, happy. It was starting to make him question a lot of the decisions he'd made way back.

His private life was a lot more carefree than hers, but much less happy. He'd taken one of the theatre staff out for a meal one night after they'd worked late and were both ready for some food. She'd reacted like most women did to his likeable charm and if he'd asked her back to his place he knew she would have been quick to accept which would have made her the first woman he'd slept with since leaving Tessa for Switzerland.

Ironically, the one he did want in his bed didn't want him. Her life wasn't the same as when he'd known her before, and if he wasn't content with what he had now, Tessa was happy with the life she'd chosen. This thought brought to mind the small Poppy's apparent attachment to himself.

Could it be that he resembled her father in some way and it drew her to him? One thing was sure, she was a sweet young thing with a loving mother and no way had he any right to interfere in that.

The sun was going down over the hills that he loved, with villages hidden amongst them that were graced by old almshouses and farms built from the beautiful golden stone that the area was renowned for.

Since returning to Glenminster, he'd never been

any further than the hospital and the town centre. He told himself it was because he'd been too busy at the hospital, but he knew deep down it was because the place was full of memories that had all of a sudden become uncomfortable to face.

So a notice in the staff restaurant announcing that the yearly picnic for staff and their families was to take place on the coming Saturday had Drake's interest immediately. The arrangements were that the coaches hired to take them to the picnic area would be waiting in the hospital car park at eight-thirty.

He hadn't mentioned it to Tessa as he'd thought she might run a mile if he told her he was thinking of going on the outing—he had discovered that she was its main organiser—but the yearning to be up there on the hills was strong and he decided that unless an emergency at the hospital occurred to prevent him, he would be there waiting for the coach like any other picnicker.

On that thought he went into the house towering behind him and climbed slowly upstairs to spend another night in the four-poster bed that graced the main bedroom with its creaking woodwork and the smell of mothballs.

Before Saturday there was Randolph's cataract removal to be done and on the morning that he was due at his private clinic Drake had a quick word with Tessa to find out how much the old guy knew about her eye problem.

'He knows nothing as yet,' she told him. 'I so much dread upsetting Randolph.'

'Yes, I can understand that,' he said, 'and if the medication does its job he need never know, but, Tessa, it's early days. There's no guarantee that it will, and then he will have to know.'

'So that will be soon enough, don't you think?' she said, and he had to agree.

'I wanted him to come and stay with Poppy and me at the cottage when the cataract has been removed,' she told him, 'so that I can supervise the drops that he'll need to have and make sure that he doesn't do any bending down. But he assures me that his neighbour in the next apartment has offered to do all that, and as she will be there all the time while I would have to be at work during the day it seemed to be the best idea. She will be making him a meal and looking after him generally, but I will call on my way home each night when I've been for Poppy to make sure that her grandfather is all right.'

'What did Poppy's father look like?' he asked.

'I've only seen a photograph obviously,' she told him, surprised at the question. 'He was quite tall, dark-haired, hazel eyes. Why do you ask?'

'Just curious, that's all,' he replied, and went on to question, 'Does she ever cry for her parents?'

'She did at first, but not any more. I got the impression that she was very much her daddy's girl, though she's not cried for him recently, and I've taught her to call me "Mummy Two" so that her birth mother, Randolph's daughter, isn't forgotten.'

'Yes. I see,' he said thoughtfully, with a glance at the clock on the wall of her office. 'He will be here any moment so I must go. If anyone asks for me, I'll be in my rooms over at the big house. Also, I'm coming on the picnic on Saturday so will you please book me a seat on one of the coaches?' He rushed on to add, 'If there's a problem with that, I shall get a bike and fetch up the rear.' Without giving her the chance to reply, he was gone, leaving her to question if his comment had been a threat or a promise.

She could imagine the expression on the face of the chairman—who always put in an appearance at the event—if he saw his top medic following the coach on a bicycle. It would seem that a ticket for the man who still made her heart beat quicken was going to be required.

But what was he up to? He surely couldn't want to spend time with Poppy—she knew how he felt about children. After that kiss in the rose garden… could it be her he wanted to see? Tessa shook her head. She had set him straight on that front. Perhaps he just wanted to be amongst the beautiful green hills to get away from work. Whatever the answer to that question, nothing had changed as far as she was concerned. Her life was sorted and it didn't include Drake.

CHAPTER FIVE

DRAKE SMILED WHEN he came back after dealing with the old man's cataract in his surgery room. There was a coach ticket on his desk with a note.

With the compliments of the picnic organiser.
A seat next to the chairman in the first coach.

He wanted to be seated next to her, he thought. Not beside someone who was going to talk about work all the way there and back. But Tessa had out-witted him, and when he strolled across to the car park on Saturday morning beneath what was prom-ising to be a hot sun he found that the two of them, mother and child in matching sundresses, would be travelling on the last coach to leave, in order to round up latecomers.

As he went to greet them Drake saw that the chairman was already settled in the first coach and he sighed at the thought of joining him. But Poppy had seen him and was approaching fast, dragging

Tessa along behind her. He said with a wry smile, 'Thanks a bunch for seating me with his lordship.'

'It seemed the right thing to do,' she said blandly.

'To you maybe,' he said, patting Poppy's dark curls as she gazed up at him. 'Tessa, how long is this thing going to go on between us? I've got the message. You don't want anything to do with me because I treated you badly. I was a thoughtless, selfish clod, leaving you as I did, but you never tried to stop me, did you?'

'No, I didn't,' she said, 'because I kept to the agreement we'd made that it was to be a no-strings affair. So how could I protest when you wanted out? It was the way you did it, as if I didn't matter, as if I didn't even exist!' Tessa stopped suddenly, remembering where they were as one of the nurses came hurrying into view with her children. 'Here are my last passengers, Drake, so if you would please go to your seat we'll be off as soon as I've given the coach drivers the go-ahead.'

'Yes, sure,' he said, and watching him go Tessa thought that she must be insane not to want to him back in her life if that *was* what Drake had in mind after his long absence.

His ambition and career had taken him from her once already, and she hadn't meant enough to him even to discuss the possibility of them staying together, making it work long distance, let alone that she might go with him. He hadn't shown a moment's regret that what they'd had was over, and nothing—

not even his dedication to restoring the sight of the blind—was ever going to lessen the hurt.

As Poppy tugged at her hand for them to follow him she shook her head and lifted her daughter up the steps of the coach they were travelling on. When the latecomers had settled into their seats they were off, driving towards a day in the sun.

'And so how is it going for you at Horizons?' the chairman of the famous hospital asked as soon as Drake was seated next to him. 'No regrets?'

'No. None,' he told him, the vision of the woman and child he'd just left as clear in his mind as the long nights in Theatre and the over-subscribed clinics that were filled with sufferers desperate for better sight.

Only the other day he'd dealt with a woman who had been diagnosed with a blocked blood vessel behind one of her eyes that had been affecting her vision quite seriously. She'd also had a cataract that had been in front of it, and that was going to have to be removed before he could judge if better sight was going to be possible for the patient.

It hadn't had the look of one of his success stories, but she had accepted it quite sensibly when told that the surgery might give her better sight but that there was a real possibility that she might lose sight completely in that eye, and the answer to that would only be revealed when the procedure was completed.

As it turned out she had been fortunate, Drake thought. When she'd removed the eye covering the next day she had cried out that she could see—and therein lay his whole reason for living, as in his life at the present there was no other joy to be had.

'How do you like your accommodation?' was the chairman's next question.

'It's all right,' Drake told him, 'but at the first opportunity I shall look for something else, not so large and more modern.'

'Yes. I suppose that's understandable as you aren't married with a family to accommodate,' the other man said. Once again the vision of Tessa and Poppy came to mind, and Drake couldn't believe that his thoughts were running along those sort of lines, especially with regard to another man's child. It was totally opposite from what he'd always decided about being burdened with family responsibilities of his own, let alone those of someone else.

The picnic was to take place in the tea gardens of a hotel in one of the area's most attractive villages, and when the last of the coaches arrived at its destination Drake was waiting for Tessa and Poppy to alight, along with its other occupants. When she saw him the 'organiser in chief' groaned.

How was she going to be able to concentrate on ensuring that all those present enjoyed themselves if she was mesmerised by Drake's presence all the time? Tessa thought. And what about Poppy? Was she going to run to him, as she'd tried to do once already?'

'If you've got things to take care of, I'll watch

Poppy until you're free,' he offered. As her small daughter was already clinging to his hand it didn't seem like the moment to argue, so she gave a brief nod and went to check on the catering that she'd ordered and find out which chairs and tables had been allotted to them for the occasion.

When that was sorted she went to look for Drake and Poppy and found him pushing her to and fro on a swing in the children's play area. He hadn't seen her and for a brief poignant moment Tessa let her heart take control instead of her hurt and it was there, the feeling that the three of them were bonded together, when deep down she knew that it wasn't so.

He turned in that moment and unaware of what was in *her* mind let her see what was in *his*. 'Here you are,' he said teasingly, 'eager to make sure that I haven't run off with your precious child! Of course I knew it would be more than my life was worth.'

'You needn't have concerned yourself about my thinking that,' she told him. 'I haven't forgotten your views on family life.'

The slight edge of bitterness that he could detect in her voice made Drake swallow his next comment. He'd been about to surprise her with the memory of his casual remark about house-hunting to the chairman.

While she'd been busy he'd taken Poppy onto the field where the other children were playing and, incredibly, he'd found it! It was there, on the other side of the hedge, his dream house, in the last stages of being built in the golden stone that he loved, windows everywhere, a terrace to sit on in the sun, at least five bedrooms at a glance...*and it was up for sale!*

He'd decided that when Tessa came to claim Poppy he was going to go across to get a closer look, let the perfection of it sink in, then find the builder whose name and phone number were on the 'for sale' sign.

Knowing none of that, she wasn't amazed at the speed with which he handed her child back to her, as if he'd had enough and been reminded exactly why he never wanted children. In fact, Tessa thought nothing of it, Drake being far from sharing her joy in parenthood.

When she and Poppy had disappeared amongst the crowd of picnickers Drake went to get a closer look at the house and discovered the builder was on the site, about to finish for the day. As he appeared around the corner of the house—his house, Drake already couldn't help but think!—the man eyed him questioningly.

'Can I have a look inside?' he asked.

'Yes, sure,' was the reply.

'Would you show me around, please?' Drake asked him. 'But only if you haven't got a sale already.'

'I haven't,' he replied. 'Wait a second, don't I know you from somewhere?'

'Only if you've had cause to visit the Horizons Eye Hospital in recent days.'

'I have,' the builder told him, surprise at the co-incidence lighting up his face. 'But it wasn't for me. It was you who treated my lad when his eye was injured during a football match at school.

'We thought he was going to lose his sight, his mother and me, but you sorted it. Goodness! What are the chances? If you decide to buy this house, I will consider it an honour.'

'It's just what I've dreamed of,' Drake told him, 'and if the inside is as beautifully designed as the outside, we have a deal! I'm sure we can come to an agreement on the price.'

'Gee whiz!' the man exclaimed. 'How long have you been house-hunting?'

'No time at all,' Drake told him. 'This could be my first and last time, viewing a property.' Gesturing towards the front door, he said excitedly, 'Lead the way!'

The inside of the house was just as attractive as the outside and when the builder told him what he looking to get for the property, he said, 'You have a deal. I'll give you the name of my solicitor and any other details that you may require. Let's shake on it now.' The builder beamed back at him. 'How long will it be before the house will be ready to move into?'

'I'd say about a month,' was the reply. 'There are a few things that I want to do to achieve the results that I have in mind, and of course if you are going to buy it you can have your say about anything that you would like done. As soon as the contracts have been signed, the keys will be yours!'

They shook hands again on that and as Drake made his way back to the picnic area he wondered what Tessa would think of what he'd just done. Would she even be interested? The last time he'd been this crazy was when he'd knocked on her door in the early morning, having only met her briefly the night before; when she'd asked him in they'd made love and it had been wonderful.

They'd carried on from there with the no-strings agreement, the one that he realised now had been mostly his suggestion. Although it had left him with a get-out clause when he'd been offered the Swiss contract, he'd paid the price with three cold, miserable years to contemplate the mistake he'd made in letting Tessa go.

Now he was back where it had all started and she didn't want him near her. She had a child who was strangely drawn to him…and, even more unusual, he was equally attracted to the little Poppy. But Tessa was doing everything she could to keep him out of Poppy's life and he found he was oddly hurt by this, unexpectedly so.

He found the two of them enjoying picnic food at one of the tables, and as he looked around him he asked, 'So how is it going?'

'Fine,' she told him. 'This sort of event depends so much on the weather' She glanced at the sky above. 'And today is perfect, especially for the children.'

It had been a good day for him too, he thought,

finding the kind of house he'd always dreamed of, and being in a position to buy it. But the way things were, he might be rattling around in it on his own like a pea in a bottle.

At the end of the day, as they walked to where the coaches were parked, Drake said, 'I've spoken to Randolph a couple of times and he's due to see me again next week for a check-up on his cataract removal. He seems quite happy with what he's had done so far, which is a start.'

'Yes,' she agreed. 'I've called on my way home each day and it would seem that he is being so well looked after by his neighbour Joan, I can almost hear wedding bells.'

'Really! Well, they do say that it's never too late,' he commented dryly. But whether Tessa had the same feelings was another matter, and until he knew what the answer to that was he needed to tread carefully.

The first coach was ready to leave, with the chairman once more settled in his seat. As Drake prepared to join him he looked down at Poppy and she gazed back up at him and said, 'I want to go with *you*.'

'Our seats are on the other coach,' Tessa told her gently, but she didn't budge and the chairman called across, 'She'll be all right with us, Tessa.'

Observing the reluctance in her expression, Drake bent down and when his face was level with

Poppy's he said, 'No, sweetheart, you belong with Mummy. I'll be waiting when you get back.' And taking her hand, he placed it in Tessa's and went to his seat.

He was true to his word, and when the last coach arrived back at the hospital Drake was waiting, and as Tessa saw him standing there she felt like weeping for the three of them, Poppy for the loss of her parents, Drake for trying to bring back the past that was dead and buried, and herself because his nearness was affecting her the same as it had always done.

'What do you have in mind now?' he asked, as Poppy ran into his arms. 'Bedtime for the young miss? Going for a meal? Or an assisted tour of the mausoleum?'

'The first one, I think,' she told him. 'It has been a long day for a child of her age.'

'Yes, of course,' he agreed, 'but, Tessa, before we separate I hope you don't think I'm deliberately encouraging Poppy to want to be near me. I know it's the last thing you would want. Do you think it could be that she sees her father in me for some reason?'

'I really don't know,' she told him hurriedly, 'and it's been a long day, Drake. Maybe we could discuss it another time.'

'Yes, of course,' he agreed, and cautioned, 'Be sure to give me a buzz if you're getting low on your medication.'

As he turned to go, Poppy lifted her face for a

kiss and Tessa turned away. Did he remember the time when all his kisses had been for her?

Sunday once again was chores in the morning and the park in the afternoon, and from the moment they got there Tessa was watching for Drake to arrive.

She wasn't to know that his intention had been to join them until he'd been called into Theatre at eight o'clock that morning, on his one day off, to deal with the emergency treatment of a guy who had received serious eye injuries on a building site. As the hours dragged by with no sign of him, Tessa had to keep reminding herself that he hadn't said he would be in the park, so she shouldn't be disappointed when he didn't come.

Looking in the mirror that morning, she hadn't been able to see any change as yet in the protruding of her eye and, desperate for reassurance, had wished him near. It must be the reason why his absence was getting to her so much, she decided, and consoled herself with the thought that at least she hadn't had to put up with Drake gazing at the park bench.

As soon as he'd received the message about the injured man Drake had assembled the members of his team who were on duty over the weekend and by the time he'd arrived they had all been in position.

One nurse was monitoring the patient's blood pressure while another was holding his hand and trying to soothe his fears while at the same time

warning him not to move his head while being examined or operated on.

Drake's assistant was hovering closely. He was
young, intelligent and keen to follow in his footsteps, observing everything his mentor did and said.
However, the sight of the man with both eye sock-
ets bleeding being wheeled into their midst on a
stretcher and transferred carefully onto the operating table had caused him to pale for a moment
or two.

The theatre sister stepped forward and gently
wiped the blood away, where possible, to allow
Drake the space to use the ophthalmoscope to check
for tearing of the iris, or ruptures of the sclera, which
could cause collapse of the eyeball or even blindness.

The atmosphere in the operating theatre was
tense when he told the patient, after examining both
eyes, 'There is a retinal tear of the left eye, which
isn't good, but it looks as if the macula is still in
place, which is the main thing, and we are now going
to sort that out.

'But the damage to your right eye is not repair-
able because there are ruptures of the sclera,' he said
gently. After passing the ophthalmoscope to an older
colleague, and then to his assistant for their obser-
vations, he told the man, 'All I can promise is that
your horizons won't have disappeared completely.'

He rang Tessa in the late afternoon and knowing
every tone of his voice she could tell that he was
feeling low.

'What's wrong?' she asked.

'I've been trying to save the eyesight of a guy from a building site who'd had his head split open, blood all over the place, and couldn't see afterwards. The damage to one of his eyes was untreatable, and in the other one there was a retinal tear that we just managed to sort out before his vision became impaired.'

'Have you eaten?' she asked with a shudder.

'No. Why?'

'Do you want to come round and I'll make you a meal?'

'Are you sure?'

'Yes.'

'Then thanks, I'd like to. Is seven o'clock all right? I've got some notes to write up, and before that the family of the injured man want a word as they've only just heard about the accident.'

'Yes, seven o'clock will be fine,' she told him, and when he'd rung off she was left to ponder why she'd issued the invitation. Had it been because she needed him near to give her reassurance about her own eyes, or because she could sympathise with Drake's frustration at not being able to save the man's vision? Or was it simply because she wanted him near for a little while?

When he tapped on the kitchen window so as not to awaken Poppy with the doorbell, Tessa was in the kitchen, with steak grilling and an assortment of vegetables bubbling on the hob. When she let him in his hunger peaked at the smell.

'This will be the first decent bite I've had in hours,' he said. He was assailed with the memory that it had been something more physical than food that had always been his first thought every time they'd been together all that time ago. That and prestige. Yet his expertise hadn't been enough today to save that poor fellow's eye; the man's injuries had been appalling. It was a miracle he hadn't lost his sight altogether.

'I need to wash up before I eat,' he said, bringing his mind back to the moment on hand.

'The bathroom is at the top of the stairs and Poppy's room is next to it,' Tessa told him. 'Please don't disturb her. If she knows you're here she will be down in a flash.'

'I wouldn't complain,' he said laughingly.

'Maybe not, but I would,' she told him, 'and you know making friends with her doesn't exactly fit in with your no-family-ties resolution, if I remember rightly.'

'Neither does the huge responsibility that you have taken on single-handed fit in with yours,' he said, suddenly serious. 'Why, for heaven's sake?'

'I thought you were hungry,' she chided, ignoring the question. 'The food is ready.'

Drake was halfway up the stairs and wishing he'd kept silent. The truth of it was he envied Tessa her life and her child more than he would ever have dreamed possible.

A vision of the beautiful house he was going to buy came to mind and he hoped that he wouldn't feel as lost and lonely in it as he did in the one he was staying in at the moment. It was hard to believe Tessa and Poppy would ever live there with him as she appeared to be content in her cosy little cottage, and was showing no signs of wanting to get any closer to him than on that first day of their meeting at the AGM.

When he sat down to eat it occurred to Tessa that they had crossed another barrier by her inviting Drake to eat in her home. When he'd finished, the feeling was still on her as he said whimsically, 'I think I'll book into a hotel for the night to get away from the smell of mothballs.'

'I have a spare room that you can use if you like that I always keep ready in case of visitors,' she told him. 'I don't like to think of you driving into town looking for somewhere to sleep after the kind of day you've had.'

'Do you get many?' he asked.

'What, visitors? Oh, yes, they come in droves,' she said laughingly.

'Sarcasm doesn't suit you,' he said softly, 'or maybe what you've just said is correct.'

'Yes, well, you're quite capable of working that out for yourself,' she told him teasingly. 'So do you want to stay the night?'

As if, he thought, with her only feet away and memories of how it used to be pulling at him. But he was crazy if he thought Tessa might want him to be part of the new life she'd made for herself.

He'd come back to Glenminster and found that she had her life sorted, not with another man but with a little orphaned girl.

He'd been dumbstruck at the sight of the small, dark-haired child standing sleepily at the bottom of the stairs when she'd opened the door to him that time, and been staggered when Tessa had explained the circumstances of her being there. But he was getting more and more comfortable with the idea of Tessa *and* Poppy in his life, though he was no closer to understanding why that might be so.

She had gone into the kitchen and was clearing away after the meal she'd made for him. With her back to him, she wasn't aware of him approaching until she felt him plant a butterfly kiss on the back of her neck, and as she swung round to face him he held out his arms. Unable to resist, she went into them.

If it hadn't been for Poppy suddenly crying out above it would have been like all those years ago when he'd called at her apartment at six o'clock in the morning and taken her into the bedroom.

But this time it was different, Tessa thought as she withdrew herself from his hold. She was no longer free and easy, she had a child, a beautiful little girl who depended on her entirely, and to reopen the floodgates of her love for Drake was not what she was intending.

The crying up above was becoming louder and

moving towards the stairs she said, 'I think you'd better go, Drake. Poppy has little nightmares when the memory of the car crash comes back and she feels frightened but doesn't know why, so I hold her close and cuddle her until she goes back to sleep.'

Moving swiftly upwards, she paused and looking down at him said in a low voice, 'I forgot for a moment where my responsibilities lie. It was crazy of me to ask you to stay, just a mad moment, that's all.' And then she was gone in the direction of Poppy's sobbing.

As he closed the front door behind him and drove back to his own place he relived the moment she had walked into his arms. It had felt so right, until Poppy had cried out. How quickly Tessa had let him see that her child came first, he thought. As if he didn't know that already.

The days, weeks and months after Drake had gone to Switzerland had been the darkest time of her life, she thought as she gazed at the child in her arms, now sleeping with dark lashes sweeping down onto flushed cheeks. It was Poppy who had brought her out of sadness and into joy as they had each healed the other's hurts.

But tonight Drake's nearness had brought back the longing she'd thought she had under control, and when he'd kissed her neck it would have gone on from there if Poppy hadn't cried out. Her daughter's anguish had brought her back to reality she thought as she laid her gently under the covers, leaving the door wide open so she'd hear any further sounds.

* * *

Drake was back in the big house and sleepless with everything that had happened at the cottage starkly clear in his mind. The meal Tessa had made him, her offer of a bed for the night had taken him by surprise, considering that she was so wary of him. Then when he'd kissed her from behind there had been her amazing response, but that had lasted only seconds before Poppy's cries had shattered the moment and Tessa had wanted him gone.

So much for the barriers coming down. He could have nursed Poppy for her, soothed whatever it was that had brought her out of her sleep, while Tessa gave her a drink and they checked her temperature. Instead, she had wanted him gone as fast as possible and before he'd known what was what he'd found himself ejected from her home.

He'd been hoping that after tonight she might let him take her to the theatre, or out for a meal some time, or both, but clearly he'd been wrong to anticipate any such thing. She was a single parent, bringing up a child she adored, and everything else came second.

There was little chance that she would want to take time away from Poppy, and he'd been crazy to think the kiss in the kitchen had meant anything to her, other than a moment's arousing of the senses.

It had been a strange day of ups and downs. He'd been able to save the vision in one eye of a man who had looked likely to lose it completely, then he'd been invited for dinner at Tessa's—and to stay the night!

He'd actually held her in his arms for the briefest of moments until they'd come down to earth and he'd been reminded that he would never come first in Tessa's life, never be her top priority. Perhaps not be in her life at all.

The next morning she knocked on the door of the big house before going to her office in the hope of catching Drake before he left for the day, and was rewarded by the look of surprise on his face as he saw her.

'I'm sorry that you didn't manage a night away from this place,' she told him awkwardly. 'But I am always most concerned when Poppy has one of her bad dreams. She's so little and she's been through such a lot.'

'And you didn't think I might have been able to assist?' he said abruptly. 'I'm not unused to dealing with children and Poppy does know who I am.'

'I didn't ask because I was so conscious of what had been happening between us at the moment of her awakening,' she explained awkwardly, 'and it seemed inappropriate that you should stay when my position as Poppy's mother was being called into account.'

Drake looked at his watch as if time was of the essence and Tessa felt her face warming. 'Yes, I suppose so,' he said dryly. 'I'm due in Theatre in five minutes, can't stop.' And closing the door behind him, he strode off towards the hospital, leaving Tessa to interpret that as she would. The sheer male attractiveness of him once again caused heads to turn, but left her with the awful feeling that those moments in the kitchen the night before meant a lot more to her than they did to him.

Yet she'd learned one thing from them. That she wasn't as far from wanting Drake back in her life as she'd thought.

As he scrubbed up for what lay ahead in the operating theatre Drake was wishing that he hadn't been so abrupt with Tessa when she'd knocked on his door. But he'd been left with the uncomfortable sensation that for the first time in his life he wanted something very much that he couldn't have. The truth was that he had no idea what he was going to do about it.

When Tessa arrived at her office, Jennifer was already there and the first item on the agenda was an event that was to take place on the coming Saturday that the two of them were organising on behalf of the hospital management.

The picnic that had only just taken place had been basically for the children and families of staff members, while this occasion was for staff and partners only in the form of a supper dance on board a floating restaurant on a nearby river.

Tessa's involvement meant that Poppy would have to spend the night at Lizzie and Daniel's place, which they didn't mind in the least, but she, Tessa, did. Her little one had been there all week during her working hours so it didn't feel right to expect more from her friends. And no doubt Drake would be at the party looking absolutely mind-blowing, while she would be bogged down with the pressures of making sure that the organising was perfect.

When she'd invited Drake for a meal and then offered him the spare room for the night it had been because he'd had a rough day in Theatre, and she'd felt sorry for him. But it had been a major lapse of her avowal not to be alone with him except during working hours, and when Poppy had cried out she'd made a big thing of it because she'd felt guilty and ashamed for breaking her promise to herself.

What he'd thought about that she didn't know— probably decided that it was a bit over the top—but he had done as she'd asked, though his manner now was abrupt to say the least.

She and Jennifer had an appointment during the morning with the manager of the river restaurant to discuss menus and floral decorations for the event and to hand over name cards for the guests seated at each table. It was time-consuming and when they'd finished it was almost lunch-time.

On arriving back at the hospital, Tessa found a message from Drake saying that he would like to see her at four o'clock if she was free, to check on the progress of the treatment of her overactive thyroid gland.

She shuddered. It was always there, the thought

of what might happen if the medication didn't solve
the problem and she had to have surgery. The only
good thing about it was that at least she would have
the best of his profession to perform it. But there
was Poppy, small and defenceless, and she had to
be able to take care of her no matter what. If Drake
could give her that she could forgive him anything.

When she arrived at his consulting rooms at exactly four o'clock he was on the phone and told whoever he was speaking to that he would get back to
them shortly.

It was the builder, as it happened, wanting to discuss the décor in one of the rooms in the house of
his dreams and, pleasurable though it was, it came
a poor second to having Tessa near for a short time,
even though it was clear that there was no joy in her.

'It's early days as yet,' he said when she sat facing him across his desk, 'but I don't see any harm in
checking to see if the treatment is working,'

It was true, he didn't, and after their lacklustre
exchange of words at the start of the day he'd been
wanting to do something to make up for his sur-
liness.

CHAPTER SIX

So FAR SHE hadn't spoken and as he beckoned her to position herself across from him, only inches away, with her chin resting in the required position, Drake thought ironically that this was probably the nearest he was going to get to Tessa after their very brief encounter of the night before.

Once he had finished his examination he asked, 'How does your eye feel now? Does it seem any less pressured?'

'Just a little maybe,' she told him, with a feeling that what he had to say next wasn't going to be uplifting.

'Mmm,' he murmured thoughtfully. 'I can't see much improvement yet, but it is early days, Tessa, so don't be discouraged.'

'It's Poppy that I think about all the time,' she told him tearfully. 'I need to be able to take care of her, Drake. She has no one else apart from her grandfather and he is way past looking after her if I should lose my sight.'

He came round to her side and looked down at

her. 'Why don't you let *me* worry about that?' he said softly. 'I do have my uses.'

'Yes, I know,' she said. 'I'm aware of how fortunate I am to have you as my ophthalmologist.' 'But how do I know that you aren't going to move on to pastures new just when I need you?'

'I didn't leave any of my patients in the middle of treatment when I went to Switzerland. There was no one left behind to fret about my absence.'

'Except me,' she said. 'I was just a plaything for you.'

'I can't believe that you remember it as such,' he said sombrely. 'You were beautiful, divine, and I let my dream of being at the top of my profession spoil what we had.'

'Oh!' she said with surprise. 'I didn't know you saw it that way.' After a short pause she continued, 'But did you have to come back from your Swiss idyll and shatter the contentment that I'd worked so hard for?'

'That was never my intention, Tessa. I love Horizons, this place is my home, and when I was offered this position I couldn't resist coming back to where I belong.'

He glanced at a clock on the wall above their heads. 'I've got a consultation in five minutes, Tessa, but before you go will you promise me that you will trust me with your eyes?'

'Yes, of course,' she replied, and thought she would trust him with anything...except her heart.

As she was on the point of leaving he said, 'What

about the event on the river boat on Saturday. Are you going?'

She was going all right, Tessa thought. There was absolutely no way to get out of it since she and Jennifer were the organisers. Drake was waiting for an answer so she told him, 'Yes, I am. Poppy is staying at Lizzie and Daniel's.'

'So, will you save me a dance?' he wanted to know.

'I can't. I'm booked for the night.'

'What?' he exclaimed. 'You must be in big demand.'

'Yes, I am,' was the reply, and she left Drake's office overwhelmed with regret for what could have been.

When Tessa took Poppy to her friend's house on the Saturday night and Lizzie saw that she was wearing the smart navy suit that she had to wear for work she said, 'What a shame you aren't allowed to wear a dress, especially since *you know who* is going to be there.'

'It's regulatory that staff involved with organising efforts away from the hospital wear work clothes,' she told her laughingly, 'and the person in question will be too occupied with his fan club to chat to skivvies.'

After watching Poppy playing happily with the twins, Tessa went, making her way reluctantly to the riverside where the fashionable restaurant that they'd hired for the night was situated.

She hadn't seen Drake since he'd checked the progress of the eye treatment and wished herself far away from a situation where the two of them would be at the same gathering. She was apprehensive about his reaction when he discovered she was far from the belle of the ball she had presented herself as, but since she and Jennifer would be there quite some time before the guests arrived, she hoped by then to have everything under control—including herself.

It was a vain hope. They were greeted with the news that the head chef was in hospital after being knocked off his motorcycle on the way to work that evening and that the manager had gone away for the weekend. So instead of organisation there was chaos in the kitchen, with Tessa assisting the missing chef's two assistants and Jennifer doing the last-minute setting up of the dining room with the help of the bar staff.

She had taken off her jacket and was wearing a long white apron and white hat as she obeyed the orders of the two remaining chefs, and was praying that all would be ready in time. So much for being in big demand that she'd teased Drake about. She would be lucky if she even saw the dance floor.

In evening dress with a corsage of lily of the valley and pale pink roses in a florist's box on the back seat of the car, Drake had intended on arriving early to make sure he got the chance to spend some time with Tessa if possible, and as he pulled up by the riverside he smiled to see that her car was already in the restaurant's parking area.

What would she be wearing? he wondered. Whatever it was, she would look divine, and with hospital and family commitments put to one side for a few hours, maybe they could spend some time together.

When he went inside, up the gangplank's gently rocking timbers, he saw that apart from her secretary, who was chatting to a couple of bar staff, there was no one else in sight from the hospital. It was still quite early, so it wasn't surprising, but he was sure he'd seen Tessa's car parked on the river bank and was determined to catch her alone for a moment before the event kicked off.

Jennifer had seen him and when he asked where Tessa was, he was pointed in the direction of the kitchen, and in a few swift strides he was pushing back its swing doors and coming abruptly to a halt.

'What on earth!' he exclaimed, as she swung round to face him while in the process of testing a large joint of beef that looked as if it had just come out of the oven. All around her was food of one kind or another, with the kitchen staff having returned quickly to their tasks, as if his interruption was not the most pressing of demands on their attention.

Tessa was still wearing the long white apron and shapeless hat, and as it deserved an explanation she said, 'The head chef was involved in an accident on his way here and is in hospital. I was just another pair of hands, but the crisis seems to be over now.'

'Why you?' he questioned. 'Who is supposed to be in charge?'

'I am,' she informed him. 'It's part of my job.'

'So when you told me that you would be otherwise engaged when I asked you to save me a dance, it was this sort of thing that you meant?'

'I'm afraid so,' she informed him, as she took off the hat, undid the apron strings and revealed that she was wearing work clothes underneath.

He groaned as he passed her the corsage of flowers that he had hoped to see her wearing and said, 'So much for that, then.' He turned without another word and went back into the restaurant area, which was gradually filling up with hospital employees.

When the band began to play Tessa surprised him a second time by appearing beside them and their instruments—with the corsage firmly pinned to her jacket—to announce that the meal would be served in half an hour's time and there would be dancing before and after.

When Drake glanced up from reading the menu at a table at the far end of the bar he observed her, slack-jawed. She was standing before him, smiling with hand outstretched and asking, 'Can we have this dance?'

'Yes, of course,' he said, 'though what about your duties?'

'I feel that two hours over a hot stove should cover that.'

'I'm quite sure that it will,' he said laughingly, 'but aren't you forgetting something?'

'What?'

'I can't dance with you without touching you and I thought that wasn't allowed.'

'Maybe just this once,' she said, smiling back at him, and he thought how beautiful she was despite the plain navy suit bedecked with his flowers.

'So let's do it,' he said, holding out his arms, and she went into them like a nesting bird under the surprised glances of those present.

Drake was holding her close when he felt her stiffen. 'There's Daniel!' she said. 'Something must be wrong with Poppy.'

'We had better go and find out,' he said, and hand in hand they hurried towards Lizzie's husband.

'Poppy jumped off a stool with a metal whistle in her mouth and it has cut open the roof of her mouth quite badly,' he said, wasting no time. 'Lizzie and the boys are on their way to A and E with her, but needless to say it's you that she wants, Tessa. I've left my engine running so we'll soon catch them up.'

'I'm coming with you,' Drake said, and after leaving Jennifer in charge of the rest of the evening Tessa, Drake and Daniel piled into the car. Tessa was holding tightly onto him and praying that it wasn't as bad as it sounded and that Poppy wasn't afraid.

As he observed the pallor of her face and the fear of what awaited her in her eyes, Drake was debating whether parenthood was worth it, taking on a lifetime burden of care, and for someone else's child into the bargain. The enchanting Poppy had almost made him change his mind about that, but tonight was going to be the testing time.

Lizzie and the twins had arrived just before them, with Poppy crying loudly while a doctor attempted to assess the damage to the inside of her mouth, which wasn't easy under the circumstances. When he saw that Tessa had arrived he said, 'I'll leave you for a few moments while your little girl calms down and then we'll see what will be the best way to deal with the problem.'

'If you can coax her to stop crying and open her mouth while I have a look, we might be lucky and find that the injury is of such a nature that it might suction back up into position while she sleeps, as I have known it do sometimes in similar circumstances.' And off he went to see someone else who needed his attention, with a promise to be back shortly.

Since arriving, Drake had kept a low profile, standing apart from those closest to Tessa, and as she held Poppy and soothed her gently he felt that she was probably wishing him miles away right now.

They'd been sharing a precious moment of togetherness back there on the dance floor, he was thinking, but within moments the magic had gone with the news of Poppy's accident.

He supposed there was a chance that she would let *him* see inside her mouth because she knew him and so save Tessa more upset. But would she want him to try, after making it clear that she didn't want him there when Poppy had woken up from a bad dream that night? His professional instincts kicked in—the little one was hurting and he couldn't stand by and do nothing.

Tessa went weak with relief when he appeared by her side and said, 'Maybe Poppy will open wide for me. Shall I try?'

'Yes,' she said desperately, as the crying had stopped since he had appeared.

When he held out his arms Poppy went into them and gave a little whimper, but didn't cry when he said gently, 'Open your mouth wide so that I can see where it hurts.' After a gulping sort of sob she obeyed.

The doctor who'd been attending her was back and gazing in amazement at the sight of his young patient co-operating with someone he recognised as Drake Melford from his much-publicised top-ranking position at the Horizons Hospital.

'If you will take my word for it, I think you could be right about your suggestion that the roof of the mouth might suction up again when Poppy goes to sleep and is still,' he told him.

The other man nodded. 'It would save the child a lot of distress if we try that first, and to have your opinion is much appreciated.'

He turned to Tessa. 'If you are willing for that to be done, I'll phone the children's ward and make the arrangement for an overnight stay for her and we'll see what tomorrow brings.'

When he'd gone, Lizzie, who had been hovering anxiously, said, 'Thank goodness for that, Tessa. It may not be as bad as it seemed at first.' Glancing across at Drake, who was still holding Poppy, she said, 'As Dr Melford is here to give his support, we'll be off. I've got to get the boys home but I'll ring you later.'

After they'd gone he said, 'I'll carry her to the ward then I'll go, as I'm sure that you must be feeling that you've seen enough of me in the last few hours. Give me a ring in the morning when you have an answer as to whether the damaged area of Poppy's mouth has gone back into position, and I'll come and pick you up.'

Tired in both mind and body, she nodded. It had been a long, exhausting day. There had been the preparations for the event on the river boat in the morning, followed by a couple of hours in the heat of the kitchens in the afternoon, which had been quite exhausting, and then the few magic moments when they'd danced carefree and happy had been shattered by the news that her child was hurt. After that nothing else had registered, except Drake being in her life once again, and this time he had been so very welcome!

By the time they reached the ward Poppy was asleep in his arms and as he laid her down carefully on the bed that had been waiting for her, with a smiling nurse standing by, Tessa was filled with thankfulness that the first part of the nightmare was over, and if the fates were kind there might be better news in the morning.

She longed to ask Drake to stay but wasn't going

to. He had been there when she'd needed him. What more could she ask?

'You know where I'll be,' he said with a wry smile. On the point of departing, he added, 'Amongst the mothballs in the big house, but not for much longer. You may find it hard to believe but I'm in the process of buying a house and can't wait to move into it.'

If she hadn't been so tired Tessa would have wanted to know the details, but she merely nodded wearily and said, 'I hope that you will be happy in your new home.' As if it was a minor item of news amongst the other matters in her mind, she pointed to the sleeping child on the bed and said, 'If you should have any reason to speak to Randolph, please don't tell him about this.'

'Of course not,' he said dryly, with the feeling that he had been chastised for bringing mundane matters into the moment, and that much as he wanted to stay he needed to relieve Tessa of his presence and let her sleep. So, with a last glance at Poppy, he went.

The night staff had found her a comfortable chair beside the bed and every so often came to check on their young patient, and in the meantime, as the hours dawdled by, Tessa was able to take in the surprising news of Drake's about-turn on his views of the time they'd spent together.

She had changed her ideas long ago—the no-babies-no-mortgages idea was long gone. All right, it was someone else's child that she loved, and her home was a small cottage, yet it all felt so right, and until Drake had come back to unsettle her she'd been content.

The moments she'd spent in his arms on the dance floor of the river boat had been exactly how she'd known they would be. They'd brought memories of that other time back in full force, and if it hadn't been for Poppy's accident she would have given in to them.

At the worst possible moment Drake had told her that he of all people had bought a house and now in the quiet night her mind was adjusting to the news. Now she was filled with questions—where? What? How…? But most of all, why? When she saw him again she hoped to get some answers.

Maybe he'd taken the step because he loved Glenminster and the villages dotted around it that were a source of delight. If the house he was buying was local, the very fact of what he was contemplating had to mean that his wanderings were over, and she didn't know how she would feel about that. Would she be able to cope with Drake at Horizons for the rest of their lives?

Poppy stirred in her sleep, gave a little moan, then opened her eyes and said croakily, 'Drink, Mummy Two.'

The nurses had left some water by her bed and when Tessa raised her up against the pillows Poppy drank thirstily, looked around her and said, 'I'm hungry.'

One of the nurses had appeared and she said,

'Not until the doctor has had a look at the inside of her mouth, I'm afraid, but she can have plenty of liquids.'

Drake was deep in thought. While Daniel had been driving them to Accident and Emergency he had told himself that tonight he would finally know what he wanted in his life, and he did.

He'd tried to stay on the edge of things and let Tessa, her friends and the doctor in charge deal with what had happened to Poppy. But he loved the child too much to stand by when she was hurt, and by taking over had admitted to himself how much she meant to him.

As for Tessa, he wanted her back in his life completely, but he knew she had doubts about how she felt about him, and like a crazy fool he'd told her about the house he was buying at the worst possible moment. Naturally she hadn't been in the least interested, with her little girl hurt and crying. He had made a proper mess of the whole thing.

When he rang the hospital in the quiet of a bright Sunday morning, ready to set off immediately if the news was good, he wasn't disappointed, at least not right away.

Tessa's voice had a lift to it as she told him that Poppy had slept through the night and what they had hoped for had happened, the roof of her mouth had suctioned back into place and the doctors there were allowing her to be discharged with an instruction that for the next few days she have only soft foods and liquids.

'Fantastic!' he cried. 'I'll come and get you.'

'There's no need,' she told him. 'I've got a taxi waiting outside, but thanks for the offer, Drake.'

'All right.' It was an effort to sound casual but he felt her rejection to his core. Tessa was clearly on her guard again.

Surely he didn't think that what had happened the night before was going to bring them back to how they used to be? Tessa thought. It would always be there, the magnetism they had for each other, but she'd lived without it for three years...no, it was nearly four, and she had no intention of altering the arrangement.

As they walked slowly towards the waiting taxi Poppy was looking around her and Tessa didn't have to question who it was she sought. Knowing that Drake had been there the night before, she would be wanting to know where he was now.

The answer to that was he'd gone to seek comfort in the only place where he could find it. In one of the villages up in the hills was the house where he'd been hoping to bring Tessa and Poppy one day.

It was only during the long night that the thought had become a certainty in his mind, and it had taken just one short sentence when she'd rebuffed him to wipe it clear.

* * *

The builder was on the job when he got there, at the top of a ladder, putting some finishing touches to the house, and Drake thought that whatever else he might have got wrong this was not it. His job at the Horizons Hospital wouldn't leave him much time for leisure, but however much it did he would spend it here in this beautiful house...lonely as hell.

'You don't look too happy,' the man said. 'Is it something to do with this place?'

'No, not at all, it's fabulous,' he told him. 'How long will it be before it's finished?'

'Three weeks, a month at the most.'

'So I'll soon be free of the mothballs.'

'I can guarantee that,' the builder promised laughingly. 'So why don't I take you for another tour of your new home, show you the progress?'

On the way home in the taxi Tessa felt like weeping. His casual acceptance of her decision to take a taxi hurt. She sighed at how foolish she was being. Was she so afraid that he would shatter her contentment? Could she not let him in just a little?

Were its foundations so feeble that she couldn't let him share in the joy of discovering that Poppy's accident had proved not so serious as they'd at first thought? Some of it had been due to him because her small daughter liked him, trusted him—which was getting to be a problem—and it was that thought that had prompted her to phone for a taxi, and which was why she was now on the way home with Poppy cuddled up close, asking where Drake was.

To add to Tessa's unease there was the moment when he'd told her about the house he was buying, and now that Poppy was fine she was burning with curiosity about where it was, when he would be moving in, what it was like—and, of course, what had prompted him to buy it.

It was Sunday once more. No chance of seeing Drake again until Monday morning at the clinic to try to make amends for her rudeness after everything he had done for her and her family, and Tessa resigned herself to a day of keeping watch over Poppy's intake of light foods and liquids, even managing to coax her to have a sleep in the afternoon.

It was evening after what had been a long day. Poppy was asleep up above when a car she didn't recognise pulled up outside the cottage with Drake behind the wheel.

With her heartbeat quickening, Tessa watched as he uncoiled himself from the driving seat and walked slowly up to the door. When she opened it to him he said quizzically, 'I waited until I was sure that Poppy would be asleep before coming, as I didn't want to be any more intrusive than I was yesterday.'

As she stepped back to let him in she swallowed hard. Drake had been there when she'd needed him and was describing it as an intrusion. She wanted to throw herself into his arms, let him back into her life totally, but couldn't because he was saying breezily,

'I got your point about the taxi, so spent the afternoon with the builder at the house I'm buying and then went to the garage to pick up the car that you see at the bottom of your drive.

'It has been on order for a few weeks and they phoned yesterday to say that it had arrived, so today I got the chance to do both of those very pleasing things.'

'Yes, I see,' she said stiffly. 'I'm sorry I didn't get the chance to ask about your decision to become a homeowner. I suppose it's because you are so weary of your present accommodation?'

'Partly, but not entirely,' he replied. 'It is more that I fell in love with it and had to have it. You may recall that I am rather inclined to be like that. But, in general, I'm learning to hold onto precious things, am changing some of my views on life.'

'And so where is it, this house that you've fallen in love with?' she asked, without taking him up on that last comment.

'In one of the villages. It will be ready soon and I shall commute daily to the hospital, but I didn't come to discuss that. I'm here to ask about Poppy's mouth. Any problems?'

'No,' she said flatly. 'It seems all right. We've had a quiet day, unlike your own, and I will be at my desk as usual tomorrow.'

'Fine, but the place won't fall apart without you.

Why not take another day to get over the weekend's traumas?'

'I'm aware that my position at Horizons is much less important than yours,' she told him wryly, 'but I'm a working mother and take my responsibilities seriously.'

'I do know that, and I admire you for it,' he said easily, 'but there must be times when you need a helping hand. You have only to ask. And now that I know that Poppy is all right I'll be off.' And before she could think of something to say that would delay his departure, he went striding back to his new car with the sheer male charisma of him turning her bones to jelly and her heart to lead.

Upstairs Poppy whimpered in her sleep and as she hurried to her Tessa was aware of the irony of the situation she found herself in. Poppy already loved Drake and would be happy to have his presence always there, but her own love for him was a battered and bruised thing that was reluctant to be brought back to life. The only cure for that was to avoid him as much as possible, but that strategy could hardly be any worse!

And as if a prod in that direction the voice of conscience was there to remind her that he wasn't the one who hadn't kept to the vows they'd made. She had been that person, and as the last rays of the sun slanted across the hilltops like the bands of gold of that other time, the memory hurt now just as much as it had then.

CHAPTER SEVEN

THE NEXT MORNING Tessa was treating it as back to normal, with herself at the hospital and Poppy at Lizzie's for the day. She would have liked to inspect the inside of Poppy's mouth before she left her, just to be sure that all was well, but was getting no co-operation as the light breakfast she'd made for her was of more interest than obeying the request to 'open wide'.

Just as she was about to give up the phone rang and Drake's voice came over the line. 'Would you like me to call round to check Poppy's mouth before you take her to your friends?' he asked. 'Or have you already accomplished that?'

She almost groaned. Here he was again, her daughter's favourite person. It went without saying that Poppy would oblige for him.

'No. I haven't,' she admitted, 'but not for want of trying. I would be grateful if you would come, Drake, as I'm concerned that there might be some damage that isn't obvious.'

'How long before you leave for your childminder's?'

'Forty-five minutes.'

'I'll be round before then.' So much for avoiding him.

But she couldn't fault Drake's concern for her child, even though he was continually turning *her* world upside down.

'Looks fine,' he said after Poppy had opened her mouth to its widest for him. 'I'll drop her off at your friend's house, if you like, to save you the journey into town after the harrowing weekend you've had.'

'It's kind of you to offer,' she told him, 'but, no, thanks, we'll be fine. I have a suggestion of my own, though, that I'd like to put to *you*.'

He was smiling, unabashed. 'Let me guess. Could it be a request that I stop interfering in your life?'

'No, it isn't. It is connected with you having some breakfast while you're here because I'm sure that coming to check Poppy's mouth means that you haven't had time to eat.'

'It's a tempting thought, but I ought to be off,' he protested weakly. 'I really haven't the time to wait while you prepare me a meal, Tessa.'

'It's ready,' she informed him calmly. 'I cooked bacon and eggs while we were waiting for you to come, and tea and toast will only take a matter of minutes, so take a seat.'

'Why?' he asked, obeying the request. 'Why are

you doing this when you've made it clear you don't want me in your life?'

She was placing the food in front of him and said, 'I don't know. I must be crazy, but I do owe you an apology for the way I behaved about the taxi. It got shelved when I heard what a lovely day you'd had.'

'Yes, it was a riot,' he said dryly, with the memory of gazing at the house he was buying and thinking again that he was going to be as lonely as hell in it.

When he'd finished eating Drake said, 'I need to see how the medication you are on for the eye problem is progressing. When are you free?'

She shuddered. The mere mention of it made her feel nervous, but he was waiting for an answer and she told him, 'Not today if you don't mind. I left my secretary to clear away after the event on the river boat and feel that I must be available to sort out any loose ends that I may have left before anything else. Would tomorrow be all right?'

'Sure,' he said easily. 'I'll give you a buzz when I've sorted out a suitable time. And, Tessa, don't feel so apprehensive at the thought. It's a trifle early for results, but we'll see... And now I must go, I've a busy day ahead of me.'

He longed to hold her close again, if only for a moment. It had been magical having her in his arms as they'd danced on Saturday night, but it had been short-lived and he wasn't going to risk a rebuff at this hour of the day. The new Tessa could be unpredictable and he needed a clear head to get through what looked to be a very busy day.

So, bending to pat Poppy's dark locks as she came to stand beside him, he smiled across at her and said, 'Thanks for the breakfast. It was a lifesaver.' And when seconds later his car pulled away Tessa felt as if the day had lost its meaning.

Drake's face was set in sombre lines as he drove the short distance to the hospital. A quick glance while at the cottage hadn't shown any big improvement in Tessa's eye, but he needed her where his equipment was to decide about that. He understood her anxiety about caring for Poppy and maybe underneath was the dread that he might muscle into their lives if she couldn't cope for any reason.

She had softened towards him, though not to the degree that she wanted him back as before. So it was going to be a case of treading carefully and doing all he could to allay her fears. Being too pushy wasn't the answer. He had to face up to the fact that the future still held a lot of questions.

Horizons had just come into sight, the old stone building that had once been a wool mill and was now used for a far worthier purpose. As Drake glanced at the hills above the thought came, Would Tessa ever want him again, need him like he was beginning to need her, and want to live in that lovely house with him?

With that thought uppermost he parked the car and the day closed in on him, with a clinic in the morning, Theatre in the afternoon and a special appointment for Randolph in the evening to discuss his next cataract surgery, which was coming up soon.

He liked the old guy and when the consultation was over said, 'Can I ask you something personal?'

'Sure, go ahead,' was the reply, because Drake was liked in return.

'Do I resemble Poppy's father in any way?'

'Yes, you do,' Randolph told him without hesitation. 'The dark hair and hazel eyes, the bone structure of your face and your height. I think Poppy is confused—sometimes she seems to think you *are* him, but then she doesn't understand why you and Tessa are so at odds. The two of you don't get on, do you?'

'We had an affair before I went to Switzerland to take up a promotion, and I hurt her a lot by behaving like an idiot and leaving her behind.'

'Ah! So that's it,' Randolph said. 'I did wonder. So are you going to do anything about it?'

Drake's smile was wry. 'I'm working on it.'

If he hadn't promised Tessa that he wouldn't mention her eye problem to Poppy's grandfather he would have told him that the unromantic but vital task of sorting out her vision had to come before anything else, and that he was hoping that tomorrow might have some answers for both of them.

Yet it *was* still early days to expect significant improvement in her eye. First the treatment had to disperse an accumulation of debris behind the eye that had built up over recent weeks before being seen to have any effect. Only time would tell if surgery was required.

When he saw her the following day she looked pale and tense and greeted him with the news that her Aunt Sophie, the younger sister of her mother, who had died when she'd been in her late teens, had phoned for a chat, and on discovering that she had an eye problem had said that she'd once had something similar and so had her mother, that it ran in their family.

As he listened to what she had to say Drake wanted to reach out to her, hold her close, and tell her that he would always be there for her, but Tessa's expression was indicating that it was strictly a doctor-patient moment, and she was hardly likely to believe him anyway, with his track record of disappearing when the mood took him.

'Yes, hyperthyroidism can be hereditary,' he agreed, 'but so are quite a few other illnesses and the medication for this one can take a while to clock in, so shall we see what it's been up to?'

When he'd finished checking the eye from all angles and had measured what was a minor reduction of the problem with the orbital area of her eye he said gently, 'We have a small success. Does your eye feel more comfortable at all?'

'Yes, a little,' she told him, and smiled for the first time since appearing before him. 'I've been reading up on these kinds of conditions and they can be quite scary, so thank you for being here for me, Drake.'

'Thanks aren't necessary,' he said, smiling across at her, and took advantage of the moment. 'How about you let me take you for a meal to celebrate the slight though most welcome improvement? To somewhere more upmarket than my previous suggestion of the staff restaurant in this place.'

There was silence for a moment of the kind indicating that the other person intended to be firm but polite. 'I'm sorry,' she said. 'I can't ask Lizzie to have Poppy more than she does already, and don't you think the two of us see enough of each other already? From a distance, maybe, which seems the most sensible arrangement, but nevertheless...'

'Oh, by all means let's keep our distance!' he said tightly. 'All I am doing is asking you out to lunch, Tessa.'

She swallowed hard. Didn't he see that her unwillingness to dine with him and take their frail relationship a step further was because of her dread that he might do the same thing again if the mood took him? Leave her behind? Which now would hurt Poppy as well as herself, and she couldn't bear the thought of that happening.

But to reject what on the face of it was just an invitation to take her for a meal had the sound of playing hard to get over something of minor importance. Finally she caved in and said, 'Yes, all right about the meal, but in the daytime during Monday to Friday so that I don't put any extra pressure on Lizzie.'

He nodded. 'All right, I'll take a couple of hours off around midday tomorrow, as long as you're able to do the same. We'll drive into the town to a smart restaurant somewhere. And now, if you'll excuse me, I have work to do.'

'Yes, of course,' she said weakly, and went back to where Jennifer observed her curiously.

In spite of her reluctance to socialise alone with Drake, the next morning Tessa had an insane longing to dress up for him, because apart from on the odd occasion he hadn't seen her in anything but her office clothes since he'd come back into her life, and putting the dark blue jacket and skirt to one side she surveyed the clothes in her wardrobe.

Gone were the days when she had revelled in making herself look beautiful for him with smart clothes and jewellery. A turquoise dress of fine linen caught her eye, mainly because he had always loved to see her in it.

If she wore it today it would have another message, one that told him she wasn't just the single mother of a small child having to work to survive, but a beautiful woman, just as he was a man who had heads turning wherever he went. If he ever asked if she had forgiven him for walking out of her life so uncaringly, she was beginning to feel that she could truthfully say that she had, but that was as far as it went.

Yet it didn't stop her from being afraid that he might come knocking on her door early one morning like that other time, and with her melting in his arms carry her upstairs... But this time she wouldn't be alone. Poppy would be there, sleeping in her pretty little room, and he would never do anything to upset the child who sometimes thought he was her father.

In the end she chose not to wear the turquoise dress. If Drake got the wrong signal it could be harder than ever to stop him from thinking it was just a matter of time before she melted into his arms again. So it was a top of apricot silk, slim-line cream trousers and high-heeled shoes that she arrived in at the office, to Jennifer's amazement.

'What's going on?' the other woman asked laughingly. 'Are you going out straight from here tonight?'

'No,' was the reply. 'Drake Melford is taking me out to lunch. I have an eye problem that is worrying me and he wants to discuss it in more relaxing surroundings than these. It will be just a matter of taking an extended lunch break, and the clothes are...er...'

'To let him see how beautiful you are out of the clothes that we spend our working days in?' Jennifer teased. 'Because when he sees you it's going to knock him out cold.'

Better cold than hot, Tessa thought wryly, so why was she doing this?

There was no sign of Drake during the morning, just a brief phone call to say he would be waiting in the car park at half past eleven, if that was all right. When she'd assured him that it was he'd rung off, and now it was just five minutes to go, and she was making her way there, wishing she'd worn her usual work clothes instead of dressing up like a Christmas tree.

He followed her outside seconds later and when he saw her his eyes widened. As far as he was concerned, the occasion came from a longing to be with her, even for just a short time, disguised as a working lunch in the middle of a busy day. The last thing he'd expected had been that Tessa would have dressed up for it. Was it a sign of forgiveness, temptation or a moment of mockery? He wished he knew, but it was as if the sun up above was shining just on them and maybe the hurts of the past would be forgotten for a while.

'It's nice to see you out of your usual work clothes for once,' he said casually and left it at that as they drove out of the hospital grounds, having no wish to say the wrong thing in the moment of meeting.

'It's good to have a change sometimes,' she said in a similar tone, and with a glance at what he was wearing thought that no one could fault Drake's appearance. His suit had the style and quality that he always kept to.

'I've booked a table at the new hotel in the gardens at the end of the shopping promenade,' he said, as the town came in sight, and thought Tessa couldn't fault that for tact. No going to one of their old haunts to pull at her heartstrings. They were too far apart for that sort of thing.

'So how is little Poppy?' he asked, when they

had been shown to a table in the restaurant. 'Is her mouth still all right?'

She smiled. 'Yes, thank goodness.'

He nodded. 'It was fortunate that it was the roof of the mouth, which in such cases can suck back upwards easily, instead of the bottom of the mouth, where injuries can be more serious.'

With a change of subject he went on to say, 'When Randolph came for an appointment the other day I asked him outright if I resembled her father in any way. He said yes and was quite definite about it. So, Tessa, I do hope you don't still think I'm using Poppy's attraction to me to ease myself into your life again.'

As their glances locked she said, 'I did, but I don't any more, Drake. It's just a most unusual co-incidence and if it makes Poppy happy, it's all right with me.'

'Just as long as I don't want to take it to its natural conclusion,' he commented dryly.

'Yes, you could say that. She has already had one father who through no fault of his own disappeared out of her life, another would be just too much for her young mind if you decided to move on again to pastures new.''

There'd been nothing green about his time in Switzerland, he thought grimly. It had been cold outside and he'd been cold inside with the misery that had always been there when he thought about how in his arrogance he'd left behind the special woman in his life.

But this getting together for a meal was supposed to help put Tessa's mind at rest as much as possible about the thyroid over-activity that was affecting her eye.

Blood tests were showing a slight improvement in the condition, but there was some way to go before he would be able to tell her anything definite. An under active thyroid was easier to deal with by far than one that was the opposite.

He could remember some years ago having to remove the four parathyroids from an elderly woman's neck because they were overworking and causing her calcium levels to rise dangerously, making such things as benign tumours appear, and causing serious kidney defects along with other life threatening illnesses, and it could have been the same with Tessa's problem.

So far there had been none of the hazards associated with the problem except for the eye protruding from the socket and there had been a very small sign of improvement the last time he'd done a blood test but there was a way to go before the problem was sorted.

So he didn't let himself be drawn about her lack of faith regarding his reliability and said, 'The medication is beginning to work and now we might see a reduction in the pressure around the optic nerve and your eye feeling more comfortable. Then it really will be time to celebrate.'

The food had arrived, it was time to eat, and they

talked about minor things until she said, 'So where exactly is the house that you're buying, Drake?'

'Why don't you let me take you to see it instead of talking about it?'

She didn't reply to that, instead asked casually, as if she wasn't bothered one way or the other, 'Are you intending living there alone or will someone be sharing it with you?'

'A couple of folks might if I can persuade them, but it will be a few weeks before it is ready for occupation,' he explained, 'and then it will be goodbye to where I'm living now, thank goodness. Would you feel like giving some advice when it comes to furnishings?'

She was observing him, startled. 'Er, yes, I suppose so, but I don't really want to be involved in something that might be wrong for others.'

He was smiling across at her and she thought he was still the most attractive man she had ever met. It wasn't surprising that from the first moment of their meeting she'd adored him and that it was taking all her willpower not to let it happen again.

The moments on the dance floor, the time when he'd kissed her in the rose garden and the brief moments of desire they'd shared in her kitchen were like an oasis in a dry land. But there was the new life she'd made for herself and Poppy with its special kind of contentment that she couldn't risk.

'It's what I like that counts, anyone else doesn't matter,' he was saying, safe in the knowledge that if they ever did have a fresh start and she and Poppy lived with him in his house up on the hillside he would be sure to like the furnishings because she would have chosen them, and if that wasn't reaching for the moon he didn't know what was.

They'd finished the meal and the clock in the restaurant said there was a short time left before they had to return to the hospital, so Drake suggested a walk in the hotel gardens and said, 'When I passed a couple of days ago there was a wedding taking place and I thought what a beautiful setting it is.'

'Yes, all right,' she agreed reluctantly, having no wish to be reminded of such things while they were together, and was amazed that he who had scorned matrimony had commented on it so favourably.

There was his obvious love of Poppy, he was buying a house, and now Drake was speaking admiringly about a wedding he'd seen. Could this be the same man who had left her all those years ago?

The gardens *were* lovely, the moments together in them filled with promise, but a promise of what? she questioned. Their time had been and gone long ago. She had branched off into a different kind of life since then, separate and fulfilling. Did she want to change?

This isn't working Drake thought, casting a sideways glance at her expression. If you are going to woo Tessa you have to come up with something better than this. Why don't you ask her to marry you outright?

The words were forming themselves in his mind,

but on the point of saying them he saw that in Tessa's expression there was nothing but the wish to get back to the hospital and reality. It wasn't the right moment, he decided, far from it, and led the way to where he'd parked the car, unable to ignore the relief in her expression.

He was expecting a speedy departure from her when they arrived back at the hospital, but instead Tessa turned to face him in the confines of the car and said, 'I'd like to return your hospitality. When would it be convenient for you to come for dinner with Poppy and me at the cottage?'

He was observing her sombrely. 'You don't have to do that because I took you out to lunch. If you remember, it was to celebrate that the over-functioning of your thyroid gland was beginning to slow down. So don't feel that you have to invite me back.'

'You don't want to see Poppy, then?'

'Of course I want to see her, but not on sufferance!'

'What makes you say that?' she protested.

Drake, the memory of his aborted marriage proposal still fresh in his head, had his answer ready. 'It might be because you were so obviously bored back there.'

'If that is what you really think you are so wrong,' she told him. 'I feel as if I don't know you any more. Your thinking is different. All the things that you didn't want as part of your life then are acceptable to you now.'

'And is that not allowed?' he asked.

'No, of course it is, but my life was sorted long ago. As I picked up the pieces of what I'd thought was a love that would last for ever I discovered that there was a lot less pain in loving a child than loving a man.'

'So you intend to stay as you are, just you and Poppy in your safe little cocoon?'

Tessa didn't answer. Her glance was on the clock on the front of the hospital building and she said hastily, 'I have a new food supplier arriving in ten minutes, Drake, I must go.'

'Yes, me too,' he agreed. 'I have a cataract removal this afternoon.'

'I do hope it goes well,' she said softly. 'That is so much more important than what I will be doing.'

'You know our patients need nourishment as well as eyesight, and Tessa, I'd like to accept your dinner invitation, if it still stands.'

She smiled. 'Yes, of course it does. I thought of lunch during the weekend so that you will have more time to be with Poppy than in the evening. Which day would suit you best?'

'Sunday would be fine if that if that is all right with you. I usually work on Saturdays.' On that promise they went their separate ways into Horizons, with their own skylines looking momentarily brighter.

When Drake arrived on the Sunday morning Poppy was on the drive, playing on a small scooter that was her latest treasure, and as his car stopped outside the gate she became still until she saw who was in it and then as he eased himself out and came towards her she began to run towards him, and as he swung her up into his arms the name was on her lips for the first time... 'Daddy!'

For Tessa, who was following close behind, it was the moment of truth. As their glances met above Poppy's dark curls the quiet contentment she had so treasured with just the two of them was disappearing. She would have to talk to Poppy about it once Drake had gone, to help clear up what must be a very confusing situation for her little girl.

Drake's smile was rueful as he placed Poppy back onto her scooter and when she'd gone whizzing off he said, 'I told you what Randolph said about the likeness, but I didn't tell you that I asked him if the poor guy would be upset if he knew that his little girl thought another man was him and he said, no, not at all, that somewhere in the ether his daughter and son-in-law would want what would make their little girl happiest. That her father, who'd been a great guy, wouldn't mind someone else taking his place if it brought comfort.'

She looked white and withdrawn, as if a cold hand was squeezing her heart. It would be so easy to give in and let Drake back into her life for Poppy's sake, but that wouldn't do. She had made a good life for the two of them out of sadness and hurt, and it hadn't always been easy with the memory of what it was like to be in Drake's arms, in Drake's bed, the kind of things that were only ever going to happen again in her dreams.

'I want us to carry on as we are doing,' she said, 'with you living in your lovely new house and Poppy and me in our home. You can see her whenever you want, but you know that it works both ways, Drake. She has to be able to see you when she needs you—you have to be there for her too.'

It was a hurtful thing to say, and she wished she could take it back the moment she'd said it. His glance was cold as he told her, 'I know how it works, Tessa. You and I had an agreement—you can't hold that against me for ever.'

Yes, but I do, Tessa thought raggedly. Can't Drake see that? I've had the foundations of my life crumble once. I couldn't face it again. But he is so confident, so keen to make sure I remember that I wasn't entirely blameless all that time ago. Should I try a second time round?

She had cooked foods that she knew he liked and watching his enjoyment of them brought back memories of the two of them arriving home from their different workplaces and while the food was cooking making love wherever the mood took them.

They had been days of reckless rapture and even more reckless promises about the lives they intended to live devoid of responsibilities. But all that had come to Drake living alone in a rented house in the hospital grounds and her a single mother with a child that wasn't his.

He was reading her mind and when the three of them had finished eating he said, 'Let's fill the dishwasher and go out into the garden for some playtime with Poppy. I see no reason why she should suffer for our lack of rapport.'

'Yes, you're right,' she agreed, holding back tears at the thought of such a farce. What Randolph had said about Poppy's father made her feel trapped. Nothing was clear and uncomplicated any more, and after Drake left in the early evening and Poppy was asleep, Tessa watched the sun go down and tried not to think about times past.

CHAPTER EIGHT

WHETHER IT WAS because of that she didn't know, but in the stillness of the night she dreamt that she was in Drake's arms and it was magical. Consequently, when she awoke the next morning she felt tired and low-spirited.

Lizzie didn't miss her lacklustre appearance when she dropped Poppy off, and wanted to know how Sunday lunch had gone. Tessa could only manage to give a silent thumbs-down as she departed to face Monday morning at the hospital.

After the trauma of Sunday she was hoping that Drake would stay out of her radius and wasn't happy to find him perched on the corner of her desk chatting to Jennifer, when she arrived.

'Hi, there,' he said in greeting. 'Just stopped by to leave you an appointment card for next week. Now that the treatment is working I need to see you more often.'

The phone rang, her secretary answered it, and while she was taking the call he said in a low voice, 'We need to talk. When can I see you alone?'

'I don't know. I'd rather not,' she told him.

He frowned. 'I'm getting a little tired of being cast as the archvillain in your life.'

'Lunchtime, then, at the big house?' she suggested reluctantly, and he nodded and went on his way, leaving her wishing that she hadn't been so obliging in agreeing to his demands. But wasn't that how she'd always been?

When she rang the bell Drake greeted her unsmilingly and invited her to take a seat in its huge sitting room. She obeyed with the feeling that what he had to say was unlikely to be good, and waited to hear what he had to say.

It was brief, to the point, and incredible.

'When I got home from your place last night there was a message waiting for me from a clinic in Canada, offering me a similar position to the one I have here, and I've arranged to go over there in a couple of weeks' time to see what's on offer.'

He was about to take temptation out of her way, and relief was washing over her, but only for seconds until reality took over. 'You can't leave us now!' she said in a strangulated whisper. 'Poppy doesn't want a father figure who is there one moment and gone the next. She has had enough hurts in her young life.'

He didn't reply to that, just commented, 'I notice that there's no concern at the thought of my departure with regard to yourself?'

'I don't care about myself,' she cried. 'You've already messed my life up by coming back, but she's so small and defenceless.'

Tears, warm and stinging, were forming behind closed eyelids as she tried to shut him out of her vision, because Poppy wasn't the only one who was defenceless when it came to Drake. So far she'd been able to cope with his return and the effect it was having on her life but not any more.

She'd already had to pick up the pieces after one of his departures, had she the strength to do it again, this time with a child to think of?

'I'm only considering the Canadian offer because you've made it clear you don't want me here,' he said, 'and Poppy will soon forget me once I've gone. If you marry at some time in the future she will have an adoptive father to go with an adoptive mother and all will be well.'

'I can't believe that you could be so smug about something so important,' she said, fighting to maintain her self-control. 'Is that it, you have nothing more to hit me with?'

'That's it,' he said levelly. 'I didn't plan it. The offer came out of the blue at what seemed to be just the right moment in both our lives.'

'Yours maybe,' she told him, 'not mine and Poppy's. Apart from anything else, you promised to be there for me with regard to treating my eye problem. What are you going to do about that, shuffle me on to whoever takes your place?'

'I'll sort something, don't worry. If I take this

offer I won't be living on the moon. There *are* airlines, you know.'

'Don't come back out of limbo again for my sake,' she told him flatly. 'What about the house that you're buying?'

'I shall still buy it and use it for holidays if I accept the offer. Or rent it out.'

Tessa was on her feet, holding onto the arms of the chair as she asked, 'And is that it? No other me, me, me kind of news you have to pass on?'

Drake shook his head wearily. 'No, nothing else. But, Tessa, you can't have it both ways. You don't want me around, but you don't like it when I'm prepared to oblige and get out of your life.'

The door was wide open, flung back on its hinges, and she had gone. As he closed it slowly behind her the room felt cold, as cold as it had been in Switzerland.

The rest of the day dragged on. She forced herself to concentrate on hospital matters with Jennifer's chatter in the background about what a lovely weekend she'd had with her new man friend, and all the time Tessa was imagining the pain of yet another separation from Drake. He was treating it as if she was to blame—maybe she was.

He'd been nothing but kind and caring and supportive since coming back into her life, and what had she been? Mistrusting? Unpleasant? It wasn't surprising that he was ready once again to go his own way, and ahead of them was an uncomfortable fortnight until he flew to Canada to investigate what was on offer for him out there, which was certain to be spectacular. It would need to be to lure him away from Horizons.

When she arrived at Lizzie's house after a dreadful day her friend's first words were, 'You look ghastly. What's happened?'

'Drake has been headhunted by a hospital in Canada and is going to see what's on offer in a couple of weeks, and it's all my fault, Lizzie. He's tired of me keeping him at arm's length and being so mistrusting and…well, I have to admit, sometimes I've been rude and hurtful—when that other time was just as much my fault as his.

'Poppy called him Daddy yesterday, which was fine by me until we got our wires crossed as usual and ended up putting on a big pretence of playing in the garden with her. Then he went, with things as bad as they've ever been between us, and as if the fates were weary of our lack of trust in each other the Canadian offer was waiting for him when he arrived back at the big house.'

Lizzie was observing her sadly. 'Tessa, when are you going to admit that you still love him?'

'Why not ask me when I'm going to climb Everest or something equally difficult? Why couldn't he be any man instead of Drake Melford? He loves Horizons and I'm driving him away from the place. The only way that I can admit to myself that I still love him is to do something that will make him stay.'

'And what might that be?'

'Move out of the area. Give him the space that he deserves without judging him all the time. Then he can carry on with his plans to buy a house in one of the villages and live there in contentment.'

'You can't do that!' Lizzie exclaimed in horror.

'I can. Before Drake leaves on his visit to Canada I shall tell him that if he proceeds with his crazy plan of moving there to be away from me, he will find me gone when he comes back to say his good-byes to the folks at Horizons.

'The hospital needs him, Lizzie, and if I can't persuade him to change his mind I will appeal to his conscience by having left when he comes back after looking the Canadian place over. Once he is airborne I shall put the cottage up for sale and find somewhere not too far away to move to, and once that has been sorted Poppy and I will go into temporary accommodation until the sale goes through.'

'Where have you got in mind?' Lizzie asked unbelievingly.

'Maybe Devon, or somewhere not quite so far away, so that I can visit you regularly and keep an eye on Randolph, and once I've found somewhere to live please don't tell anyone except Daniel where I am, will you?'

'Of course I won't,' she assured her, staggered at the scenario that was unfolding before her. 'We shall miss the two of you so much,' she told her sadly.

'Please don't make it any harder,' Tessa begged, with her glance on Poppy playing happily in the garden with the twins.

Driving past the park on their way home, she brought the car to a halt. Workmen were delivering new benches and putting the old ones into a truck. The one that had such sweet and sour memories was the next one to go.

'Can I buy it?' she asked, pointing to the bench in question.

'Yes,' she was told. 'Unwanted things such as these are sold and the money goes to charities. This lot are fifty pounds each, including delivery.'

'You have a deal,' she told them. 'I live on the road that goes past the eye hospital.'

'Right, we'll drop it off now if you like,' one of them said, and with a sick feeling that both she and the bench were surplus to requirements she led the way.

'Where do you want it?' he asked, when they arrived at the cottage. 'On the patio at the back, please,' Tessa told him, having no wish for Drake to see it if he should happen to drive past. When they'd gone she stood observing it in silence as Poppy whizzed to and fro on her scooter.

It was a strange thing to choose as a memento of a dead love affair, she thought, but if every time she sat on the bench it brought Drake near in her self-imposed exile, it might take some of the hurt away.

Randolph rang in the late evening. It seemed that Drake had told him about his proposed Canadian trip and he wanted to know what if anything was going on between them.

'Nothing is going on,' she told him uncomfortably. 'He has the chance of a fantastic opportunity over there and is flying across to see what is on offer.'

'Surely you don't want him to leave you and Poppy back here while he goes to live and work in another country?' he questioned.

'It has happened to me before, Randolph, and what Drake does is his own affair. We have no claim on him.'

'No, of course not,' he agreed vaguely, and rang off, leaving Tessa with another problem to worry about. Randolph wasn't going to want to be far away from his granddaughter.

After Monday's day of despair Drake rang her office the next morning and said in clipped tones that he would want to check her eye once each week before he left on his Canadian trip, so how about on the mornings of the two Fridays before he flew out in the afternoon of the second one?

'Er, yes,' she agreed, remembering how she'd accused him of leaving her in the middle of the treatment if he took a job abroad.

'So shall we say first thing on each Friday?' he suggested. 'I'm going to be pushed to get all my commitments here dealt with before I leave.'

'How long do you expect to be away?' she asked, as if only mildly interested, when, in fact, she was aching for him to stay.

'I have no idea, but does it matter?' he questioned. 'You aren't going to miss me.'

She didn't reply to that. Just rang off and sat gazing through the window to where the hills that they both loved so much and the gracious town nestling beneath them seemed to be saying, If you can persuade Drake to refuse the Canadian offer and stay here, you won't have loved in vain.

She rang him back a few moments later and said, 'You shouldn't leave Horizons because of me. The hospital needs you, Glenminster needs you. So I've decided to leave the hospital and the area in order to give you some space. Perhaps you could keep that in mind while you're being shown around the Canadian set-up.' Tessa rang off before he could comment. *Coward*, she thought.

But he rang back only minutes later and said, 'I'm free for a short time and am hoping that it will be long enough to tell you what I think about your ridiculous idea, Tessa. I am quite capable of sorting out my affairs without you offering yourself as a sacrificial lamb. Don't even think of taking Poppy to some strange place because of me!

'I made a mistake coming back and I'm going to rectify it. It's as simple as that, and I'm expecting that by the time you come for your appointment on Friday you will have seen sense.' Drake put the phone down without knowing that she was going to proceed to Plan B regardless.

It was a week of miserable activity: putting the cottage up for sale without a 'for sale' sign until he had flown to Canada on the second Friday, searching for a place to move to that would meet her needs and Poppy's, somewhere that was not too near and not too far, and when she'd found the right sort of place—if ever there could be such a thing without Drake—starting afresh with little enthusiasm.

She'd spoken to the chairman and explained that she might have to leave without the usual month's notice. He'd been surprised but quite amenable as Tessa had served Horizons well over the years, and when she'd asked that the possibility of her leaving be kept private he'd also agreed, and wondered at the same time if it had anything to do with his top man being headhunted by a Canadian hospital.

When Tessa went for the check-up early on the Friday morning of that first week, Drake was waiting. She'd had a blood test the day before in the endocrine clinic with better results than before and once he had done his examination of the offending eye he said, 'It begins to look as if I won't need to cross the Atlantic to check progress. The medication that you're on seems to be working fine'.

For a moment she felt weak with relief. But that thought was swiftly followed by the realisation that everything had its price. His next and last consultation would be her final goodbye to him, and it would be beyond bearing.

It was early September. Poppy had a place reserved at the nearest pre-school, but now it was beginning to look as if she was going to receive that part of her education elsewhere. Tessa still hadn't found a suitable place for them to live until she saw a house similar to the cottage for sale in a Devon coastal resort. It had a good pre-school nearby, and she decided to drive down there during the coming weekend to look the place over.

The idea would have been great if it hadn't been that with every mile in that direction on the Saturday her concerns regarding Poppy being separated from Lizzie's twin boys, and Randolph fretting because he wasn't going to see enough of her, were assuming gigantic proportions, and halfway there she stopped the car in a lay-by and decided to turn back.

Not because she'd changed her mind about leaving but because the place she'd been heading towards was too far away for an easy relationship to be maintained with Lizzie's boys and, of course, Poppy's beloved grandfather. How could she be so cruel as to contemplate taking his granddaughter so far away?

Yet those thoughts didn't solve the problem of leaving Horizons and Glenminster and all that they stood for to stop Drake from moving to Canada. Tessa knew that she had only herself to blame for the situation she found herself in. How had it come to this? At first she would have been delighted that he was leaving her alone—when had she changed her mind?

When she pulled up in front of the cottage the thought came that one week had already gone before

Drake flew out there and she was floundering with no idea where to go before he came back.

The phone was ringing as she put the key in the lock and on answering it she was surprised to hear her Aunt Sophie on the line once again. But when Tessa heard what she had to say it was as if someone, somewhere was looking after her.

'I did so enjoy our chat,' said the sixty-year-old keep-fit fanatic, 'even though I caused you alarm when I mentioned the thyroid connection between the women of our family. I would love to see you and Poppy and wonder if you and your little girl would like to come and stay with me for a while. I have lots of room and you'd be most welcome for as long as you'd like.'

'We'd be delighted,' Tessa said weakly.

Sophie, her mother's younger sister, lived on a part of the coast not too far away for Randolph to see his granddaughter quite often and Poppy to see the twins, yet distant enough for them to be away from Glenminster as far as Drake was concerned. If she liked it there, maybe she might see a house that would be suitable for them with a school close by, and even a hospital not too far away where she could put her training to good use.

'So when can you come?' her aunt was asking.

'Would next weekend be too soon?' she questioned.

'Not at all,' was the reply, and Tessa sank down onto the nearest chair, relieved yet tearful. Everything would work out for the best now, wouldn't it?

* * *

During the week that followed, the talk around the hospital was that Drake would be crazy not to accept the offer from a much larger and more prestigious hospital than their own, but would be sorely missed. As Tessa listened to the gossip she prayed that her departure would keep him where he belonged, enjoying life in the house that he was so set on buying, instead of having to give up the dream.

The fact that she also was involved in departure plans wasn't known generally as the chairman was keeping his word and Jennifer was too head over heels in love with the new man in her life to take much notice of what was going on anywhere else.

The more Drake thought about a move across the Atlantic the less he was looking forward to it. He'd gone to Switzerland for prestige and had got it, wrapped around with regrets over what he'd lost in the process.

It had stood to sense that in the time he'd been gone she would have found someone else to fill the gap he'd left, but nothing could have prepared him for the enchanting small child that Tessa had adopted who had all her love and devotion.

She had offered in recent days to move out of the area so that he would stay, but no way was he going to allow her to do that. He wanted her in his life now more than ever, and would be devastated if she wasn't there when he got back from Canada.

If he hadn't already agreed to attend the appointment with the Canadians he would forget the whole thing. He hadn't seen anything of her in days, and when she came for his last examination of her eye this Friday he was going to repeat what he'd said about her not leaving Glenminster.

Almost everything Tessa possessed was going to be put into storage once Drake had gone until she found the right place to live, and when she called at Randolph's on the way home on the Thursday night before her last Friday of residence in Glenminster there was a chill in the air that indicated that Poppy's grandfather was not pleased with her plans for the future.

'We aren't going to be too far away,' she told him reassuringly. 'I will bring Poppy to see you as often as I can.'

'And are you going to give me a new address where I can get in touch?' he asked crustily.

'I will when I've got one,' she promised, 'and in the meantime I've made a temporary arrangement with my Aunt Sophie and will give you her phone number.'

'So what has Drake to do with all of this?' he wanted to know.

'Everything and nothing,' was the reply, and he had to be satisfied with that.

That same morning Tessa had told Jennifer that the following day would be her last at Horizons and her secretary had gazed at her in astonishment.

'So no fanfare of trumpets at *your* departure,'

she'd said incredulously. 'I wouldn't be surprised if there's a brass band if Drake Melford decides to leave us. The general feeling is that no one wants him to go, but you can't begrudge him what has to be the opportunity of a lifetime.'

Tessa had turned away. What would everyone think if they knew she was responsible for him considering the move to Canada? She prayed that her leaving Glenminster would not be in vain. That when Drake came back and saw she was gone he would stay and be happy, and perhaps having given up on her might one day meet someone less difficult to love.

It had come, the final check-up for her eye problem with Drake, and she made her way to his consulting room with dragging steps.

What she was hoping was that he would return to the place they both loved and that, whatever decision he'd made while in Canada, he wouldn't leave Horizons once he discovered that she'd gone. She wanted him to be happy in the house of his dreams and fulfilled with the work he did at the hospital, while she would seek a return to the contentment of sorts that she'd found while they'd been apart.

Tessa looked tired, he thought when she appeared. There was a crease across her brow and a listlessness about her that indicated inward weariness. But one thing was sure, she would be relieved to see him go after the telling off he'd given her.

Yet there was no way he could let her disappear

from his life, he loved her too much. He was going to make one last attempt to show her how much he cared when he came back from Canada, and if she still didn't want him near, well, he would just persist until she did.

For one thing, his beautiful house was meant to be lived in, not used as a holiday home, and for another was the knowledge that a little girl wanted him as her daddy and he wasn't going to let her down on that.

He'd told Tessa that he was going to accept the offer from the Canadians in a moment of frustration and ever since had wished he'd kept silent.

'What time is your flight?' she asked in a polite but disinterested kind of voice. She didn't want him to call at the cottage later in the afternoon and find her in the middle of moving.

'Half past three,' he said, and with a wry smile, 'I imagine that you are just being polite with that question as the only real emotion you are feeling with regard to my departure has to be relief.'

She flashed him a tired smile. 'I thought I was here for an eye check. Is the mind-reading a freebie?'

'No, just an observation. so if you would like to open wide we will see what has been going on behind those beautiful eyes over the last week.'

Tessa could feel tears rising, and when Drake had finished the examination she said, 'Before you tell me the final results, whether they be good or not so good, I will never forget how you have been there for me with this whole unexpected eye thing.' Before he could answer she took a photograph of a happy, smiling Poppy out of her bag and, giving it to him, said, 'I thought you might like this.'

'Yes. I would indeed,' he said, as he looked down at it. 'But I would have liked one of the two of you more.'

'I'm sure you are only saying that to be polite.'

'Not necessarily,' was the reply, and cut that discussion short. 'Your results, Tessa. The eye is back to normal. Keep on taking the medication for another couple of months to be on the safe side and it should be fine. If at any time you are worried about your vision let me know immediately.'

'Are you definitely going to accept the position if they offer it to you?' she asked, choking on the words. 'I meant what I said that day on the phone.'

'Maybe you did, and maybe I won't take the job over there. What matters is that irrespective of whatever I decide to do I find you here when I come back in two weeks' time. Don't make any sacrifices on my account, Tessa. The Canadian job is already mine if I want it.'

'And you are going there because of me?' she choked.

She held out her hand to wish him goodbye, but ignoring it he looked down onto her upturned face and kissed her just once, then, releasing her, opened the door for her and closed it behind her with a decisive click.

Speechless at the finality of the moment, Tessa

went back to her office to watch for Drake's departure from the big house in time to catch his three-thirty flight.

When a taxi arrived and his baggage had been put in the boot he paused for a moment before seating himself in the back of the vehicle and glanced across to where her office was. It took all her willpower not to rush outside and beg him to stay, but thankfully it wasn't his final departure.

That, she hoped, would not come, and she prayed that when he returned Drake might forget about Canada on finding her gone and decide to stay in Glenminster where he belonged. Otherwise what she was planning to do would be a waste of both their lives.

Her furniture would be going into storage in the late afternoon and the park bench, which was covered by waterproof sheeting on the patio at the back of the cottage, was going to be transported by haulage to her aunt's home, later in the day.

All that she would have to do at the end of her last working day at the hospital would be to check that all was secure at the cottage and collect Poppy from Lizzie's house for the last time before they went to the bed and breakfast place where she had booked them in for the night.

It had been a painful farewell for the two friends, who had kept what was happening in the background from the children to avoid tears, but she was determined to make a fresh start with Poppy, and Lizzie at least understood her reasons, even if she didn't agree with the decision.

Tessa had brought a snack with her to serve as their evening meal at the bed and breakfast place and once they'd eaten she consoled a fretful Poppy, who didn't like the strange place she had brought her to with the assurance that the next day they would be at the seaside. Then she'd tucked her up in the big double bed that graced the room and, once she was sleeping, eased herself in beside her daughter and tried not to think about those last moments she'd spent with Drake in his consulting room.

After an early breakfast she stopped off at the cottage to see if the bench had been picked up yet and was relieved to see that it had. Then one of the strangest days Tessa had ever known got under way, and as the miles flashed past the enormity of what she was undertaking was beginning to register.

It was fortunate she'd managed to leave while Drake was away, she thought. She couldn't have done it with him being anywhere near, and now the die was cast and the future that not so long ago had looked contented was in front of her. She tried not to think of it as bleak—indeed, thinking of Poppy's joy at going to the seaside helped her to smile.

She had been anxious to make sure that her scooter was in the car boot before they set off, and now she was asleep after such an early start when she'd been bewildered by what was happening but excited too because they were going to be staying at the seaside and she had brought her bucket and spade on the promise of it.

Tessa had found her looking wistfully through the window at the front of the cottage a few times since the day when she'd invited Drake to lunch, but she hadn't mentioned him, except for one night when Tessa had heard her cry 'Daddy' in her sleep.

But now in the excitement of what was going on in her life he wasn't mentioned and Poppy didn't watch out for him as before.

They received a warm welcome from her aunt, who had prepared a double bedroom for the two of them, and had a lovely meal ready for the travellers at the end of a long day, and when Poppy was asleep later in the evening Sophie said gently, 'Tessa, you have the look of someone who is running away from something. Is it a man?'

'Yes,' she said. 'The love of my life left me, then he came back, and now he's leaving again. I can't cope.'

'Did he leave you for another woman?' her aunt asked.

Her smile was wry. 'No, it was his career that I had to compete with.'

'And what was that?'

'Eye surgery, ophthalmology.'

'And where is he now?'

'Debating whether to accept a position in Canada to get away from how I've been pushing him away.

I felt that if I left Glenminster he might decide to stay as he loves the place.'

'It sounds as if you care for him a lot.'

'Yes, I do. But I hurt so much when he left me that I'm afraid of it happening again, and to make matters worse Poppy is drawn to Drake like a magnet. He and I feel that she thinks he's the father that she lost in the car crash as we are told that he looks very much like him.'

'So stay here as long as you like,' Sophie said. 'Let your hurts heal by the sea and the golden sands, and, Tessa, you will know when the time is right to decide who you want to spend the rest of your life with.'

When the plane touched down in the UK Drake gave a sigh of relief. The journey had seemed to take for ever and he wanted to get back to Glenminster with all speed. He was going to ask Tessa to marry him, and if she refused he was going to keep on asking until she said yes.

The Canadian set-up had been excellent and he'd thought a few times that not so long ago he would have accepted the offer immediately, grabbed it with both hands like a precious gift. But he was no longer the same person as the one who had left Tessa with scarcely a word of goodbye and had spent the next three years wishing he hadn't.

He had bought a ring of sapphires and diamonds while he'd been in Canada, regretting all the time having told her that she was the reason why he was contemplating leaving Glenminster. It had been said in a moment of frustration. He loved the place and dreamt all the time of sharing his new house with her and Poppy.

On leaving the airport, he hired a taxi to take him straight to the cottage. It was late evening, but not so late that he would expect Tessa to have gone to bed, and he didn't want to waste a moment before being with her.

But as he turned away from paying the driver Drake saw that it was in darkness. There was a 'for sale' board on display in the front garden and his heart sank. Unconvinced, he rang the doorbell several times but got no response, and then went round to the back, only to find no signs of life there either. He thought grimly that it was going to be his turn to be left in despair and it served him right, but where to start looking for Tessa and Poppy?

Were they staying with Lizzie and Daniel? It seemed the most likely place. He checked the time. The autumn dusk was falling over the town. It wasn't fair to pressure Lizzie for Tessa's location until he was calmer, and maybe she wouldn't want to tell him where she was even then.

A better report on what had been happening while he was away might be available from Horizons tomorrow. Surely someone there would know where Tessa was, either the chairman or her secretary maybe.

He unpacked, had a shower and sat outside on the terrace of the house he had found so depressing and soulless, though it felt almost cosy after seeing Tessa's cottage dark and empty in the autumn night.

That day in his consulting room when he'd told her that if he liked the set-up in Canada he would take the job to get away from her was starkly clear in his mind and he'd never stopped regretting making the comment. Now he knew it must have pushed her too far.

CHAPTER NINE

THE NEXT MORNING he rang the chairman at home to ask if he had any knowledge of where Tessa had moved to and was told he had no idea, that the only thing he knew was that Tessa had asked him if he would allow her to skip the usual four weeks' notice.

He'd agreed reluctantly, and she'd left the same day that Drake had flown out to Canada.

'And since you're back, have you come to a decision about the job in Canada?' finished the chairman.

'I'm staying here,' Drake told him. 'I care for Horizons too much to go elsewhere.' And amidst the other man's relief he thought, and that goes for Tessa too when I find her. I care too much for her to ever want to be anywhere other than here with her. She has given up much that meant a lot to her to make me stay. But surely she knows that if she isn't with me, life will be meaningless?

After that he went to what had been Tessa's office to have a word with her secretary and saw that a temporary replacement was already sitting behind her desk, which added another ominous note to his enquiries, and when Jennifer said that she hadn't known that Tessa was leaving until the very last moment and had no idea where she was planning to move to he gave up on that one.

He could no longer ignore the fact that Lizzie and Daniel were the only people who would know where she was, and he hoped he could persuade them to tell him. He'd had an exhausting day, bringing his appointments up to date and taking the clinic that his staff had been in charge of during his absence, but like the cottage of the night before there was no answer when he rang the doorbell. Luckily, a neighbour told him they were on holiday. So using the moment to ask a question he said, 'Have Lizzie's friend and her little girl gone with them?'

'No, just the four of them—Lizzie, Daniel and the children,' he was told.

So much for that, Drake thought grimly, pointing the car back towards Horizons. As he was driving past the park his eyes widened: the bench had gone! All the benches had gone, and been replaced by new ones. Was it a sign, telling him that it really was over between the two of them? He wouldn't take no for an answer this time, he was going to find her and tell her how he felt. He should have done it ages ago, but somehow his pride and her prickliness had got in the way. This time would be different.

After his unsuccessful visit to Lizzie's house Drake rang Randolph, who told him that he didn't know where Tessa and Poppy were, but she had promised to be in touch the moment they were settled somewhere new, and that was it.

'What is it with the two of you?' he asked. 'Anyone can see that you are meant to be together.'

'Not quite everyone,' Drake told him. 'Tessa doesn't, and I'm to blame for that.'

The old man sighed. 'So work your magic on her. We both want her back here, don't we?'

'Yes, we do,' he told him flatly. 'I'm doing my best. I'll find her.'

They were having a picnic on the beach, Tessa and Poppy with Lizzie and her family, who had just arrived in the area for a short holiday further along the coast so as not to draw attention to Sophie's house guests, though it was unlikely that anyone from Glenminster would be visiting the isolated coastal village.

Her aunt had gone to a keep-fit class in the village hall, and the children were splashing in the shallows after making a sandcastle.

But the adults were having a serious talk as Lizzie reported that Drake was apparently back from Canada and hadn't been tempted by what was on offer there, from the looks of it. She had rung the hospital in the guise of a prospective patient and been told that Dr Melford was back and was taking appointments as he would be staying on the staff of Horizons for the foreseeable future.

'So Drake is back where he belongs,' Tessa said. But the relief at his decision to stay was complicated by not knowing how she was going to endure a future that was grey and empty, like that of an exile from a promised land, and as if Lizzie had read her mind she had a question to ask.

'So are you going to go back there now you're sure that he isn't leaving?'

Tessa shook her head. 'No, not unless I'm asked.' And for the rest of the afternoon she picnicked and played with the children until the light began to fade, then Lizzie and her family, who were leaving the next morning to travel further along the coast for another few days, said their goodbyes with a promise to see her again soon.

Almost a week had gone by and it was as if Tessa had disappeared off the face of the earth, Drake thought. No one at the hospital had seen her or knew of her whereabouts. There was no sign of Lizzie and Daniel having returned from their holiday, but he would try again tonight, he vowed, and if they were still away he would ask the obliging neighbour if she'd had any messages from them that might point him towards locating Tessa.

The house had the same look of being unoccupied as on the other occasion when he'd called, but this time he rang next door's bell and the same woman as before appeared.

'I've been looking out for you,' she said. 'They'll be back tomorrow. I got a card a couple of days ago. It seems they've been staying at a place called Bretton Sands.'

'Fine!' he said. 'I'll call round tomorrow night and surprise them.' And went on his way thinking that he'd heard the name before, but it didn't sound like somewhere Tessa would make a beeline for. The kind neighbour had also said the first time he'd called that Tessa and Poppy weren't with them, so he was still none the wiser.

It was in the middle of the night that he awoke wide-eyed and raised himself up off the pillows. At the time of Tessa's aunt phoning and mentioning that the women of their family were prone to thyroid issues he had recalled that she was the one that Tessa had once told him lived in a remote village miles down the coast. Was it possible that was where she'd gone?

There was no way he could set off now to find out. A full day in Theatre and on the wards was ahead of him, but he could set off the moment he'd finished, and if he found himself to be mistaken he could drive all night and get back in time for the next day's duties.

If Tessa was to be found in the place that he was heading for, someone else would have to take his appointments until he came back down to earth… And there was the ring. If he took it with him it might bring him his heart's desire, the woman he loved as his beautiful bride.

The day that followed seemed never-ending but Drake's attention to his patients was faultless. Blindness was everyone's terror and if it was possible to prevent it, he had the skills to help.

His last case of the day was a middle-aged woman brought in as an emergency with an eye injured from the cork of a bottle of home-made wine flying off explosively when she'd been trying to open it, and was in a state of shock.

This time he decided to let his second in command take over while he watched, and while he inspected the eye with the ophthalmoscope Drake listened to his comments, and then took over to see if he agreed with his findings that the blow from the cork had been prevented from doing serious damage by the eyelid's reflex action, and that the bruising and soreness would disappear in a few days.

It seemed that his findings were correct and he said, 'Well done!' and left him to give the good news to the anxious patient.

As soon as he had been home to change Drake set off to find what he now knew was real love, the kind that Tessa had wanted, the kind that was ready to give rather than take, and prayed that he'd find her at the place off the beaten track called Bretton Sands.

Poppy was asleep, sun-kissed and wind-blown after all the fun she'd had with her friends on the beach, and as Tessa moved restlessly from room to room, with Lizzie's news uppermost in her mind, her aunt said, 'There's a full moon and the tide is out. Why don't you go for a stroll along the sands while I keep an eye on Poppy?' and because of all things she needed quiet and the time to think, she followed the suggestion.

Outside it was warm, with moonlight turning the sea to silver, and when Tessa left the sand behind and came to rocks she perched herself on the first one she arrived at and sat silhouetted against the night sky.

Drake had parked the car and was moving along the short promenade, seeking someone to ask where he might find Tessa's Aunt Sophie. He wasn't sure of her surname, which would make the questioning tricky. Even trickier was the fact that there was no one to ask, the place being deserted.

As he approached the end of the paved area and was about to turn back he saw her, seated on a rock, gazing out to sea. He said her name softly, and the wind must have carried it out towards her for it could not have been loud enough for her to hear.

Tessa turned, startled, and as their glances held she exclaimed, 'Drake! How did you know where to find me? No one knows I'm here except Aunt Sophie, Lizzie and her family…and Randolph.'

He was smiling. 'I'd tried everywhere else and no one knew where you'd gone, until on a second visit to Lizzie and Daniel's place yesterday their neighbour said she'd had a card from a place called Bretton Sands, which didn't ring a bell at first. But in the middle of last night it dawned on me that your Aunt Sophie lived somewhere along that coast, and as soon as I'd finished for the day I was on my way, praying that I hadn't got it wrong.'

'Why did you change your mind about leaving Horizons?' she asked softly from her perch on the rock.

'Because I love you, and know that you love me, or you wouldn't have left Glenminster for my sake.' He produced the ring and said, 'I bought this while I was in Canada. Will you let me put it on your finger and in the near future place a wedding ring next to it? Will you marry me, Tessa?'

'Yes,' she said, finding her voice, and when she stretched her arm across the divide that separated them he put it on her finger. Looking down at the sapphires and diamonds, she said, 'It's beautiful, Drake. I shall feel truly blessed wearing it. The only way I knew to show you how much I loved you was by moving out of Glenminster to give you a reason for staying.'

'Yes, I know,' he said softly, 'but you overlooked one thing. I can't live without you.'

He opened his arms and took her hands in his and as she stepped down from the rock and was safe inside his hold he said laughingly, 'What do you think Poppy will say when she hears about this?'

'It goes without saying, she'll be delighted,' she told him, and then he kissed her and at last life was how she had longed for it to be.

CHAPTER TEN

THEY HAD TO sort out where Tessa and Poppy were going to sleep when they arrived back in Glenminster the following day. Drake had spent the night in Bretton Sands' only hotel and had been greeted rapturously by Poppy the next morning.

There was no way they could sleep at the cottage as even the bedding had gone into storage, but there was one thing that hadn't, and it had been an emotional moment when he'd seen the park bench on Aunt Sophie's patio.

'Where on earth has that come from?' he'd asked huskily.

'I was driving past when the workmen were taking them away and I bought it from them as I had to have something to remember you by,' she'd told him.

'What a lovely surprise,' he'd said, holding her close, 'and when we get back I have a surprise for you.' Turning to her aunt, who had been beaming at them in her delight at seeing her niece so happy, 'You must come and stay with us, Aunt Sophie, when we are settled. I'm indebted to you for looking after my precious ones.'

And now Drake was inside the hospital, rearranging his appointments so that he could take a couple of days off while they arranged their wedding. It was, of course, going to take place in the gardens of the hotel where he'd taken Tessa for lunch that day, and she was making up the other four-poster bed in the big house so that she and Poppy would have somewhere to sleep until the night of the wedding.

When he came in and saw what she was doing Drake said, 'For once this place won't seem so cheerless tonight, we might not even notice the creaking. Are you ready for the scenic tour?'

She smiled across at him. 'Of course. Is it the surprise that you promised?'

'It is indeed because I don't want you to get any wrong ideas that I might be expecting you to live in this place.'

He couldn't wait to take her and Poppy to see his new home, and was hoping that they would love it as much as he did. Tessa would adore the idea of planning the furnishing of its empty rooms in the short time they had before the wedding, and the large garden was just crying out for some children's swings and slides.

When they arrived at the village that Horizons had chosen for its yearly picnic that day, Tessa recalled how Drake had been quick to pass Poppy back into her care after minding her and had strolled off casually towards a house that was for sale in the last stages of construction.

She'd thought nothing of it at the time, but now here he was, turning the key in the lock, sweeping her up into his arms and carrying her over its threshold, and as she looked around her it was easy to tell why he loved the place.

It was light and airy, with clean lines, spacious rooms and fabulous views from the windows. All it needed now was to be furnished, for them to put the finishing touches to it that were their choice. As Poppy gazed around her in wonderment he said gently, 'This is where we are going to live. Do you like it?'

'Yes!' she cried. 'Can the boys come to play?'

'Of course they can. We are all going to have a lovely time living here, aren't we, Mummy?' he asked Tessa.

She nodded, and told the man who had once held her heart in careless hands, and had come back to give *his* into *her* keeping, 'Yes. We are. It will be wonderful beyond words.'

'We have such a lot of time to make up for, Tessa,' he said softly. 'Does that make you glad or sorry?'

'Just so glad,' she whispered. 'Happy that we are together at last.'

Lizzie and Poppy were the bridesmaids on the day of the wedding with Randolph giving the bride away and the chairman in the role of Drake's best man, while the vicar from the local church was to marry them.

It was autumn and the day had dawned with fruit ripening on the trees and everywhere to be seen were the bronzes and golds of the season.

The wedding wasn't a big family affair as neither bride nor groom had many relatives, their parents having been lost to them at different times over the years, but plenty of staff from Horizons who weren't on duty were there to offer their best wishes.

Tessa's white wedding dress had lily of the valley looped along the hemline and she was carrying a bouquet of the palest of pink roses. As Drake, standing beneath an archway of the same kind of flowers, watched her walking slowly towards him along the main walkway of the hotel gardens, he recognised them.

Lily of the valley and pink roses had been the flowers in the corsage he had given her that night on the river boat when she'd fastened it to her suit and asked him to dance, and the thought brought even more joy to a day that was already overflowing with it.

The marriage had taken place. The gold band of matrimony was in place next to the beautiful sapphire and diamond ring. The festivities were over and Poppy was asleep in the back of the car after all the day's excitement. But when they arrived at the house, she opened her eyes as Drake carried her upstairs and said, 'Can I sleep in my bridesmaid's dress, Daddy?'

'I don't see why not,' he said, and when he'd laid her gently against the pillows they watched her eyelids droop, and before they'd got to the door she was asleep again.

It was late afternoon and a September sun would soon be setting on their special day. As they strolled around the garden of their new home, with the park bench safely inside a flower-decked arbour, Drake said with laughing tenderness, 'How long do you think we should wait before we give Poppy a brother or a sister?'

'No time at all,' Tessa suggested laughingly, and she could tell that he thought it was a good idea.

EPILOGUE

THEY HAD MADE love with the evening sun laying strands of gold across them while Poppy slept in dreamland. It had been as good as it had always been, wild, sweet and passionate.

But instead of it being the end for them, it was only the beginning of lives that would be built on the rock of their love for each other, instead of the shifting sands of desire and a need for acclaim.

* * * * *

HIS LITTLE
CHRISTMAS MIRACLE

EMILY FORBES

PROLOGUE

'AND SO IT BEGINS,' Kristie said as she stuck her head into her cousin's bedroom.

'So what begins?' Jess asked as she tied off her plaits and pulled a red knitted hat over her white-blonde hair. She picked up her sunglasses and ski gloves and followed her cousin out of their family's five-star apartment.

'Operation Find Jess a Boyfriend,' Kristie replied.

'What! Why?'

'Because you're almost eighteen and you have no idea what you've been missing. It's time to find you a gorgeous boy. One you won't be able to resist, someone who can kiss their way into that ivory tower of yours and sweep you off your feet. We've talked about this.'

They had but Kristie was always talking about boys in one way or another and Jess mostly ignored her. Kristie was boy crazy—she fell in love every couple of weeks—but Jess was different. Most boys Jess met seemed immature and silly. She didn't see what all the fuss was about. Seventeen- and eighteen-year-old boys were just that. Boys. And Jess wanted Prince Charming. And Prince Charming would arrive in his own time. She didn't think Kristie was going to be able to conjure him up.

'I think you're forgetting something,' Jess said as they dropped their skis onto the snow and clicked their boots into the bindings, ready to tackle their first day on the slopes of the Moose River Alpine Resort.

'What's that?'

'I'd never be allowed to find my own boyfriend. Everyone I've ever dated has been a friend of the family.'

'*You're* not going to find him, I'm going to find him for you,' Kristie explained. 'And let's be honest, you'll never get laid if you only date guys your dad picks out. For one they'd be too terrified of what he'd do to them if he found out and, two, I'm sure your dad deliberately picks guys who are potentially gay.'

'That's not true,' Jess retorted even as she wondered whether maybe it was.

But surely not? Some of those boys had kissed her and while the experiences certainly hadn't been anything to rave about she'd always thought that was her fault. The boys had been cute enough, polite and polished in a typical trust-fund, private-school, country-club way, but not one of them had ever set her heart racing or made her feel breathless or excited or any of the things she'd expected to feel or wanted to feel, and she'd decided she was prepared to wait for the right one.

'Maybe I don't want a boyfriend,' she added.

'Maybe not, but you definitely need to get laid.'

'Kristie!' Jess was horrified.

'You don't know what you're missing. That's going to be my eighteenth birthday present to you. I'm going to find you a gorgeous boy and you're going to get laid.'

Kristie laughed but Jess suspected she wasn't joking. Kristie didn't see anything wrong with advertising the fact that she wanted to hook up with a boy but Jess could think of nothing more embarrassing. Despite the fact that they spent so much time together their personalities were poles apart. Less than three months separated them in age but Kristie was far savvier than Jess, not to mention more forthright and confident.

'This is your chance,' Kristie continued. 'We have one week before your parents arrive. One week with just my parents, who are nowhere near as strict. That's seven days to check out all the hot guys who'll just be hanging around the resort. You'll never get a better opportunity to hook up with someone.'

'Maybe I don't want to hook up with anyone. Promise me you won't set me up,' Jess begged. Kristie's seven-day deadline coincided with Jess's eighteenth birthday. Her parents were coming up to the resort to celebrate it with her and once they arrived Jess knew she wouldn't have a chance to be alone with a boy. Surely not even Kristie could make this happen in such a short time even if Jess *was* a willing participant. And while she wasn't averse to the *idea* of the experience, she wanted it her way. She wanted the romance. She wanted to fall in love. She wanted to be seduced and made love to. *Getting laid* did not have the same ring. Getting laid was not the experience she was after.

But then she relaxed. She might get a chance to kiss a boy but even though Kristie's parents were far more lenient than her own she still doubted that she would get an opportunity to lose her virginity.

'We won't be allowed out at night,' she said when Kristie didn't answer.

Kristie laughed again. 'Do you think you're only allowed to have sex after midnight?' she called back over her shoulder as she skied over to join the lift line for the village quad chair. 'No one is keeping tabs on us during the day. We could sneak off whenever we wanted.'

Sex during the day! Jess hadn't considered that possibility. But it still wasn't going to happen. As much as Kristie wanted her project to get off the ground, Jess couldn't imagine getting naked in the middle of the day. In her fantasy she imagined soft lighting, perfumed candles, the right music and a comfortable bed. Preferably her own bed. With clean sheets and a man who adored her. A quick fumble in the middle of the day with some random guy from the resort, no matter how cute, just wasn't the same thing.

'Today is the beginning of the rest of your life. It's time you had some fun,' Kristie told her as she joined the line. 'This place will be crawling with good-looking boys. We'll be able to take our pick.'

Getting a boy's attention was never a problem. Jess knew she was pretty enough. She was petite, only one hundred and sixty centimetres tall, and cheerleader pretty with a heart-shaped face, a chin she thought was maybe a bit too pointy, platinum-blonde hair, green eyes and porcelain skin. Finding a boy who ticked all her boxes was the tricky part. And if one did measure up then getting a chance to be alone was another challenge entirely.

Kristie's joke about Jess's ivory tower wasn't completely inaccurate. Jess did have dreams of being swept off her feet, falling madly in love and being rescued from her privileged but restricted life. It seemed to be her best chance of escaping the rules and boundaries her parents imposed on her. She couldn't imagine gaining her freedom any other way. She wasn't rebellious enough to go against their wishes without very good reason.

But she couldn't imagine falling in love at the age of seventeen and she wasn't about to leap into bed with the first cute guy who presented her with the opportunity. That didn't fit with her romantic notions at all. But although Jess could protest vigorously, it didn't mean Kristie would give up. And she proved it with her next comment.

'What about him?' she asked as they waited for the quad chair.

Jess looked at the other skiers around them. It was just after nine in the morning. The girls had risen early, keen to enjoy their first morning on the slopes, but everyone else in the line was ten years younger or twenty years older than them. They were surrounded by families with young children. All the other teenagers were still in bed, and Jess couldn't work out who Kristie was talking about.

Her cousin nudged her in the side. 'There.' She used her ski pole to point to the front of the line and Jess realised she meant the towies.

Two young men, who she guessed to be a year or two older than she was, worked the lift together. They both wore the uniform of the mountain resort, bright blue ski jackets with a band of fluorescent yellow around the upper arm and matching blue pants with another yellow band around the bottom of the legs. A row of white, snow-covered mountain peaks was stitched across the left chest of the jacket with 'Moose River Alpine Resort' emblazoned beneath. Their heads were uncovered and Jess could see one tall, fair-headed boy and another slightly shorter one with dark hair.

They had music pumping out of the stereo system at the base of the lift. It blasted the mountain, drowning out all other noise, including the engine of the chairlift. Jess watched as the boys danced to the beat as they lifted the little kids onto the chair and chatted and flirted with the mothers.

The fair one drew her attention. He moved easily, in time with the music, relaxed, unselfconscious and comfortable in his skin. Jess couldn't ever imagine dancing in front of strangers in broad daylight. She wasn't comfortable in a crowd. But there was something erotic about watching someone dance from a distance. She wouldn't normally stare but she was emboldened by her anonymity. He didn't know her and from behind the security of her dark sunglasses she could watch unobserved. Like a voyeur.

Kristie shuffled forward in the line and Jess followed but she couldn't tear her eyes away from the dancing towie. Watching the way his hips moved, she felt a stirring in her belly that she recognised as attraction, lust, desire. Watching him move, she could imagine how it would feel to dance with him, how it would feel to be held against him as his hips moved in time with hers. She found her hips swaying to the beat of the music, swaying in response to this stranger.

The song changed, snapping her out of her reverie, and she watched as he mimicked some rap moves that had the kids in front of her in stitches. The dark-haired one was chatting to a mother while the fair one lifted the woman's child onto the seat before giving him a high five. He lifted his head as he laughed at something the child had said and suddenly he was looking straight at Jess.

Jess's pulse throbbed and her stomach ached with a primal, lustful reaction as his eyes connected with hers. They were the most brilliant blue. A current tore through her body, sending a shock deep inside her all the way to her bones. She was aware of Kristie moving into position for the lift but she was riveted to the spot, her skis frozen to the snow. She was transfixed by eyes the colour of forget-me-nots.

'Careful. Keep moving unless you want to get collected by the chair.' It took Jess a second or two to realise he was talking to her. He had an Australian accent and in her bewildered and confused state it took her a moment to decipher it and make sense of his words. While she was translating his speech in her head he reached out and put one hand on her backside and pushed her forward until she was standing on the mat, ready to be swept up by the chairlift. Jess could swear she could feel the heat of his hand through the padding of her ski suit. She was still standing in place, staring at him, as the chair swung behind her and scooped her up, knocking into the back of her knees and forcing her to sit down with a thump.

'Have a good one.' He winked at her as she plopped into the seat and Jess felt herself blush but she kept eye contact. She couldn't seem to look away. *Let me off*, she wanted to shout but when she opened her mouth nothing came out. Her eyesight worked but she appeared to have lost control of all her other senses. Including movement. She was enchanted, spellbound by a boy with eyes of blue.

'They were cute,' Kristie said as the lift carried them up the mountain and Jess forced herself to turn her head and look away. Maybe that would break the spell.

'I guess,' she said. She felt like she had a mouthful of marbles as she tried to feign indifference. Kristie would have a field day if she knew what Jess had really been thinking.

'What do you think?' Kristie asked. 'Worth a second look?'

The girls had the quad chair to themselves but that didn't mean Jess wanted to have this discussion. She knew if she agreed it would only serve to encourage Kristie's foolish plan.

'You're not serious!' she cried. 'I don't think they're my type.' She suspected she'd have nothing in common with them. She knew she wouldn't be cool enough.

'Why not?'

'You know the reputation those guys have.' The towies—usually an assortment of college students taking a gap year, locals and backpackers—had a reputation as ski-hard-and-party-harder people.

But Kristie was not about to be deterred. 'So…' she shrugged '…that all adds to the excitement and the challenge.'

'I'm not going to hook up with a total stranger,' Jess said. Obviously the lessons of her upbringing were more deeply ingrained in her than she'd realised. Her movements were carefully orchestrated, her whereabouts were always mapped out, and she'd never really had the opportunity to mingle with strangers. Prince Charming was going to have his work cut out for him.

'I know your parents want to know where you are every minute of the day but they're not here,' Kristie replied, 'and despite what they tell you, not every spontaneous situation is dangerous and not every stranger is a psychopath. I'm not saying you have to marry the guy, just have some fun.'

'He looked too old for me,' Jess protested.

'You're always complaining about how immature boys our age are. Maybe someone a bit older would suit you better. Shall we head back down? Take another look?'

The quad chair took them to the basin where all the other lifts operated from. No one skied straight back down to the bottom of this lift unless they'd forgotten something and needed to return to the village. Jess didn't want to be that overtly interested. She needed time to think. 'No. I want to ski,' she said as they were deposited in the basin.

The slopes were quiet at this hour of the day and it wasn't long before Kristie decided she was overheating from all the exercise and needed to discard some layers. Jess suspected it was all an act designed to invent a reason to return to their apartment and hence to the quad chair, but she was prepared to give in. She knew she didn't have much choice. She could have elected to stay up on the mountain but they had a rule that no one skied alone and she had to admit she was just a tiny bit curious to have another look at the boy with the forget-me-not-blue eyes. After all, there was no harm in looking.

But by the time they had changed their outfits and returned to the quad chair there were two different towies on duty. Disappointment surged through Jess. It was silly to feel that way about a random stranger but there had been something hypnotic about him. Something captivating.

They rode the lift back to the basin where they waited in line for another quad chair to take them to the top of the ski run. As they neared the front the two original towies appeared, each with a snowboard strapped to one foot as they slipped into the singles row and skated to the front of the line.

'G'day. Mind if we join you?'

Jess and Kristie had no time to reply before the boys had slotted in beside them and Jess found herself sandwiched between her cousin and the boy with the tousled, blond hair and amazing blue eyes. He shifted slightly on the seat, turning a little to face her, and the movement pushed his thigh firmly against hers.

'Have you had a good morning?' he asked her. 'You were up at sparrow's.'

'Pardon?' Jess frowned. His voice was deep and his accent was super-sexy but the combination of his stunning eyes and his Aussie drawl made it difficult to decipher his words. Or maybe it was just the fact that she was sitting thigh to thigh with a cute boy who was messing with her head. Either way, she couldn't think straight and she could make no sense of what he was saying.

'Sparrow's fart,' he said with a grin before he elaborated. 'It means you were up really early.'

His blue eyes sparkled as he smiled at her but this time it was the twin dimples in his cheeks that set Jess's heart racing. His smile was infectious and she couldn't help but return it as she said, 'You remember us?' She was surprised and flattered. The boys would have seen hundreds of people already today.

'Of course. Don't tell me you don't remember me?' He put both hands over his heart and looked so dramatically wounded that Jess laughed. She'd have to watch out—he was cute and charming with more than a hint of mischief about him.

And, of course, she remembered him. She doubted she'd ever forget him, but she knew his type and she wasn't about to stroke his ego by telling him that his eyes were the perfect colour—unforgettable, just like him. She knew all the towies were cut from the same cloth, young men who would spend the winter working in the resort and then spend their time off skiing and drinking and chasing girls. They would flirt with dozens of girls in one day, trying their luck, until eventually their persistence would pay off and they'd have a date for the night and, no matter how cute he was, she didn't want to be just another girl in the long line that would fall at his feet.

'Well, just so you don't forget us again, I'm Lucas and that's Sam,' he said, nodding towards his mate, who was sitting on the other side of Kristie.

'I didn't say I'd forgotten you,' Jess admitted. 'I remember your accent.' But she wasn't prepared to admit she remembered his dancing or had been unable to forget his cornflower-blue eyes. 'You're Australian?'

'Yes, and, before you ask, I don't have a pet kangaroo.'

'I wasn't going to ask that.'

'Really?'

'I might not have been to Australia but I know a bit about it. I'm not completely ignorant.'

'Sorry, I didn't mean to imply that,' Lucas backtracked.

'It's okay.' She'd stopped getting offended every time people treated her like a cheerleader but while she was one she was also a science major. 'I know most of you don't have pet kangaroos and I know you eat that horrible black spread on your toast and live alongside loads of poisonous snakes, spiders and man-eating sharks. Actually...' she smiled '...I'm not surprised you left.'

Lucas laughed. 'I'm not here permanently. I'm only here for the winter. It's summer back home. I'll stay until the end of February when uni starts again.'

'So where is the best place to party in the village?' Kristie interrupted. 'What's popular this season?'

Kristie knew the village as well as anyone—she didn't need advice—but Jess knew it was just her cousin's way of flirting. To Kristie that came as naturally as breathing.

'How old are you?' Sam replied.

'Nineteen,' she fibbed. She was only three months older than Jess and had only recently turned eighteen but nineteen was the legal drinking age.

'The T-Bar is always good,' Sam told them, mentioning one of the après-ski bars that had been around for ever but was always popular.

'But tonight we're having a few mates around,' Lucas added. 'We're sharing digs with a couple of Kiwis and Friday nights are party nights. You're welcome to join us.'

'Thanks, that sounds like fun,' Kristie replied, making it sound as though they'd be there when Jess knew they wouldn't. Which was a pity. It did sound like it might be fun but there was no way they'd be allowed out with strangers, with boys who hadn't been vetted and approved. Although Kristie's parents weren't as strict as hers, Jess's aunt and uncle knew the rules Jess had to live by and she didn't think they'd bend them that far.

'We're in the Moose River staff apartments. You know the ones? On Slalom Street. Apartment fifteen.'

'We know where they are.'

They were almost at the top of the ski run now and Jess felt a surge of disappointment that the ride was coming to an end. The boys were going snowboarding and Jess assumed they'd be heading to the half-pipe or the more rugged terrain on the other side of the resort.

They wouldn't be skiing the same part of the mountain as she and Kristie.

She pretended to look out at the ski runs when she was actually looking at Lucas from behind the safety of her sunglasses. She wanted to commit his face to memory. He was cute and friendly but she doubted she'd ever see him again. He wasn't her Prince Charming.

CHAPTER ONE

JESS ZIPPED UP her ski jacket as she stood in the twilight. She was back.

Back in the place where her life had changed for ever.

Back in Moose River.

She remembered standing not far from this exact spot while Kristie had told her that day marked the beginning of the rest of her life, but she hadn't expected her cousin's words to be quite so prophetic. That had been the day she'd met Lucas and her life had very definitely changed. All because of a boy.

Jess shoved her hands into her pockets and stood still as she took in her surroundings. The mountain village was still very familiar but it was like an echo of a memory from a lifetime ago. A very different lifetime from the one she was living now. She took a deep breath as she tried to quell her nerves.

When she had seen the advertisement for the position of clinic nurse at the Moose River Medical Centre it had seemed like a sign and she'd wondered why she hadn't thought of it sooner. It had seemed like the perfect opportunity to start living the life she wanted but that didn't stop the butterflies in her stomach.

It'll be fine, she told herself as she tried to get the butterflies to settle, *once we adjust*.

In the dark of the evening the mountain resort looked exactly like it always had. Like a fairy-tale village. The streets had been cleared of the early season snow and it lay piled in small drifts by the footpaths. Light dotted the hillside, glowing yellow as it spilled from the windows of the hotels and lodges. She could smell wood smoke and pine needles. The fragrance of winter. Of Christmas. Of Lucas.

She'd have to get over that. She couldn't afford to remember him every few minutes now that she was back here. That wasn't what this move was about.

In a childhood marked by tragedy and, at times, fear and loneliness, Moose River had been one of the two places where she'd been truly happy, the only place in the end, and the only place where she'd been free. She had returned now, hoping to rediscover that feeling again. And while she couldn't deny that Moose River was also full of bittersweet memories, she hoped it could still weave its magic for her.

She could hear the bus wheezing and shuddering behind her, complaining as the warmth from its air-conditioning escaped into the cold mountain air. It was chilly but at least it wasn't raining. She was so sick of rain. While Vancouver winters were generally milder than in other Canadian cities there was a trade-off and that was rain. While she was glad she didn't have to shovel snow out of her driveway every morning, she was tired of the wet.

Jess could hear laughter and music. The sound floated across to the car park from the buildings around her, filling the still night air. She could hear the drone of the snow-making machines on the mountain and she could see the lights of the graders as they went about their night-time business, grooming the trails. She glanced around her, looking to see what had changed and what had stayed the same in the seven years since she had last been here. The iconic five-star Moose River Hotel still had pride of place on the hill overlooking the village but there were several new buildings as well, including a stunning new hotel that stood at the opposite end of Main Street from the bus depot.

The new hotel was perched on the eastern edge of the plaza where Main Street came to an end at the ice-skating rink. There had been a building there before, smaller and older. Jess couldn't recall exactly what it had been but this modern replacement looked perfect. The hotel was too far away for her to be able to read the sign, although she could see the tiny figures of skaters gliding around the rink, twirling under the lights as snow began to fall.

She lifted her face to the sky. Snowflakes fell on her cheeks and eyelashes, melting as soon as they touched the warmth of her skin. She stuck out her tongue, just like she'd done as a child, and caught the flakes, feeling them immediately turn to water.

But she wasn't a child any more. She was twenty-four years old, almost twenty-five. Old enough to have learned that life was not a fairy tale. She didn't want a fairy-tale ending; she didn't believe in those any more but surely it wasn't too late to find happiness? She refused to believe that wasn't possible.

Seven years ago she'd had the world at her feet. She'd been young and full of expectation, anticipation and excitement. Anything had seemed possible in that winter.

In the winter that she'd met Lucas. In the winter that she'd fallen in love.

Sometimes it seemed like yesterday. At other times a lifetime ago. On occasions it even seemed like it was someone else's story but she knew it was hers. She was reminded of that every day. But as hard as it had been she wasn't sure that she would do anything differently if she had her time again.

She could still remember the first moment she had laid eyes on him. It was less than two hundred metres from where she now stood. She'd been seventeen years old, young and pretty, shy but with the self-assurance that a privileged lifestyle gave to teenagers. In her mind her future had already been mapped out—surely it would be one of happiness, wealth, prosperity and pleasure. That was what she and her friends, all of whom came from wealthy families, had been used to and they'd had no reason to think things would change. She'd been so naive.

At seventeen she'd had no clue about real life. She'd been happy with her dreams. Her biggest problem had been having parents who'd loved her and wanted to protect her from the world, and her biggest dream had been to experience the world she hadn't been allowed to taste.

To her, Lucas had represented freedom. He'd been her chance to experience the world but the freedom she'd tasted had been short-lived. And the real world was a lot tougher than she'd anticipated. Reality had slapped her in the face big time and once she'd been out in that world she'd found there had been no turning back.

Reality was a bitch and it had certainly killed her

naivety. She'd grown up awfully quickly and her clueless teenage years were a long way behind her now.

She was still standing in the car park, mentally reminiscing about that winter, when an SUV pulled up in front of her at a right angle to the bus. The driver put down his window. 'Jess? Jess Johnson?' he said.

Jess shook her head, clearing the cobwebs from her mind. 'Sorry,' the driver said, misinterpreting the shake of her head. 'I'm looking for a Jess Johnson.'

'That's me.'

The driver climbed out of the car. 'I'm Cameron Baker,' he introduced himself as he shook Jess's hand. Cameron and his wife, Ellen, owned the Moose River Medical Centre. He was Jess's new boss. 'Let's get your gear loaded up. Is this everything?'

Jess looked down at her feet. The bus driver had unloaded her belongings. Three suitcases and half a dozen boxes were piled beside her. All the necessities for two lives.

'That's it,' she replied. 'I'll just get Lily.'

She climbed back into the bus to rouse her sleeping daughter.

She scooped Lily up and carried her from the bus. She was keen to introduce her to Moose River but that would have to wait until tomorrow.

This was Lily's first visit to the mountain resort. Jess had avoided bringing Lily here before now. She'd made countless excuses, telling herself Lily was too young to appreciate it, but she knew that was a lie. Jess had been skiing since she was four and Lily was now six and there were plenty of other activities here to keep young children entertained for days. Lack of money had been another excuse and even though Jess hadn't been able to afford to bring her that was still only part of the truth. The reality was that Jess hadn't wanted to return. She hadn't wanted to face the past. She'd thought the memories might be too painful. But it was time to give Lily a sense of where she had come from. It was time to come back.

Cameron loaded their bags and Jess climbed into the back of the vehicle, cradling a sleepy Lily in her arms as he drove them the short distance to their accommodation. The job came with a furnished apartment, which had been one of a number of things that had attracted Jess to the position, but she hadn't thought to enquire about any specifics, she'd just been relieved to know it had been organised for her and she was stunned when Cameron pulled to a stop in front of the Moose River staff apartments.

She picked Lily up again—fortunately Lily was small for her age and Jess could still manage to carry her—and followed Cameron inside the building, counting off the apartment numbers as they walked down the corridor. Thirteen, fourteen, fifteen. Cameron's steps started to slow and Jess held her breath. It couldn't be. Not the same apartment.

'This is you. Number sixteen.'

She let out her breath as Cameron parked the luggage trolley, loaded with boxes and bags, and unlocked the door. There'd been a brief moment when she'd thought she might be staying in apartment fifteen but she might just be able to handle being one apartment away from her past.

She carried Lily inside and put her on the bed.

'I'm sorry, they were supposed to split the bed and

make up two singles,' Cameron apologised when he saw the bedding configuration.

'It doesn't matter,' Jess replied. 'I'll fix it tomorrow.' She couldn't be bothered now. She had enough to think about without fussing about the bed. She and Lily could manage for the night.

'Ellen has left some basic supplies for you in the fridge. She promised me it would be enough to get you through breakfast in the morning,' Cameron said, as he brought in the rest of Jess's luggage.

'That's great, thank you.'

'I'll let you get settled, then, and we'll see you at the clinic at eleven tomorrow to introduce you to everyone and give you an orientation.'

Jess nodded but she was having trouble focusing. She was restless. There were so many memories. Too many. More than she'd expected. Thank goodness Lily was dozing as that gave her a chance to shuffle through the thoughts that were crowding her brain. She paced around the apartment once Cameron had gone but it was tiny and in no more than a few steps she'd covered the kitchen and the dining area and the lounge. All that was left was the bedroom and a combined bathroom-laundry. There wasn't much to see and even less to do as she didn't want to disturb Lily by beginning to unpack.

She crossed the living room, opened the balcony doors and stepped outside. Night had fallen but a full moon hung low in the sky and moonlight reflected off the snow and lit up the village as if it was broad daylight. To her left was the balcony of unit fifteen, the two-bedroom apartment that Lucas had stayed in seven years ago. The apartment where she and Kristie had gone on the night of the party was only metres away.

She could see the exact spot where she'd been standing when Lucas had first kissed her.

He had been her first love. He had been her Prince Charming. She'd fallen hard and fast but when he'd kissed her that first time and she'd given him her heart she hadn't known there would be no turning back.

Now, at twenty-four, she didn't believe in Prince Charming any more.

CHAPTER TWO

'MUMMY?'

The sound of Lily's voice startled her. Jess was still on the balcony, standing with her fingers pressed against her lips as she recalled the first kiss she and Lucas had shared. She shivered as she realised she was freezing. She had no idea how long she'd been standing out there in the cold.

She didn't have time for reminiscing. She had responsibilities.

Lily had wandered out of the bedroom and Jess could see her standing in the living room, looking around at the unfamiliar surroundings. She was sucking on her thumb and had her favourite toy, a soft, grey koala, tucked under one arm. With white-blonde hair and a heart-shaped face she was the spitting image of Jess, just as Jess was the image of her own mother.

'I'm hungry,' Lily said, as Jess came in from the balcony and closed the doors and curtains behind her.

'You are?' She was surprised. Lily wasn't often hungry. She was a fussy eater and didn't have a good appetite and Jess often struggled to find food that appealed to her daughter, although fortunately she would eat her vegetables.

'Let's see what we've got.' Jess opened the fridge, hoping Cameron had been right when he'd said that his wife had left some basics for them. She could see bread, milk, eggs, cheese and jam.

'How about toasted cheese sandwiches for dinner?' she said. 'Or eggs and soldier toast?'

'Eggs and soldier toast.'

Jess put the eggs on to boil and then found Lily's pyjamas. By the time she was changed the eggs were done. Lily managed to finish the eggs and one soldier. Jess slathered the remaining soldier toasts with jam and polished them off herself.

Lily was fast asleep within minutes of climbing back into bed, but even though Jess was exhausted she found she couldn't get comfortable. Lily, who was a restless sleeper at the best of times, was tossing and turning in the bed beside her and disturbing her even further. She would have to split the bed apart tomorrow; she couldn't stand another night like this.

She got up and put the kettle on, hoping for the hundredth time that she'd made the right decision in moving to Moose River.

It seemed surreal to think that returning to the place where things had started to go wrong had been the best solution, but she'd felt she hadn't had much choice. She'd needed a job with regular hours and this one had the added bonus of accommodation, which meant she could be home with Lily before and after school and she wouldn't need to leave Lily with a childminder or take extra shifts to cover the rent or babysitting expenses. She also hoped that living in Moose River would give Lily the opportunity to have the childhood she herself had missed out on. A childhood free from worry, a child-hood of fun and experiences.

She carried her decaf coffee over to the balcony doors. She drew back the curtains and rested her head on the glass as she gazed out at the moonlit night and let the memories flood back. Of course they were all about Lucas. She couldn't seem to keep thoughts of him out of her head. She hadn't expected Moose River to stir her memory quite so much.

What would he be looking at right now? Where would he be?

Probably living at Bondi Beach, running a chain of organic cafés with his gorgeous bikini-model wife, she thought. They would have three blue-eyed children and together his family would look like an advertisement for the wonders of fresh air and exercise and healthy living.

But maybe life hadn't been so kind to him. Why should it have been? Why should he be glowing with health and happiness?

Perhaps he was working in a hotel restaurant in the Swiss Alps and had grown fat from over-indulging in cheese and chocolate. He could be overweight with a receding hairline. Would that make her feel better?

What was it she wanted to feel better about? she wondered. It didn't matter where Lucas was or what he was doing. That was history. She'd woken up to herself in the intervening years. Woken up to real life. And he wasn't part of that life. He was fantasy, not reality. Not her reality anyway.

Jess shook herself. She needed to get a grip. Her situation was entirely of her own choosing and she wouldn't change it for anything, not if it meant losing Lily.

She sighed as she finished her coffee. Her father had

been right. Lucas hadn't been her Prince Charming and he wasn't ever coming to rescue her. Wherever he had ended up, she imagined it was far from here.

Their first fortnight in Moose River went smoothly. Lily settled in well at her new school. She was thriving and Jess was thrilled. She loved the after-school ski lessons and Jess was looking forward to getting out on the slopes with her this weekend and seeing how much she'd improved in just ten days. It was amazing how quickly children picked up the basics.

She wondered about Lily's fearless attitude. If Lily wanted something she went after it, so different from Jess's reticence. Was that nature or nurture?

Jess had vowed to give Lily freedom—freedom to make her own friends and experience a childhood where she was free to test the boundaries without constant supervision or rules. A childhood without the constant underlying sense that things could, would and did go wrong and where everything had to be micromanaged.

Moose River was, so far, proving to be the perfect place for Lily to have a relaxed childhood and Jess was beginning to feel like she'd made a good decision. Lily had made friends quickly and her new best friend was Annabel, whose parents owned the patisserie next to their apartment building. By the second week the girls had a routine where Lily would go home with Annabel after ski school and have a hot chocolate at the bakery while they waited for Jess to finish work. Jess had been nervous about this at first but she'd reminded herself that this was a benefit of moving to a small community. She'd wanted that sense of belonging. That sense that people would look out for each other. She wanted somewhere where she and Lily would fit in.

Initially she'd felt like they were taking advantage of Annabel's mother but Fleur was adamant that it was no bother. Annabel had two older siblings and Fleur insisted that having Lily around was making life easier for everyone as Annabel was too busy to annoy the others. Jess hated asking for favours, she preferred to feel she could manage by herself even if she knew that wasn't always the case, but she was grateful for Fleur's assistance.

Her new job as a clinic nurse was going just as smoothly as Lily's transition. Her role was easy. She helped with splints, dressings, immunisations and did general health checks—cholesterol, blood pressure and the like. It was routine nursing, nothing challenging, but that suited her. It was low stress and by the end of the two weeks she was feeling confident that coming here had been the right decision for her and Lily.

Not having to work weekends or take extra shifts to cover rent or child-care costs was paying dividends. She could be home with Lily in time for dinner and spend full, uninterrupted days with her over the weekends. It was heaven. Jess adored her daughter and she'd dreamt of being able to spend quality time with her. Just the two of them. It was something she hadn't experienced much in her own childhood and she was determined that Lily would have that quality time with her. After all, they only had each other.

She checked her watch as she tidied her clinic room and got ready to go home. Kristie was coming up for the weekend—in fact, she should already be here. She was changing the sheet on the examination bed when Donna, the practice manager, burst into the room.

'Jess, do you think you could possibly work a little later today? We've had a call from the new hotel, one of their guests is almost thirty-six weeks pregnant and she's having contractions. It might just be Braxton-Hicks but they'd like someone to take a look and all the doctors are busy. Do you think you could go?'

'Let me make some arrangements for Lily and then I'll get over there,' Jess said when Donna finally paused for breath. Jess was happy to go, provided she could sort Lily out. She rang Kristie as she swapped her shoes for boots and explained the situation as she grabbed her coat and the medical bag that Donna had given to her.

Thank God Kristie was in town, she thought as she rang Fleur to tell her of the change in plans. Of course, Fleur then offered to help too but Jess didn't want to push the friendship at this early stage. She explained that Kristie would collect Lily and take her home. She could concentrate on the emergency now. It was always a balancing act, juggling parenting responsibilities with her work, but it seemed she might have the support network here that she'd lacked anywhere else.

Jess hurried the few blocks to Main Street. The five-star, boutique Moose River Crystal Lodge, where her patient was a guest, was the new hotel on the Plaza, the one she'd noticed on the night they'd arrived. She and Lily had walked past it several times since. It was hard to miss. It wasn't huge or ostentatious but it was in a fabulous position, and she'd heard it was beautifully appointed inside.

In the late-afternoon light, the setting sun cast a glow onto the facade of the lodge, making its marble facade shine a pale silver. On the southern side of the main entrance was an elevated outdoor seating area, which would be the perfect spot for an afternoon drink on a sunny day; you could watch the activities in the plaza from the perfect vantage point.

A wide footpath connected the lodge to the plaza and in front of the hotel stood a very placid horse who was hitched to a smart red wooden sleigh. Lily had begged to go for a ride when they had walked past earlier in the week but Jess had fibbed and told her it was for hotel guests only because she doubted she could afford the treat. She had meant to find out how much it cost, thinking maybe it could be a Christmas surprise for Lily, but she had forgotten all about it until now.

She walked past the horse and sleigh and tried to ignore the feeling of guilt that was so familiar to her as a single, working mother, struggling to make ends meet, but walking into the lobby just reinforced how much her life had changed from one of privilege to one much harder but she reminded herself it was of her own choosing.

The lobby was beautifully decorated in dark wood. Soft, caramel-hued leather couches were grouped around rich Persian rugs and enormous crystal chandeliers hung from the timber ceiling. It looked expensive and luxurious but welcoming. Although it was still four weeks until Christmas, festive red, green and silver decorations adorned the room and a wood fire warmed the restaurant where wide glass doors could open out onto the outside terrace. Jess tried not to gawk as she crossed the parquet floor. She'd seen plenty of fancy hotels but this one had a warmth and a charm about it that was rare. Maybe because it was small, but it felt more like an exclusive private ski lodge than a hotel.

She shrugged out of her coat as she approached the reception desk.

'I'm Jess Johnson, from the Moose River Medical Centre. Someone called about a woman in labour?'

The young girl behind the desk nodded. 'Yes, Mrs Bertillon. She's in room three zero five on the third floor. I'll just call the hotel manager to take you up.'

'It's okay, I'll find it.' Jess could see the elevators tucked into a short hallway alongside the desk. The hotel was small so she'd have no trouble finding the room. She didn't want to waste time waiting.

She stabbed at the button for the elevator. The doors slid open and she stepped inside.

Jess found room 305 and knocked on the door. It swung open under her hand. There was a bathroom to her left with a wardrobe on the right, forming a short passage. Jess could see a small sofa positioned in front of a large picture window but that was it.

She called out a greeting. 'Mrs Bertillon?'

'Come in.' The faceless voice sounded strong and Jess relaxed. That didn't sound like a woman in labour.

A woman appeared at the end of the passage. She was a hotel employee judging by her uniform. 'She's through here.' The same voice. This wasn't Mrs. Bertillon. 'I'm Margaret. I was keeping an eye on Aimee until you got here,' she explained, and Jess could see the relief on her face. She'd obviously been waiting nervously for reinforcements. 'I'll wait outside now but you can call for me if there's anything you need,' she said, hurriedly abdicating responsibility.

Jess introduced herself to Aimee and got her medical

history as she washed her hands and then wrapped the blood-pressure cuff around her patient's left arm. This was her first pregnancy, Aimee told her, and she'd had no complications. Her blood pressure had been fine, no gestational diabetes, no heart problems. 'I've had some back pain today and now these contractions but otherwise I've been fine.'

'Sharp pain?' asked Jess.

'No. Dull,' Aimee explained, 'more like backache, I suppose. Ow…'

'Is that a contraction now?'

Aimee nodded and Jess looked at her watch, timing the contraction. She could see the contraction ripple across the woman's abdomen as the muscles tightened. This wasn't Braxton-Hicks.

'Your waters haven't broken?' she asked, and Aimee shook her head in reply.

Once the contraction had passed she checked the baby's size and position, pleased to note the baby wasn't breech. But she wasn't so pleased when she discovered that Aimee's cervix was already seven centimetres dilated. Aimee was in labour and there was nothing she could do to stop it.

'Where is your husband?' Jess asked. She'd noticed a wedding ring on Aimee's finger but wondered where Mr Bertillon was.

'He's out skiing,' Aimee replied. 'Why?'

Jess smiled. 'I thought he might like to be here to meet your baby.'

'It's coming now?'

'Mmm-hmm.' Jess nodded. 'You're about to become parents.'

'Oh, my God.'

'Does your husband have a mobile phone with him? Would you like me to call him for you?' Jess asked.

'No. I can do it. I think.' Aimee put a hand on her distended belly as another contraction subsided. 'If I hurry. Jean-Paul will be surprised. This was supposed to be our last holiday before the baby arrived and it wasn't supposed to end like this.' She gave a wry smile. 'Maybe we've been having too much sex. Is it true that can bring on labour?'

Jess couldn't remember the last time she'd had too much sex. She could barely remember the last time she'd had *any* sex. She nodded. 'But not usually at this stage. I think your baby has just decided to join the party.' She concentrated on Aimee. Thinking about sex always made her think about Lucas, especially since she was in Moose River, but now wasn't the time for daydreaming. Aimee needed all her attention.

Aimee's cell phone was beside the bed. Jess passed it to her and then picked up the hotel phone and asked for an ambulance to be sent. Aimee needed to go to the nearest hospital that had premature birthing facilities, which meant leaving Moose River.

Another contraction gripped Aimee and Jess waited as she panted and puffed her way through it. Jess checked her watch. The contractions were two minutes apart. How long would the ambulance take? She had no idea.

Once that contraction had passed and Jess saw Aimee press the buttons on her phone to call her husband she went to gather towels from the bathroom. She stuck her head out into the corridor and asked Margaret to fetch more towels from Housekeeping.

'How did it go? Did you reach Jean-Paul?' Jess asked when she returned to Aimee's side.

'No. It goes straight to his message service.' Aimee gasped and grabbed her belly as another contraction ripped through her. 'He's gone skiing with a snowcat group so I can only assume he's out in the wilderness and out of range.'

Margaret came into the room with an armful of towels and Jess asked if there was any way of getting a message to Jean-Paul.

'Yes, of course,' Margaret replied. 'Will you be all right on your own with Aimee while I organise that?'

Jess nodded. Margaret wasn't going to be of any further use. It was the ambos Jess wanted to see. Jess tucked several of the towels underneath Aimee. She knew it was probably a futile exercise but if Aimee's waters broke she was hoping to limit the damage to the hotel bedding. Another contraction gripped Aimee and this one was accompanied by a gush of fluid. Fortunately it wasn't a big flood and Jess suspected that meant the baby's head was well down into Aimee's pelvis.

Jess used the time between contractions to check Aimee's cervix. Eight centimetres dilated. This was really happening. If the ambos didn't hurry she would have to deliver the baby. What would she need?

She'd need to keep the baby warm. She put a couple of the clean towels back on the heated towel rail in the bathroom.

Aimee's cries were getting louder and she had a sheen of perspiration across her forehead. 'I want to push,' she called out.

'Hang on,' Jess cautioned, and she checked progress again.

Oh no. The baby's head was crowning already.

Jess felt for the cord. It felt loose and she just hoped it wasn't around the baby's neck.

'Okay, Aimee. This is it. You can push with the next contraction.'

Jess saw the contraction ripple across Aimee's skin. 'Okay, bend your knees and push!'

The baby's head appeared and Jess was able to turn the baby to deliver one shoulder with the next contraction and the baby slid into her hands. 'It's a girl,' she told Aimee. Jess rubbed the baby's back, checking to make sure her little chest rose and fell with a breath and listening for her first cry before she placed her on Aimee's chest and fetched a warm towel. She took one-minute Apgar readings and clamped the cord just as the ambos arrived. Relief flooded through her. She'd done the easy bit, now they could finish off.

'Congratulations, Aimee.'

'Thank you.' Aimee's smile was gentle but she barely lifted her eyes from her baby. She was oblivious to the work the ambos were doing. Nothing could distract her from the miracle of new life.

Jess could remember that feeling, that vague, blissful state of euphoria. She tidied her things, packing them into her bag as she thought about Lily's birth. Like Aimee, she'd done it without the baby's father there.

She hadn't wanted to do it alone but she hadn't had a lot of choice. She hadn't expected their relationship to end so suddenly. She hadn't expected a lot of things.

By the time she'd discovered she was pregnant the ski fields had closed for the season and Lily's father had been long gone, and despite her best efforts she hadn't been able to find him. So she'd done it alone and she'd done her best.

She snapped her medical bag closed with shaky hands. Now that the drama was over her body shook with the adrenalin that coursed through her system. She stripped the bed as the ambos transferred Aimee and her baby onto a stretcher and wheeled them out the door.

She could hear voices in the hallway and assumed that Jean-Paul had been located. That was quick. She could hear an Australian accent too. That was odd. Jean-Paul didn't sound like an Australian name. She listened more carefully.

A male voice, an Australian accent. It sounded a lot like Lucas.

Her stomach flipped and her heart began to race. She was being ridiculous. It had been seven years since she'd heard his voice, as if she'd remember exactly how he sounded. She only imagined it was him because he'd been in her thoughts.

It wouldn't be him. It couldn't be him.

But she couldn't resist taking a look.

She picked up the medical bag and stepped out into the hallway. The ambos had halted the stretcher and a man stood with his back to her, talking to Aimee.

'We've got a message to your husband,' he was saying. 'We'll get him back as quickly as possible and I'll make sure he gets brought to the hospital.'

The man was tall with broad shoulders and tousled blond hair. Jess could see narrow hips and long, lean legs. His voice was deep with a sexy Aussie drawl. Her heart beat quickened, pumping the blood around her body, leaving her feeling light-headed and faint.

It was him. It was most definitely him.

She steadied herself with one hand against the wall as she prayed that her knees wouldn't buckle.

It was Lucas.

She didn't need to see his face. She knew it and her body knew it. Every one of her cells was straining towards him. Seven years may have passed but her body hadn't forgotten him and neither had she. She recognised the length of his legs, the shape of his backside, the sound of his voice.

The ambos were pushing the stretcher towards the elevator by the time she found her voice.

'Lucas?'

CHAPTER THREE

JESS FELT AS if the ground was tipping beneath her feet. She felt as if at any moment she might slide to the floor. She could see the scene playing out in front of her, almost as though she was a spectator watching from the sidelines. She could see herself wobbling in the foreground and she could see Lucas standing close enough to touch. If she could just reach out a hand she could feel him. See if he really was real. But she couldn't move. Life seemed to be going on around her as she watched, too overcome to react.

He turned towards her at the sound of his name.

'JJ?'

She hadn't been called JJ in years. It had been his nickname for her and no one else had ever used it.

She couldn't believe he was standing in front of her. Lucas, undeniably Lucas. He still had the same brilliant, forget-me-not-blue eyes and the same infectious, dimpled smile and he was smiling now as he stepped forward and wrapped her in a hug. She fitted perfectly into his embrace and it felt like it was only yesterday that she'd last been in his arms. Memories flooded back to her and her stomach did a peculiar little flip as her body responded in a way it hadn't for years. She tensed, taken by surprise by both his spontaneous gesture and her reaction.

He must have felt her stiffen because he let her go and stepped away.

Her eyes took in the sight of him. He looked fabulous. The years had been kind to him. Better than they'd been to her, she feared. His hair was cut shorter but was still sandy blond and thick, and his oval face was tanned, making his blue eyes even more striking. He had the shadow of a beard on his jaw, more brown than blond. That was new. He wouldn't have had that seven years ago, but he hadn't got fat. Or bald.

Her heart raced as she looked him over. He was wearing dark trousers and a pale blue business shirt. It was unbuttoned at the collar, no tie, and he had his sleeves rolled up to expose his forearms. He looked just as good, maybe even better, than she remembered.

Her initial surprise was immediately followed by pleasure but that was then, just as quickly, cancelled out by panic. What was he doing here? He wasn't supposed to be here. He was supposed to be in Europe or Australia. Eating cheese in Switzerland or surfing at Bondi Beach. He wasn't supposed to be in Canada and especially not in Moose River. *She* was the one who belonged here. *She* was the Canadian.

'What are you doing here?' she asked him.

'I'm the hotel manager.'

'In Moose River?'

'It would seem so.' He grinned at her and her stomach did another flip as heat seared through her, scorching her insides. He didn't seem nearly as unsettled as she was about their unexpected encounter. But, then, he'd always adapted quickly to new situations. He seemed to thrive on change, whereas she would rather avoid it.

The ambos and Aimee and her baby had disappeared and a second elevator pinged as it reached their floor.

'Are you finished up here?' he asked.

Jess nodded. It seemed she'd lost the power of speech. It seemed as though Lucas had the same effect on her now as he'd had seven years ago.

'I'll ride down with you,' he said.

He waited for her to enter the elevator. She tucked herself into the corner by the door, feeling confused. Conflicted. She wasn't sure what to think. She wasn't sure how she felt. One part of her wanted to throw herself into his arms and never let him go. Another wanted to run and hide. Another wanted desperately to know what he was thinking.

Lucas stepped in and reached across in front of her to press the button to take them down to the lobby. She hadn't remembered to push the button, so distracted by him she wasn't thinking clearly.

He was standing close. She'd expected him to lean against the opposite wall but he didn't move away as the elevator descended. If she reached out a hand she could touch him without even straightening her elbow.

He was watching her with his forget-me-not-blue eyes and she couldn't take her eyes off him. His familiar scent washed over her—he smelt like winter in the mountains, cool and crisp with the clean, fresh tang of pine needles.

The air was humming, drowning out the silence that fell between them. She clenched her fists at her sides to stop herself from reaching out. She could feel herself being pulled towards him. Even after all this time her body longed for his touch. She craved him.

They stood, for what seemed like ages, just looking at each other.

'It's good to see you, JJ.' His voice was a whisper, barely breaking the silence that surrounded them.

He stretched out one hand and Jess held her breath. His fingers caught the ends of her hair and his thumb brushed across her cheek. The contact set her nerves on fire, every inch of her responding to his touch. It felt like every one of her cells had a memory and every memory was Lucas.

'You've cut your hair,' he said.

'Many times,' she replied.

Lucas laughed and the sound was loud enough to burst the bubble of awareness and desire and longing that had enveloped her.

She didn't know how she'd managed to make a joke. Nothing about this was funny. She was so ill prepared to run into him.

Last time he'd seen her she'd had long hair that had fallen past her shoulders. She'd cut it short when Lily had been born and now it was softly feathered and the ends brushed her shoulders. She'd changed many things about herself since he'd last seen her, not just her hair. It was almost a surprise that he'd recognised her. She felt seventy years older. Not seven. Like a completely different person.

She *was* a different person.

She was a mother. A mother with a secret.

The lift doors slid open but Jess didn't move. Lucas was in her way but even so she didn't think she was capable of movement. She needed the wall to support her.

Her legs were shaking. Her hands were shaking. She knew her reaction was a result of the adrenalin that was coursing through her system. Adrenalin that was produced from a combination of attraction and fear. Why had he come back? And what would his presence mean to her? And to Lily?

'Mr White.' A hotel staff member approached them. Lucas had his back to the doors but he turned at the sound of his name and stepped out of the elevator. 'Mr Bertillon is nearly back at the lodge. He's only a minute or two away. What would you like me to do?'

'I'll meet him here. Can you organise a car to be waiting out the front? We need to get him down the mountain to the hospital asap.'

Jess pushed off the wall and forced her legs to move. One step at a time, she could do this. Lucas turned back to face her as she stepped into the lobby. 'Have you got time for a coffee? Can you wait while I sort this out?'

Jess shook her head. 'I have to get back to the medical centre,' she lied. She had no idea how to deal with the situation. With Lucas. She had to get away. She needed time to process what had just happened. To process the fact that Lucas was here.

'Of course. Another time, then.' He put a hand on her arm and it felt as though her skin might burst into flames at his touch. Her pulse throbbed. Her throat was dry. 'We'll catch up later,' he said.

Jess dropped the medical bag off at the clinic before trudging through the snow back to her apartment. Seeing Lucas had left her shaky and confused and she used the few minutes she had to herself to try to sort out her feelings.

He said they'd catch up later. What would he want?

She definitely wasn't the naive teenager from seven years ago. She wasn't the person he would remember.

What would she do? She needed to work out what to tell him. How to tell him.

She shook her head. This was all too much.

She'd have to try to avoid him. Just for a while, just until she worked out what having all three of them in the same place would mean for her and Lily. Just until she solved this dilemma.

Seven years ago she'd fallen in love. Or she'd thought she had. Seven years on she had convinced herself that maybe it had just been a bad case of teenage hormones. Lust. A holiday romance. But seeing him today had re-inforced that she'd never got over him. How could she when she was reminded of him every day?

She knew she wouldn't be able to avoid him for ever. Moose River wasn't big enough for that. They were bound to bump into each other. But even if avoidance was a possibility she suspected she wouldn't be able to resist him completely. Curiosity would get the better of her. She'd been thinking about him for seven years. She would have to fill in the gaps. But as to exactly what she would tell him, that decision could wait.

She opened her apartment door and was almost knocked over by an excited Lily.

'Mum, where have you been? Kristie is here. We've been waiting for you for ages.'

'Yes, darling, I know. I'm sorry I'm late,' she said as she kissed her daughter.

Normally, seeing Lily's little face light up when she arrived home after a long day at work was enough to lift her spirits. Normally, it was enough to remind her of why she worked so hard and why she'd made the choices she had, but today all she could think of was all the secrets she had kept and wonder how much longer she had until the secrets came out.

She felt ill. The living room was warm but she was shivering. Trembling, Kristie got up and hugged her and Jess could feel herself shaking against her cousin's shoulder.

Kristie stepped back and looked at Jess while she spoke to Lily. 'Lily, why don't you go and try on that new skisuit I got for you? I think your mum would like to see it.' She waited for Lily to leave the room and then said to Jess. 'What's going on? Did it go badly with the patient?'

'No, that was all fine,' Jess replied. She'd been going to stop there but she knew Kristie would get the news out of her eventually. She'd always known when something was bothering her and she'd always been able to wheedle it out of her. She decided she may as well come clean now. 'It's Lucas.'

'What do you mean, "It's Lucas"? What's he got to do with anything?'

Jess collapsed onto the couch. 'He's not in Switzerland or on Bondi Beach. He's here.'

'Here? In Moose River?'

'Yes.'

'What's he doing here?' Kristie sat down opposite Jess.

'He's managing the Crystal Lodge.'

'The new hotel? How did you find that out?' she asked, when Jess nodded.

'I saw him there.'

'You've seen him?'

She nodded again.

'Oh, my God! What did he say? How did he look? What did *you* say?'

'Not much. Good. Nothing.' She couldn't remember what she'd said. All she could remember was how he'd looked and how she'd felt. How those eyes had made her catch her breath, how her knees had turned to jelly when he'd smiled, how her heart had raced when he'd said her name, and how he'd wrapped her in his arms and she'd never wanted to leave. How, after all these years, she still fitted perfectly in his embrace.

'Look, Mum, it's pink.' Jess jumped as her reverie was interrupted by Lily modelling her new skisuit. 'Isn't it pretty?'

'It's very nice, darling,' she replied, without really looking at her mini-fashionista. She was finding it hard to focus on anything other than Lucas. 'Now, why don't you get ready for a bath while I do something about dinner.'

Lily stamped her foot. 'I want to stay in my suit and I don't want dinner.'

'You need to eat something and you don't want to get your new suit dirty, do you?'

Lily folded her arms across her chest and scowled at her mother. 'I don't want dinner.'

'I bought Lily a burger and fries after school. She won't be going to bed hungry,' Kristie said.

'She ate it?'

'She ate the fries and about half the burger.'

Jess was pleased. Maybe the fresh mountain air was stimulating her appetite. Maybe a compromise could be reached.

'Okay, you don't need to eat but you do need to have a bath and put your pyjamas on. Then you can hop into bed, put the headphones on and watch a movie on the laptop.'

That was a bribe and a compromise but it worked. Lily thought she was getting a treat and she stopped complaining. It worked for Jess too as it meant she and Kristie could talk without fear of being overheard. She knew Kristie would continue to pump her for information and she didn't want to discuss Lucas in front of Lily.

By the time Jess had bathed Lily and got her settled with her movie Kristie had ordered a pizza and poured them both a glass of wine. The moment Jess emerged from the bedroom she could tell she was in for a grilling.

'What are you going to do?' Kristie asked, as Jess drew the curtains on the balcony doors and shut out the night.

'Nothing.'

'You can't do nothing! He deserves to know.'

'Why? My father was right. Obviously the week we spent together didn't mean as much to him as it did to me. If Lucas wanted to be a part of my life he's had plenty of time to look for me before now.'

'You know you don't believe that,' Kristie said. 'You didn't believe your father seven years ago and you don't believe that now. If we could have found Lucas all those years ago he'd be part of your life already.'

'But we couldn't find him and my life is fine as it is,' she argued.

'But what about Lily? Doesn't she deserve to know?'

Jess greeted Kristie's question with stony silence.

'You can't put off the inevitable,' Kristie added. 'It's not fair to Lucas and it's not fair to Lily.'

'But I have no idea what type of man he is now,' Jess countered. He might not be the person she remembered. *Did* she even remember him? Maybe everything she remembered had been a product of her imagination but she knew one thing for certain—she wasn't the person he would remember.

She'd dreamt of Lucas coming back into her life but now that he was here she was nervous. His return brought complications she hadn't considered and consequences she wasn't ready for. She wasn't ready to deal with having him back in her life. She rolled her eyes at herself. Who said he would even want to be part of her life? Or Lily's? This wasn't a fairy tale. This was reality.

She sighed. One thing at a time. That was how she would deal with this. She would gather the facts and then work out her approach, and until then she would stay as far away from him as possible.

'I need some answers before I tell him anything,' she said.

'You can't avoid him for ever.'

'I just need some time to process this,' she said. No matter how much she'd wished for one more chance, now that the moment was here she wasn't ready. 'Whatever we had was over a long time ago. It was a teenage romance—it's water under the bridge now.'

'It might be,' Kristie argued, 'except for the fact that the bridge is sleeping in the other room. There's always going to be something connecting you to him.'

And Jess knew that was the crux of the matter.

Lily.

'You can't keep her a secret any more, Jess.'

CHAPTER FOUR

IT TOOK A lot to frustrate Lucas. He was normally a calm person, level-headed and patient, all good attributes when working in hospitality, but right now he was frustrated. Seeing Jess again had hit him for six. It was a cricketing term but one that perfectly matched how he was feeling. He could cope with the day-to-day issues that arose with the hotel, he'd even coped with the delays and revisions while it had been redeveloped, but he couldn't cope with Jess's disappearance. Not again.

By the time he'd waited for Aimee Bertillon's husband and seen the ambulance off, all the while itching to return to Jess but doing his best to hide his impatience, she had vanished. She had said she couldn't wait and it seemed she'd meant it.

He knew he wouldn't be able to settle, he wouldn't be able to concentrate on work, not while thoughts of Jess were running rampant through his head. He told his PA that he was going out. No excuses, no reasons. He needed to think and he always thought better if he was outside in the fresh air. If she wasn't going to wait for him, he'd go and find her. He changed his shoes and grabbed his coat and walked to the medical centre.

'Can I help you?' The lady behind the desk had a name badge that read 'Donna'.

'I hope so. I'm looking for one of your doctors, Jess Johnson.'

'She's not a doctor,' Donna told him.

Now he was confused as well as frustrated. 'I've just seen her. I'm Lucas White from the Crystal Lodge. I called for a doctor and she came.'

'Jess is a nurse. All our doctors were busy so she agreed to go and make an assessment. Was there a problem? She's gone for the day but is there something I can help you with?'

A nurse.

Lucas shook his head. 'No. Nothing. Thank you.' The only thing he wanted was to know where she was and he didn't imagine that Donna would give him that information. He'd have to come back.

Jess was a nurse. He wondered what had happened. She'd been planning on becoming a doctor—why hadn't she followed her dream?

Night had fallen when he stepped back outside and the temperature had dropped. He pulled his scarf and gloves out of his coat pocket—he'd learnt years ago to keep them handy—and wandered the streets, still hoping to find her.

If he'd known on the day she'd been yanked from his life that he wasn't ever going to see her again he would have tried harder to keep hold of her. When she'd disappeared he'd been left with nothing. Nothing but a sense that he needed to prove himself.

He had left Moose River to return home, vowing he would make it back one day. Vowing to make something of himself. For her. It had been an impulsive, young man's promise, one that seven years later he might have thought would be long forgotten, but even though there had been plenty of other women over the years he'd never got Jess out of his system. She'd been an irresistible combination of beauty, brains, innocence and passion. She had worn her heart on her sleeve and she'd shared herself with him without reservation.

At times it was almost impossible to believe they'd only had seven days together. That one week had influenced him profoundly. It had made him the man he was today, determined to succeed. Determined to find Jess again and prove himself worthy.

It had taken longer than he would have dreamed. If someone had told him at the age of twenty that it would take him almost seven years, he would have thought that was a whole lifetime. But he had done it and he was back.

When the opportunity had presented itself in Moose River he'd jumped at it. At the time it had seemed as though all the planets had aligned. The timing had been right, he'd been ready to spread his wings, and the opportunity to be back in Moose River had been too good a chance to pass up. He'd wanted to prove himself and what better place to do it than in the very place where his dreams had all begun.

He'd returned as a successful, self-made man but things hadn't gone quite as he'd expected. The hotel hadn't been the problem. It had been Jess. He'd been back in Moose River for nine months and hadn't caught sight of her until today. He hadn't imagined that he'd find her, only to have her disappear again. Maybe she didn't feel the same desire to catch up. Maybe she hadn't kept hold of the memories, as he had. Maybe she barely remembered him.

Although he'd seen in her face that she hadn't forgotten him. He'd held her in his arms and it had felt like yesterday and he knew she'd felt it too.

But things had not gone according to his plan. The reunion he'd always pictured had gone quite differently.

But he wasn't a quitter, he never had been, and he wasn't about to start now. He'd found her and he wasn't going to let her disappear again.

He walked past the building where Jess's family had had their apartment all those years ago. He'd called in there before but this time he knew she was in town. She had to be staying somewhere. He pushed open the lobby door and pressed the buzzer for the penthouse.

No answer. That would have been far too easy.

He continued walking and eventually stopped and leant on a lamppost. He looked across the street and recognised the building. He was in front of the Moose River staff apartments. He counted the windows and stopped at unit fifteen. It was in darkness but he could see lights in the gap between the curtains in apartment sixteen. His gaze drifted back to the dark windows of fifteen as his memory wandered.

Jess had given him her heart but he hadn't really appreciated it at the time. He'd been young and hungry for adventure. He hadn't realised what he'd had with her. Not until she'd been long gone. And by then it had been too late.

No one else had ever measured up to her. Or not to his idealisation of her anyway. Perhaps he was looking back on the past with rose-tinted glasses but there had been something special about her and he'd never met anyone else like her. And he'd travelled to almost every corner of the globe. He'd been constantly on the go since he'd left Moose River. He'd immersed himself in the hospitality trade before he'd even finished studying, learning the lessons that enabled him to take the next step, getting the knowledge and experience to embark on a solo project. Getting ready to prove himself to Jess and her father.

But he wasn't to know his efforts were to be in vain.

Apartment fifteen remained dark. He wasn't going to solve the puzzle that was life or even the problem that was Jess and her whereabouts while standing out here in the cold. There were plenty of issues waiting for his attention back at the lodge. He could make better use of his time. He pushed off the lamppost and trudged back through the snow. He'd continue to search for her tomorrow.

Lucas had been up since five. He'd been unable to sleep and he'd done half a day's work already. It was Thanksgiving weekend in the United States and the official start of the ski season in Moose River, Canada. Crowds were building and the Crystal Lodge was fully booked. This was what he'd wanted. What he'd been working towards. No vacancies. He wanted Crystal Lodge to become one of the premier hotels in the resort. But now he feared that wasn't enough. Jess was back and he wanted her too.

He loved his job, he loved his life and he'd thought that he was happy with his success, but seeing Jess yesterday had shown him that all his success was nothing if he had no one to share it with. Seeing her yesterday reinforced that he'd spent seven years making something of himself, of his life, and he'd done it for her. But had she moved on? What would be the point of making himself worthy of Jess if she didn't want to have anything to do with him?

He stood by the window of his office and watched the snow fall. It had started early this morning and the forecast was for heavy falls over the weekend. It was perfect for the start of the season.

Next week all the Christmas decorations would be up around the village. They were already multiplying at a rapid rate and Lucas knew his tradesmen were at work this morning, building a frame for the thirty-foot tree that would be on display in front of the hotel on the plaza. He planned to switch on the lights on the tree next weekend to coincide with the opening of the Christmas market that was to be held in the plaza. There were plenty of things needing his attention, he had plenty to keep him occupied, but all he could think about was Jess.

He needed a break from the indoors. He muttered something to his PA about inspecting the progress on the framework for the tree and then wandered through the village, retracing his steps to all the places he and Jess had spent time seven years ago. Not that he expected to find her in the same places but he was happy to let his feet lead the way as it left his mind free to reminisce.

He headed up the hill, past the popular après-ski venue, the T-bar, and skirted the iconic Moose River Hotel, which set the standard for accommodation and was the hotel that Lucas measured the performance of Crystal Lodge against. The village was blanketed in snow. It was as pretty as a picture but everyone was bundled up against the weather and he knew he could walk right past Jess and never know it. He may as well return to the lodge and do something more productive.

He was halfway down the hill, passing the tube park, when he spotted her. She was leaning on the railing at the bottom of the slope and he could see her profile as she watched people sliding down the hill in the inflatable rubber tubes. She was wearing a red knitted cap and he had a flashback to the day he'd first met her. How the hell did he remember that? The sound of laughter floated up to him as people raced down the lanes and Lucas felt like laughing along with them. He'd found her.

'JJ!'

Jess turned around at the sound of her nickname. Her heart was racing even before she saw him. Just hearing his voice was enough to make her feel like she was seventeen once more and falling in love all over again. He was smiling at her and she couldn't help but smile back, even as she cursed her heart for betraying her brain.

'I was hoping to bump into you.'

That was ironic. She'd been hoping to avoid him.

'You were? What for?'

'Old times' sake. I wanted to invite you for coffee. Or dinner?'

'I don't think so,' Jess replied. She was nowhere near ready to spend one-on-one time with Lucas. She knew she owed it to him to catch up but she wasn't ready yet. She needed time to prepare. She needed time to plan a defence. And she definitely needed more than twenty-four hours.

'Jess!'

Kristie was flying down the slope towards them in a double tube. The snow had been falling too heavily to make for pleasant skiing with a beginner so she and Kristie had opted to bring Lily to the tube park instead. But she hadn't anticipated that they'd bump into Lucas. Not here.

She used the interruption to her advantage, choosing to wave madly at her cousin and hoping to divert Lucas's attention.

'Is that Kristie?'

'Yes.' Kristie had Lily tucked between her knees and she was screaming at the top of her lungs as they raced alongside the person in the adjacent lane. Kristie always took things to the extreme and Lily was yelling right along with her, looking like she was having the time of her life.

Jess could remember coming to the tube park with Lucas. She could remember sitting in the tube between his thighs with his arms wrapped around her and yelling with delight, just like Lily was now. Life had been so much simpler then but she hadn't appreciated it at the time.

'Who's that with her?' Lucas asked, as he spotted Lily.

Jess had successfully diverted Lucas's attention away from herself, only to focus it on Lily. The one thing she didn't want.

She was tempted to tell him that Lily was Kristie's but she knew she'd be caught out far too easily in that lie. 'That's my daughter,' she said.

'You have a daughter?'

Kristie and Lily hopped out of the tube and Kristie started dragging it back to the conveyor belt that would take them back to the start of the lanes at the top of the hill. Lily waved to Jess but followed Kristie. Luckily, she wasn't ready for the fun to end yet so didn't come over to her mother. Jess was relieved. She didn't want to have to introduce Lily to Lucas. Not yet. She definitely wasn't prepared for that.

'She's the image of you,' Lucas said, as Lily stepped onto the conveyor belt. 'How old is she?'

'Five.' Jess's heart was beating at a million miles an hour as she avoided one lie only to tell another.

Lily was, in fact, six, but luckily she was small for her age. While Jess didn't want to give Lucas a chance to put two and two together, she wasn't completely certain why she'd lied. She didn't expect him to remember that it had been seven years ago that they had spent one week together. It was obvious he hadn't forgotten her but to think he would remember exactly how many years had passed might be stretching things. Just because that time had become so significant to Jess, it didn't mean it would be as important to him. Why should it be? It had been just one week for him. For her it had been the rest of her life.

'Is that the reason you don't want to catch up? You're married?'

Jess shook her head. 'No.'

'Divorced?'

'No, but I still can't go to dinner with you. Life is more complicated now.' She had to think of Lily. But she knew she was also thinking of herself. She wasn't ready for this.

'I guess it is.' He nodded his head slowly as he absorbed her words. 'But, if you do find yourself free at any time, or if your complications become less complicated, you know where to contact me.'

He didn't push her. He didn't suggest she bring Lily

along to dinner and Jess knew he wanted to see only her. Alone.

Was it possible that her father had been right? If she'd been able to find Lucas all those years ago would he have wanted to know about Lily or would he have chosen to have nothing to do with her? She didn't think that was the sort of person he was. But what would she know? It wasn't like they'd had time to really get to know each other.

She wondered if he'd ever thought about being a father. Maybe he already was one. The question was on the tip of her tongue but she bit it back. Did she want to know more about him? Did she want to know what his life was like now? What if he had children of his own? Other children? Would that be too painful?

Surely it was better, safer, easier if she kept her distance.

He smiled. His forget-me-not-blue eyes were shining and his dimples flashed briefly, tempting her to say, *Wait, yes, of course I'd love to have dinner with you*. But she nodded and let him go.

She watched him walk down the hill and thought about how different her life could have been.

Jess stood at the balcony doors as the last rays of the sun dipped behind the mountain. She had thought that spending the morning at the tube park would have exhausted Lily but she seemed full of beans and Jess didn't have the energy to cope with her at the moment. Thank goodness for Kristie. She had taken Lily off to the shops, leaving Jess alone to think.

She looked to her left, down to the village. In the foreground she could see the balcony of apartment fifteen,

Lucas's old apartment. She tried to look past it as she didn't want to think about him but she knew she couldn't help it. Her mind had been filled with memories of him all day and right there, on that balcony, was where they had shared their first kiss.

When Lucas and Sam had invited them to their party Jess had never imagined actually going. But Kristie had managed to come up with a semi-believable story about a school friend's birthday and before she'd known it Jess had been at Lucas's door.

He and Sam had been sharing the apartment with two other boys and it had already been crowded when they'd arrived. People had spilled out of the living room into the corridor between the flats, overflowing into the bedrooms and out onto the balcony. But somehow Lucas had met her and Kristie at his front door.

He'd smiled at her and his blue eyes had lit up. His grin had been infectious and full of cheek and Jess had known right then that he would love creating mischief and mayhem. 'You look great,' he told her.

She and Kristie had spent ages getting ready, all the while ensuring that it had looked effortless. Kristie had straightened Jess's hair so that it hung in a shiny, platinum cascade down her back. She had coated her eyelashes with mascara to highlight her green eyes and swiped pink gloss over her lips.

She'd been nervous about coming to the party, worried about being in a room full of strangers, but one smile from Lucas and all her nervousness had disappeared. He hadn't felt like a stranger. She'd felt safe with him. She'd trusted him. All those years of listening to her parents telling her to be wary of strangers, of forbidding her to go out alone, and what had she done at the first opportunity—she'd disappeared to a party with a stranger just because he'd been cute and he'd flirted with her. He'd been so gorgeous and she'd been pretty sure she was already in trouble but she'd been unable to resist.

Even Kristie couldn't have predicted this turnaround in such a short time. Jess, who'd never gone against her parents' wishes, had been rebelling big time because a cute boy had smiled at her and made her laugh. She hadn't known him but she hadn't cared. She would get to know him. She'd felt like she'd been where she was supposed to be. Here. With him.

He took the drinks they carried, opened one for each of them and handed them back before stashing the rest into a tub that had been filled with snow. Kristie had used a fake ID to buy the pre-mixed cans of vodka and soda and they'd shared one as they'd walked to the party. Jess had needed it for courage; she hadn't really planned on having another one but she supposed she could nurse one drink for the evening. It's not like anyone would pay attention to what she was doing.

'I'm glad you could make it,' he said to her, as Kristie spotted Sam and made a beeline for him.

'We almost didn't.'

'How come?'

'We're not normally allowed to go to random parties.'

'Who would stop you?'

'Our parents.'

'So you're not nineteen, then?'

Jess frowned. What did her age have to do with anything? 'What?'

'If you were nineteen you'd be making your own decisions.'

They'd fibbed to her aunt and uncle about where they were going but she'd forgotten that Kristie had also lied to the boys about their age.

'I'll be eighteen next week.' She hoped that wouldn't matter. She wasn't sure what she wanted to happen but she wanted a chance to find out. She didn't want Lucas to decide she was too young but he didn't mention her age again.

'So you've sneaked out and no one knows where you are. Are you sure that's wise?'

'You seemed trustworthy.' Jess smiled. 'And as long as we're home before midnight, everything should be fine,' she added, aware that she was babbling. Normally if she was nervous she'd be tongue-tied but she had forgotten to be nervous. Was it the half a drink she'd had or was there something about Lucas that made her feel comfortable?

'What trouble can you get into after midnight that you can't get into before?' he asked.

'You sound like Kristie.'

'You have to admit I have a point.' Lucas was standing very close to her. When had he closed the distance? She was leaning with her back against a wall and he was standing at a right angle to her, his left shoulder pressed against the same wall, inches away from her. His voice was quiet and he had a mischievous look in his blue eyes.

'I don't know the answer,' she said. 'I just know we need to be home before our curfew. I don't want anyone looking for us and finding out we're not where we said we'd be. I don't tend to get into trouble.'

'Not ever?' He grinned at her and suddenly Jess could imagine all sorts of trouble she could get into.

Trouble, mischief and mayhem. All sorts of things she'd never exposed herself to before.

She shook her head. 'I've never had the opportunity.'

Her parents knew where she was every minute of the day and Jess knew how stressed they would be if she ever sneaked off and went against their wishes. She had never wanted to test the boundaries before, aware of how upset they would be. But neither they nor her aunt and uncle had any idea where she was tonight. If she was careful she could have some fun and they would be none the wiser.

'Maybe you just haven't recognised opportunity when she's come knocking,' Lucas said. 'Or maybe you need to create it.'

His last sentence was barely a whisper. His head was bent close to hers and she held her breath as he dipped his head a little lower. He was going to kiss her! She closed her eyes and leant towards him.

'Hey, Lucas,' someone interrupted. 'Your shout.'

'You've gotta be kidding me.' He lifted his head and turned to face the room. Over his shoulder Jess could see a couple of his mates holding empty beer bottles up in the air and laughing, and she knew they'd deliberately interrupted the moment. Jess could have screamed with frustration. She'd never forgive them if she'd missed an opportunity that she couldn't get back. What if the moment was gone for ever?

'Come on.' He took her by the hand and her skin burned where his fingers wrapped around hers. He pushed through the crowd until they came to a pair of doors that opened onto a balcony. He led her outside to where there were more tubs filled with snow and beers.

He let her go as he grabbed a couple of beers in each hand and asked, 'Will you wait here?'

She wasn't sure what she was waiting for but she nodded anyway. She seemed destined to follow his lead. Something about him made her finally understand what got Kristie all hot and bothered when it came to boys. Her hormones were going into overdrive and she was certain she could still feel the imprint of his fingers on hers. She couldn't think about anything except what it would be like to be kissed by Lucas. He was cute and confident, his accent was completely sexy and the way he looked at her with those brilliant blue eyes made her want to leap in, even though she didn't have the faintest idea about how to do that. But she suspected he knew what to do and she would happily let him teach her.

He took the beers inside and when he came back to her he was holding two coats and another drink for her that she didn't really want. He handed her the can, not realising she hadn't finished her first drink.

'You're not having anything?' she asked.

'I don't feel like drinking tonight.'

He was looking at her so intensely that even with her limited experience Jess knew exactly what he did feel like doing and the idea took her breath away.

'I don't want this either,' she said.

Lucas reached out and closed his hand around hers. It was warm, really warm in contrast to the cold drink. He took the can from her and stuck it into a tub with the beers.

Lucas was making Jess feel light-headed and giddy and she didn't want alcohol to interfere with her senses. She wanted to remember this moment, how it made her feel. She finally felt as if the world made sense.

She had always believed in love at first sight. She didn't know why, but she liked the idea that people could recognise their soul mate the very first time they saw them and she imagined that this was how it would feel. Like you couldn't breathe but you didn't need to. She felt as if she could exist just by looking into Lucas's eyes. She felt as though she didn't need anything more than that. Ever.

'I thought we could stay out here,' he said. 'There'll be fewer interruptions and, you never know, we might find the only thing that interrupts us is opportunity.' He was standing only inches from her. She could see his breath coming from between his lips as little puffs of condensation that accompanied his words and it was only then she noticed the cold. He opened one of the coats and held it for her as she slipped her arms into the sleeves. It smelt like him, fresh and clean with a hint of pine needles, but it swamped her tiny frame.

'How long are you staying at the resort?' he asked, as he rolled the sleeves up for her. He had closed the balcony doors and while they could still see the party through the glass the music was muted and they had the balcony to themselves.

'A little over two weeks. Until the New Year.'

'Do you come here often?'

'We spend most Christmas vacations here.' That was true of the past nine years. Prior to that, when her brother had been alive, they'd spent every second Christmas in California with her mother's family. But that had all changed after Stephen had died. But she didn't think Lucas needed to hear that story. Tonight wasn't about her family. It wasn't about her past. Tonight was about her. Tonight was her chance to experience all the things that Stephen's early death had robbed her of.

'Christmas in the snow,' he said. 'I'm looking forward to seeing what all the fuss is about. This will be my first white Christmas.'

'Really?'

He nodded.

'I'll have to make sure you get the full festive season experience, then,' Jess said with a smile. She'd worry about how to actually achieve that later.

'Don't worry, I intend to.'

He was watching her closely and she started to wonder if she had food caught between her teeth. Why else would he be staring at her like that? 'What is it?' she asked.

'I want to know what you're thinking,' he told her.

'About what?'

'About me.'

She hesitated before answering. She could hardly tell him she thought he was gorgeous or that he might well be her soul mate. He might appreciate her honesty but then again he might think she was completely crazy. She played it safe. 'I don't know anything about you.'

'What would you like to know?'

'I have no idea.' She wasn't very good at social conversations. She'd never really had to talk to a stranger before. She usually only got to talk to people with whom she already had some sort of connection—family, school friends or family friends. There was never anything new to learn about any of them. Every one of them was the same. Rich, well educated and well spoken, they all lived in Vancouver's exclusive suburbs, had private school educations, holiday homes, overseas vacations and were gifted new cars on their sixteenth birthdays. She was surrounded by trust-fund children. Lucas was a clean slate and she didn't know where to begin.

'Well, why don't I start?' he said.

'All right.'

'Do you have a boyfriend?'

She shook her head. 'No. Why?'

'I want to kiss you and I want to know if that's okay.'

Jess's green eyes opened wide. He was offering her a chance to experience freedom. To do something spontaneous, something that hadn't been sanctioned by her parents.

She'd broken so many rules tonight, what was one more? And, besides, there wasn't actually a rule forbidding her to kiss boys. It was more that she was rarely given the opportunity. And that was what it was all about, wasn't it? Opportunity.

Her freedom in Moose River was on borrowed time and if she didn't grab the opportunity with both hands now she knew she'd miss it altogether. She didn't have time to stop and think. She didn't have time to weigh up the options and the pros and cons. Her time was finite. It was now or never.

She didn't do anything she would regret. Not that night at least. Lucas was cute and he was interested in her and there was no one in the background, keeping tabs on her. For the first time ever she could do as she pleased. And she wanted to kiss Lucas.

'Have you made up your mind yet?' he asked.

He bent his head. His lips were millimetres from hers.

She'd wanted a chance to make a decision for herself. But some decisions, once made, couldn't be reversed. Right then, though, she wasn't to know that this kiss would mark the moment when she stood at the crossroads of her life. She wasn't to know that this would be the moment when she decided on a path that would change her life for ever.

She nodded, ever so slightly, and closed her eyes in a silent invitation.

His lips were soft. The pressure of his mouth on hers was gentle at first until his tongue darted between her lips, forcing her mouth open. She let him taste her as she explored him too. She felt as though he'd taken over her body. She felt as if they had become one already, joined at the lips. Her nipples hardened and a line of fire travelled from her chest to her groin, igniting her internally until she thought she might go up in flames. Her body was on fire as she pushed against him, begging him to go deeper, to taste more of her.

She could feel herself falling in love with each second.

He could kiss her as much as he liked for the rest of for ever if he kissed like that.

CHAPTER FIVE

'JESS? JESS!'

Jess turned around from the window as the sound of Kristie's voice dragged her back to the present. She needed to focus. Judging by Kristie's tone, it seemed she might have been calling her for a while. 'What?'

'Lily was talking to you.'

'What are we doing tonight, Mummy?' Lily asked, but Jess couldn't think. Her mind was still filled with thoughts of Lucas and it took her a moment to come back to the present. She was distracted but that wasn't Lily's fault and it wasn't a good enough reason to ignore her daughter.

Kristie rescued her. 'How would you like to do something special with me, Lily?' she offered.

'Like what?'

'It'll be a surprise. I know you love surprises. Go and pack a bag with your pyjamas and a toothbrush while I think of something.'

Kristie waited for Lily to leave the room. 'You should ring Lucas and see if he's free for dinner.'

'What? Why?' How was it possible that Kristie could read her mind?

'I know you haven't stopped thinking about him

since this morning, probably since yesterday. I know you said you were going to avoid him but you can't pretend you don't want to see him. You've been miles away all afternoon. So the way I figure it is you might as well go and see him while I'm here to look after Lily. I'll take her on a sleigh ride, she's desperate to do that—she won't even care what you're doing.'

'She told you she wants to go on a sleigh ride?' That was enough to stop Jess from thinking about Lucas. 'Would you mind doing something else? I really want to do that with her. I'm saving up to take her as a Christmas surprise.' Her heart ached. She knew Lily wanted to take a sleigh ride from Crystal Lodge more than anything and even now that she knew Lucas's involvement with the lodge she wasn't going to let it derail her plans. Logistics weren't the issue but money was. She didn't have the cash to spare so, until she got her first pay cheque, the sleigh ride would have to wait.

Jess could see Kristie biting her tongue and knew she wanted to offer to pay for it but she'd learnt the hard way that Jess was determined to make it on her own.

Kristie looked at her but didn't argue the point. 'Sure. Can I take her to our apartment?' she asked. 'I won't tell her it belongs to our family—we can drink hot chocolate and toast marshmallows in front of the fire and watch the replay of the Thanksgiving parade. She can have a sleepover and then you can have the night free to do as you please.'

Jess wasn't convinced this was a good idea. 'You know what happened last time we hatched a plan like that,' she said. 'I ended up pregnant.'

Kristie just shrugged and smiled. 'Lily would like a sibling. She'd probably like a father too. I think this is fate intervening. Leading you to decisions that I know you don't want to make. Perhaps you should let fate dictate to you. I think you owe it to Lucas to meet up. Don't you?'

'No,' Jess replied.

She'd refused to wear a dress. As if that meant she had some control over the situation. She didn't want to feel like she was going on a date. They were just two old acquaintances catching up. She tucked her jeans into her boots and tugged a black turtleneck sweater over her head. Jess did put on make-up—she was too vain not to—but kept it simple. Foundation, mascara, some blush and lip gloss. She still wanted to look pretty but not desperate. Adding a red scarf for some colour, she headed out the door.

She'd insisted on meeting him at the hotel. This wasn't a date so he didn't need to collect her, she was quite capable of walking a few streets. She stepped from the plaza into the lodge. Tonight she had more time to take in her surroundings and she stopped briefly, gathering her thoughts as she admired the room. There were two beautifully decorated Christmas trees in the lobby, one at each end, and the lobby itself was festooned with lights, pine branches, red bows and mistletoe.

The lodge was celebrating Christmas in style and decorations were multiplying in the village too. The Christmas spirit was alive and flourishing in Moose River and Jess smiled to herself. As a child she had loved Christmas. She had looked forward to it all year, partly because the festive season also included her birthday, but it had been her favourite time of year for so many reasons. Until her brother had died.

After Stephen's death Christmas had lost its sparkle. She knew he was always in her parents' thoughts, particularly her mother's, especially at certain times of the year, including Christmas, and that had taken the shine off the festivities. Even though he wasn't spoken of for fear of further upsetting her mother there was always the underlying sense that someone was missing and Christmas had never been the same. Until Lily was born. And now Jess was desperate to have the perfect Christmas. She wanted to create that for Lily and she had hoped that being in Moose River would give her that chance. This was her opportunity to put the sparkle back.

She felt someone watching her and she knew it was Lucas. Jess turned her head. He had been waiting for her by the bar and now he was walking towards her, coming to meet her in the lobby.

Seeing him coming for her made her feel as if she was coming home but she resisted the feeling. She belonged here in Moose River so she should already feel at home, she shouldn't need Lucas to make her feel that way.

He was wearing a navy suit with a crisp white shirt and a tie the colour of forget-me-nots. She'd never seen him in a suit before. His hair had been brushed, it wasn't as tousled as she was used to, and she fought the urge to run her fingers through it and mess it up a bit. He looked handsome but she preferred him more casually styled. But perhaps the old Lucas wouldn't have fitted into this fancy hotel. She wondered how much he'd changed. Probably not as much as she had. The thought made her smile again.

He smiled in response. A dimple appeared in his

cheek, a sparkle in his eye. Now he looked like the Lucas she'd fallen in love with.

He reached out and took both her hands in his then leaned down and kissed her cheek, enveloping her in his clean, fresh scent. The caress of his lips sent tingles through her as her body responded to his touch. She could feel every beat of her heart and every whisper of air that brushed past her face as his lips left their imprint on her skin. Despite what she thought, her body didn't seem to remember that this wasn't a date or that seven years had passed. Her body reacted as if it had been yesterday that Lucas had been in her bed.

She'd been on a few dates over the past few years but she'd eventually given up because no one else had ever had the same effect on her as Lucas had. The attraction she'd felt for Lucas had been immediate, powerful and irresistible, and she'd never felt the same connection with anyone else. Not one other man had ever made her feel like she might melt with desire. Not one of them had made her feel like she was the centre of the universe, a universe that might explode at any moment. What was the point in dating? she'd asked herself. Why waste time and energy on someone who wasn't Lucas? If she couldn't have Lucas she'd rather have nothing.

And it seemed he hadn't lost the ability to make her feel truly alive. Just a touch, a glance, a kiss could set her off. She'd need to be careful. She'd need to keep her wits about her and remember what was at stake.

'JJ,' he said, and his voice washed over her, soft and deep and intimate. How could she feel so much when so little was said? 'Thank you for coming.'

As if she'd had a choice.

Despite her show of determination to Kristie earlier

in the day, she'd known her resolve wasn't strong enough to withstand the temptation of knowing that Lucas was only a few streets away. She'd known she'd pick up the phone and call him.

'I hope you don't mind if we stay in the hotel to eat?' he asked.

'I'm not dressed to eat here,' she said, as she took her hands out of his hold and shrugged out of her coat. Jeans and an old sweater were not five-star dining attire, even if the jeans hugged her curves and the black top made her blonde hair shine like white gold.

He ran his eyes over her and Jess could feel her temperature rise by a degree for every second she spent under his gaze. She could see the appreciation in his eyes and the attention felt good.

'You look lovely,' he said as he took her coat. It had been a long time since she'd wanted to capture a man's interest and despite telling herself this wasn't a date it was nice to know that Lucas liked what he could see. 'And you're safe with me. I can put in a good word for you if need be.' He was laughing at her and she relaxed. His words reminded her of their first night together all those years ago. She'd felt safe then and she felt safe now.

'Are you sure? I don't want to drag down the standards.'

'Believe me, you're not lowering our standards.' He ran his gaze over her again and Jess's breath caught in her throat as she saw his forget-me-not-blue eyes darken. 'We're fully booked for the weekend and I'd like to be close to hand in case there are any issues.'

She was worried that eating in the hotel would give him the upper hand. He would be in familiar surroundings and she felt underdressed and out of place. But, then again, she consoled herself, this wasn't a competition, it was a friendly dinner.

'Are you expecting problems?' she asked, as she walked beside him into the restaurant. He had his hand resting lightly in the small of her back, guiding her forward. His touch was so light she should hardly have felt it but she could swear she could feel each individual fingertip and her skin was on fire under the thin wool of her sweater.

'There are always teething problems with a new project—the only unknown is the scale of the disaster,' he said, as he checked in her coat and greeted the maître d'.

She followed him to a table positioned beside the large picture windows looking out over the outdoor terrace and onto the plaza. Lucas pulled out her chair for her and reached for a bottle of champagne that was chilling in a bucket next to her. He popped the cork and poured them each a glass.

'To old friends,' she said, as they touched glasses.

'And new memories,' he added. 'It's good to see you, JJ.'

She took a nervous sip of her champagne as the waiter approached their table.

'We're not ready to order yet,' Lucas told him.

'It's fine, Lucas,' Jess told him. 'You must know what's good—why don't you choose for us both?' She sounded breathless. She was nervous, on edge from conflicting emotions—guilt, lust, fear and desire—and she doubted she'd be able to eat anything anyway. The sooner he ordered the sooner she'd be able to escape before she said or did something she might regret. She'd been desperate to see him but now she was worried that she'd made a mistake.

She looked out the window as Lucas gave the waiter their order. Christmas lights were strung up around the terrace and stretched across to the plaza. They surrounded the ice-skating rink and looped through the bare branches of the trees. The ice and snow sparkled under the glow of the lights as skaters glided around the rink. It was the perfect image of a winter wonderland.

'It's a beautiful view,' she said, as the waiter departed, leaving them alone again. She got her breathing under control and returned her gaze to Lucas. 'It's a beautiful hotel.'

'You like it?'

'It's perfect. Just looking at it makes me happy. Someone has done a very good job.' The entire lodge—the furnishings in the rooms, the decorations in the lobby and the views from the restaurant—all conspired to make her feel as though the hotel was giving her a warm hug. Or maybe that was Lucas.

'Thank you,' he said.

'You?'

Lucas nodded. 'This is my vision.'

'Really? I thought you were the hotel manager.'

'That's my official title but this is my hotel.'

'Yours? You own it?'

'Yes. This is my baby.'

'You dream big, don't you?' she said.

'What do you mean?'

'You told me you wanted to work in the hospitality industry when you finished university. You never said you actually wanted to own a hotel.'

'You remember that?'

I remember everything about you, she thought, but she said nothing. She just nodded as the waiter placed their first course on their table.

'I have you to thank for that,' he told her.

'Me?'

'I started planning this the day you vanished from my life.'

'I didn't vanish,' she objected. 'My father dragged me away. I didn't have a choice.'

'In my mind you vanished. I never saw you again. I looked for you, every day, until the end of the season, until the day I left, but you had disappeared.'

'You looked for me?' She'd never dared to imagine that he would have thought about her.

'Of course. Did you think I would just let you go? Especially after what happened that day. I went back to your apartment the next day but there was no answer. Eventually I found the caretaker and he told me you'd all left. I was sure you would get in touch with me and I kept looking, thinking maybe you'd be back before the season ended. When that didn't happen I started writing to you, long letters that I was going to post to your family's apartment, but I never finished them.'

'Why not?' How much simpler might things have been if he'd done that. Then she might have been able to find him when she'd needed to.

'I was never good with words. I decided that words were empty promises and that I was better off showing you what I wanted you to know. It's taken longer than I thought. But now we have a chance to fill in all the gaps. To catch up on what happened that day and in the past seven years.'

Jess could remember every second of that day. Every

moment was imprinted on her brain, each glorious moment, along with every humiliating one. It had certainly been a birthday to remember.

She had wanted to sleep with him from the moment he'd kissed her. After that first night at his party she would have gladly given him anything he'd asked for but for as long as she could remember she'd fantasised about her first sexual experience and it had involved a big bed, clean sheets, flowers, music and candles. Not a single bed in a shared flat. Getting naked in Lucas's flat in a bedroom he'd shared with Sam had not been an option and so she'd had to wait and hope for a different opportunity. And then, on the morning of her birthday, her aunt and uncle had announced they were going cat skiing, leaving the girls on their own, leaving Jess free to spend the afternoon with Lucas.

They had spent any spare moments they'd had together since meeting seven days earlier. With Kristie's help Jess had sneaked off at every chance she'd had. She'd never done anything like that before but being with Lucas was more important than being the perfect daughter. Lucas had unleashed another side to her personality and she hadn't been able to resist him.

On her eighteenth birthday her aunt and uncle's plans had given her the ideal opportunity to create the perfect setting in which to let Lucas seduce her. It had to be that way. Lucas would have to seduce her as she didn't know where to start. She would create the opportunity for seduction and Lucas would have to do the rest.

And, just as Kristie had predicted several days earlier, Jess found herself planning sneaky afternoon sex. Only it had been more than that. She had gifted her virginity to Lucas. She had offered herself to him. She had offered him her body and her heart and he had taken them both. She had given herself to Lucas and in return he had given her Lily. It had been the perfect birthday. Up to a point.

'That day didn't end quite how I'd expected,' she said.

'No. Me neither. But I have to know what happened to you. Where did you go?'

'We left Moose River that night.'

'All of you?'

Jess nodded.

'Because of me?' Lucas asked.

'Because of both of us,' Jess said. 'But mostly because of my father. I still don't know how I'd forgotten they were arriving that night. I can't believe I lost track of time so badly.' She'd been swept away by Lucas and once she'd had a taste of him she hadn't been able to get enough. He had brought her to life. Her body had blossomed under the touch of his fingers and the caress of his lips. He had introduced her to a whole new world. A world of pleasure, fulfilment and ecstasy. He had consumed her body, her mind and her heart, and she had forgotten about everything else, including the imminent arrival of her parents.

Everyone had got more than they'd bargained for that day.

Jess could still remember the moment she'd heard them arrive. The moment her ecstasy had turned to dread. The moment her fantasy had become a nightmare.

Lucas's head had been buried between her thighs and he had just given her another orgasm, her second of the day, when she'd heard the front door of the apartment slam. And then she'd heard Kristie's loud, panicked voice welcoming them. Jess had known Kristie had been trying to warn her. Thank God she'd been there and had been able to stall them just long enough for Lucas to scramble to the bathroom. Jess could still recall how his round white buttocks, pale in contrast to his Aussie tan, had flexed as he'd darted to the bathroom. She'd just had time to throw his clothes in after him and then pull on her sweatpants and a T-shirt before her father had come into her room to wish her a happy birthday.

Their hurried dressing hadn't been enough to fool him. He'd taken one look at their semi-dressed state and the rumpled bed and had gone completely berserk. Being caught out by her parents hadn't been anywhere near how she'd imagined that afternoon would end.

Her father had been furious with her, upset and disappointed, and disparaging of Lucas. He'd thrown him out without ceremony after a few well-chosen remarks before making Jess pack her bags. Her aunt and uncle had arrived home from their day of cat skiing in the middle of the circus and both girls had then been bundled into the car and returned to Vancouver, where Jess had been subjected to endless lectures about abuse of trust and lack of respect for her aunt and uncle as well as for her parents' rules.

'I was so worried about you.' Lucas's words broke into her reverie. 'I thought your father was going to have a fit.'

'He was always over-protective but his reaction was extreme, even by his standards. I was so embarrassed by the way he spoke to you. I still haven't forgiven him for that.'

Lucas smiled as the waiter delivered their appetisers. 'I feel I should thank him.'

'*Thank* him?'

Lucas nodded. 'His diatribe started me on this mission. He accused me of being a good-for-nothing bum and I wanted to prove him wrong.'

Jess looked around her at the opulent hotel. 'You did all this to get back at my father?'

'I wanted to prove to him that I was worthy of his daughter. He was my inspiration but I did this for you.'

'For me?'

He picked up her hand and Jess felt his pulse shoot through her. His thumb traced lazy circles in her palm and her body lit up in response to his touch. It gave life to her cells and awakened her dormant senses. She felt seventeen again, full of newly awakened hormones.

'Your father suggested I would never measure up to his expectations. But it was your expectations I was worried about. I wanted to be someone who was important to you. I wanted to be someone who could fight for you. Who could protect you. I didn't stand up for you that night and I want you to know that won't happen again.'

'I'm not the same person I was then, Lucas.'

She remembered that awful day as if it were yesterday. The shame. The heartbreak. She had felt as though things could never be worse. Until she'd found out that, really, they could. In fact, they could be a *lot* worse.

Everything had changed after that, including her. The only thing that hadn't changed, apparently, over the past seven years was how Lucas affected her. As his eyes locked onto hers she knew she would jump right back into bed with him tonight if he asked. She could feel every cell in her body yearning for him. She felt as though if she didn't keep tight control of her emotions her body would dissolve. The heat between them was enough to melt her core and she could feel herself burning.

She could get lost in him so easily and she couldn't let that happen. She needed to resist him, needed to keep her distance, but when he looked at her like he was doing now, like she was the only person in the world, she didn't think she had the willpower to stay away. Sitting there, looking in to his blue eyes, she could pretend that her life was still simple and easy and privileged.

But that wasn't the truth.

She fought the urge to give in to him. To do so would mean telling him all her secrets. She knew that it was inevitable but she was terrified of what he would think when he found out. Would he forgive her? Would he reject her? Would he reject them both?

What a complicated situation. Coming back was supposed to be the answer. It was supposed to help her get her life on track, to give her and Lily the freedom she craved, but all she'd got were complications and confusion. All she'd got were more questions and fewer answers.

She suspected it would be impossible to get out of this with her heart intact and she wasn't sure if she could stand to lose him a second time. But that wasn't going to be her choice to make.

She picked up her glass as it gave her a chance to remove her hand from his, which was the only thing to do if she wanted to think straight. There were things she needed to tell him.

Jess sipped her champagne, steadying the glass on her lip to disguise the shake in her hand. All the times she'd wished he'd been with her and now here he was.

It was time for the truth. She couldn't keep her secret any longer. She took a deep breath and put her glass down on the table. Starting the tale would be difficult but she feared it wouldn't be the worst part.

'Lucas, there's something I need to tell you.'

CHAPTER SIX

'I'M SORRY TO INTERRUPT, Mr White, but there's an emergency.'

Before Jess could begin to explain, before she could begin to divulge the secrets she'd been keeping, she was interrupted by a tall, thin, young woman dressed impeccably in a tailored black skirt suit, who appeared beside their table. The gold name tag on her lapel read 'Sofia' and her dark hair, cut in a shiny blunt bob, brushed her shoulders as she leant over to speak to Lucas.

'What is it?'

'A child is missing.'

Lucas was out of his seat before Sofia had finished her sentence. 'Are they hotel guests?' he asked.

'No.' Sofia named one of the smaller lodges and Jess recognised the name. It was an old lodge on the edge of the village. 'The search and rescue team has been mobilised but because of the heavy snowfalls they are having trouble finding tracks and have requested all hands on deck.'

'Of course.' Lucas turned to Jess. 'I'm sorry, I'll have to go. I'm part of the volunteer S&R team. We assist the professionals when we're needed.'

'Is there anything I can do?' Jess asked.

'What did you have in mind?'

'I don't know. I could help to look or at least make cups of tea. Someone always does that job.' There had to be something she could do.

'Sofia, can you see if you can rustle up some warmer clothes for Jess and some snow boots while I get changed?'

Jess took that to mean he had given permission for her to accompany him and she followed Sofia and got changed as quickly as possible. She didn't want to hold Lucas up.

Outside the snow was still falling. The Christmas lights around the plaza were doing their best to shine through the weather as Jess wondered what sort of Christmas the family of the little boy would get. She hoped he'd be found.

She could see pinpricks of light throughout the village and up and down the mountain. The lights bobbed in the darkness as the searchers panned their flashlights across the snow. There had to be hundreds of them.

The snow muffled all sound but Jess could hear the occasional voice calling out a name. Otherwise, the village was eerily quiet and Jess guessed that the S&R team didn't want any unnecessary noise that might mask something important. Like the cry of a young child.

Lucas strode out, heading for the lodge where the little boy had gone missing and where the S&R was now being co-ordinated. Jess hurried along beside him. When she slipped on the snow he reached for her hand to steady her. He kept hold of her as they approached the lodge from the rear but he wasn't talking. Jess assumed he was focusing on what lay ahead and she kept quiet too. She didn't want to disturb him or any of the other people who were out searching.

They reached the lodge and Lucas held the door open for her and followed her inside. He made his way directly to a table that had been set up in a lounge area to the right of the entrance and introduced himself to the man who was sitting there. He had a two-way radio in one hand and a large map spread out in front of him.

'The boy's name is Michael. He is seven years old and he was reported missing twenty minutes ago.' The search co-ordinator gave them the little information he had.

'Where was he last seen?'

'He and his brothers were playing in the snow behind the lodge. His brothers came inside thinking he was behind them but he wasn't.'

'Where is the search area?' Lucas peppered the man with questions.

'The lodge is at the epicentre of the search and we've spread out from here. There are people searching at one-hundred-metre intervals from here.' The co-ordinator pointed to concentric circles that had been marked on the map with red pen. 'This is the area we're covering so far.'

'Can someone show me exactly where he was last seen?'

'If you go around the back of the lodge you'll see the snowman the boys were making. That was the last confirmed sighting.'

'I'd like to start from there,' Lucas said, 'unless there's anywhere more specific you want me to begin?'

'There was no sign of him there.'

'I'd like to check again.' Something about Lucas's tone suggested he wasn't really asking for permission. He was a man with a plan.

The co-ordinator nodded. 'Okay. Take these with you,' he said, as he handed him a whistle and a torch.

Lucas turned to Jess. 'JJ, come with me.'

Jess followed him back outside with no real idea about what he expected of her or how much help she could be. She'd have to trust him to direct her.

She hurried to keep up with him as he stomped through the snow around to the back of the lodge. Jess's borrowed boots sank into the snowdrifts that had formed against the walls of the lodge and she was out of breath by the time she rounded the back corner. A lonely, misshapen snowman stared at her as she gulped in the cold air.

Lucas was standing beside the snowman, looking left and right. The snow around the snowman had been flattened and trampled by dozens of feet, the searchers' feet, Jess assumed, although most traces were already being covered by the fresh snow that continued to fall. Jess knew the footsteps of Michael and his brothers would have been obliterated long ago, making the search even more difficult.

Lucas lifted his head and Jess could see him looking up at the roof of the lodge.

'What are you looking for?' she asked.

He took three steps towards the lodge and stopped beside a large mound of fresh snow, which looked as though it had been pushed into a heavy drift by a snowplough. 'This pile of snow has fallen from the roof.' He pointed up to the roof. 'See how that section of roof is clear of snow?' Above their heads a large section of the lodge roof was bare. The weight of the fresh snowfall had caused the snow beneath to slide off the roof and land in a heap on the ground, a heap that was five or six feet high. 'I've seen this once before. We need to check this drift. Michael could be buried under here.'

Lucas knelt in the snow and started digging with his gloved hands while Jess stared at the huge mound. She felt her chest tighten with anxiety and she struggled to breathe. She felt as though she was the one trapped and suffocating.

How long had Michael been missing? It must be close to half an hour by now. *How long can someone survive without air?* Not long.

She knew that. She'd lived that. Her own brother had suffocated.

Jess was frozen to the spot, paralysed by the memories. She couldn't go through this again.

'JJ, give me a hand.' Lucas was looking at her over his shoulder. His busyness was in stark contrast to her immobility but she didn't think she could move.

'JJ, get down here.'

Lucas raised his voice and his words bounced off the walls of the lodge and echoed across the snow, jolting Jess out of her motionless state.

She knelt down beside him and started digging. If she didn't want to go through this again she only had one option and that was to do everything in her power to save this child. Digging like a mad woman now, she could feel the sweat running between her breasts and her arms ached with the effort of shifting the snow, but she wasn't going to let this be another tragedy. She hadn't been able to save her brother but she'd been eight years old then. She wasn't going to let another little boy die.

'Michael, are you there, buddy? Hang on, we're

going to get you out.' Lucas was talking constantly as he frantically tore at the snow.

Jess's vision was blurring as the blood pumped through her muscles. Her breaths were coming in short bursts and her heart was pounding but she wasn't about to stop. She dug her hands into the pile of snow again and her fingers hit something hard. Something firmer than the recently fallen snow.

'Lucas! There's something here.'

Lucas helped her to scrape the snow away and Jess could see something dark in the snow pile. Clothing? A jacket?

'It's a boot,' he said. 'Keep clearing the snow,' he told her as he pulled the whistle from his pocket and blew into it hard. The shrill sound pierced the still night air and Jess knew it would be heard for miles. Lucas gave three, short, sharp blasts on the whistle before yelling, 'Some help over here.'

Jess's movements intensified. She had to hurry. She had to clear this snow.

'What is it?'

'Have you found him?'

They were bombarded with questions as other searchers arrived on the scene.

'He's here,' Lucas replied. 'We need to clear this snow.'

Jess had cleared the snow to expose Michael's foot and ankle and now that they could work out in which direction he was lying Lucas could direct others to start clearing the snow to expose Michael's head. There was a sense of urgency, though the snow muffled the sound so there was nothing loud about the panic but it was there, under the surface. Every minute was vital, every second precious.

In under a minute the snow had been cleared to reveal a child's body. A young boy, curled into a foetal position with one arm thrown up to cover his face. He wasn't moving.

'Call the ambos,' Lucas said to the crowd that had gathered around them. He whipped off one of his gloves and placed his fingers on the boy's neck to feel for a pulse. 'Pulse is slow but present.'

Jess bent her head and put her cheek against Michael's nose. 'He's not breathing.'

'We need to roll him,' Lucas said. 'Clear some snow from behind him.'

'I can't let this happen again, Lucas. We have to save him.'

'We're doing everything we can, JJ.'

'We have to hurry.'

The snow had been cleared now and Jess held the boy's head gently between her palms as Lucas rolled him. Stuffing her gloves into her pocket, she started mouth-to-mouth resuscitation as they waited for the ambulance. She had to do something. She had to try to save his life.

Clearing Michael's airway, she tipped his head back slightly and breathed into his mouth, watching for the rise and fall of his chest. She was aware of his parents arriving on the scene as she continued to breathe air into their son's lungs. She heard them but she couldn't stop to look up. Everything else had to be blocked out. She could feel tears on her cheeks but she couldn't stop to wipe them away, she had to keep going.

'JJ, the ambos are here.' Lucas rested his hand on her shoulder and finally she could stop and hand over to someone who was better qualified than her.

She was shaking as Lucas helped her to her feet. She knew the tip of her nose was red and cold and she could feel the tightness of the skin on her cheeks where the tears had dried and left salt stains. Her toes were numb and her fingers were freezing.

Lucas put his arm around her. 'Come on, let's get you warmed up.'

She knew Lucas wanted to get her out of the cold and she knew she should probably listen to him but she couldn't do it. 'I can't leave yet,' she told him, as she pulled her gloves back onto her hands. She had to stay. She had to know how this ended.

Lucas didn't argue. He kept his arm around her as they stood together while the ambulance officers inserted an artificial airway and attached an ambu bag and Jess was grateful for his additional warmth. She could hear that the ambos were worried about head and thoracic injuries but they weren't giving much away. They ran a drip of warm saline and loaded Michael onto a stretcher as they continued to bag him. At least they hadn't given up.

Jess and Lucas waited until the ambulance drove away, heading for the hospital, and then, somehow, Lucas wangled a lift for them back to Crystal Lodge.

Jess was exhausted and Lucas practically carried her inside when they reached the lodge. 'Do you want me to run you home?' he asked.

'Not yet.' She could barely keep her eyes open but she wanted to stay in Lucas's embrace for just a little longer.

'Come to my suite, then, and I'll organise something warm to drink.'

Jess didn't have the energy to argue, even if she'd wanted to. He led her into an office behind the reception desk and unlocked a door in the back wall. The door opened into the living room of his suite. The room was cosy and, even better, it was warm.

Lucas steered her towards the leather couch that was positioned in front of a fireplace. A wood fire burned in the grate. It was probably only for decoration—Jess assumed there would be central heating—but there was something comforting about a proper wood fire.

He undid her boots and pulled them from her feet. He rubbed the soles of her feet, encouraging the blood back into her extremities, and Jess almost groaned aloud with pleasure.

There was a knock on the door as Lucas propped her feet on the ottoman and one of the housekeeping staff wheeled in a small trolley. 'Dessert, Mr White.'

Lucas lifted the lid to reveal a chocolate pudding, apple pie and a mug of eggnog.

He took the eggnog and added some brandy and rum to it from bottles that stood on a small sideboard. 'That'll warm you up,' he said, as he passed it to Jess before pouring himself a shot of rum. He dropped a soft blanket over Jess's lap and sat down beside her. She lay next to him with her feet stretched out to the fire and his arm wrapped around her shoulders. Lying in front of the fire in Lucas's embrace with a warm drink and warm apple pie, she thought this might be heaven.

'Do you think Michael will be all right?' she asked.

'He has a good chance. His pulse was slow but the cold temperature means his systems had shut down and that may save him.'

'But we have no idea how long he wasn't breathing.'

'Maybe he'd only just stopped breathing. If there was an air pocket in front of his face he could have survived for thirty minutes or maybe a little longer in those con-

ditions, provided the snow wasn't heavy enough to crush
him. We'll just have to hope that we found him in time.'

'How did you know where to look for him?'

'I saw a similar scenario once before in Australia
when a child was in the wrong place at the wrong time
and was buried by a pile of snow that slid off a roof. No
one picked up on it at the time so people were searching in the wrong places. It's stuck with me. I'll never
forget the possibility that that can happen.'

'What happened that time?'

Lucas shook his head. 'We weren't so fortunate back
then. By the time we found him it was too late. We were
lucky tonight.' He took a sip of his rum. 'You said you
couldn't let this happen again. You know what it's like,
don't you? To lose someone. You've been in that situation before too, haven't you?'

Jess nodded.

'Do you want to talk about it?'

'It was my brother.'

'Your brother?' She could hear the frown in his voice
and his arm around her shoulders squeezed her against
him a little more firmly.

She let her head drop onto his shoulder. 'He died when
he was six.'

'In an accident?'

'Yes, one that had a lot of similarities to tonight.'

'Was it here?'

'No. We spent most of our winter holidays here but
Mum used to take my brother and me to spend our
summer holidays in California with her family. Dad
would join us for a week or two but it was usually just
Mum and her sisters and our cousins and we'd spend
the summer at my grandparents' beach house. We loved

it. We were pretty much allowed to do as we pleased for six weeks. That summer we were digging a big hole with tunnels under the sand. We'd done this before but not with tunnels and one of the tunnels collapsed, trapping Stephen and one of my cousins in it. We managed to get my cousin out but not Stephen. The weight of the sand crushed him and he suffocated. His body was recovered but it was too late.'

'JJ, that's awful. I'm so sorry.' Lucas dropped a kiss on her forehead, just above her temple. It felt like a reflex response but it lifted her spirits. 'How old were you when it happened?'

'Eight.' Jess sipped her eggnog. She could feel the warmth flow through her and the kick of the added brandy gave her the courage to continue. 'My mother has never gotten over it. I think she feels a lot of guilt for not watching us more closely but we'd done similar things plenty of times before without any disasters. I think the combination of stress and guilt and trauma was all too much. We've never been back to California. Stephen's death cast a shadow over our family, a shadow I've grown up under, and it's shaped my life. I didn't want another family to go through what we've been through.'

'What did it do to you?'

'After he died my mother changed. She couldn't be around people. She couldn't bear the thought that they would ask about Stephen or ask how she was coping. She wasn't coping. With anything. She shut herself off from everyone, including me. Dad said she couldn't cope with the idea that something might happen to me too so her way of coping was to ignore the outside world and me.

'Dad, however, was determined that nothing was going to happen to me. One tragedy was enough. So I was protected, very closely and very deliberately. I wasn't allowed any freedom. Mum and Dad had to know where I was and what I was doing every minute of the day, which is why Dad flipped out when he caught us together. His whole mission in life had become to protect me from harm and there I was, in bed with a stranger. His reaction was completely out of proportion with what we'd been doing but it was a case of his mind jumping to the worst possible conclusions of not knowing what else I'd been up to without his knowledge. My whole life has been influenced by Stephen's death. In a way it's still influencing me.'

'How?'

'It had a lot to do with why I came back here with Lily.'

'Lily? That's your daughter?'

Jess nodded. She hadn't realised she hadn't told him her name. She wondered if he liked it.

'Before Stephen died I was allowed to walk to school with my friends and go on sleepovers and school camps. After he died that all changed. I didn't want Lily to grow up like that. But because I'd spent most of my childhood being taught to be fearful I found it hard to relax. When she was a baby I was very uptight, I was worried about what she ate and panicked every time she got a cold.

'I was nervous about leaving her with childminders while I studied and worked and when she started school I realised that I was bringing her up the same way my parents had brought me up. I was wrapping her in cotton wool and I didn't want that. I wanted her to have the childhood that I'd missed out on. I wanted her to be able to walk to school and to her friends' houses without me worrying that something would happen to her. I wanted her to grow up somewhere safe.'

'And what about Lily's father? What does he think about you moving here?'

'Lily doesn't know her father.'

'Really? What happened to him?'

Was now the right time to tell him? No, she decided, she needed to have a fresh mind.

'Sorry,' he apologised, when she didn't answer straight away. 'It's probably none of my business.'

If only he knew how much of his business it actually was.

She had to tell him something. 'Nothing happened to him. I was young. We both were.' She tipped her head up and looked at Lucas, met his forget-me-not-blue eyes and willed him to understand what she was saying. 'I loved him very much but our timing was wrong. It was no one's fault but Lily and I have been on our own for as long as she can remember.'

She knew she had to tell him about Lily but where did she start? *How* should she start?

She stifled a yawn. It was too late to have this conversation tonight; they were both exhausted. A little voice in her head was telling her that she was making excuses but she didn't have the emotional energy to have the discussion now.

She pushed herself into a sitting position. 'It's getting late,' she said, making yet another excuse. 'I'd better get home.'

'Are you sure? I hate to think of you going out in the cold just when you've thawed out.' She could hear the smile in his voice and knew she couldn't afford to look at him. If she saw him smiling at her she'd find it hard to refuse. Although he might not be intending to cause trouble he'd done it once before and she suspected it could easily happen again.

Mischief and mayhem. That's how she'd first thought of him and it still seemed to fit. Mischief, mayhem and trouble.

She was tempted to stay right where she was, on the couch in front of the fire wrapped in Lucas's arms. It felt safe. Lily was having a sleepover with Kristie so she could do it but she knew that it would just complicate the situation. Seven years ago she'd fallen for the charms of a good-looking boy and she knew she could easily fall again. She couldn't let herself get involved.

She reached for her boots, busying herself with putting them back on. 'I have to go. I have Lily, remember?'

'I'll walk you home, then.' Lucas stood and took her hand to pull her to her feet. He helped her into her coat and then took her hand again as they walked through the village. She kept her hand in his. There was no harm in that, right?

'This is where you're living?' He sounded surprised to find she was in the old accommodation block. 'We're back where it all began.'

He pushed open the door and Jess knocked the snow from her boots before stepping into the foyer. She hesitated inside, not wanting Lucas to walk her to her door, afraid of too much temptation.

'Thanks for getting me home safely and thank you for an interesting evening.' She sounded so formal but that was good. She was keeping her distance.

'My pleasure. We should do it again.' Lucas's voice was far from formal. It was full of promise and suggestion and Jess could feel her body respond. If he could do that to her with his voice she hated to think what he could do with a touch.

'Without the drama,' she said, as she fought for control. She was still conflicted and confused. She could feel the attraction but she knew she couldn't pursue it. Not yet. She couldn't let her hormones dictate to her.

'Definitely.' Lucas's voice was a whisper. He bent his head and his lips were beside her ear. Then beside her mouth.

Her hormones took over again as confusion gave way to desire. She wasn't strong enough to resist him. She never had been.

She turned her head and then his lips were covering hers. He wrapped his arms around her waist and pulled her close. Her hands went behind his head and kept him there. She parted her lips and tasted him. He tasted of rum and chocolate. He tasted like a grown-up version of the Lucas she'd fallen in love with.

His kiss was still so familiar and it made her heart ache with longing. She had seven years of hopes and dreams stored inside her and Lucas's lips were the key that released them. They flooded through her and her body sang as it remembered him. Remembered how he tasted and felt.

His body was still firm and hard. His hair was thick. He smelt like winter and tasted like summer. He felt like home.

She clung to him, even though she knew she shouldn't be kissing him. She knew she was only complicating matters further but she had no resistance when it came to Lucas. Absolutely none. She knew she'd have to find some.

She pulled back.

'We should definitely do *that* again,' he said as he grinned at her, and she was tempted to take him up on his suggestion there and then.

No. Find some resistance. Find some resolve, she told herself, and find it right now. 'I'm not sure that's wise.'

'Don't blame me.' He pointed up and she saw a sprig of mistletoe hanging from the ceiling. 'Someone has gone to all that effort, I thought it would be a shame to let it go to waste.'

A shame indeed. She smiled but she'd have to let it go for now. She wanted the fantasy but she was worried that the reality might be very different.

CHAPTER SEVEN

'LUCAS, WE HAVE a situation.'

Lucas looked up from his computer screen. His PA was standing in his doorway, smiling. She didn't look too perturbed by the 'situation'.

'What is it?'

'I think you'd better come and see,' Sofia replied.

Lucas followed her out of his office. He glanced around as he crossed the lobby. Everything looked to be in order. Sofia continued across the floor and exited the lodge out onto the plaza. It was late in the afternoon, the ski runs had closed and streams of people were coming and going through the village. Sofia gestured with an open palm towards the bay where the lodge sleigh was parked. Three young girls, one with her platinum blonde hair tied in two short pigtails, stood beside it.

Lily. Even if he hadn't seen her at the tube park last weekend he would have recognised her. She was just a down-sized version of her mother.

Lucas frowned. What possible reason could Lily have for being here? It had been almost a week since he'd seen Jess and he'd never met her daughter.

Since the kiss, he'd been snowed under with work, the hotel was at full capacity and he'd had some staffing and maintenance issues that had taken up a lot of his time, and although he had invited Jess and Lily to dinner during the week Jess had graciously refused. He wasn't sure if she was avoiding him or not but he'd been too busy to push the invitation. Nevertheless, his curiosity was now piqued.

'What do they want?' he asked Sofia.

'A sleigh ride.'

'I've got this,' he told her.

He'd been kicking himself since last weekend when he'd discovered that Jess had a child. He couldn't believe he'd been such an idiot. He should have come back to Moose River sooner. He'd thought he'd had time, he'd thought he could afford to wait until he'd achieved his goals. They were both young and he hadn't considered for one moment that Jess would have moved on. Not to this extent.

But a child wasn't a deal-breaker. Not in any way. If Jess had been married, that would be a different ball game but he could work with her being a mother. If she'd let him. And he was intrigued to find out more about Lily. This might be the perfect opportunity.

He approached the girls. One looked to be Lily's age, maybe a year older, and the other he guessed to be twelve or thirteen.

'Lily?' he asked. 'I'm Lucas. This is my hotel. Is there something I can do for you?'

Lily looked up at him and he was struck again by the resemblance to Jess. She was frowning and she got the same little crease between her eyebrows that her mother got when she was unsure of something. 'How did you know my name?' she asked.

Lucas smiled to himself. He'd been imagining that

Jess had mentioned him to Lily. He'd been flattered and encouraged to think she might have but obviously that wasn't the case.

'I know your mum. You look just like her. What can I do for you?'

'Is this your sleigh?' Lily asked, as she pointed at the brightly painted red sleigh that had 'Crystal Lodge' stencilled across the back of it in ornate gold lettering.

Lucas nodded. 'It is.'

'We wanted a sleigh ride. We have money but this man…' Lily looked up at François, the sleigh driver with an accusatory expression '…says he can't take us.'

'François isn't allowed to take you unless you have an adult with you,' Lucas explained.

Lily folded her arms across her chest and frowned. Lucas expected her to stamp her tiny feet next and he almost laughed before realising that would probably not be appreciated. Not if she was anything like her mother. Lily looked up at him with big green eyes that were nearly too big for her face. She was a *lot* like her mother. 'You could come with us,' she said.

'Me?'

Lily nodded. 'You said you know my mum. You could take us. We have money.'

'Where did you get the money from?'

'Annabel's mum,' Lily said.

Lucas turned to the other two girls. 'Is one of you Annabel?' he asked.

The older girl pointed to the younger one. 'She is,' she said. 'I'm Claire, her sister.'

'Is the money supposed to be for a sleigh ride?' Lucas asked.

Claire shook her head. 'No. We were going ice skating but Lily and Annabel ran off here.'

'Where is your mum?'

'She's at work,' Claire told him. 'She owns the bakery.'

'The patisserie?' he asked.

Lily giggled and her laughter set her pigtails swinging. 'You don't say it right,' she told him.

'Don't I? That's probably because I'm Australian. I don't speak French.'

'That's why you sound funny,' she said, as if everything made perfect sense now. 'I know all about Australia.'

'How much can you know? You're only five.'

'I am not. I'm six.'

Lucas was curious. He was sure Jess had told him Lily was five. 'How do you know about Australia?'

'My mum told me.'

Now he was even more curious. He'd been wondering about Jess's circumstances, he'd spent too much time in the past week thinking about her if he was honest, but there was a lot to consider. Why wasn't she living in her family's apartment? Why had she taken basic accommodation? And what had happened to Lily's father? Why wasn't he in the picture? And why would she talk to Lily about Australia? He couldn't ask Lily directly but he had another solution.

'I need to call your mum,' he told Claire. 'Would you girls like to meet Banjo while I do that?' he asked.

'Who's Banjo?'

'He's the horse.'

Lily and Annabel jumped up and down and clapped their hands.

'You've met François,' Lucas introduced the sleigh driver, 'and this is Banjo.' He was a handsome draught horse. He was dark brown but had distinctive white lower legs with heavy feathering and white markings on his face. Lucas rubbed his neck and the big horse nuzzled into his shoulder. 'Would you like to feed him? He loves apples.'

'Yes, please.' The girls all answered as one.

'Hold your hand flat like this,' Lucas took Lily's hand and flattened her fingers out. François passed him an apple that had been cut in half and he placed it in the centre of her palm. 'Banjo will take it off your hand but keep your hand flat.' He guided Lily's hand to the horse and held her fingers out of the way. 'He won't be able to see the apple so he'll sniff for it.'

Lily giggled as the horse's warm breath tickled her hand. He took the apple and Lucas let Lily rub his neck as he crunched it. Banjo shook his head and Lily pulled her hand away.

'François will give you each an apple to feed Banjo while I ring the patisserie,' Lucas said, as he took his cell phone from his pocket. He got the number and spoke to Fleur. He explained the situation and also explained he was an old friend of Jess's and offered to drop the girls off to her.

As he finished the call Sofia reappeared, carrying a small cardboard cake box, a flask and some takeaway coffee cups. 'What are those for?' Lucas asked.

'I thought the girls might like some hot chocolate and something to eat on their sleigh ride.'

Lucas raised an eyebrow. 'How did you know?'

Sofia smiled and shrugged. 'You're a soft touch.'

'All right,' he asked the girls, 'who would like a lift home in the sleigh?'

'Really?'

'Yep.'

His offer was met with a chorus of squeals and as Banjo had finished all the apples that were on offer to him Lucas helped the girls into the sleigh before climbing up to sit on the driver's seat beside François.

The sleigh had been decorated with pine wreaths, bells and ribbons, and François had also decorated Banjo's harness with bells and tinsel. The shake of his head as he started to pull the sleigh set the bells ringing. Lucas asked François to take them for a turn around the plaza before heading to the patisserie. He'd acquiesced on the ride as he wanted a chance to chat to Lily, wanted to find out what she knew about Australia, but sitting up next to François while Lily sat in the back wasn't going to get him the answers he wanted.

He delivered Annabel and Claire to their mother and told Fleur that he would take Lily to collect Jess.

'Banjo can take you to your mum's work, Lily. Would you like to sit up front next to François?' Lucas asked, and when Lily nodded he lifted her onto the driver's seat. This seat was higher than the passenger seat to allow François to see over Banjo, and the position afforded Lily an uninterrupted view of the Village. The sun had set and the streets and the plaza were glowing under the Christmas lights. Lucas grabbed a fur blanket from the back of the sleigh and tucked it over Lily's lap.

On the seat next to them was the cardboard box Sofia had given him. Lucas peeked inside. Sofia had packed some pieces of cake and Lucas's favourite chocolate biscuits. The girls had finished their hot drinks but hadn't had time to eat anything. He showed the contents of the box to Lily as Banjo set off again, pulling the sleigh through the snow. 'Would you like a piece of cake?'

'No, thank you, I don't really like cake.'

'How about chocolate biscuits, then? I know you like chocolate.'

'How do you know that?'

'Who doesn't like chocolate? And these are the best chocolate biscuits ever. I get them sent over to me from Australia,' he told her.

'Really?' she asked, as she picked one up and bit into it.

'Do you like it?'

Lily nodded.

'So that's something you know about Australia—we make good chocolate biscuits. Tell me what else you know.'

'I know about the animals.'

'Do you have a favourite?'

Lily nodded again. 'Mum says I remind her of a platypus but I like the koala best,' she said with a mouthful of chocolate biscuit, 'because it's so cute. I know what the flag looks like too but I like our flag better. Did you know you've got the same queen as us?'

'I did know that.' Lucas smiled. She really was adorable.

'I can sing "Kookaburra sits in the old gum tree".'

'Did your mum teach you?'

'No, I learnt it in school. Mum taught me "Waltzing Matilda".'

Lucas remembered teaching that song to Jess and explaining what all the words meant. Why had Jess told Lily so much about Australia? 'Did you know that in

Australia it's summertime now? It's so hot at Christ-mastime we all go to the beach for a swim.'

'That's silly. Who would want to go to the beach on Christmas?'

'Yeah, you're right.' Lucas had come to love a white Christmas but that might be because it reminded him of Jess. It was far more romantic to think of cuddling by a warm fire with snow falling outside than sweating under a blazing sun, battling flies and sand. He loved summer but he didn't have to have it at Christmastime.

Lucas checked his watch. It was almost five. 'We'd better get you to the medical centre,' he told Lily. 'Your mum will be finishing work soon and I promised Fleur I would have you there on time.'

'Oh.' Lily pouted. 'Is that the end of my sleigh ride?'

'I have an idea. Does your mum like surprises?'

Lily nodded. 'She likes good surprises. She says I was a good surprise.'

'Excellent. Why don't we go and pick her up from work in the sleigh? Do you think she'd like that?'

Lily nodded, her green eyes wide.

'That's healed up nicely, Oscar,' Jess said as she re-moved the stitches in the chin of a teenage boy. He had come off second best in a tussle between the snow-boarding half-pipe and his board and Jess had assisted Cameron when he'd fixed him up a week earlier. She snipped the last stitch and pulled it from the skin. 'See if you can stay out of trouble now, won't you?' Oscar was a regular visitor to the clinic and Jess suspected his skills on his snowboard didn't quite match up to his enthusiasm.

'I'll try,' he said, as he hopped up from the examination bed. 'But maybe I should make a time for next week just in case I need it.'

'I don't want to see you again for at least two weeks.' She laughed. 'Off you go.'

Oscar was her last patient for the evening and she checked her watch as she typed his notes into the computer. She was finishing on time and was looking forward to collecting Lily from Fleur's and getting home. Sliding her arms into her coat, she switched off the computer and pulled the door closed as she prepared to leave for the day. Heading into the reception area to say goodnight to Donna, she was surprised to find Lily there.

'Hi, Lil, what are you doing here?' She frowned as she bent down to give her daughter a kiss.

'We have a surprise for you.'

'We?'

Lily took her hand and led her outside. Lucas was standing on the porch.

He looked gorgeous. He was wearing a grey cashmere coat that contrasted nicely with his forget-me-not-blue eyes. His coat looked smart and expensive. Her own coat was several years old and Jess was well aware of the contrast in their wardrobes.

'Lucas,' she greeted him.

'Hello, JJ.' He smiled at her and her heart beat a tattoo in her chest.

She hadn't seen him for a week and the sight of him took her breath away all over again. How was it possible that she could forget the effect his smile had on her? It was like seeing the sun coming out when she hadn't noticed it was missing. She'd never thought her day needed brightening until Lucas had popped into it.

But that didn't explain what he was doing there. In front of her work. With her daughter. Lily didn't know Lucas. He didn't know Lily. She had deliberately kept them apart. She didn't want him getting to know Lily. Not until she'd decided what to do. So what on earth were they doing together? What was going on?

'Why are you here?' she asked. 'Why are you *both* here?'

'Lily went walkabout.'

'What's walkabout?' Lily wanted to know.

Lucas looked at Lily as he explained. 'It's something we say in Australia. It means you went wandering.'

'What? Where?' Jess was worried. She had wanted Lily to be able to roam around the village safely, she'd felt confident that it would be possible, but she realised now that she'd assumed Lily would be wandering with her permission. Not taking off on a whim whenever the mood struck her. 'Did you find her?'

'No.' Lucas was shaking his head. 'She came to the lodge.'

'Why? What for?' Why would Lily go to Lucas? Jess turned to her daughter. 'Lily, what's going on?' She could hear the note of panic in her voice but there was nothing she could do to stop it.

'Jess, it's all right.'

Lucas's voice was calm, his words measured. He was always very calm, very matter-of-fact and practical. A whole lot of personality traits that Jess was sure she could use but it wasn't his place to placate her.

'Don't tell me it's all right!' she hissed at him.

'Lily, Banjo looks hungry.' Lucas turned to Lily, ignoring Jess's outburst. 'Why don't you go and ask François if he has another apple that you can give him?'

Jess watched as Lily went down the steps at the front of the clinic to where the Crystal Lodge sleigh was waiting in the snow. She hadn't even noticed it she'd been so distracted by Lucas and Lily arriving on her doorstep. She assumed Banjo was the horse, a very large but fortunately placid-looking horse.

Once Lily was out of earshot Lucas turned back to Jess. 'Lily was quite safe. I thought this was what you wanted—for her to be able to feel safe in the village?'

'Within reason,' Jess snapped. 'I didn't expect her to roam the streets alone or take off without notice.' Who knew what might happen? All Jess's insecurities, deeply embedded into her psyche by her parents, came to the fore.

'Is this about Stephen?' Lucas asked. He was watching her carefully with his gorgeous eyes. Was he waiting to see if she was going to explode with anger or dissolve into tears?

Jess had to admit that in a way it did all relate back to her brother. She nodded. 'I wanted Lily to have the freedom I never had but I expected to know where she was. She's too young to be getting about on her own. She'd supposed to have someone with her.'

'She wasn't alone. Annabel and Claire were with her. Claire was supposed to be taking them ice skating.'

'So what happened? How did Lily end up with you?'

Lucas shrugged. 'She wanted a sleigh ride so I gather she convinced Annabel to take off with her and they came to the lodge to see if they could use their ice-skating money for a ride instead.' he said, as if that was a perfectly natural request to make of a complete stranger.

'And you said yes, I see.' Jess was annoyed. Not only had Lily gone and found Lucas, she'd also managed to wangle a sleigh ride out of him. She'd been planning that as a holiday surprise and Lucas had taken that gift away from her. She knew it wasn't his fault—he hadn't done it deliberately—but it still irked her.

'I did clear it with Fleur first,' he told her. 'You should be proud of Lily. She wanted something badly enough to go after it. That shows initiative, determination and commitment, and I thought she deserved to be rewarded.'

He would think that, Jess thought, even though she knew her bitchy attitude was unfair.

'And I didn't think you'd mind, especially if you got to share it with her.'

'What do you mean?'

'We've come to give you a lift home in the sleigh. We thought we'd take the long way around. What do you say? Am I forgiven?' He held his hands out, palms open, beseeching her, and she couldn't stay mad. She knew she shouldn't be cross with him anyway, he had only been trying to do something nice for Lily and for her.

And he was right. Did it matter that she hadn't organised it? She should be happy. Lily was safe and she was getting her treat. And it wasn't costing her anything. Well, not money at least. It was costing her some pride and now she would owe Lucas a favour.

He smiled at her. His dimples flashed and his blue eyes twinkled. She would owe him a favour, but when he smiled at her she figured she could live with that.

She sighed. 'I'm sorry I snapped at you. And, yes, you're forgiven.'

'Good. Shall we?' He bent his elbow and Jess tucked her hand into the crook of his arm as he led her down the steps to the sleigh. She put one foot onto the running board and felt Lucas's hands on her hips as he helped her up. She sank into the soft leather seat as Lucas lifted Lily up beside her. He climbed in on the other side of Lily and tucked rugs around them all.

François clicked his tongue at Banjo and the big horse moved off slowly, bells jingling.

'Mummy, I can't see,' Lily complained.

She was tucked between Jess and Lucas and was too small to see past them or over the front of the sleigh.

'Hold up, please, François, while we do some reshuffling,' Lucas said.

Lily and Jess swapped seats so Lily could see out of the side of the sleigh but this meant that Jess was now sitting beside Lucas. Their knees were touching under the blanket and Jess was very aware of the heat of his body radiating across to her. He took up a lot of space and she could have shifted closer to Lily to give them both some room but she didn't want to. It felt good to sit this close to him.

'How has your week been?' he asked, as Banjo set off again.

'It was busy. Apparently the resort is almost at full capacity, I suppose you know that, but we also really notice the influx of the tourists as we get an increase in patient load.'

'Do you still think you've made the right choice taking this job?'

'Definitely. It's so much better than my old job in so many ways. No shift work, no weekends. Three minutes from home. It's heaven.'

'What are your plans for the weekend?'

'I'm not sure. Nothing much. We'll probably do a bit of skiing. Lily has been having lessons after school so I like to see how she's progressing. She's been pestering me for a sleigh ride since we arrived in Moose River but I won't need to do that now.' She smiled at him, all traces of her earlier irritation having vanished. The sleigh ride was relaxing and romantic, even with Lily in tow. It was a lovely end to the working week and sitting beside Lucas was the icing on the cake. 'Thank you.'

'My pleasure.'

She could see his forget-me-not-blue eyes shining in the light of the streetlamps. He looked very pleased with himself. As he had every right to be.

He was humming carols—something about it being lovely weather for a sleigh ride together—as François took them on a circuit around the village. Lucas's hand found hers under the blanket. He squeezed it gently and didn't let go.

Jess rested her head on his shoulder. She didn't stop to think about what she was doing. It just felt natural. It felt good. Banjo headed up the hill where François stopped to let them take in the view of the village, which was spread out before them. The lights sparkled and danced and the sounds of happiness drifted up to them on the breeze. Jess sighed. Sitting in the sleigh, listening to Lucas humming, and seeing Lily's smile, she imagined this could be what her life would be like if they were a real family. Cocooned in their own little bubble of contentment.

She suspected that anyone looking at them now would assume that's what they were. A blond family, bundled up in their furs, being pulled through the snow on a sleigh. They could be the perfect image on a festive season card.

Only it wasn't the truth.

Lucas wasn't her reality. He wasn't her Prince Charming.

She still didn't know if he even wanted a family.

Telling him everything might ruin it all.

Banjo had begun picking his way back down the hill and within minutes François had guided him to a stop in front of her apartment block. It was late now. It was time for dinner.

Lucas helped them down from the sleigh and walked them to the door.

'I know you have other priorities and I don't want you to feel as though I'm intruding on your life, but I would really like to spend some time with you. With you and Lily,' he said, as he held the door open. 'Tomorrow evening is the first Christmas market for the season and we're switching on the lights on the Christmas tree out the front of the lodge. I'd like the two of you to be my guests for the tree lighting. What do you think?'

Jess thought she should refuse politely but she couldn't. She wanted to see him too and Lily would love it.

If Lily and Lucas wanted something badly enough, they would both go after it. That was definitely a trait of nature, not nurture, but why shouldn't she do the same? She and Lily could spend time with Lucas, it would give her another chance to see how he interacted with Lily, another chance to watch him. Was it her fault if having Lily there meant she had to hold onto her secret for one more day?

'We'd love to,' she said. 'Thank you.'

CHAPTER EIGHT

THE THIRTY-FOOT FIR tree stood sentinel over the plaza. Lily craned her head to see to the very top where the star was perched, and even Jess looked up in awe. She'd noticed the framework being erected—that had been difficult to miss too—but the tree itself, with its spreading limbs, was simply enormous. Its dark green foliage had been decorated with myriad silver balls and shining stars and bells that rang when the breeze stirred the branches. A light, shaped like a candle, was attached to the end of each branch. It must have taken hours to decorate but the effort was well worth it. It was beautiful.

Lucas came to them as they stood under the tree. He had his grey cashmere overcoat on again with a black scarf wrapped around his throat. Jess had made more of an attempt to dress up tonight. She'd chosen her smartest woollen coat in a winter white and had taken time with her make-up.

'Ladies, your timing is perfect.' Lucas greeted them with a smile and Jess was pleased she'd made the extra effort.

Lucas had reserved a table for them on the outdoor dining terrace in front of the lodge. They had an uninterrupted view across to the tree as well as down to the plaza, where the colourful tented market stalls had been set up. Carol singers were performing at the edge of the terrace and Lucas ordered eggnog for everyone as they sat down.

As the eggnog was served Lily handed Lucas a box wrapped in Christmas ribbon.

'What's this for?'

'For you,' Lily told him. 'To say thank you for the sleigh ride.'

Lucas undid the ribbon and lifted the lid to reveal cookies in various Christmas shapes—stars, angels, reindeer, bells and sleighs. Each cookie had been decorated with icing and had a small hole in the top through which red ribbon had been threaded.

'Mum and I made gingerbread for the school Christmas cookie swap and I thought you might like some.'

'Thank you, Lily, they look delicious,' he said, as he lifted out a star.

'You can't eat them yet!' Lily admonished him. 'You're supposed to hang them on the tree. That's why they've got ribbons in them.'

'I see that now. Have you hung some on your tree?'

'We don't have a tree.'

'You don't?'

'I haven't got around to it,' Jess told him. She wasn't actually planning on having a tree, mainly because she didn't have any decorations for it. She hadn't brought decorations with them to Moose River—that hadn't seemed a necessity when she'd been choosing which belongings needed to fit into their luggage—but now that she was immersed in the festive spirit of the village she regretted her decision. It wasn't likely to change, though. She could get a tree but she still didn't have the money to splash out on new decorations. Of course, she wasn't about to tell Lucas that. Fortunately Lily piped up and redirected the conversation.

'Do you have a Christmas tree inside?' she asked.

'I do,' Lucas replied.

'I think you should hang them inside, then, so they don't get snowed on.'

'I think that's a very good idea.'

The carol singers were singing 'O Christmas Tree' and as they neared the end of the song Lucas stood up.

'That's my cue,' he said. 'Would you like to come with me, Lily? We need to start the countdown for the lights.'

He took Lily's hand and a lump formed in Jess's throat as she watched the two of them make their way to the tree. He was being so sweet with her. She didn't know what she was worried about. He would love Lily.

Actually, she did know what she was worried about. She was worried he'd think less of her for keeping the secret. She didn't want that but there was no way around it. She knew she had to tell him the truth. She just hadn't decided when.

Lucas took a cordless microphone from his pocket and switched it on. He looked confident and relaxed and very sexy.

'Welcome everyone to the inaugural lighting of the Crystal Lodge Christmas tree. I'd like to invite you all to help count us down from ten to one before we flick the switch. Lily, would you like to start us off?'

Lily looked up at Lucas and beamed. Jess thought her smile was so wide it was going to split her face in two. She was looking at Lucas as if he was the best thing that had ever happened to her, and Jess knew Lily would only benefit from having Lucas as a father. There would be no downside for Lily. Jess had to do the right thing.

Lucas handed Lily the microphone. 'Ready? From ten.'

'Ten!' Lily's voice rang out across the plaza and then the crowd joined in.

'Nine, eight, seven, six, five, four, three, two, one!'

As they reached 'one', the lights were switched on, accompanied by a massive cheer. The tips of the candle lights were illuminated and now glowed brightly against the night sky. The tree had a light dusting of snow and looked magical.

As the carol singers launched into another set of carols Lucas and Lily returned to their table.

'Did you see that, Mum?'

Jess had tears in her eyes as she got out of her chair and hugged her very excited daughter. 'I did, darling, you were fabulous.' Over the top of Lily's head she mouthed 'Thank you' to Lucas.

'Can we go to the market now?' Lily asked, and Jess knew she wasn't going to be able to sit still.

'Would you like to come with us or are you busy?' she invited Lucas.

'No, my duties are all done for the evening. I'd love to walk with you.'

They strolled through the market, stopping at any stall that caught their attention. There was a good variety selling food and gifts, everything from scarves, knitted hats and delicate glassware to souvenirs, Christmas decorations, hot food and candies.

Lucas stopped at a stall selling decorations. 'Lily, I think I need a few more decorations for my inside trees, to go with your cookies. Would you like to choose some for me?'

Lily agonised over her choices but eventually had filled a bag with a varied assortment of ornaments. Jess wasn't sure how they would match in with the smartly decorated trees in the lodge's lobby but seeing the pleasure on Lily's face she knew that wasn't the point. Lucas was doing all sorts of wonderful things for Lily that Jess couldn't afford to do but she couldn't begrudge him. Not when she could see how much pleasure Lily was getting from it.

Jess stopped at the next stall, which was selling barley candy. This was a Canadian Christmas tradition and one she could afford. It was also one she'd shared with Lucas years ago. She chose three sticks of the sugary sweets, one shaped like Santa, one a Christmas tree and the third a reindeer, and let Lily and Lucas choose one each.

They sucked on the candy as they wandered through the market. Lily skipped in front of them, in a hurry to see what lay in the stalls ahead. She stopped at one that displayed some intricate doll's houses, complete with delicate furniture and real glass windows, and spent ages admiring the display as Lucas and Jess talked.

'What are your plans for Christmas?' Lucas asked. 'Are your parents coming up to the resort?'

Jess shook her head. 'I don't think so.'

'Really? I thought that was a family tradition for you?'

Jess had no idea what her parents' plans were. They could be spending Christmas here but even if they were their celebration wouldn't include her and she wasn't going to explain why that tradition had come to an end.

She stopped to buy a bag of hot cinnamon doughnut holes, hoping that would distract him from any further questions.

'What about you?' she asked, as Lily traded her barley sugar for the bag of doughnuts.

'I'll be hosting the Christmas lunch at the lodge. A buffet extravaganza.'

'A bit different from your traditional Christmas,' she said.

'I've grown to prefer a white Christmas.' Lucas smiled. 'It feels more like a celebration to me.'

They had reached the ice-skating rink at the end of the first row of market stalls and they sat on a bench to eat doughnut holes and watch the ice skaters. Lily leant on the railing, leaving Jess and Lucas free to talk. Jess sat at one end of the bench, which was a long bench with plenty of room, but Lucas chose to sit right next to her.

'What has Lily asked Santa for?'

'It's the same thing every year, a baby sister.'

'I take it from your tone you have no plans to give her what she wants.' He was smiling.

Jess shook her head. 'I'm not doing that again. Not on my own.'

Lily came back to Jess and handed her the empty doughnut bag. 'Can we go ice skating?' she asked.

'I guess so.' Jess knew it was only a few dollars to hire the skates.

'I might have to sit this one out. I'm a terrible ice skater. I'm Australian, remember, there's not much ice where I come from.'

Disappointment flowed through Jess. She hadn't stopped to think that this might be something Lucas wouldn't enjoy. But, taking a leaf out of his book, she decided persistence might pay off. 'Lily and I will help you,' she suggested. 'We can hold your hands.'

Lucas flashed his dimples at her as he grinned and said, 'There's an offer too good to refuse. Let's do it.'

He scooped Lily up and she squealed with delight as he carried her over to the hire kiosk to choose skates. It seemed his charm worked equally as well on Lily as it did on her.

Jess tied Lily's skates and then she and Lily each took one of Lucas's hands and stepped onto the ice. Lucas struggled to get the idea of gliding on the slippery surface but his innate sense of balance meant she and Lily had no trouble keeping him upright as they skated around the rink.

They'd managed to negotiate their way twice around the rink before Lily saw one of her friends from school and skated off, leaving Jess alone with Lucas.

'Did you want to keep skating?' she asked him.

'Definitely,' he replied. 'I'm not going to pass up an opportunity to have you all to myself.' He pulled his gloves off his hands and put them into his pocket. He held out his hand and Jess slipped her gloves off too and gave them to him before putting her hand in his outstretched palm. His skin was warm but Jess knew she wouldn't care how cold it got, she wasn't going to put her gloves back on.

They did a couple more laps of the rink hand in hand and then Lucas let her go.

'Are you going to try by yourself?' she asked.

'No,' he said, as he put his arm around her waist and pulled her in closer. 'I still need to lean on you.'

Jess knew that was a bad idea—he wasn't steady enough on his skates yet—but before she could protest he'd pushed off and within a few feet their skates had tangled. Lucas stumbled and grabbed the railing that ran around the edge of the rink and just managed to keep his feet, but his momentum as he tried to regain his balance spun Jess around so that she was now facing him. They leant together on the railing as Lucas straightened up.

He was laughing. 'Sorry about that,' he said. 'Actually, I'm not sorry, it's put you right where I want you.'

She was almost nose to nose with Lucas and she could feel her cheeks burning but it wasn't from the cold. It was from being so close to him. Jess lifted her chin and looked into his forget-me-not-blue eyes. She could feel his breath on her cheek. Warm and sweet, it smelt of cinnamon doughnuts. She was close enough to kiss him.

Lucas dipped his head. She knew what he was going to do. But she couldn't let him kiss her. Not here. Not yet. But she couldn't move away. She was transfixed by his eyes. She held her breath as she watched his eyes darken from blue to purple as he closed the distance.

Jess felt something tugging on her coat.

'Mummy, I feel sick.'

Jess looked down. Lily was beside her. 'Lily? What's the matter?'

'I feel sick,' she repeated.

Was she dizzy from skating? Jess wondered. She did look a bit pale. Jess let go of Lucas to put her hand on Lily's forehead. She felt warm but Jess found it hard to tell if that was just because of all the layers she was bundled up in.

'Too much sugar, probably,' Jess said. 'We'd better get you home.'

'I can't walk,' Lily grumbled.

'I'll give you a piggyback,' Lucas offered, and Jess looked at him gratefully.

Lily didn't need to be asked twice. She whipped her skates off, pulled her boots back on and wasted no time hopping onto Lucas's back, where she held on tight and buried her face in his neck as he carried her home.

'You're making a habit of getting us home safely,' Jess said, as Lucas put Lily onto the couch.

'I'm happy to be of service,' he said with a smile. 'Are you going to be all right?'

'We'll be fine. Thank you.' It wasn't quite the ending she'd pictured to the night but there wasn't anything she could do about that.

Jess was browning onions to add to the meatballs she was planning to make when there was a knock on the apartment door. 'Can you answer that, please, Lily?'

'Who is it?' she called out to Lily as she heard the door open.

'It's a Christmas tree!'

Jess wiped her hands on a tea towel and stepped out of the kitchen. A pine tree filled the doorway. 'What on earth…?'

Lucas's face appeared around the side of the tree. He was grinning at Lily. 'G'day.'

'Lucas!' Lily jumped up and down and clapped her hands as she shouted. All trace of yesterday's illness had well and truly disappeared. 'Who's the tree for?'

'You. I thought it might cheer you up if you were sick but you look like you're feeling much better.'

'I am better but, please, can I still have it? I *love* Christmas trees, they're so pretty.'

'It's not pretty yet but it will be once we decorate it.'

'That's very sweet of you,' Jess interrupted before the excitement took over completely, 'but I haven't got time to be fiddling around with a tree.'

'What's the problem?' Lucas asked, as he leant the tree against the door frame and stepped into the apartment.

He looked as disappointed as Jess knew Lily would be but as much as she would have loved to have a Christmas tree she hadn't the budget for one. She'd thought about decorating the room with a small pine bough and maybe spending an afternoon making kissing balls with Lily as a compromise, but that was as far as she'd got. 'It's always so difficult to get it secure and then in a couple of weeks I'll just have to work out how to get rid of a dead tree.'

'That's why I'm here. I will make sure it won't topple over and I promise I will dispose of it when you're ready. All you need to do is tell me where you'd like it.'

'Lucas, have a look.' Jess waved an arm around at the cramped living space. 'There's nowhere for it to go.'

'Why don't I put it in front of the balcony doors? How much time do you spend out there in this weather anyway?'

He smiled at her and Jess remembered how it had been when she'd been seventeen. She would have given him the world when he'd smiled at her. She had. And she thought she still might.

But she wasn't ready to give in just yet. 'I like to look at the village lights,' she protested.

'How about, for the next three weeks, you look at the lights on the tree instead?'

He made a fair point but she didn't have any decorations and that included lights. 'I don't—'

'Have lights,' Lucas interrupted. 'No dramas. I do. I have everything you need. Just say yes.'

Did he have everything she needed? Should she say yes? It was a tempting offer.

'Please, Mum?'

Why was she refusing? She'd dreamt of giving Lily a perfect Christmas and Lucas was here, offering to help make that happen. She'd offer him one last chance to excuse himself. 'I'm sure you've got better things to do too,' she said to Lucas.

'Nope. It's Sunday. I'm taking the day off. This'll be relaxing.'

Jess laughed. 'You think? Why don't you go out snowboarding? Wouldn't that be more fun?'

'It'll be snowing for the next four months, there's plenty of time for that. Christmas is in three weeks, which makes this a priority.'

She couldn't resist a combined assault. 'All right, if you're sure.' She gave in. 'But you and Lily will have to manage without me. I've got a mountain of mince-meat waiting to be turned into dinner.'

'No worries. We'll be right, won't we, Lily?'

Lily nodded her head eagerly.

Jess would actually have loved to help but she'd already said she didn't have time. But Lucas didn't argue—he didn't seem to mind at all, leaving Jess feeling mildly disappointed. Had he only come to see Lily?

Lucas tossed his coat onto the sofa and then Lily helped him to carry all the paraphernalia into the apartment. He'd brought everything they would need, including all the decorations Lily had bought at the market the day before plus candy canes and some of the gingerbread. The tree was only small, maybe a touch over five feet tall, and Jess had to admit it was perfect for the compact apartment.

Jess watched out of the corner of her eye, unable to resist an opportunity to watch Lucas. She forgot all about the onions on the stove as she watched his arms flex and his T-shirt strain across his shoulders as he hefted the tree inside and fitted it into the stand.

The smell of burning onions eventually returned her focus to the kitchen and she pitched the singed batch and chopped a second lot as Lucas and Lily trimmed the tree. He had even brought Christmas music—Jess could hear it playing on his phone while they worked.

'What are you listening to?' she asked.

He named a well-known Australian children's group. 'This is their Christmas album.'

'Why do you have their music?'

'I downloaded it for Lily. I thought she'd enjoy it,' he explained. 'Surely you recognise the songs, even if you're not familiar with the artists?'

'I will by the end of the afternoon,' Jess quipped. 'You seem to have it stuck on repeat.'

Lucas laughed and the sound filled the space. It was a lovely sound, better than the music, and Jess wished she could hear that whenever she liked.

'We like it, don't we, Lily?'

'Yes, it's fun.'

Jess felt even more left out as she listened to them laugh and sing along to Lucas's music. But she'd had six years of having Lily to herself. It was time Lily got to know Lucas.

But was she ready to share? What implications would

it have? He said he'd come back for her but what if he
changed his mind? What if he only wanted Lily? What
if he wanted to take her away? What was best for Lily?
Should she turn her world upside down? Could Lucas
give her things that she couldn't?

She knew he could.

He already had.

The tree was finished and Lily had switched the
lights on. It looked very pretty and lifted Jess's spirits.
'Would you like to stay for dinner?' she invited Lucas.
'We're having spaghetti with meatballs.'

'I don't want to be rude but I don't eat pasta.'

'Oh.' Her heart dropped. It seemed he didn't want to
spend time with her.

'Would it be all right if I just had the meatballs?'

'I don't want spaghetti either,' Lily said, but Jess
wasn't all that surprised. Lucas was Lily's new idol so,
of course, she'd want to imitate him. She hadn't stopped
talking about him all day and it had almost been a relief
when he'd arrived at their door. At least then Jess hadn't
had to listen to Lily's running commentary any more,
but having Lucas there in the flesh had added other
frustrations. She could see him and smell his winter-
fresh pine scent but she couldn't touch him.

Lucas and Lily sat opposite Jess with their bowls of
meatballs sprinkled with cheese. Jess could see some
similarities. Lily may look just like her but her green
eyes were more changeable. Tonight, sitting next to
Lucas, Jess could see that flash of forget-me-not blue
in them. It was odd that she'd never noticed that before.

Looking at them sitting opposite her, Jess had another glimpse of what it would be like to be a family,

and she wondered what Lucas would say if she told him the truth tonight.

But she couldn't tell him in front of Lily. Despite how he'd treated Lily over the past couple of days, she couldn't assume that his reaction would be positive. Being nice to an old friend's daughter was one thing, finding out he was a father might be another thing entirely. Jess couldn't risk upsetting Lily if Lucas's reaction wasn't what she hoped. This wasn't a conversation she could launch into on the spur of the moment. They needed time alone, without interruption. She needed a plan.

Perhaps she should ask Fleur if Lily could have a sleepover with Annabel. She didn't like to ask for favours but given the circumstances it was probably her best option. Either that or get Kristie to come up to the resort to babysit. Kristie had been right. Lucas deserved to know the truth.

Christmas was fast approaching and Lily's calendar was chock-full of activities, far more so than Jess's was. In the past week alone she'd had the Christmas cookie swap, a Christmas lunch, yesterday had been Annabel's birthday party and tonight she was supposed to be going back to Annabel's for a sleepover, but right now it didn't look as though that was going to happen.

Lily had started vomiting after the party and fifteen hours later she hadn't stopped and Jess was beginning to worry. She called the clinic for advice as she spooned ice chips into Lily's mouth. She tried to think what she would advise a stressed parent in this situation if she was the nurse who took the call, but sleep deprivation and worry made it difficult to think clearly.

Donna answered the clinic phone and put her straight through to Cameron.

Jess explained the situation and Lily's symptoms. 'She's been vomiting since four o'clock yesterday, she's complaining of abdominal pain—that's not unusual but she's extremely lethargic.'

'Do you think it could be her appendix?'

Jess had thought about that but Lily's symptoms didn't fit and she'd just assumed it was a usual childhood stomach ache, which Lily seemed to get plenty of, but what if it was more serious than that?

'I've checked but what if I've missed something?'

'I'll come over as soon as I can.'

Jess sat with Lily and fretted while she waited for Cameron. This was one of the things she hated about being a single parent. There was no one to share the worry with.

'Has she had a temperature overnight?' Cameron asked when he arrived.

'No.'

'No, not now or, no, not at any stage?' Cameron clarified.

'Not at any point.'

'Any urine output in the last four to six hours?'

'No.'

'When was her last bowel movement?'

'Yesterday?' Jess wasn't one hundred per cent sure.

Cameron examined Lily and checked for signs of appendicitis. 'I agree with you. I don't think it's her appendix. How quickly did she get sick after the party?'

'Pretty quick. A couple of hours.'

'Too soon for it to be food poisoning. And no one else has had any gastro?'

Jess shook her head. She'd spoken to Fleur and between the two of them they'd rung and checked with the other parents.

Cameron motioned for Jess to follow him out of the bedroom. 'I think it would be best to take her down to the hospital. They should run some tests. She could have a bowel obstruction but she'll need an X-ray to check that out.'

'A bowel obstruction!' That was not good news.

'It's one possibility and I think it should be investigated. The hospital will be able to run blood tests and get the results faster than I can up here on the mountain. I can treat her for dehydration but that's treating the symptoms, not the cause. Would you like Ellen to drive you? She's not working today.'

'Thanks, but I'll call a friend.' Jess didn't want to impose on Cameron or his wife any more than necessary. She had made plans to have dinner with Lucas tonight and it looked like she was going to have to call him to cancel but she hoped he would offer to drive them down the mountain. 'If he can't take us, I'll call Ellen.'

'All right, I'll let the hospital know to expect you.'

Just as she'd hoped, Lucas offered to drive them. She'd rather he was with her than Ellen. They were both busy and probably neither had the time to spend being her taxi service but Lucas had more invested in Lily—he just didn't know it yet.

Lily didn't vomit at all on the hour-long trip to the hospital, which Jess was grateful for. Lucas dropped them at the entrance to the emergency department and went to park the car. The hospital was small. At the bottom of the mountain it was still more than an hour out of Vancouver, but it did have modern facilities. Jess carried Lily inside and walked straight up to the desk.

'This is Lily Johnson. Dr Cameron Baker was calling ahead for us.'

The nurse on duty took them straight into a partitioned cubicle. There wasn't a lot of privacy but Jess knew most patients in an emergency department had bigger priorities than to be fussing about privacy. Jess ran through all Lily's symptoms with the nurse while she took Lily's obs and then listened as the nurse repeated them to the doctor, who had introduced himself as Peter Davis.

'This is Lily. Age six, weight sixteen kilograms. She has been vomiting since yesterday afternoon but nothing for the past two hours. Complaining of stomach pains. Afebrile. BP normal. No diarrhoea.'

'Current temperature?'

'Thirty-seven point two.'

'No allergies?' He looked at Jess.

'No,' she replied.

'What has she eaten?'

'Nothing since yesterday afternoon.'

'What did she eat yesterday?'

'I don't really know. She went to a party but none of the other children are sick, I checked.' Jess knew the doctor was thinking about food poisoning as one option.

'Has there been any gastro at the school?'

'No. Nothing.'

'No major illnesses? No surgeries?'

Jess shook her head again.

'Any episodes of rumbling appendix?' Peter continued to question her.

'No, and her GP didn't seem to think it was her appendix. He thought she could have a bowel obstruction.'

Jess was getting distressed. She didn't want to tell the doctor what to look for—she knew there was a routine, she knew he would want to eliminate more common possibilities first, and there was no need to run unnecessary tests if Lily's problem was something simple, but she wanted to make sure he didn't miss anything or ignore something more significant. A bowel obstruction could be nasty and Jess really hoped it wasn't the case but nothing else seemed to fit.

'No diarrhoea, you said?' he asked as he conducted the rebound test, checking for appendicitis.

'No.'

'Can you cough for me, Lily?'

Lily coughed obediently and didn't show any signs of discomfort.

'Is there any past history of recurrent diarrhoea or blood in her stools?'

'No.'

'I'll run a drip to counteract her dehydration and organise an abdominal X-ray. See if that can shed any light on the situation.'

Jess held Lily's hand as the nurse inserted a canula and connected a drip. Lily was very flat but that might have been related to lack of sleep. Jess wasn't feeling so bright herself.

The nurse fixed a drip stand to a wheelchair and helped Lily into the seat, explaining she would take her over to the radiology department. Jess walked beside the wheelchair and tried to keep a positive frame of mind, but it was difficult when she could see Lily so pale and quiet, with needles and tubes sticking out of her.

Jess waited as the X-ray was taken. Then she waited for the result.

'The X-ray was inconclusive,' Dr Davis told her. 'We'll do a CT scan next but I'm not sure we're looking in the right place.'

'What do you mean?' Jess was confused.

'Her pain has eased considerably and she's stopped vomiting. I don't think it's all as a result of the medication. I think she may have purged her system of whatever was upsetting her. Has she *ever* had any allergy testing done?'

Jess shook her head.

'Is there any family history of allergies or gastrointestinal problems?'

'She's a fussy eater with the usual childhood stomach aches but no allergies that I know of.'

'Any auto-immune deficiencies?'

'Not on my side, but I'm not sure about her father's side.' It was obvious that the tests weren't giving the doctor the answers he was expecting but Jess didn't have any other answers for him. She would have to talk to Lucas. She had to know what was wrong with Lily and Lucas could hold the key. 'I'll see what I can find out,' she said.

Knowing Lily wouldn't be able to see her while she was in the CT scanner, Jess returned to the waiting room to see if Lucas had appeared. She needed to find him. She needed answers. The time had come. She had secrets that needed to be told.

He was in the waiting room when she returned. He stood up when she walked in and came towards her with his arms open. She stepped into his embrace.

'How're you doing?' he asked. 'How's Lily? Do they know what's wrong?'

'They're still not sure. The doctor was thinking appendicitis or a small bowel obstruction but the X-ray was inconclusive. They're doing a CT scan now but the doctor seems to be leaning towards an allergy of some sort. He was asking about her family history but, of course, I only know half of the answers.'

'Well, there's not much you can do about that,' Lucas said, 'unless you can track down Lily's father.'

Jess took a deep breath. The time had come. 'I have,' she told him.

'What? Have you spoken to him?'

'Yes and no. Will you come outside with me? I need some fresh air.' She knew she had some explaining to do but she wasn't about to go into the details in the middle of the emergency department. Jess stepped out through the automatic sliding door. There was a bench just outside. She sat and waited until Lucas was sitting beside her.

It was time.

'I know where Lily's father is,' she said. She took another deep breath. 'It's you. You're her father.'

CHAPTER NINE

'WHAT?' LUCAS SHOT straight back up off the bench as if it was electrified. 'What the hell are you saying?'

'Lily is your daughter.'

'What? No. She can't be.'

Jess nodded. 'You're her father.'

'She's mine?' He shook his head in disbelief. 'I have a daughter?'

Lucas paced backwards and forwards in front of the bench while Jess waited nervously. What was going through his head?

He stopped and looked at her, a puzzled expression in his forget-me-not-blue eyes. 'You're sure about this?'

'Of course I'm sure.'

'But why haven't you told me?' Lucas stood in front of her, rooted to the spot. He ran his hands through his hair and stared at her with a fixed, unseeing expression. 'How could you keep this from me? *Why* would you keep this from me?'

'I'm sorry.'

'What for?' He was looking at her now, his blue eyes boring into her as if he was searching for any more secrets she had yet to divulge. 'For telling me? For not telling me? For keeping her a secret? Which one of those things are you apologising for?'

Jess felt ill. She swallowed nervously and she could taste bile in her throat. 'I'm sorry for telling you the way I did. I didn't mean to blurt it out like that.'

'How could you have kept this a secret?'

'I didn't mean to. I tried to find you.'

'When?'

'When I found out I was pregnant. Kristie and I hired a private investigator but after a month the PI told us we were wasting our time. Do you know how many Lucas Whites there are in Australia? And not one of them was you.'

'When was this?'

'It was April. The ski season was over, the resort had closed for the summer and you would have been home in Australia.'

Lucas's legs folded and he sat back down on the bench. His face was pale. He looked ill. 'I...'

'What is it? Are you okay?' Jess asked.

He looked up at her and she could see dismay in his blue eyes. 'April?'

Jess nodded.

'I wasn't in Australia then,' he said.

'What? I thought you were going back to university?'

Lucas was shaking his head. 'That was my plan. But my plans changed. I went home but I couldn't settle into uni. The father of one of my mates offered me a job in his new hotel and I jumped at the chance. It was a fantastic opportunity, I was going to get to do everything from housekeeping to bartending to running the activities desk and administration, so I took a year off uni. That April, I was in Indonesia.'

'I was looking in the wrong place.' Jess sat on the bench beside him. She was close to tears. All that time spent searching for Lucas, only to find now that she'd been looking in the wrong haystack.

'I'm sorry, JJ. I should have written like I'd planned to, but I thought I had time. I hadn't expected consequences.'

'Neither of us did, I guess,' she sighed. 'But I had to deal with the consequences and I've done the best I could.'

'But what about more recently? Did you look for me again?'

'Of course. I was eighteen, pregnant and alone— do you think I wanted to do this by myself? I searched again when Lily was born but I was still concentrating on Australia and the harder I looked without success the more I believed you didn't want to be found. My father told me you wouldn't want a baby, that you wouldn't want to become a father with a girl you barely knew, and I didn't want to believe him but in the end I didn't have a choice. I couldn't find you.'

'Lily is my daughter.' Lucas stood up and Jess could see him physically and mentally settling himself. He straightened his back and squared his shoulders and focused his forget-me-not-blue eyes on her. 'I need to speak to the doctor.'

'What for?'

'You said he was asking about allergies and family history. We need to tell him to test Lily for celiac disease.'

'What? Why?'

'I'm a celiac and if I really *am* her father then there's a good possibility she has it too.'

'Lucas…' Jess was about to say 'Trust me' but she decided that was a poor choice of phrase. 'Believe me, you're her father.'

'You said Lily had a lot of parties last week. If she has celiac disease and she's overloaded on gluten, that could explain the vomiting. We need to let the doctor know. He needs to run tests.'

'What sort of tests?' Jess felt she should know the answers but it was strange how everything she'd ever learnt seemed to have vanished from her head. Right now she was a patient's mother, not a nurse, and her head was filled with thoughts of Lily and Lucas. There was no room in it for facts about a disease she'd never had to deal with. A disease that quite possibly her daughter had inherited from her father.

Jess needed to focus. Lily was the priority here; she'd have to sort through all the other issues later, when her head had cleared and the dust had settled.

'I think it's just a blood test initially,' Lucas was saying. 'It's been fifteen years since I was diagnosed. We'll have to speak to the doctor.'

He headed back into the hospital with Jess at his heels. Dr Davis was standing beside the triage desk.

'Do you have the CT results?' Jess asked.

He nodded. 'There was no sign of a blockage on the CT scan either.'

'We'd like you to test Lily for celiac disease,' Lucas said.

'Why?' he asked Jess. It was his turn to be puzzled now.

'Apparently her father has celiac disease,' Jess replied.

Dr Davis frowned. 'And you didn't think to tell me?'

'I didn't know.'

'Lily is my daughter,' Lucas interrupted, 'and I have celiac disease.'

'She's never been tested?' Dr Davis asked.

'We were estranged,' Jess said.

At the same time Lucas said, 'I didn't know I had a daughter.'

Neither of the answers made things any clearer for the doctor.

'Look, that's all irrelevant,' Lucas continued. 'The bottom line is I have celiac disease, Lily is my daughter and her symptoms sound consistent with celiac disease. Even if she was asymptomatic, there's a high possibility she has it too. We'd like her tested.'

Dr Davis was nodding now. They'd managed to get his attention but if Jess thought she was going to be the one in control she was mistaken. Lucas was used to being in charge; she'd forgotten how much he relished it and he didn't mince his words with the doctor. He'd become like a wild animal protecting his offspring and nothing was going to stop him from getting what he wanted for Lily. Not this doctor and certainly not her.

If Lucas thought there was a strong chance that Lily had celiac disease they needed to find out for sure, but listening to him now and looking at his body language she knew that if she thought he would bow out of their lives, out of Lily's life, without a whimper, she was mistaken. She knew he would want to be involved, she knew he would fight for Lily, but where would that leave her?

'A blood test isn't conclusive. There are other digestive diseases with similar presentations,' the doctor explained.

'I know that but it's a start,' Lucas replied.

'What do you test for?' Jess asked.

'The best test is the tTG-IgA test. It's the most sensitive and is positive in about ninety-eight per cent of patients with celiac disease.'

'Positive for what?'

'Tissue transglutaminase antibodies. They'll be present if the celiac patient has a diet that contains gluten. But if they've already been avoiding gluten you may get a false negative. Does Lily eat food that contains gluten?'

Jess nodded.

'The result might still depend on whether or not she eats *enough* gluten.'

'It's our best chance,' Lucas insisted. 'Can you run the test?

'I can order it but I'm also going to admit her overnight. I want to keep her here while we run the tests. If it turns out to be appendicitis or a bowel blockage, she's better off here. I'll go and make the arrangements.'

'Now what?' Jess asked Lucas, as they watched the departing figure of the doctor.

'We wait. The important thing is finding out what's wrong with Lily. Celiac disease isn't life-threatening but if left untreated or undiagnosed it can cause irreversible damage to her small intestine. You know that— you're a nurse. If that's all it is it can be controlled by diet. Just cut out gluten. It's much easier to manage now than it was years ago. The important thing is to get it diagnosed.' He ran his hands through his hair, making it more tousled than it normally was. He sighed and shook his head. 'I'm going to wait outside. Come and get me if there's any news.'

That didn't sound like he wanted company.

He headed for the exit and Jess waited inside. Alone. And wondered if she'd done the right thing. But she'd done what she'd had to for Lily's sake.

Lily was brought back from the radiology department and Jess sat with her as the nursing staff got her settled into a ward bed. Her blood was taken and a sedative was added to her drip and Jess stayed with her until she fell asleep.

Lily hadn't vomited since they'd arrived at the hospital and Jess would have been happy to take her home. She would have gladly put all this behind them but the doctor's reasons for admitting Lily were valid ones. She would stay at the hospital for as long as it took to diagnose Lily's problem. But what about Lucas? Had he waited? Was he still in the hospital or had he got out while he still could? She couldn't have blamed him, her announcement must have come as quite a shock. She should have broken the news differently.

She owed him an apology.

She found him sitting on a bench outside the emergency department with his head in his hands. He lifted his head as she sat beside him but he didn't look at her. He ran his hands through his hair as he stretched his legs out, before tipping his head back and resting it against the wall. He was casually dressed in jeans and lace-up workman's boots with a T-shirt under his coat. His hair was tousled but his infectious grin was missing. What had she done?

He sighed and finally looked at her. His forget-me-not-blue eyes were dark purple. He looked exhausted. 'You should have told me.'

'I know.'

'I understand you couldn't find me but for the past two weeks I've been right here. You've had plenty of opportunity to say something and you still chose not to. Why? Why would you continue to keep this a secret? Did you not think I deserved to know I had a child?'

'I was waiting for the right time. I didn't know what you'd think. I needed to find out what kind of person you had become. I didn't know if you wanted to be a father. If you didn't want Lily then she would be better off never knowing about you. Better that than for her to know that her father didn't want her.'

'Of course I would want her. How could you think otherwise?'

'You don't miss what you've never had. She might not matter to you.'

'How can you say that? Of course she matters, and think of all the things I've missed. I missed her being born, I missed her starting school, losing her first tooth, taking her first step, saying her first word. My God, JJ, I don't even know when her birthday is.' He listed all the milestones that Jess had witnessed. She hadn't taken them for granted but she had revelled in them.

'Her birthday is September thirteenth.'

He ignored her olive branch. 'And what about Lily?' he continued, as if she hadn't spoken. 'You thought I wouldn't miss her but what about her? Do you think she doesn't miss having a father?'

Jess had felt the absence on Lily's behalf and Lily herself commented when she saw her friends' families. But did she really know what she was missing? Jess suspected she did—Lily knew what other people's fathers were like. She just didn't know her own.

He had made a good point.

'Yes, she misses it,' she admitted. 'She would love to have a father. She would love you.' Jess could feel tears of regret welling in her eyes but she tried to fight them back. She didn't want to turn on the waterworks, she didn't want Lucas to think she was looking for sympathy—she didn't deserve sympathy. But she did hope to make him understand. She was scared that if he didn't understand he was going to hate her, and how would she live with that?

'And when she asked about her father? What were you planning on telling her?'

'I hadn't worked that out yet. I didn't think we'd ever see you again.' Jess's voice was quiet. There were so many things she'd refused to think about. So many things she'd just tried to ignore. It looked like those days were over now.

'Did you think you were the only one who could love her?'

Jess shook her head. 'No.' *But I was worried you wouldn't love me.*

'I thought I knew you, JJ. I came back here to prove myself to you but I wasn't prepared for this.'

'What are you going to do?'

'I don't know but I want to see Lily.'

'What are you going to say?' Jess was worried. Was she about to lose everything?

'Nothing yet,' he said as he stood up. 'I'm not an idiot. This is a shock for me, it's going to be a shock for her too. I just want to see my daughter. Is that too much to ask?'

Jess shook her head and walked with him to the ward. She hesitated outside the door to Lily's room.

'Aren't you coming in?' Lucas asked.

'I wasn't sure whether you wanted me to.'

'Lily might think it's odd if she wakes up to find me by her bed. You're the one she'll be looking for.'

Lily was still asleep. Lucas stood by her bed. He didn't speak, just stood and watched her. Jess knew that feeling. She used to spend hours just watching Lily sleep when she'd been a baby. She looked like a little angel.

She stirred and murmured. She opened her eyes and recognised Jess but didn't wake fully. 'I need Ozzie,' she said.

Jess pulled the little grey koala with white-tipped ears and a shiny black nose out of her handbag and tucked it under Lily's arm. Lily never liked sleeping without Ozzie. She hugged the soft toy into her chest and closed her eyes again.

'Is that...?' Lucas spoke.

Jess nodded. It was the koala he'd given her for her eighteenth birthday seven years ago.

'You've kept it?'

'It was all I had of you.' Jess could hear the catch in her throat. The little koala had been the cutest thing she'd ever seen, aside from Lucas, and it had become her most treasured possession throughout her pregnancy, and now it was Lily's.

'Does Lily know where you got it?'

'No.' Jess shook her head and turned as she heard the door open.

Dr Davis stepped into the room and he held a piece of paper in his hand. 'I have the blood-test results,' he told them. 'Lily has tested positive for TTG antibodies and the test also showed elevated antigliadin antibodies.

'What does that mean?'

'It means Lily *could* have celiac disease.'

'Could?'

'The blood test isn't definitive,' he reminded her.

'So what do we do now?'

'You can take her home once this drip has run through, provided she has something to eat and keeps it down.'

'She doesn't need to stay overnight?'

'No. With her history and the blood test and scan results I think a bowel obstruction is unlikely so provided she eats, doesn't vomit and can urinate, you can take her home. But she will need an endoscopy and biopsy of her small intestine in order to confirm the diagnosis.'

'A biopsy? What for?'

'To look for inflammation of the intestinal lining and changes to the villi. That's a more definitive indication of celiac disease. Lily will need to see a specialist for the endoscopy. It will be done under a GA. I'll organise a referral. Has she seen a gastroenterologist in the past?'

Jess shook her head. 'No.'

'Who would you recommend?' Lucas asked. 'Who is the best paediatric gastroenterologist in Vancouver?'

'Stuart Johnson.'

Jess had known that would be the answer. 'Is there anyone else?' she asked.

'Of course,' Dr Davis replied, 'but you asked who the best is and in my opinion Dr Johnson is. But I can give you some other names if you prefer.'

Lucas jumped in before Jess could protest any further. 'He will be fine. We'll take that referral.'

'Okay. Do you have any other questions? I'm not an expert but at this stage I wouldn't panic. It looks like celiac disease may be the problem and if that's the case it's one of the easier gastrointestinal problems to control. Just make sure you keep Lily eating some gluten. If you stop before she sees the specialist they may not be able to make an accurate diagnosis. If she has a diet that is already low in gluten we could see a false negative. The recommendation is that she should continue to eat two slices of bread, or the equivalent amount of gluten, per day.'

Lucas waited until the doctor had left the room before he turned to Jess. She knew what he was about to say.

'What is the matter with Stuart Johnson?' he asked. 'Do you know him? Is he a relative? What's wrong with him?'

'He's my father.'

'Your father! Your father is a gastroenterologist?'

'Yes.'

'And he's the top dog?'

'What's going on, JJ? If your father is the best in his field, why did you ask for a different referral? Why don't you want to take Lily to him?'

Jess had managed to delay the discussion until Lily had been discharged and they were in Lucas's car on the way home. Lily seemed to have fully recovered from whatever it was that had upset her. There was no trace of the vomiting, she'd had a good sleep and appeared to have no lingering ill-effects. Jess, on the other hand, was exhausted, physically and emotionally, but she knew Lucas wasn't going to let matters lie.

Lily was cuddling Ozzie while she listened to Lucas's Christmas music through the headphones on his cell phone when he raised the subject again, and Jess figured she might as well get the conversation over with while Lily was out of earshot and otherwise occupied. Maybe it would be easier if Lucas was concentrating on driving and couldn't interrogate her or pin her down with eye contact. 'What do you remember about my father?' she asked.

'That's a loaded question. The only time I came across him was on your birthday when he called me all sorts of colourful names and threw me out. You probably don't want to know my impressions of him as a person.'

'And you're asking why I don't want him to be Lily's specialist?'

'If he's the best in the business then I assume his behaviour that night isn't a reflection on his skills as a doctor. I'm prepared to separate the two. If he's the best I want him to see Lily.'

'My father and I aren't in contact any more.'

'What?' Lucas slowed the car as he took his eyes off the road and looked at her. 'At all?'

Jess shook her head.

'Since when?'

'Since Lily was born. I haven't seen him for six years. He's never met Lily.'

Lucas flicked his gaze back to her a second time. 'If we are going to have any chance of working things out between us, for Lily's sake, we need to operate on a policy of full disclosure. No more secrets. I think it's time you told me everything.' His hands were tight on the steering-wheel and Jess could hear in his voice the effort he was making to stay calm.

She took a deep breath and said, 'Remember I told you how Stephen's death shaped us into the family we became? How I was protected, supervised, guarded almost, from that day on? I went to school, I spent time with Kristie and we came up here as a family. I went to parties but only if Dad had thoroughly researched the event. I understood his reasons—he was determined to do everything he could to keep me safe—and it didn't really bother me until I met you.

'That was when I finally understood Kristie's point of view when it came to boys. For the first time I was prepared to disregard my parents' wishes. For the first time I was prepared to take risks, to ignore their rules, to lie to them or to my aunt and uncle. I couldn't resist you and I couldn't forgive my father for dragging me away from you, for separating us. You were my first love. I couldn't resist you and I gave you everything. My heart and my soul.'

'You gave me everything except for our child,' Lucas said, as he glanced in the rear-vision mirror.

Jess clenched her hands in her lap as she willed herself not to cry. Lucas's words were like a sledgehammer against her already brittle heart and she could feel how close it was to shattering. She had done her best but it didn't seem as though he was prepared to believe that. Maybe, given time, he would trust her again. She'd never deliberately kept Lily from him and maybe one day he would realise that.

She checked back over her shoulder to where Lily lay with her eyes closed. She was either sleeping or listening to music but either way she wasn't paying them any attention. Jess needed Lucas to understand what had happened. She needed to try to explain.

'That's not fair. I told you I tried to find you. If my father had had his way you wouldn't have Lily now either. She is the reason I haven't seen him for six years.'

'Lily is?'

Jess nodded. 'My relationship with Dad had been strained ever since we left Moose River. He was still furious that I'd lied to my aunt and uncle and that I hadn't followed the rules, and finding out I was pregnant was the icing on the cake. I thought that maybe it would be good news, maybe it would help to ease the pain of Stephen's loss, but Dad was convinced it was going to ruin my life. He didn't want me to keep the baby and, as I've explained, he convinced me that you wouldn't want to be a father. He used the argument that you'd never tried to contact me. He was quite persuasive and I even started to question whether you'd given me your real name.'

'Of course I had.'

'I know that now but you have to understand that I was only eighteen and not a very mature eighteen. I was naive and uncertain and scared, and Dad's argument was quite convincing.'

'What did he want you to do? Did he want you to terminate the pregnancy?'

'No! He would never have asked me to do that. We may have had our differences of opinion on lots of things but that wasn't one of them. After losing a child of his own, he wouldn't have wanted me to terminate a pregnancy. He wanted me to give the baby up for adoption.'

'But why?

'He was worried that I was too young. That having a baby at the age of eighteen would ruin my life, my plans for the future. He tried to convince me that there were other options, that I didn't have to be a single mother. Obviously, I refused to give her up. I hadn't planned on getting pregnant but I had a baby growing inside me and it was my job to protect her. Plus she was yours— I couldn't give her up.

'So I decided to keep the baby and prove to my father that I could manage on my own, that I didn't need his help. I was going to prove I could handle the consequences. It was stupid really. I had no idea about anything but I resented my father for taking me away from you and I wasn't going to let him take my baby as well. So I sacrificed the bond I had with my father for the love I felt for Lily. I told my father I was keeping the baby and if he thought I was making a mistake then I would do it on my own and he need have nothing to do with me or his grandchild.'

'Was it a mistake?'

'I certainly hadn't planned on getting pregnant but being with you wasn't a mistake. And Lily isn't a mistake.' Jess glanced back again at her sleeping daughter. Their daughter. Lily was perfect and Jess had never regretted her decision. 'I was a naive teenager with no clue but a massive stubborn streak. It hasn't been easy but I don't regret it.'

'I'm sorry, JJ. It's been tough on you and I'm sorry to have to ask you this, but don't you think it's time you swallowed your pride and moderated your stubborn streak? Don't you think you should try to sort things out with your father? For Lily's sake?'

Jess shook her head. 'No. Too much has happened. I'm not sure I can go back.' Her entire life had changed and all the decisions she'd made, for the right or wrong reasons, had brought her to where she was now. She didn't think her decisions could be reversed that easily. She didn't know if she could do it. 'Couldn't we just ask for a couple of other names? It would be a lot easier.'

'But your father is the best. You're telling me you don't want your daughter, our daughter, to have the best medical attention we can give her? Because I sure as hell do.'

'Let me make some calls,' Jess begged, as Lucas indicated and turned the car onto Moose River Road.

'Let me see what other specialists I can come up with. Please? Just give me twenty-four hours.'

'I'll do you a deal. I'd like to spend some time with Lily so assuming she's feeling okay tomorrow I will pick her up in the morning and she and I can do something together while you sort out a specialist. We both have some decisions to make.'

Jess was worried. Was this going to be the beginning of deals and bargaining? Was Lily's time now up for negotiation? But she couldn't refuse his request. Not if she wanted to win the argument over the specialist.

Lucas parked his SUV in front of the Moose River Apartments. He carried a drowsy Lily inside for Jess but he didn't stay. He didn't stop under the mistletoe and he didn't speak to Jess again. It was as if he didn't even notice she was there.

Whatever Jess had dreamt of having was surely gone. She wasn't going to get the fairy-tale ending. They weren't going to be the perfect family on a Christmas card. She'd be lucky if she was left with anything at all.

But was that just what she deserved?

CHAPTER TEN

'HOW DID YOU GET ON?'

Lucas spoke to Jess as she walked into the stables behind the lodge but there was no 'Good morning'. No 'How are you?' There were obviously more important things on his mind.

Lily had spent the morning with Lucas while Jess was supposed to be organising a specialist appointment. Lily had chosen to groom Banjo and she barely looked up when Jess arrived. It was obvious that Lily had enjoyed the morning far more than Jess had. She seemed quite content with Lucas's company and Jess knew Lily was smitten with him. Why wouldn't she be? He had that same effect on her. Did neither of them need her? Would they be just as happy with each other? Without her?

Everything was changing and Jess was worried.

Jess shook her head in response to Lucas's question as she tried to stem the rising fear in her belly.

'Lily, why don't you finish up with Banjo and then François can bring you to the restaurant for a hot chocolate when you're all done? Your mum and I have some things we need to talk about.'

'Okay,' Lily said. She barely looked up, content just to be with Banjo.

'Have you made a specialist appointment?' Lucas asked as they left the stable to return to the lodge.

Jess had spoken to Cameron but she'd got nowhere with alternative options. She shook her head. 'I couldn't get anything until well into the New Year,' she admitted. 'The doctors Cameron could call in favours from are both on holidays and Lily's condition isn't considered serious so no one else would squeeze her in.'

'I'm sure your father would see her earlier,' Lucas argued. 'I understand your history with your father—you were eighteen and on your own—but I'm here now and if you think I'm not going to be an active part of Lily's life you're mistaken. One way or another I will make sure she gets a diagnosis and the treatment she needs. If she is a celiac then staying on a gluten diet could be doing her more damage. If she is a celiac she'll feel a whole lot better once gluten is eliminated from her diet and we can't do that until she's had the biopsy. We already have a referral to your father,' he continued. 'If you prefer I'll take Lily. You don't need to come. You owe me this much.'

Jess shook her head. She'd already come to the same conclusion. She didn't want Lily to suffer any more than necessary. She knew what she had to do. 'I know she needs the appointment. I'll make the call but I'll take her. Lily is my daughter. She'll need me there.'

'She is also my daughter and that is something else I wanted to speak to you about. When are we going to tell her the truth?'

'Can it wait until the holidays? There's a lot for her

to digest and I think it will be better if she has time to think about it.' Jess honestly felt it would be better to wait a little longer but she also didn't want to deal with the repercussions.

'I'll wait,' Lucas agreed. 'But only until the end of the school term. She finishes on Friday, right?'

Jess nodded.

'I'll take you both to dinner on Friday night, then,' he said, as he held the door for her to step into the lobby. 'We can speak to her together. I'd like to be able to tell my parents about her before Christmas. I was planning on going back to Australia at the end of the ski season and I would like to take Lily too.'

Jess stopped dead in her tracks. He wanted to take Lily!

Black spots danced in front of her eyes and she thought she might either faint or throw up but if she couldn't stand the idea of giving her baby up at birth there was no way she was going to give her up now after six years of being her mother. She might not be able to deny him but she wasn't going to give up without a fight. She stood up as tall as possible and willed her vision to clear. She clenched her fists and tightened her thigh muscles as she tried to stop her knees from shaking. 'No.'

Lucas was frowning. 'What do you mean, "No"?'

'I left Moose River seven years ago, heartbroken and pregnant. Lily was all I had left.' Her voice was quiet but firm. 'I'm sorry I couldn't find you. I'm sorry I didn't try again. I'm sorry that you never posted me those letters and I'm sorry that you've missed six years of her life. I was foolish and I'm sorry but I'm not going to let you take her away from me. I've lost my brother and my mother and my father. Lily is all I have left. I won't let you take her from me.'

'I don't think you were foolish.'

'You don't?' After everything she'd admitted to he wasn't going to crucify her?

'No.' He shook his head. 'I've never said that.' He put his hand on her elbow and guided her to one of the soft leather couches in the lobby. He sat beside her and put his hand on her knee and only then did Jess stop shaking.

'You've made it this far on your own and from what I can see you've done a great job with Lily. She's a great kid and she's lucky enough to have a mother who loves her. I admit I wish I'd known about her before now but I know I have to take some of the blame for that. And I don't intend to take Lily away from you. I'd like to take her to Australia—she's got a whole family over there who would love to meet her—but I'm only talking about going for a holiday. My life is here now. My business is here and my daughter is here. I'm not going to abandon her and I would never take her from you. I assumed you would come with us.'

'Really?' Relief flooded through Jess and she thought she might burst into tears. Her emotions had been running high for days and being close to tears was almost becoming a permanent state for her. 'Even after everything I've done?'

'What's done is done, JJ,' he replied. 'We can't undo the past. We need to move on and Lily has to be our priority. She's the important one. We need to do what's best for her. We need to make sure she feels loved and secure and we need to sort out her health. So will you make an appointment to take Lily to see your father?'

'Yes.' She had no choice. She owed it to Lily and to Lucas. She would have to mend the relationship with her father. After seven years of making all her own decisions it seemed as though her time was up. Fate, or maybe Lucas, was taking over.

Jess was sweating as she picked up the phone and dialled her father's office number. She had never forgotten it, even after all these years. She just hoped he still had the same secretary. How would she explain her request if her father's admin staff had changed?

She'd delayed phoning her father's office until this morning. She'd spent last night trying to work out how to word her request. It seemed strange to be calling to ask for a favour from her father when she hadn't spoken to him in over six years. But it looked like it was time for Jess to be the bigger person and put her stubborn streak to one side, as Lucas had suggested.

She sighed with relief when Gabrielle answered. Jess launched into the speech she'd rehearsed before she could chicken out and she had just hung up the phone when there was a knock on her door. It opened and Cameron stepped in to her clinic room.

'Jess, has Lily gone on the school excursion to go dog sledding?'

What a strange question. Jess frowned and nodded.

'I don't want you to panic, everyone is okay at this stage, but there's been an accident.'

You couldn't tell someone not to panic right before delivering that sort of news. Jess shot out of her seat. 'What is it? What's happened?'

'There's been an accident on one of the chairlifts.'

Jess's hand flew to her mouth as her heart plummeted in her chest. *'Lily.'*

'The children are all okay at this stage but the lift has stopped working and there are people trapped in the cars. I thought you might want to go up the mountain. I'm sure the authorities will contact everyone but I wanted you to know.'

Jess changed her shoes and grabbed her coat. She didn't need to be asked twice.

She raced out of the building and collided with Lucas.

'What are you doing here?' She looked up at him as his arms went around her to steady her. One look at his face told her that he'd heard about the accident too. Of course, he was part of the search and rescue unit.

'What have you heard?' she asked.

'Not a lot at this stage except that no one seems to be injured yet and that a group of six- and seven-year-olds are involved. I thought that might mean Lily. But no one will notify me because I'm not her next of kin. I didn't know if you would call me so I came to you.'

'Have you been called in to the rescue?'

He shook his head and let her go. 'No, this is a mission for the trained team. I came to find out if Lily was in the gondola and to take you up the mountain.' He gestured to his left where a snowmobile was parked at the bottom of the steps. 'It'll be faster than taking the chair lift to the basin and then walking.'

She didn't waste time arguing. She pulled a knitted cap from her pocket and tugged it onto her head as Lucas handed her a pair of snow goggles. She followed him down the steps and climbed onto the snowmobile behind him. She tucked herself against his back and wrapped her arms around his waist. He was solid and muscular. He felt safe. Maybe he really was her knight in shining armour after all.

There was no denying he was a good man. Maybe they would be okay. She and Lucas would work things out. She'd make sure of it. For Lily's sake.

After several minutes Jess felt the snowmobile slow and knew they'd reached the basin. She peered around Lucas's shoulder and saw a group of people, parents of children in Lily's class, gathered around the base of one of the gondola pylons.

Lucas switched off the engine. The lift was motion-less and the silence was eerie. Jess had expected noise and activity but everyone seemed to be standing around. Immobile. Uncertain.

They dismounted and Jess removed her goggles. She needed a clearer picture.

They were close to the edge of a gully. The gondola cable stretched across the ravine and Jess's eye was drawn to where it dipped lower. She could see what looked like two cars close together. Weren't they nor-mally further apart than that? Or was she just looking at it from a funny angle?

'What's going on? Why isn't anything happening?' she asked Lucas.

'I'm not sure. I'll go and find out.'

He was back within minutes, bringing Fleur and her husband, Nathan, with him. Fleur's eyes were puffy and her nose was red but she wasn't crying at the moment. Jess hugged her tightly. 'Where are the girls?' she asked.

Fleur pointed down into the ravine to where it looked as though two cars had collided. 'They're in one of those cars.'

'Oh, no!'

'The girls are okay, JJ,' Lucas told her. 'There's a teacher in the gondola with them and she is in contact via her cell phone. No one is badly injured. The second car hasn't come loose but access is difficult.'

Jess released Fleur and turned to Lucas. 'When will they get them out?'

'It's going to take time. It's complicated. No one is getting out of any of the cars until the rescue team are certain that it is safe to do so. They're worried that emptying or moving the cars that haven't been involved in the derailment may cause the unstable cars to fall.'

'They could fall?' Jess clutched Lucas's arm.

'At the moment they think the cars are stable.'

'At the moment! I don't understand how this could happen. How is something like this even possible?'

'Apparently the emergency brake was accidentally activated, which caused one car to derail. The grip holding that car to the cable must have been faulty and when the cable jolted the car bounced and the grip released, but when it slid back into the other car they locked together and so far that has prevented it from falling. But because of where the cars are, getting to them will be tricky. They're talking about rigging up a second cable from tower to tower so that the mountain rescue team can access the gondolas from above. They'll have to secure the cars and then use harnesses and stretchers to lower everyone to safety. It's going to take time,' he repeated.

Jess wrapped her arms around herself. Despite the chill in the air she could feel herself breaking into a sweat. Fear gripped her heart and squeezed it tight. She couldn't bear to think of all the things that could go wrong. She couldn't bear to think of Lily up there, scared and in danger.

Lucas pulled her against his chest. She didn't want to imagine going through this on her own. Whatever happened, she knew she could rely on him. He would be there for Lily and she knew he'd be there for her too. He had promised her that much. She needed to give him something in return.

'If Lily is okay I promise I will give you whatever you want,' she said as she looked up at him. 'We'll tell her the truth tonight.'

Lucas hated feeling useless. He hated not being needed. He'd organised the lodge to send up hot refreshments but that had been the sum total of his assistance, and he wished there was more he could do. Standing around waiting while other people were being constructive didn't sit well with him. His child was trapped in one of the cars and he could do nothing.

He knew this rescue required the expertise of trained personnel and he didn't want to put anyone at risk by having people who were not fully qualified sticking their oar in, and that included him, but it didn't stop him from feeling inadequate.

Fleur and Nathan had gone to get something to eat, leaving him alone with Jess. She hadn't wanted to join the larger group of parents who waited anxiously to hug their children. She said she didn't want to talk to anyone. She sat on the snowmobile and chewed her lip while he paced around in the snow.

The whole process was slow going. Lucas and Jess had been on site for two hours and the gondolas had only just been secured. It was bitterly cold and unpleasant but no one was going anywhere. Hot drinks, soup and blankets were being passed around to the parents and some shelters had been brought up the mountain in an attempt to provide some protection from the biting wind. The wind was blowing straight up the gully, rocking the cars. The wind was strengthening and in Lucas's opinion the rescue team had managed to secure the cars just in time. Any longer and the wind would have made the project even more difficult, treacherous even, but at least the sky was clear. No snow was forecast and that was something to be grateful for. That was one less thing for the mountain rescue team to have to contend with.

'Do you want to sit down for a while?' Jess asked him.

He shook his head. 'I can't sit still. I'm finding it hard enough knowing that other people are being useful while I'm hanging around, twiddling my thumbs.'

Jess had promised him that if they got through this they would tell Lily the truth and he had to believe that everything would be okay. But it was proving difficult. He'd only just discovered the truth and he wasn't prepared to have Lily taken away from him now. 'I wish there was more I could do.'

'You're helping me.' Jess smiled up at him and reached out one hand.

'How?' he asked as he took her hand in his.

'It's nice to know I'm not alone. I'm glad you're here.'

He let her pull him down to sit beside her on the snowmobile. He wrapped his arm around her shoulders and tried to be content with the moment while avoiding thinking about all the things that could go wrong. He could sit still if Jess needed him to. She could anchor him. Sitting with her tucked against his side would settle him.

'Talk to me about Lily,' he said. Talking might keep his mind occupied. It might keep him too busy to worry and there was so much he didn't know about his daughter. He was still coming to terms with the idea that he was a father. He felt the weight of responsibility, to both Lily and Jess, but he was looking forward to the changes this development would bring. He didn't expect it to be easy.

There was a lot he and Jess needed to sort out but he was determined they would manage. He wished he hadn't missed six years of his daughter's life but that was as much his fault as Jess's and all he could do now was make certain he got to share the rest with them both. He refused to think that he wasn't going to get that chance and, in the meantime, he needed to learn as much about Lily as he could. He needed to get to know his daughter.

'She was born at half past six in the morning, six twenty-eight, to be exact, and she weighed seven pounds, five ounces.' Jess's voice lifted as she spoke about their daughter. This conversation wasn't just helping him. It was keeping her mind occupied too. 'She was in a hurry and she didn't come quietly. She hasn't been afraid to let me know what she's thinking ever since. She can be quite stubborn.'

Lucas smiled. 'Sounds like someone else I know.'

Jess nudged him in the side and said, 'She's got plenty of you in her as well.'

'Really?' He was surprised at how pleased he was to hear that. 'Good traits, I hope?'

'Mostly,' Jess teased. 'She's becoming quite a confident skier. I suspect she got her sense of balance from you, and her fearlessness—those things definitely didn't come from me. She has a very strong sense of self and have you noticed she has your ears?'

'I'm glad she got a little bit of me. There's no doubting she's your daughter, but it's nice to know I had something to do with it.'

'Don't worry, there's plenty of you in her. Her eyes aren't always green, they change colour depending on what she wears and if she wears blue they can look like yours. She started walking when she was thirteen months old and lost her first tooth at the beginning of this year. She loves roast chicken and carrots and Disney princesses and her koala and your horse, Banjo. Her favourite colour is pink and she loves to sing.'

Jess paused as around them noise started building. Low murmurs became a buzz of anticipation and people were on the move. The rescue crews in their bright yellow jackets were going past, carrying harnesses, and the ski patrol and ambos carried stretchers and first-aid kits. Lucas knew what that meant.

He stood and reached for her hand. 'They're starting to evacuate the cars.'

They hurried closer and stood waiting. The derailed car was the first to be evacuated but eventually it was Lily's turn.

Jess burst into tears when she spied Lily being lowered from the gondola in a harness. She ran through the snow and scooped her into her arms.

'My precious girl, are you all right?'

'I'm fine, Mum.' She was beaming. 'That was the best excursion *ever.*'

'She sounds okay to me.' Lucas grinned but relief washed over him too.

Jess laughed and wiped the tears from her cheeks. 'You've only been on one other excursion, Lil.' She brushed Lily's hair from her forehead and dropped a kiss there. Her fingers ran gently over the spot she'd just kissed. 'You've got a nasty bump on your head here— are you sure you're okay?'

'I was leaning on the window when the other gondola car crashed into us and I bumped my head. You should have heard the big bang it made.'

'Your head or the car?' Lucas asked.

Lily giggled. 'The car. It sounded like thunder and we all fell on the floor.'

Snow cats had been sent up the mountain to ferry the children back to the medical centre, where they would be checked for any injuries, frostnip or concussion. Jess climbed into the vehicle with Lily, she wasn't prepared to let her out of her sight, and Lucas took the snowmobile back down the mountain and met them at the clinic.

'Is she *still* talking?' he said, as he watched Lily gossiping with a group of friends as they drank hot chocolate and waited to be given the all-clear after their ordeal.

'The whole adventure has given her plenty to say. This is the most excitement she's ever had. She definitely takes after her father.' Jess spoke quietly but her words were accompanied by a smile. 'I always avoided drama.'

'Nature versus nurture?' he asked.

'It looks that way.'

Lucas took Jess's arm and gently pulled her to one side of the bustling waiting room. The noise level was high and he was fairly sure they could talk without being overheard but he made sure he kept Lily within sight. For Jess's sake and his own. 'Will you bring her over to the lodge when you're finished here? I'd like to talk to her tonight.'

Jess frowned and a little crease appeared between her eyebrows, making her look exactly like her daughter. Their daughter. 'I don't know. Don't you think she's had enough for one day?'

'I was as worried as you were up on the mountain, JJ. I want to be part of Lily's life and I want that to start today. I don't want any more missed moments. She's resilient. Look at how she coped with the events of today. She'll cope with this. Besides, it's good news.'

Jess paused and Lucas held his breath. He didn't want to wait. He wanted to be acknowledged as Lily's father.

Finally she nodded. 'All right. I'll take her home for a warm bath and then we'll come over.'

'Lily, your mum and I have something to tell you.'

Lily paused momentarily with one hand on Banjo's neck. It had been Jess's suggestion that they go to the stable and he had agreed without reservation. Grooming Banjo was a soothing, familiar activity for Lily and it meant they didn't have to sit awkwardly in the hotel to have this conversation. 'Is it a surprise?' she asked. 'I love surprises.'

'It was a surprise for me,' Lucas told her. 'But it's something I'm very excited about. Something I've wished for for a long time.'

'Lil, you know how I've always said you were made up of bits and pieces?' Jess asked her.

Lily nodded and tilted her head as she replied, 'Like a platypus.'

'That's right. Well, the outside bits of you are just like me,' Jess said, 'but some of the inside bits of you are different. Parts of your insides are funny and other parts are curious and other parts are brave, much braver than me, and you get those parts from your dad.'

Lily frowned and Lucas was reminded of how Jess had looked earlier in the day. 'I don't have a dad.'

'Everyone has a dad somewhere, sweetheart. I just lost your dad for a while and it took me a long time to find him again.'

'Is he nice?'

'He's very nice.'

Jess smiled at Lucas as she spoke to their daughter, and Lucas finally had what he'd wished for. He remembered the expression on Jess's face the night she'd told him about her relationship with Lily's father. How she'd looked when she'd told him that she'd loved Lily's dad. He'd seen the love in her eyes that night and he'd wished she'd been talking about him. He hadn't known then that he was Lily's father but she had that same expression in her eyes tonight. She'd said she loved him then. Did she love him still?

'Will he like me?' Lily wanted to know.

'He will *love* you. Very much. But I think he might want to tell you that himself.'

'When can I see him?'

'He's right here, Lily.'

'Where?'

'It's me, Lily,' Lucas told her 'I'm your dad.'

'Really?'

'Really.' He nodded. 'And I think I'm the luckiest dad in the world.'

'This is the best day ever,' Lily said, as she threw her arms around his neck and burrowed in against his chest.

He'd been worried about her reaction to their news. Holding his child in his arms was the most incredible feeling and he would have been devastated if Lily hadn't wanted him. He didn't think he would be able to give her up after this. What would he have done if she hadn't been as thrilled about the news as Jess had assured him she would be? What if she hadn't been as excited as he'd hoped she would be?

He wondered how Jess was feeling. He looked over the top of Lily's head. Jess was smiling but he could see a glimmer of tears in her eyes. How did she feel about having to share Lily?

Lily had fallen asleep on his couch after polishing off her dinner. Lucas looked at his sleeping daughter. Her blonde head was resting on Jess's lap and she had Ozzie, the koala, tucked under her arm. She was beautiful. She was perfect.

'What is it?' Jess asked him.

'I think it's incredible that we made her.' He'd never felt that anything was missing in his life but now that Jess was back in it, and Lily too, he wondered how he could not have known that there should be more. 'And that she accepted me so easily.'

'She thinks you're fabulous.'

'She does?'

'Why wouldn't she? You own a horse and sleigh.' Jess was smiling at him and his heart swelled with love for her and their daughter. His family.

He needed to make that his reality.

Thinking of family made him think of hers. 'Have you spoken to your father yet?'

Jess shook her head. 'Not exactly. But I did speak to his secretary this morning. Luckily she's been working for him for ever and she has booked Lily in for the biopsy on the Wednesday before Christmas. I meant to tell you but with all the drama today I forgot,' she said as she stifled a yawn.

'But you didn't speak to your father.'

'No. I couldn't do it. Talking to him on the phone didn't seem right but I don't know what to do. I don't want to have our first conversation in six years just before Lily goes into the operating theatre—that won't be any good for any of us—but I'm running out of time.'

'Sleep on it,' he said, as she stifled another yawn. 'A solution will present itself.' He had an idea that might just work. 'And why don't you take my bed for the night?' he offered. 'There's no point in waking Lily to take her home.'

Jess shook her head. 'Thanks, but if you bring me a blanket I'll be perfectly happy to sleep in front of the fire. I need to stay close to her, I don't want her to wake up in unfamiliar surroundings without me. Not after the day she's had.'

'I'll move her to my bed, then, and I'll take the couch.'

He picked Lily up. She was feather-light in his arms and snuggled in against his chest, still fast asleep. Jess followed him into his bedroom and pulled the comforter back. He tucked Lily under it before dropping a kiss on her forehead.

They stood together and watched Lily sleep. 'I still can't quite believe I have a daughter. It's incredible.

Thank you, JJ. For giving me this gift. For being strong enough to make what must have been a tough decision. Do you mind sharing Lily with me?'

Jess shook her head. 'Of course not. I never wanted to do this on my own and having you in Lily's life will be a good thing for her—provided we can figure out how it's all going to work.'

'We will,' he agreed, 'but not tonight. There have been enough decisions made today.' He turned Jess to face him. 'But I do have one more question for you. I want to be a part of your life too.'

'You will be. We'll always be connected through our daughter.'

'I want more than that. I want a chance to have a relationship with you that goes beyond us as parents. I want more. I want you.'

'You want me? After everything I've done?'

'Look around you, JJ. Everything I've done has been with you in mind. I know I said I wanted to prove a point to your father but I wouldn't have bothered with that if it wasn't for you. You were the reason I've done this. You were the reason I came back. I admit I've got more than I bargained for but I'm thrilled about that. The past is the past. I meant it when I said there's no point dwelling on it. It can't be changed. We all had a hand to play in the mess we made—me, you and your father—but what's done is done. It doesn't change how I feel about you or Lily. All we can do is look to the future. We have the rest of our lives to make up for lost time.'

'Really?'

'That was my plan.' He was smiling, grinning like a lovestruck fool. He loved her and he wanted to be 'the one' for her. He wanted them to be a family. 'Do you have other plans that I should know about?'

Jess shook her head. 'No.'

'Good.' He took Jess's face in his hands, cupping her cheeks gently between his palms, and tipped her head up. Her green eyes were wide, her lips plump and pink. He wanted her to be his. He wanted to claim her for his own.

He bent his head and covered her lips with his, pouring his love into her and sealing it with a kiss. She tasted like vanilla ice cream, innocent and sweet, and he made a promise to himself that he would take care of her, of her and Lily, if she would let him. He would convince her, he would persuade her, he would charm her and love her until she agreed to give herself to him. And then he would be content.

CHAPTER ELEVEN

JESS'S HEART POUNDED in her chest and her arm felt as if it weighed a tonne as she reached for the door handle of the lodge suite. Her hand was shaking and her palms were clammy. 'I don't think I can do this,' she said to Lucas.

He'd told her he would take care of things but she hadn't expected him to do it so quickly and she also hadn't expected her father to agree to Lucas's suggestion, but it seemed as though she had been wrong on both counts because her father was here, in Moose River, and he was waiting for her.

'It'll be okay, JJ, and I'll be just outside if you need me. Remember, this time I've got your back.' Lucas's voice gave her the courage to turn the handle. 'You can do this.'

She pushed the door open. 'Daddy?'

He was halfway across the room, coming to meet her. He was tall and still trim, although his dark hair was greyer than she remembered. He was sixty now. She'd missed his sixtieth birthday and he'd missed her twenty-first. For what? Why?

Because she was stubborn.

But his arms were open, forgiving, inviting. She

burst into tears and stepped into his embrace. 'I'm sorry, Dad,' she said, as his arms tightened around her. He'd only ever wanted to protect her and she'd repaid him by cutting him out of her life.

She closed her eyes and sobbed and let him hug her as he'd done when she'd been a child. She could feel the tension in her shoulders ease. She could feel the forgiveness in his embrace and all the anxiety that had been building up, all her nervousness over this meeting slipped away as he held her.

'I'm sorry too, Jessie.' He stepped back to look at her, pulling a clean handkerchief out of his pocket and handing it to her.

She smiled through her tears. 'You still carry a handkerchief.' It was one of the many things she remembered about him. Her father wore cufflinks and always had a clean hankie in his pocket.

'Always,' he replied. 'Some things never change. It's good to see you, sweetheart.'

'You too, Dad.' Jess looked around the room. She could smell coffee. There was a pot and two mugs on the sideboard. Only two cups. 'Is Mum here?' she asked.

'No. I wasn't sure how receptive you were going to be. She wouldn't be able to handle any confrontation.'

Jess was disappointed and she felt her shoulders drop. 'I wasn't planning on being confrontational,' she told him. She hadn't been planning anything. This had all been Lucas's idea. But it was silly to feel disappointed about her mother's absence when she hadn't even been sure if she herself wanted to come to the meeting. Why should her mother feel any differently?

Her father must have heard the disappointment in her voice. 'I'm sorry, Jessie. But we'll work it out. This is the first step. I promise I'll do everything I can to make sure we will be a family again.' He reached into his pocket and pulled out his wallet. 'I have something I want to show you.' He flipped his wallet open and handed it to her.

He'd always had a photo of her and Stephen as children in the plastic sleeve but that was gone now. Jess stared at the replacement. Her own eyes stared back at her. The photo was one of her and Lily. It was a photo Kristie had taken on Lily's sixth birthday.

She sat on the sofa and slipped the photo out of the sleeve. Behind it was the old photo of her and Stephen. She held the picture of Lily in her hands and looked up at her father. 'Where did you get this?'

'Kristie gave it to Aunt Carol. She gave it to me.'

'Why?'

'I asked for it.' Her father dragged an armchair across the floor, positioning it at an angle to the sofa, so that he was nearby without crowding Jess. 'I know I wasn't very supportive when you told me you were pregnant and were planning on keeping the baby. I didn't understand how you could make that decision at the age of eighteen but when you cut me out of your life I felt like I'd lost both of my children, first Stephen and then you. Kristie was my link to you, to you and to Lily. I tried to keep in touch with you but when you returned all my letters I had to rely on your aunt and uncle to give me news over the years. I couldn't stand the thought of you being lost to me for ever.'

Her father had sent her a letter, along with a birthday card and a sizeable cheque for Lily, every year. Kristie had always delivered it for them but Jess hadn't realised things had been going back in the other direction. Jess had kept the cards—she had boxed them up and put them away for Lily—but she had returned the letters and the cheques, still determined to prove she could manage on her own. Determined to prove she didn't need anything from her father.

But all this time he'd been hearing about Lily. She didn't know why she was surprised. If she'd ever given it any thought she would have figured out that Aunt Carol would have passed on any information her parents asked for. All this time he'd been following Lily's progress. Despite Jess's actions he had never stopped being her father or Lily's grandfather. He had never given up hope.

'I'm sorry I was stubborn. I'm sorry I've kept you out of our lives,' she apologised. 'I returned your letters but I've kept your cards for Lily. I was going to give them to her one day.' She wanted him to know that. It was important.

'Thank you, Jessie.' Her father reached for her hand and Jess gave it to him. 'I've missed you. Do you think we might have a chance to start fresh?'

'I wasn't sure if I could forgive you for separating me from Lucas. I loved him then, I love him still.' Jess felt her father tense and she hurried to continue, to put his mind at ease. 'But he says we need to leave the past behind if we want to move forward and I think he's right. I would like a chance to start again.' She stood up. 'Would you like to meet Lily?'

'Now?'

Jess nodded.

'She's here?'

'She's in the lodge. Lucas is waiting outside. He'll fetch her.'

'I'd love to, Jessie, and if it's all right I'd like to meet Lucas too. After all, I have him to thank for bringing you back into my life.'

Jess nodded. 'Okay. Give me a minute.' She was smiling as she left the suite. Lucas was waiting for her, just as he'd promised.

'You look happy.'

She walked over to him and threw her arms around him, hugging him tightly.

He picked her up and held her close. 'What was that for?' he asked, as he set her back down on her feet.

'It's a thank-you. I think it's going to be okay. Dad wants to meet Lily.'

'That's good. I've already asked Sofia to bring her up and I've ordered some champagne and afternoon tea for you too.'

'You knew it would go well?'

'I could tell when I spoke to him on the phone that he was keen to reconcile. I was pretty sure this would all turn out okay and I'm glad it has so far.'

'He wants to meet you too.'

'Now?'

Jess nodded and Lucas followed her back into the room.

'Dad, this is Lucas White. Lucas, my father, Stuart Johnson.'

Jess's heart was in her throat. *Please, be nice, Dad.*

Stuart was looking at Lucas closely but he stayed silent. He extended his hand and Jess exhaled as they shook hands. They seemed far more relaxed than she was. Perhaps this would turn out all right after all.

'Good to meet you properly at last, sir. I apologise for not taking responsibility before now—'

Stuart cut him off and Jess held her breath again. 'That's all right. I think I owe you an apology. I was hasty in my judgement of you and it cost me my daughter and my granddaughter. Thank you for bringing them back to me.'

'I want you to know that I intend to make it up to Lily,' Lucas said. 'And to Jess. I have the means and the desire to make it up to both of them and I'm not one to shy away from my responsibilities.'

Lucas stood next to her and she took his hand and squeezed it. He circled her waist with his arm and pulled her close, and Jess could almost feel her life turning around. With Lucas beside her, perhaps things would be okay. With him beside her, anything seemed possible. She'd felt lost, adrift and alone with no one except Lily and Kristie. She never would have admitted it, she was too stubborn, but now perhaps she could. With Lucas back in her life and her father and maybe even her mother, she and Lily wouldn't be alone any more.

Maybe she had a chance of finding happiness after all.

Jess was wearing scrubs and was sitting in the operating theatre at the foot of the bed while her father prepared for Lily's biopsy. The anaesthetist gave Lily a very light general anaesthetic and when she gave Stuart the all-clear he slid a flexible tube, complete with a tiny camera, down Lily's oesophagus, through her stomach and into the small intestine. Jess could watch the images on the monitor above their heads. Stuart examined the intestinal lining and took half a dozen samples at various points.

'What are you looking for?' Jess asked. She'd researched the procedure and the disease and she knew she was asking just to hear her father's voice. It was hard to believe he was back in her life.

'Atrophy of the villi and inflammation of the mucosal tissue,' he explained. 'There's a pathologist waiting for the samples as we speak so the results should be back almost immediately.'

The whole process took less than fifteen minutes and the light anaesthetic Lily had been given was reversed quickly. Then it was just a matter of more waiting.

Lucas and Jess were sitting with a drowsy Lily in the day surgery recovery area when Stuart ducked in between surgeries.

He kept his mask on as he spoke to them.

'The results are back. The villi are shrunk and flattened, indicating partial atrophy, and there is an increased presence of lymphocytes and some other changes consistent with inflammation. The Marsh classification is given as Marsh III.'

'What does that mean?'

'It means Lily has celiac disease.'

'Should I have done something about this earlier?' Guilt swamped Jess again.

Her father shook his head. 'From what I've read in her history from the emergency department, any symptoms she did have were so mild they could have been attributed to any number of things. Because it is commonly an inherited condition, finding out Lucas's history was the red flag. I know it's called a disease but you should think of it more as a condition. It's easily controlled as long as you are prepared to be vigilant with Lily's diet. I'm sure Lucas will agree with me, it's not difficult to manage. Once Lily has a gluten-free diet the villi and her intestine will recover.'

'How long does that take?'

'Usually around three to six months, but provided she sticks to a gluten-free diet there won't be any long-term effects. If she doesn't adhere to a strict gluten-free diet there can be other complications but there'll be time to discuss those later. I'll tee up an appointment with a dietician and a counsellor. It'll be okay, Jessie, we'll get through this.' He squeezed her hand. 'I have to get back into Theatre. Will you be all right?'

Jess reached for Lucas's hand and smiled at her father. 'We'll be fine.'

Lily was up bright and early on Christmas morning. She'd had no ill effects following the biopsy and had taken the news about her celiac disease in her stride, just like everything else. In all honesty, Jess suspected Lily was pleased to know that she and Lucas had something tangible in common.

That had been one problem solved. Jess had been busy ticking boxes over the past few days and things were going well. With Lucas's help she was mending her relationship with her parents, both her mother and her father. Lucas had invited them to the lodge for Christmas lunch and they were coming, along with Kristie and her parents. It would be the first family Christmas in many years and Jess and Lily were both excited. Lucas was helping to repair all the damage Jess had done but fortunately everyone seemed prepared to forgive her.

The only other thing still to be finessed was her relationship with Lucas and how they would parent Lily. But Jess knew they would get there. One thing at a time.

Lily was bouncing up and down on Lucas's bed, where she and Jess had spent another night while Lucas had slept on the couch. Jess felt bad about kicking him out of his own bed yet again but he had insisted. He wanted to be there when Lily woke up, he said. He'd missed all of her Christmases to date and he didn't want to miss another one. It was a good argument and Jess had happily agreed.

'Is it time for presents yet?' Lily was asking.

'We'll go and see if your dad is awake.' It was going to take some time to get used to saying that but Jess liked how it sounded.

'Merry Christmas to my girls,' he said, as he kissed them both and handed Jess a coffee.

'Did Santa come?' Lily asked.

'There seems to be a very big present by the fireplace that wasn't there last night,' Lucas was grinning. 'Shall we take a look?'

An enormous gift sat in front of the fireplace and Lily wasted no time in tearing the paper off it to reveal a magnificent doll's house. It was one she had admired at the Christmas market and had working lights and delicate furniture. A curved staircase led from the first to the second floor and a hollow chimney ended in a small fireplace in the lounge that was complete with tiny logs that lit up with fake flames at the flick of a switch. It was elaborate and beautiful.

'I think Santa might have stolen your thunder,' Jess said with a smile as Lily flicked the lights on and off before picking up a tiny music box that was inside the doll's house. She turned the handle on its side and squealed with delight as it played 'Waltzing Matilda'. 'You might not be her favourite today,' Jess added.

'Santa had six years to make up for but I've still got a few tricks up my sleeve.'

He handed Lily a small box. Nestled in tissue paper was a carved wooden sleigh. It had been painted red, just like the Crystal Lodge sleigh. Lily lifted it carefully from the box. Attached to it was a perfect replica of Banjo. 'I love it, Daddy, it looks just like Banjo.'

'Okay, Dad's turn, Lil,' Jess told her, once they'd all finished admiring the tiny horse.

Lily handed Lucas a flat, heavy parcel and then went to play with her doll's house as he unwrapped his gift, revealing a photo album.

He turned the pages of the album. It was filled with photographs of Lily, beginning on the day she'd been born and continuing to her sixth birthday. As Jess described each picture, telling Lucas something about each occasion, Lily's curiosity got the better of her. Fascinated as always by photographs of herself when she'd been younger, she abandoned the doll's house temporarily and climbed onto Lucas's lap. She snuggled against his chest and added to the commentary as he turned the pages. 'That's me when I lost my first tooth,' she said, 'and that's me when I was in the nativity play last year. I was a shepherd. And that's me on the day I started school in Moose River.'

'It's brilliant, JJ,' Lucas said, as he reached the end of the album and closed the book. He leant behind Lily and kissed Jess lightly on the lips. 'Thank you.'

'I have something else for you too,' she said, as she handed him a large, thin envelope. Inside was one sheet of paper.

Lucas slid it out. 'It's Lily's birth certificate.'

Jess nodded. 'I've had it amended,' she said. She

pointed to the word 'Father'. In the box underneath it said 'Lucas White'.

'This is the most perfect gift.'

'It's going to be a perfect Christmas,' Jess replied.

'I hope so. But there's one more thing to do before we reach perfection.'

'What's that?'

'Your present.' Lucas turned to Lily, who had returned to play, and Jess had to smile when she saw that Lily was busy showing mini-Banjo through the house. 'Lil, it's time for Mum's surprise.'

Lily put Banjo down and dived under the Christmas tree to retrieve a gift bag.

Lucas picked up Jess's hand and looked into her eyes. 'JJ, I loved you seven years ago and I love you still. You are beautiful and smart and I never forgot you. I love you and I love Lily. I want us to be a family.' Without letting go of her hand, he got down on one knee beside the couch. Lily was bouncing up and down on the cushion beside Jess, clutching the gift bag. 'Jess Johnson, will you do me the honour of becoming my wife? Will you marry me?'

Jess's eyes filled with tears.

'No! Don't cry, Mum.'

'It's all right, Lil, these are happy tears,' Jess said as she choked back a sob. 'You are my first and only love,' she said to Lucas. 'I have loved you and only you since the moment you first kissed me and, yes, I will marry you.'

Lily threw her arms around them both. 'Hooray,' she shouted.

'Okay, Lily, you can hand over the bag now,' Lucas said, when Lily finally released them.

Inside the bag was a tiny jewellery box. Jess pulled it out and lifted the lid. A princess-cut diamond ring glistened in dark blue velvet. Lucas pulled it from the cushion.

'Just as you have rescued me I promise to always protect you for as long as you need me. I promise to love you and Lily and to keep you safe. Always,' he said, as he slid the ring onto her finger before kissing her.

'I think she likes it,' Lily said, as Jess held her hand out so they could all admire it.

'You knew about this?' Jess asked her.

'Lily helped me choose the ring,' Lucas replied. 'She's nearly as good at keeping secrets as you are.'

'No more secrets. I promise.'

Lily was tugging Jess's arm. 'Now do you think I can have a baby sister?'

Jess smiled and looked into Lucas's forget-me-not-blue eyes. 'We'll see what we can do.'

EPILOGUE

JESS LAY ON a beach towel and let the autumn sun warm her pale skin as she watched Lucas and Lily playing in the famous Bondi surf. Lucas had swapped his snow-board for a surfboard and he was giving Lily her first surfing lesson. She was proving to be a natural, showing Jess once again that nature was just as strong as nurture.

Lucas came out of the water, leaving Lily to practise her surf moves with his youngest brother. He jogged up the beach to Jess and she didn't bother to pretend she wasn't checking him out. They'd been in Australia for a month and Lucas was tanned and fit and gorgeous. And all hers. He stood over her, blocking the sun and giving her a very nice view of his sculpted chest and strong thighs. His board shorts dripped water on the sand as he towelled his hair dry, leaving it even more tousled than normal.

She smiled up at him. 'Lily's having a great time. She's picked it up really fast. She must take after her dad.'

'Your husband,' he said, as he flopped down onto the sand beside her and kissed her.

They had married in Moose River in February and had just celebrated their three-month anniversary with a second ceremony with Lucas's family. It had been a whirlwind few months and Jess was exhausted but elated. She wouldn't change a thing.

'Happy?' he asked.

'Extremely,' she replied, as she rolled onto her side to look at Lucas. Some days she still couldn't believe her good fortune. Lucas was back in her life, he'd given her back her family and he'd given her himself too. She was happy and she had everything she needed. She reached out and picked up her husband's hand. 'But, in the interest of full disclosure, because I promised no more secrets, there is something I need to tell you.'

'Is it that you love me?'

'I do. But that's not a secret.'

'I know, I just like to hear you say "I do".' Lucas laughed and kissed her fingers. 'Sorry, go on.'

'You know how Lily always asks for a baby sister for Christmas? I've been thinking…'

'You think we should make a baby?' Lucas's forget-me-not-blue eyes lit up.

Jess shook her head. 'That wasn't what I was going to say.' She smiled as Lucas's face fell. She knew he was going to love her news. 'It's too late for that. We've already done it.'

'What?'

'I'm pregnant.'

'You are?'

Jess nodded. 'The baby is due the week before Christmas. So it looks as though Lily will get her Christmas wish this year. She's going to have a sibling,' she said, as she brought Lucas's hand to her belly.

'That is fantastic news, JJ. The best.'

'All those things you missed out on with Lily, I

promise you'll be there for every one of them this time around. Do you think that sounds okay?'

'I do.'

Jess closed her eyes and smiled as his lips covered hers.

This was the perfect start to the first day of the rest of their lives.

* * * * *

COMING SOON!

We really hope you enjoyed reading this book. If you're looking for more romance, be sure to head to the shops when new books are available on

Thursday 29th November

To see which titles are coming soon, please visit **millsandboon.co.uk**

LET'S TALK
Romance

For exclusive extracts, competitions
and special offers, find us online:

- �f facebook.com/millsandboon
- 🐦 @MillsandBoon
- 📷 @MillsandBoonUK

Get in touch on 01413 063232

For all the latest titles coming soon, visit
millsandboon.co.uk/nextmonth